BRIDGE
of
ETERNITY

EDMUND CLARK TRAVIS

Independently Published

ISBN -13: 978-1-960499-94-3

ACKNOWLEDGEMENTS

All scripture quoted in this work is taken from the Concordant Version of the Bible when available. This was the work of A. E. Knoch. Today, both the Old Testament and the New Testament are available. The address is Concordant Publishing Concern, 15570 Newhaven Road, Santa Clarita, California, 91350, USA.

Special recognition is due Mr. A. E. Knoch, as editor and publisher of the Unsearchable Riches booklet for most of his lifetime. Also recognition for material used in the radio message of chapter 19.

I wish to give recognition to Vladimir Gleeson, now many years deceased, for material quoted from his book and for permission to reprint, given by The Concordant Publishing Concern.

Great is my appreciation for both Mr. Gelesnoff and Mr. Knoch for providing the study of the eons, laying the foundation for building the entire plan and purpose of God concept, as brought out in this book. This study teaches that the eons are not associated with "eternal" things but rather are a link between eternity, as it was before the eons and eternity, as it shall become when the eons have run their course.

Many thanks to the authors of The Companion Bible and their critical, explanatory, and suggested notes and 198 appendixes. Special thanks are due W. E. Bullinger, also deceased, principal contributor to that work. It is now published by Kregal Publications, a division of Kregal, Inc. PO Box 2607, Grand Rapids, Michigan, 49501.

Recognition is due the following authors and their works. It was a pleasure to study these writings while preparing this novel.

Theresienstadt: Hitler's Gift to the Jeius, NorbertTroller, University of North Carolina Press.

Survival in Auschwitz: The Reaivakening, Prima Levi, Summit Books New York.

The Warsaw Ghetto, Joe E. Hevdecker, I. B. Touris & Co. Ltd. London.

The History of the Holocaust, Yehuda Bauer, Franklin Watts-New York, London, Toronto, Sidney.

Safe Sun, Mary-Ellen Siegel

The Ages in the Scriptures (direct quotation), Vladimir Gelesnoff, Concordant Publishing Concern.

Eonian: Everlasting or Age-Lasting, Grace I. Todd, Concordant Publishing Concern.

The Problem of Evil & The Judgments of God, A. E. Knoch, Concordant Publishing Concern.

I would like to acknowledge the following individuals for the help they have given:

Miriam Dowler-Brown (now deceased), for material furnished through her association with the Winterset Public Library concerning the legends of the haunting of the Roseman Covered Bridge.

Mrs. Signe Somers, for the inspiration she gave for many years. She too is long deceased. Well, do I remember her quoting her favorite verses of scripture, 1 Timothy 4:9-11, which also became one of my favorites and was used prominently in this writing.

Members of Bible study classes over the years, especially Elwood and Jackie Gustafson, and Jack and Connie Rahn during more recent years, and especially Elwood for the forty-five years of Bible discussions with him.

My sister Doris Young, for the excellent help in recalling names and events concerning our hometown and stored in her memory from out of the past—things I had long forgot.

Marilyn, my wife for 65 years—giving special acknowledgement to her—for patiently reading and rereading this manuscript throughout the time of its development.

(All these friends and loved ones are now deceased.)

WORDS FROM THE AUTHOR

Some of the childhood experiences described in this book are true; however, the embellishment of most makes it imperative to consider the work as fiction. Above all, if a reader were to visit the small town in which I grew up, they would be disappointed should they look for things depicted in the final pages. The delicious apple tree did indeed originate there. It is said that 70% of the world's supply of apples would find their origin traced to that one tree, having grown out of an old stump during the Civil War years of the 1860s. It has always been the desire of my heart to see it given the recognition it deserves, but to this date, the "retreat" is found only in this author's imagination.

The scriptural concepts are a different matter. It is my hope that none of these will be regarded as fiction but as truth according to my understanding. Tertius was the writer of Romans on behalf of Paul. He says God is able to establish the Romans in accord with Paul's evangel. This came in accord with a revelation of a secret hushed in the Old Testament. But now it is manifested through those prophetic scriptures according to an injunction of God being made known to all nations for faith-obedience.

In the early verses of Isaiah chapter 6, the Old Testament prophet Isaiah, we are told, sees the Lord sitting on His throne in His temple and seraphim standing above. Isaiah is in awe for he is of unclean lips. One of the seraphim with snuffers in hand touches his lips with a glowing coal. Depravity is taken from him, and the Lord asks, "Whom shall I send? And who shall go to this nation?" And Isaiah says to Him, "Behold me! Send me!" This was the message of the grace of God, and the new covenant He is to go to the people and say to them:

"Go and say to this people:
Hear ye to hear, yet ye must not be understanding.
And see ye to see, yet ye must not be knowing."

It was to remain hushed up until the land was barren and no people remained. Yet a tenth remained for they turn back. The holy seed became a monument to its grace. The message of the grace of God is contained in the book of Isaiah but remained hushed up until the days of Paul's ministry. Paul's evangel is the revelation of that secret. Most, if not all, of Paul's evangel or the evangel of God was taken from the book of Isaiah. The following passages are from Isaiah but are now seen to refer to Paul.

Hearken, ye coastlanders, to me!
And attend, ye folkstems, from afar!
Yahweh, from the belly, called, me;
From the bowels of my mother He mentioned my name.
And He is constituting my mouth as a sharp sword.
In the shadow of His hand He hides me.
And He is constituting me a choice arrow.
In His quiver He conceals me. (Isa. 49:1-2)

And from Isaiah 49:7, we read the following:

A slight thing is it for you to become My servant.
To raise up the tribes of Jacob, And the dispersed of Israel to restore.
Behold! I give you also for a light of the nations,
To become My salvation unto the ends of the earth.

These are just two of the passages in Isaiah referring to Paul. Not only would he restore the two houses of Jacob, but also he would enlighten all nations to the truth of salvation. That which was hushed has been revealed through Paul. However, most of what was revealed and taught to the body of Christ was hushed once again after the close of Paul's ministry. Today, those difficult passages are not taken literally or are denied through teachings of the eternal torment doctrine.

Here are two great passages of Paul's writings showing how

Christendom does not take his words literally. "I am now rejoicing in my sufferings for you, *and am filling up in my flesh, in His stead, the deficiency of the afflictions of Christ,* for His body, which is the ecclesia of which I became a dispenser, in accord with the administration of God, which is granted to me for you, *to complete the word of God*—the secret which has been concealed from the eons" (Col. 1:24-26). The second is from 2 Corinthians 12:9. Paul pleaded with the Lord to remove the splinter from his flesh. The Lord said to him, *"Sufficient for you is My grace, for My power in infirmities is being perfected."*

The truths I have seen came slowly over more than fifty years of Bible study. All understanding came as a gift through the Holy Spirit and perseverance, and that too probably came through the Holy Spirit.

CHAPTER 1

Mark Christopher Hayes picked up the handful of marbles that lay strewn over the ground and then returned to the top step leading to the back porch. On the lawn lay a string forming a circle, into which he attempted to toss some marbles. "One out of eleven! Boy! That's the way I do everything. I never do nothin' good," he said disgustedly.

From the rear of the little four-roomed bungalow with its imitation red brick siding, Mark gazed down across the shallow hillside and over the garden and creek beyond. Directly in front of him lay a thick film of rock dust covering the cornfield wedged securely between Clanton Creek and the railroad right-of-way. The same dirty-white layer of limestone dust covered the ground everywhere he looked. A heavily traveled gravel road, passing in front of their house, wound its way through the valley. Every passing vehicle stirred up a thick cloud of swirling dust, casting it high in the air to be carried well out over the landscape by the gentle breeze. The limestone quarry up in the hills laid idol for several years but had been reopened early in the spring.

He sat thinking about the heat and the dust, wondering if most other places might be just as boring. "I reckon every place has stuff like this goin' on," he said aloud. "Whoever named this town, though, sure missed it. Should a been called Rock Valley. Yeah! Rock Dust Valley!" Mark chuckled. "Reckon they weren't digging no rocks out of the hills back then," he said as an afterthought.

The year was 1939. The day was a day in mid-August. Mark had been up only a short time, but already, he knew it was headed for being a real scorcher. That was the kind of days they'd been having for three weeks now, but it really wasn't uncommon for an Iowa August. But no rain had fallen. A slight breeze persisted, yet being such a warm breeze, it provided little relief from the high temperatures and stifling humidity.

What a far cry this was from only a few months before when the valley was alive with beauty: green lawns and freshly manicured. Fruit trees in blossom dotted the community, and flowers bloomed in an array of color not to be matched until another spring. Naturally picturesque, it was always a beautiful community that time of year; probably the reason spring would remain Mark's favorite season for as long as he lived.

But there were no signs of spring present now.

Mark loved the outdoors and virtually lived the summer vacations out in the sun wandering around the countryside. Having blue eyes and his blonde hair bleached even lighter by the summer sun, his dark brown skin seemed a contradiction of his normally fair complexion. Each morning, he stood before the mirror giving his face a swipe with the washcloth and his teeth a couple of quick brushes with his toothbrush. He always followed that by meticulously combing his hair. Every hair must be in just the right place. One had to question why, for he didn't touch a comb again until the next morning, and it didn't stay where it was combed anyway.

Barefoot and in bib overalls from the moment he arose in the morning until he went to bed, he spent the entire summer that way, except during Sunday morning church and Sunday school services. He was a quiet eleven-year-old, with a smile that seemed to stretch from ear to ear and well liked by most of those who knew him. He was sensitive in many ways, showing respect for all his family members, especially Jason, his brother, even though Jason was almost six years older.

Mrs. Hayes was a small-framed woman, frail looking but in excellent health, and a hard worker. She always made her own house dresses of fascinating colorful gingham print designs. A matching apron complimented by bric-a-brac or lace trim to give a refreshing neatness to her general appearance usually accompanied them. She always looked neat with her hair tied at the back of her head in a bun. Mark couldn't remember his mother ever wearing her hair differently. And being prematurely gray, he couldn't remember a time when she hadn't seemed old to him. She was in her forties when she gave birth to Mark, the youngest in a family of four girls and two boys. Mrs. Hayes was a splendid Christian woman and truly dedicated to being a living example of good Christian conduct. Friends looked upon her in just that way, and Mark was sure no one ever accused her of being hypocritical as he had heard it said about others in the community. His Sunday schoolteacher once said to him, "Mark, if ever there was a saint on earth, it surely was your mother." His father referred to various ones as being hypocrites but never had he heard him say it about her.

His mother enjoyed working in the garden in the morning before the heat of the day set in. Just now she was arriving at the well after finishing her work. "I suppose you came up here for water, you little critter. Don't you hiss at me! Go on! Shoo! I'm not giving you a drink!"

Mark rose from the step and started walking toward the well to find out what his mother's conversation was all about. "Are you talking to a snake?" he questioned.

"I suppose it comes up here hoping to find water," she said, watching the snake as it slithered off into the garden. "Go on!" she shouted. "I wish it would stay down by the creek. Those things give me the willies. They are kind of pretty, though, bright colors. God made snakes just like He made everything else, I guess. Maybe someday, I'll know why."

"That must be the snake Jason saw the other day," Mark said. "Thought it might be a spreading viper. Said he had a notion to kill it, but when it spread out its head and hissed at him, he had another notion beating the first one all to the devil."

Mrs. Hayes watched Mark's eyes grow larger as he spoke. "It's only a hognose snake."

"You mean they got a nose like a hog?" Mark asked.

"I suppose when they flatten their heads, maybe. They wouldn't hurt anyone. They do look kind of scary all right, but it's all just a big show. Some folks call them puff adders. I call them bluff adders. When you call their bluff, they pretend to be dead."

Those years were difficult for many, and it was especially so for people living in small towns. For them, the depression was still very much a reality. Mark's father was a sheepshearer by trade. They charged by the head, and a good shearer could shear a hundred sheep in a day if conditions were right. Mr. Hayes was good at his work. While the pay was excellent for those times, the working season lasted only about three months at most. For the remainder of the year, it was necessary to find whatever work could be found and get by the best way possible. He butchered for the farmers, did small carpenter jobs, and, in general, did whatever it took to put food on the table for his family. There weren't many groceries in the house at times, but they never went hungry.

"I suppose you're about ready for breakfast?" his mother asked, assuming Mark was getting hungry.

Mark was really never eager to eat breakfast, but there wouldn't be much way out of that. Breakfast in his house was the one meal rarely ever avoided.

"Your daddy and Jason left early this morning. Dad thought if they got an early start today, they could finish building the corncrib for Mr. Martin." Mr. Martin lived in the Old Town. She rinsed her hands in the water she pumped from the well, being careful not to be wasteful and staying alert for the possible return of the snake.

"The Old Town" was an odd name for a community, but it was only a nickname, and it came by it quite naturally. The original town was named Peru and set on the rim of the hills to the northwest of the long narrow valley. It was a small community and well centered within the boundaries of Iowa's rich farmland. In the year 1886, the Chicago Great Western railway obtained right-of-way along a sweeping path from Oelwein down through southern Iowa. This completed a line connecting Chicago with Kansas City, by way of Des Moines, and passing through the very heart of the nation's corn-growing country. Because of the abundance of corn, it was a major livestock producing area. The railroad's importance was recognized. A year later, the town was moved to the valley.

The new community took the name—they did place the name East in front of it, though it was rarely used—the old location simply became known as the Old Town.

"Mr. Sullivan wants your daddy to butcher a beef for him," his mother said as they walked toward the house. "Says there's no hurry. Says Dad can do it whenever he isn't busy. Everyone's good to us that way. They know Dad needs the work."

As Mark opened the screen door for his mother, he observed a smile on her face. She didn't often talk to him about things of that nature, mostly because of the hard times. That was grown-up talk anyway. But Mark knew she had something good to tell him because, as always, she gave herself away with her smile.

"Mr. Sullivan always gives your daddy the beef's head whenever they butcher. I thought I'd make mincemeat from some of the hamburger," she said. Her smile broadened. "I know how much you and Jason like mincemeat pie."

"Hmmm! That's my favorite kind of pie."

"When you're through eating and finish your piano lesson, I want you to go to the post office," his mother told him. "We should get the light bill today. And I can use some things from the store too. I'll make a list."

Mark didn't care for the idea of the list for groceries, but thinking about the mincemeat pie made it somewhat easier.

Passing by Molly Patton's house, he saw her hoeing in her garden. Oh, boy! I'll never get to town now, he thought.

"Hello there," Molly said, as he approached. "How are you this miserably hot morning?" she said, always wanting things to sound worse than they really were.

"Just fine," Mark replied. "How are you?"

She was the same everyday Molly. About two inches of white slip showed below the hem of her dress. At least one comb was about to fall from her hair. Never was it easy to get away from Molly, but he couldn't be rude. And as long as she could talk about her troubles, very little conversation was required of him. Mark wasn't much of a conversationalist anyway. Molly did take advantage of his inexperience, making him a captive audience.

"My rheumatism hurts something awful," she said, holding her hand on her hip. "Had such a headache all night, couldn't sleep. Couldn't find any aspirins. Mrs. Marshall's in the hospital, found a tumor on her brain, just like the tumor that took old man Breckenridge. Don't hold out much hope for her, I guess. Sure hope I don't have a tumor. I 'spect if the devil's picking on me, though, he's leaving someone else alone."

Mark's mother had told him to be polite and listen to her troubles. She said it probably did Molly good to find someone who would listen since she was lonely. Often, he didn't hear what she was saying, but he didn't think she noticed.

After listening to her troubles for a time, Mark excused himself by stressing urgency for picking up the light bill at the post office for his mother, as though it was a matter of great importance.

"I hope Mary's well," she said. She turned once again to her hoeing. "Tell your mama to stop and see me. I get so blue."

Molly kept talking, but Mark pretended not to hear. He continued to walk toward town.

As he walked, his thoughts went back to events of his younger years. Molly would bring a pillow to the evening church services. Thinking about it brought back memories of the smell of the vanilla extract Molly wore for perfume—a pleasant sweet odor. When the singing was over and the preaching began, he would lie down in the pew between Molly and his mother and go to sleep. His mother didn't mind him sleeping. She knew he wouldn't stay awake very long anyway. Just staying awake through the prayers and the singing seemed to be enough.

Mark still liked Molly a lot, but in getting older, it was embarrassing to have her fuss over him, and her complaining was a problem. It was getting harder to listen to, and he didn't know how to handle it. And it was becoming more and more noticeable.

Molly was instrumental in his acceptance of Jesus Christ as his personal Savior. An evangelist came to their town. Services were held nightly for an entire week. The man was not an evangelist of the Methodist denomination, and meetings among members of other denominations were not permitted to conduct services in their building. So the meetings were held in an old service garage not being used at the time. Planks were set on cement blocks, and several rows of seats were assembled in the same manner. An upright piano was brought in, and everything was arranged at one end of the large room. The room was dark. The planks were uncomfortable. The evangelist brought the hymnals, and everyone sang while his wife played the piano. She played well, adding a fine dimension to the services. The week wore on. The crowds grew larger. It became evident God's work was just as productive in that dingy old building as it was in the permanent church.

Mark had suffered from a toothache for several days when it was discovered the tooth was badly ulcerated. Though attending all the meetings while having the toothache, on one particular evening, the pain became more than he could endure quietly. Molly asked the evangelist to "lay hands" on Mark and pray for the ulcerated condition. During the meeting, the pain subsided. Much was made of the healing "miracle." On that evening, Mark expressed the desire to accept Jesus Christ, long since associating Molly Patton with the experience.

The memory of the experience was clear, but something about the way they persuaded people to go to the altar never seemed right. He wasn't sorry he gave his life to Jesus Christ, that wasn't the problem, but even at his young age, it didn't seem honest. Something so important as salvation should be dealt with more sincerely. To Mark, it was as though they were saying whatever it takes to get people to the altar is quite all right, just get them there. But to him, it was dishonest and made him feel uncomfortable.

The pianist alternated between hymns, playing "Just as I Am" at one evening service, then playing "Softly and Tenderly, Jesus Is Calling" the next evening. She played the same hymn repeatedly, endlessly it seemed, and softly, while the evangelist pleaded with the people of the congregation to come forward. After a while, the pastor began using choice expressions to create a sense of fear and then began describing what one's imagination was able to picture in his mind of what a horrible place hell must be. This was eventually finalized by asking the congregation to think of what it would be like to spend eternity there, with no possible hope of ever escaping from the terrible place. Endlessly, they would remain, writhing in pain and screaming in torment, never again having the opportunity to accept Jesus Christ as their Savior.

Of course, Mark wanted to be with Jesus Christ, and he was sure he would be, but there was confusion in his mind. Could fear of hellfire and brimstone be the basis for producing a proper relationship? If God was good, He would never treat people that way. If God is love, as they also teach, how could He make anyone suffer forever and ever?

Mark reached the end of Main Street. There was Ben Pritchard at the window ledge of the post office, half standing, half sitting. “Oh no!” he said aloud. “He won’t let me out of there without picking on me about something.” It seemed to Mark, Ben took special interest in teasing him. After hesitating, he decided to go on in and get it over with. Walking through the door, Ben immediately greeted Mark.

“Hello, Hayes,” he said.

“Good morning, sir,” Mark replied. Trying to avoid Ben, he moved directly to the counter. “Do we have any mail, sir?” he asked the postmaster.

But Ben was not to be ignored. “Sir!” Ben shouted, as though hardly believing what he heard. “John! Did you hear what Hayes called me? He called me sir. Hayes gave me a title,” he taunted.

The postmaster ignored Ben. “Nothing for you, Mark, except the light bill.”

Ben wouldn’t let up. “Nobody ever called me, sir. Did you hear what Mark called me, John? He called me sir.”

“Oh yes, Ben, I heard!”

As Mark reached the door, Ben added his last bit of humor. “Hayes,” he said, very deliberately, “from now on, I want you to call me ‘Sir Ben.’ Don’t forget!” he said, calling in a louder voice as Mark left the post office. “Sir Ben!” he shouted again.

As Mark started across the street, he heard Ben give out a loud guffaw. Ben was still laughing when Mark was halfway up the block.

He tried hard to convince himself Ben hadn’t upset him, but there was no hiding it. “Always tries to make me look dumb, ”he said to himself. Ben did tease Mark a great deal. Mark had always thought it was done in jest, but today, he had been made fun of, purely and simply.

Only after arriving home was Mark to realize he forgot to pick up the groceries. His mother heard him coming and was surprised to find there were none.

“Oh, Mama!” he exclaimed dejectedly. “I forgot! I’ll go back and get them.”

"It's all right," she said. "I won't need them till suppertime. You can get them later. I'll probably think of something else anyway. Is that the light bill?" she asked, upon seeing the yellow envelope poking out of his hip pocket.

The way Ben acted left Mark quite upset and wanting to get away to be alone. He sure didn't want to talk to his mother about it. Being afraid she would sense something was wrong, he quickly handed her the envelope and went outside.

"How come everything happens to me?" he asked himself.

"I don't think Dad likes me. Ben tried to make me look dumb. God took my puppy. Even God picks on me. You'd think He'd want me to have a friend, someone to like me. "

Three weeks had passed since Mark's puppy, Tippy, was hit by a car and then soon died of its injuries. They were almost home from a long walk, returning by way of the gravel road, when the car struck Tippy. Badly hurt, a neighbor thought it best the puppy should be put to sleep. Mark couldn't bear to let him do it. He sat up far into the night with him, but the injuries were more than the little dog could cope with. He died that night. It was almost as though a part of Mark died with him.

How he missed Tippy. Tippy would be a great comfort if he was only there. Mark remembered how he would get down in the grass on his knees and forearms and put his hands over his ears so Tippy could try to lick them. They played for hours that way. Right now, Mark would give anything if Tippy could lay his little chin on his arm. They used to take naps together lying out on the grass. Whenever Mark felt bad or was just lonely, Tippy was there trying to make him feel better. And he always felt better just from the comfort of knowing his puppy was with him.

But Tippy wasn't there now. Mark went over to the little grave he had made for him at the edge of the garden and laid down on the ground facing the marker he set on his grave. A tear rolled down his cheek. "Why did Tippy have to die? I don't know if I did right when I wouldn't let Mr. Simpson put him to sleep. He was hurt bad. He suffered a lot too. At least, though, he wouldn't a suffered as much," he reasoned. "Maybe I should a let Mr. Simpson put him to sleep, but then I wouldn't a known if he'd a got well," he continued to reason. The tears came streaming over his cheeks. "Why did You let my puppy die?" he asked aloud.

Mark was sobbing bitterly.

Through his tears, he reached out to God in prayer. "Please, God, I don't really think You don't like me, but could You maybe show me You're not angry? If You'd do something big a-a-and important, like You did in the Bible, then I'd know. Then I'd know You like me. Don't You see, if You like me, then people will have to like me too, amen?"

Just then, the sound of a voice was heard coming from nearby.

"You there! Son!" the voice was saying.

Mark looked in the direction of the creek from where the sound of the voice came. He saw a blurred figure standing. Mark's eyes were still filled with tears. After wiping his eyes with the back of his hand, the figure became clearer. A man was standing about twenty feet away so not to startle him. When he knew Mark had seen him, he came near.

"Hello, sir!" Mark said, wiping his eyes again.

"My, the world must have come to an end," the stranger said.

Mark was puzzled. "What do you mean, sir?" He could see the man clearly now. He reminded Mark a great deal of his own father, for he was of the same general build. This man needed a shave, though it was only of a day or two extra growth. His clothes were quite soiled, a straw hat set squarely on his head, and a knapsack hung from what looked like a broom handle riding on his shoulder. A long narrow scar appeared on his right arm. His face, neck, and arms were of a deep tan. That was in sharp contrast with the white skin showing at the bottom of his rolled-up sleeves, revealing evidence of having spent much of his time out in the sun.

But there was something different about this man. Mark felt an overwhelming sense of comfort and assurance from his presence. It wasn't something he could explain—the fact was, it seemed to defy explanation—but there was an instant bonding toward this man. Was it the gentleness of his voice, the kindness seen in his expression, or the soft gentle look from his eyes? There seemed no real reason for so much assurance, but whatever it was, Mark felt an immediate sense of security. There was complete confidence nothing was to be feared from this stranger.

"I'm thinking from all those tears, something pretty earth shattering must have happened."

"No, sir! It ain't nothing like that."

The man saw the marker over the mound in front of Mark. "What's all this?" he asked. "Must have been a good friend of yours?" "Yes, sir! My puppy."

"I had a puppy when I was a lad," the man told him. "He was about the best friend I ever had."

"You did, sir!" This excited Mark. "I mean you really had a puppy?" Being sure he had found someone who would know exactly how he felt, he asked, "Did he die, sir?"

"He lived to be an old dog, fourteen years old when he died, almost as old as I was." The man spoke more slowly now. "He went blind then just plain died of old age."

"Did you miss him, sir? I mean, when he died, did you miss him?"

"You bet I did! Even as a fifteen-year-old boy, I shed some tears when he was gone, especially when I laid in bed at night," he confided. "How did your puppy die?"

"He was hit by a car, sir. Mr. Simpson, he's our neighbor, he said even a dog doctor couldn't make him well."

Mark observed the man was dirty and in need of having a bath and something cleaner to wear. "Would you like to take a bath in the woodshed?" he blurted.

"I think my most important need is something to eat." The stranger smiled affectionately.

Mark was embarrassed when he realized he had implied the man needed a bath. "I-I'm sorry, sir, I'll ask Mama if she'll fix you something to eat."

Entering the house, he told his mother about the man in the garden. "He's hungry a-a-and needs a bath too, but mostly, he just wants something to eat."

Many hoboes walked the tracks in those difficult times. Almost always, they were assured of being given a meal at one of the houses as they passed through town. Mrs. Hayes knew she must be cautious about whom she trusted.

"I think I should meet him first," she said. "Let's talk to him, and we'll try to decide whether he seems to be a good person."

"Oh, he's a good man," Mark assured her. "He had a puppy when he was a lad. He cried at night after it died too."

"You rather like him, don't you?" she said. She smiled at Mark. "Let's talk to him."

They went to the garden to welcome the man, finding him stooped over the marker Mark had put on Tippy's grave and reading the inscription on it.

"Must have been a fine puppy," the man exclaimed, as Mark and his mother approached.

"Tippy was nearly full grown when he died," Mrs. Hayes told him. "Mark was so attached to him. It was a shame the puppy died." "I believe there's a reason for all things which happen," the stranger assured her.

Those words impressed Mark. His mother said those words many times. She should be impressed too, he thought.

"I don't have anything very fancy to fix for dinner, but I can make you some baloney gravy on toast."

His mother seemed to be apologizing. That was a special treat when she made it for Mark. There was no question his mother had approved of the stranger. He hoped the man would like the gravy as much as he did.

"Ma'am, I don't recall ever eating baloney gravy, but it sure sounds good to me. I can't accept your offer, though, until you let me earn the meal."

Even Mrs. Hayes sensed the man's sincerity.

Mark had heard his father say many times, "No hobo's gonna eat from my table 'til he's earned it first." Mrs. Hayes would have liked for him to make the offer, but she probably wouldn't have asked. She was pleased when the offer came from him.

Mark headed for the woodshed. "I'll show you where we keep the ax," he said.

"There's some stove length wood in the woodshed needing to be split for the cookstove. You might split a few armloads. That should more than pay for the food you eat," she said.

My Beautiful Nature Land

Where I spent my boyhood days,
wand'ring o're the countryside:
in my world! In my wonderful world!
Passing years brought little change
to that place I loved to be, come with me
to my beautiful nature land.

When I'm sad and the sky begins to gray,
I'm not alone! God is there to light my way.
He brings the sun and dries away,
the tears like fallen rain,
in my beautiful nature land.
From the sunrise, to the sunset,
all His handiwork I see.
Whether sunshine or in shadows,
He is ever near to me.
I can see, where the broad horizons flow,
and far beyond—everywhere the breezes go—
I wander; and ponder all my dreams.
I'm enchanted, and 1 look away in awe,
into a world, governed by a natural law—
and like the stream, go aimlessly,
yet find my winding way
in my beautiful nature land.

CHAPTER 2

When the visitor reached for the ax, Mark noticed the bulging muscles in his arms and the roughness of his hands. He didn't resemble any hobo Mark imagined. Most hobos had to work for their meals he supposed, but this man was accustomed to hard work.

Mark wasn't disappointed. Watching, he saw the man lean the wood against the chopping block and take a swing. Never had he seen anyone swing an ax so hard and with such ease. Quickly, he set the wood up again and swung the ax. In amazement, he watched the pile of split wood grow larger. Many times, the wood remained standing while he swung the ax again.

"That oughta be plenty, sir," Mark said to the man, thinking he would be glad his work was done.

The man stopped for a moment to wipe the perspiration from his forehead. "Baloney gravy sounds pretty special to me. I think I'd better do a special job to earn it."

Quickly, Mark ran into the woodshed to get more wood for the man to split. Gathering up the wood, he carried it back into the shed. The man didn't stop until he had finished every piece of wood Mark brought to him. Then he helped cord it neatly inside the shed again. "You sure aren't afraid of work," the man said.

That seemed a curious statement to Mark. The stranger was doing all the work, but before he could respond, they heard his mother call to tell them dinner was ready.

"If you'd tell me where, I might wash up."

"I'll get some water," Mark interrupted.

He picked up a bucket and ran to the well where he Pilled it about half full with water. After filling the washbasin, they both washed their hands.

Mark loved baloney gravy and never had it sounded better than at that moment. "Sir!" he began to reason. "If you don't think you can eat all of it, I might be able to eat some."

The man chuckled. "Perhaps there will be enough for both of us." His eyes twinkled as he spoke.

The two of them entered the kitchen just as Mark's mother poured the gravy into a bowl. It was a large bowl, steaming and filled to the brim. The house was filled with pleasant aroma from the gravy. Removing a piece of toast from the top of each of the oil-stove burners, she replaced them with another slice of bread. It was only eleven o'clock. Mrs. Hayes wasn't hungry, but she had set a place for Mark across the table from his guest.

After being seated, the man bowed his head and closed his eyes to silently pray before beginning to eat. Mark and his mother noticed it at the same time. Mrs. Hayes interrupted, "You may say grace for both of you if you like. Dad doesn't want us to pray when he's here, but when we're alone, we always return thanks."

Once again, the man bowed his head, and this time, he prayed aloud. "Father of Jesus Christ, and our Father too," he began, "thank You for providing this need. Thank You—"

Mark listened intently as the stranger prayed. He spoke clearly and seemed to know exactly what he was about to say. And he was quite sincere and intimate, as though he was in the very presence of God and in awe of His Being. Mark had never heard anyone pray with so much confidence and obvious closeness with God.

"And bless Mark."

Mrs. Hayes often prayed with Mark, and he always waited with anticipation for her to speak his name. There was something special about hearing his name in his mother's prayers. God would surely hear the requests she made on his behalf, and he fully expected them to be answered. He could feel the same confidence now in hearing this man pray for him.

"Would you help Mark accept the death of his puppy? Father, help him to understand the need for these unhappy experiences. Help him to love others, and especially, Father, teach him what You would have him accomplish in this life."

"What did he mean? God should help me understand unhappy

experiences?" He couldn't imagine God wanting him to be unhappy, though he obviously was. How could he ever accept Tippy's death? He would probably never be happy without him.

"And, Father," the man continued, "You know of the great need there is for rain in this area. We ask You to bring an end to this drought, even today if You can find it in Your will to do so.

"Now again, we ask Your blessing on this food before us, and indeed, Lord, bless the one who prepared it for us. Thank You for all things even before we receive them. We ask it in the name of Your Son, Jesus Christ. Amen!"

Mark was impressed with the man's prayer, and he was sure he would remember every word for a long while. He sat for a time just thinking about the words spoken. "I know God will answer his prayers for me. But they do seem like hard ones."

"By Henry! This is good food!" Mark heard the man exclaim. "I never would have believed baloney gravy could taste this good." The man had seen the faraway look on Mark's face. He said teasingly, "Don't you like baloney gravy anymore?"

Upon finishing the meal, Mark reminded the man they could heat some water on the kerosene stove in the woodshed. They carried water from the well and heated it. Mark brought an extra bucketful so the man could cool it to his liking, then he entered the house to find his mother collecting clothes to give to the man.

"These things belonged to Grandpa Carson," his mother said. "If your friend can wear any of them, he's welcome. Grandpa would be pleased to know someone would get some good out of them. They're perfectly good clothes," she added. "Someone should be wearing them." The man carried his own razor and razor strop and finished shaving just as Mark returned with the clothes. After dressing, he came from the woodshed. Mark could hardly believe this was the

same man. The clothes fit well, and he looked very neat in them. Being deeply appreciative for the thoughtful gesture, he thanked Mrs. Hayes several times.

While Mark sat on the porch waiting for his friend to finish dressing, he had prayed silently, pleading with God to cause the man to stay and visit with him.

Walking toward the garden, Mark asked shyly, "Sir, why do you think God made my puppy die?"

"Hmmm." The man pondered the answer he should give.

"This is where me and Tippy used to play a lot," Mark said, as they reached a grassy area under the trees. "Here in the shade."

The man's expression was one of genuine concern for Mark's dilemma. "Son, it's true, God does all things according to His Own counsel, but He doesn't always explain His reasons to us."

He was well aware of the need for answering such questions cautiously and in a meaningful way for a boy Mark's age.

"We should always try to find solutions to our questions which are in keeping with God's plan and purpose."

Mark didn't understand those words, but he was confident the man knew what he was talking about.

"First, I believe every creature coming into this world has a part in God's plan. It doesn't just apply to people. Makes no difference—a horse, a cow, your puppy. I think most domestic animals are considered to be living souls."

"You mean, even Tippy is important to God, sir?" he asked. "Oh! You bet he is, Mark. Its true humanity is the first object in God's purpose, but the rest of creation will find its place in God's program through humanity. We may not know the reason for Tippy being here. We may not even know why he died after being with you such a short time. But you can be very sure of this much—someday, Tippy will know."

"Son, I guess what I'm trying to say is God didn't bring anything into this world without a perfectly sound reason for doing so. Tippy has a place in eternity just as sure as there is a place for you and me." Again, the man looked at Mark with concern. "We just need to exercise the faith God gives us. Remember this. Everything,

which happens, is for the good of all, even including the fact all of us must die. By Henry! We'll all die just like Tippy did." He smiled affectionately.

"That means Tippy might get saved too. That's what you mean, isn't it, sir?" Mark said, looking for assurance. "But, sir!" he added then shrugged his shoulders and said, "I don't know nothing about a plan and purpose."

"Oh my!" the man exclaimed. "I guess you wouldn't know about that. Well, we better do something about it?"

He paused for a moment, and then placing the thumb of his

right hand under his chin, he began sliding his forefinger up and down over his lips. After a time, having reflected on his thoughts concerning the matter, he said to Mark, "I guess I've never put the subject into words. We talk about the good things, which are part of it, but we don't attempt to put it all together. Well," he said, "let's build a framework to cover God's plan and purpose. After we've done that, you can fill in your own details. When you learn the basic truth, you can study for your own answers."

Again, the man placed his thumb under his chin and slid his forefinger up and down over his lips while he contemplated the words he should select. Mark soon learned whenever the man thought seriously about something, he responded in the same way. A bond was forming between the two, and without a doubt, the bond was one of love. Perhaps the man simply enjoyed talking about the Bible so much he could talk to anyone. Mark was sure it was true, but he also liked to think the feeling he was experiencing was one his friend shared with him.

The stranger collected his thoughts and then became more comfortable as he stretched out on the grass. He began his story.

"A long, long time ago," he said, beginning slowly, "so long ago, there was no such thing as time yet. There was creation existing in the heavens." He made a sweeping gesture across the heavens to show he referred to the entire universe. "The earth had become chaos and void, but there was a problem."

"God had a problem?" Mark asked in astonishment.

"No! No! Not a problem for God! Creation continued to exist through that incredibly long period. But those celestial beings existed only by God's faith, a reflection of God, but only a reflection.

"They were exposed to His goodness, but there was no appreciation for what it meant. The reason creation didn't know God was because it had no faith of its own to believe. God planned all along to bring His entire creation to a place of perfection and become everything to every one of those creatures.

"But first, God made the eons."

Again, Mark interrupted, for the term puzzled him, "I never

heard that word, sir—eons."

"Oh my," the man exclaimed again, realizing the truth of the statement, immediately. "You'll have to learn about that word. It's a very important one." After hesitating briefly, he then began his explanation.

"The eons, Mark, have to do with time. It wasn't until then in God's plan and purpose that the duration of anything could be measured because time didn't exist before. Scientists tell us creation had continued on and on for billions of years. But actually, we can't consider it as being years or even as time at all.

"An eon is simply a long segment of time, and eons are several of those long segments placed one after another. They're a part of eternity for sure but a very special part. You see, Mark, compared with eternity, the eons are short, like the tick of a clock compared with, say, a million years. But they're a part which God set aside for the purpose of bringing His creation to perfection."

The stranger's illustration of time amazed Mark, as he tried to imagine such a comparison. He truly was engrossed in the story.

"Mark," his friend began to explain, "all that former creation was only the faith of God in an invisible form. The purpose for the eons was for God to bring His creation here in a form that He might ultimately be revealed to them in a visible and tangible way. As the original creation was a reflection of God's faith, the eons reveal faith to us in visible form. Those invisible celestial beings became visible human beings. Can you grasp that, Mark? You and I and all humanity are those powers and authorities of the universe in visible form. But humanity still isn't able to comprehend faith any better than the celestial beings were. God had made the eons in Christ Jesus, and now the faith of God will be revealed to all humanity through Jesus. This is a very important part of God's plan and purpose.

"I'll bet you remember the Bible story of Adam when he and Eve were tempted by the serpent to eat of the tree of the knowledge of good and evil."

"I sure do," Mark exclaimed. "God told them they could eat of the tree of life and live forever. But if they ate of the tree of the knowledge of good and evil, they would die. But one day, the serpent met them out in the garden and told them they wouldn't die. He said God knew they would be like Him if they did."

"Well, you know what happened, don't you, Mark? Their souls did begin to die. Every human being inherited the same dying state that Adam received. You know, Mark, people say if Adam hadn't sinned, we wouldn't have all this evil to endure. We could go on living in the garden of Eden and enjoying a life without problems. But God intended it to be just as it happened. This entire humanity has to die because those celestial beings have to die in order to become a new creation and they could only die in these fleshly bodies.

"Of course, they had to be adapted to this physical environment. Every form of life becomes substance, something we can reach out and touch. It's a matter of an invisible creation becoming fleshly and visible. God 'made' the human from the soil of the ground. Then He breathed life into him, and He became a living soul. He called him Adam because he was like God. Because of the flesh, these bodies are very frail, very delicate compared with forms enduring for eternity. When we get hurt, we experience pain. Our bodies become ill. We experience hunger and thirst. When things go wrong, we become angry. A loved one dies, and we know sorrow. We experience many terrible hardships while in this life. Tornadoes and hurricanes cause us to lose our homes. Floods sweep away our possessions. Fire takes our possessions and the lives of our families. Auto accidents and train accidents—"

Mark interrupted at this point. "I wanted to ask you about that, sir. I don't see why God had to bring us into all that. If there weren't no pain and nobody was hungry, then why would God mess it all up?" he asked. "I already know God brings tornadoes and floods. I even know He caused my puppy to die. I just don't know why He does it."

Of course, the interruption came as no surprise to Mark's friend, for he had quite purposely set up the picture for Mark to ponder. "The reason was, Mark," he proceeded to explain, "creation had to be made in such a way for it to die, but He also had to prepare for a way for us to live again and become a new creation. All those things prepare us to become the new creation God intended it to be."

"Boy! I don't understand that, sir!" Mark exclaimed.

"I realize, son," the man said apologetically. "That's a difficult subject. Let's try and follow this matter through and see what God had in mind. The Law of Moses was given to God's people. If they had lived up to its requirements, they would have become a new creation. But all those intricate details of the law made it impossible for anyone to live up to them. Nevertheless, the people believed they must go on trying to live up to it. The more the people tried, the more wicked they became, and the more unhappy God became with them. Finally, God became so annoyed, He gave them over to the penalties of the law—that means, what the law promised to do to them if they did not keep the law, came upon them. If God didn't do something differently, they would become as Sodom and Gomorrah."

"I remember that story. Lot's wife was turned into a pillar of salt because she looked back," Mark said, feeling proud he remembered.

"You're right again, Mark. But God had a far greater solution in mind. All that was brought about by the works of Satan. That was the very reason God created him. The truth is, even if they had lived up to the law, they still would not have come to know God. His purpose for Satan was for him to try and test every human being to miss the mark that the law had established. God knew man could not live up to it, but man was learning righteousness—that is the goodness God required. That paved the way for God to bring about His solution to bring salvation to all creation.

"Do you know what that solution was, Mark?"

"I think it was Jesus," Mark said, though not being quite sure that was the right answer.

"You are absolutely right. God sent His only-begotten Son to live that holy and flawless life for us. He lived up to every single word the law required. It was a concept of God, a-a concept based upon His faith in the future shed blood of His Son, Jesus Christ. God knew by faith, every creature would come to know Him through the plan He was following in order to accomplish it. God would bring His Own Son, the very image of Himself, into the eons to live holy and flawlessly. Then His Son would die for all our sins, and God would raise Him from the grave. That was accomplished when Jesus died on the cross and was resurrected. No longer is sin charged against anyone. No man has ever been capable of living that kind of life, but Jesus lived it for us. It never was a matter of an individual here and there being able to live by their own faith, like the denominations of the world teach. It isn't as though there are some people who are able to stir up a hidden grain of faith somewhere in their being. But all humanity shall believe, for through His Son, God transfers His faith to every creature to each in his or her own order.

"Well, Mark, you can see now God had good reason for the suffering we must go through. What had to come about didn't take God by surprise. He always knew it would be that way. Before He brought one creature into existence, He knew what it would have to go through. He knew He couldn't make a universe of beings and then leave them alone to work out their own salvation. He knew what would be required before any creature could know Him. He knew He must provide a way for every creature to become righteous. The Bible tells us the suffering of this life is not worthy of the glory, which is in store for us in eternity. It is by way of these fleshly bodies, Mark, that God is carrying out His plan. He was providing a way for creation to know their Creator."

Mark had no problem comprehending the picture his friend had conveyed to him. He had been confused about a lot of things, and this seemed to offer many solutions. But even though he understood, he had some difficulty in having to face the possibilities of danger from tornadoes and floods and such. "You said God teaches us through all these bad things, but it would be a lot easier if we didn't have to suffer," he said.

"That's very true, Mark, it would be nice if we didn't have to suffer, but all our suffering is necessary for carrying out God's plan to provide us with faith of our own. God is actually transferring His Own faith to us. He is becoming everything to every creature. But first, every creature must realize they are nothing apart from Him. It begins with humanity.

"Mark, I want you to realize that there is a lake of fire and many people will be cast into it, but that is still part of the eons. Every human being hears the evangel of Christ, and the truth of the evangel of Christ is placed upon every conscience. Now it is a matter for everyone to believe what they have heard. Many do believe in this life, but many do not and must be chastised. That means those who do not believe in this life must be corrected for evil they have done and ultimately receive faith to believe what they already know. At the consummation of the eons when the last trump sounds, those in the lake of fire will be raised up incorruptible and, together with all humanity, will become immortal. Victory will have overcome death to all creatures.

"I want you to think about something, Mark. Try to answer this question for me: Where is the glory of the stars at midday? We gaze into the heavens at noontime, but we see only clouds"—he pointed toward the heavens—"or blue sky or sunlight," he added. "There's no beauty of the stars to reveal themselves at noontime. Until there's a dimming of the sunlight, the beauty of the stars cannot be revealed. Darkness reveals their splendor. That's the way it is with the goodness of God. Until there is darkness, we cannot appreciate the beauty. Until there is evil, we cannot appreciate the goodness."

This had stirred up a great interest for Mark. "I think I can believe that, sir. Reverent (sic) Harper keeps talking about how most people are gonna go to the bad place." Mark gritted his teeth and pulled his shoulders upward, realizing he had almost repeated something he shouldn't have. "Sometimes, it seems like nobody's gonna go to heaven. Wait 'til I tell Mama. She believes everything Reverent Harper says."

Mark was even more excited now. This gave him reason to believe there was much more for Tippy, more than just dying and having all hope come to an end. "Reverent (sic) Harper always says Jesus died lor everyone. Then he makes everybody scared they're not gonna make it after all. Now I know everybody's gonna be saved, and I like that a whole lot better."

"I think I understand too," Mark exclaimed. "I think Tippy learned all God wanted him to know. He was a smart little dog, and I think that's why he died when he was little," Mark concluded.

CHAPTER 3

They were entering the most uncomfortable hour of the day. The heat was more intense and even warmer than on the days before. In the morning, a gentle breeze stirred among the trees, but now it was quite still and more humid than ever. The stranger took a handkerchief from his pocket and blotted the perspiration from his forehead.

Before his friend left the woodshed after bathing and getting dressed, he observed some boards and a cardboard box filled with parts necessary for making a go-kart. Obviously, Mark's intentions had been to build one, but for some reason, the plans hadn't been carried out. Having little doubt Mark needed some diversion from the rather deep conversation they were engaged in, he inquired about the go-kart.

"Dad's been gonna build it all summer, but he don't have time," Mark said. "He don't want me to use his tools when he's not here. I don't know why, he takes all the good ones with him anyway. I sure wish I had a go-kart." He showed signs of dejection as he spoke. "All my friends got one. They go up to the church and ride down the hill on the sidewalk. Allen lets me ride on his sometimes, but he'd rather I didn't. It's real nice, and boy, does it go fast!"

"What's to keep us from building one right now?"

"Do you know how, sir?"

"Well, I've built a few for the youngsters in my neighborhood," he said. They began walking in the direction of the woodshed. "Come to think of it, by Henry! I've never heard any complaints. Sure! We can come up with something pretty nice, judging by the parts I saw in the woodshed. Looked to me like you have everything you need—good set of wagon wheels, axles. Those are the most important things. That old lawn mower wheel has a chip in it, but we can smooth it out and use it for a steering wheel. You might see if your mother has some empty sewing thread spools we can use for pulleys. We're going to need those." They arrived at the woodshed and stood looking over the box of parts. "You've got rope here. Looks like just the right size," he added.

"Mama already gave me the spools. They're on my dresser, sir." Mark could hardly contain his excitement. He had practically given up on having a go-kart of his own. With this man building it, it would probably be the best go-kart in town.

"Looks like things are pretty well organized. We'll have it built in no time. That is if you think your daddy won't mind."

"He won't mind! He'll be glad he don't have to build it, sir," Mark explained.

They worked together as the man cut the boards to the proper length and drilled the hole for the steering column. Mark decided it best to let the man use his own judgment. It did save time, for he was uncertain how it should be done anyway. In just over an hour, the go-kart was completely built.

"All it needs now is a coat of paint," the stranger said.

"I don't have no paint, sir," he said. "I can buy a whole can down at Bishop's for a dime, though. They got all colors. I think I want to paint it blue."

Mark rode down the hill a couple of times. He was as proud as any boy could be, and his face beamed with happiness. "Boy! Will Allen be surprised when he sees this! You can ride on it too, sir."

"I don't think so, Mark." The man chuckled as he spoke. "I'm afraid I'm better at building carts than I am at hanging on while they go flying down the hills."

Quickly, Mark pushed the cart up the incline so he could ride down again. But as elated as Mark was, his primary concern was still the presence of the man he had come to love so very much in the short time of their acquaintance. When he reached the bottom of the hill, he saw the man walking slowly toward the creek. Realizing he was leaving, he called to the man. "Please don't leave, sir. Won't you stay for a while longer?" he said. By then, he was following after the man. Tears filled his eyes as he began running to the place where the man had stopped to wait for him.

It was apparent the man only needed good reason to remain a while longer. The tears in Mark's eyes made the decision easy. "It's mighty hot to be walking down the tracks the way the sun's bearing down. Why not," he said. "I haven't anything in particular to do." They walked to the spot where they were seated when Mark listened to the story of God's plan and purpose. "I want you to know something, son," he spoke softly, and Mark could tell just from having come to know him so well, he had something important to say.

Placing his hand on Mark's shoulder, he said, "I never had a son of my own. I would have been proud to have a son like you. I think God must have something pretty special in store for you."

If ever there had been doubt about Mark's love for the man, it was certainly gone after hearing those words. He reached both arms around the man, hoping he would understand how he felt. "I already missed you, sir, and you weren't even gone yet."

Just then, Mrs. Hayes called from the back porch.

"I'm in the garden, Mama," Mark answered.

She closed the screen door and walked to where Mark and his guest were sitting. "I'm sorry," she apologized. "I didn't know your friend was still here. I just thought maybe you should go to the store before long, but there will be time later."

"We built a go-kart. I'm gonna paint it tomorrow. Before that, we talked about life and why bad things happen," he explained to his mother. "I'm finding out why people die, even why Tippy died when he was so little."

"Oh my! Sounds like a mighty important subject to me. That's something we all need to know more about." She smiled as she spoke, as though being sure no one had the answers to those questions.

"I'm afraid I've done most of the talking, but your son is a good listener. He knows how to make a person think. It does us good to be pressed to give answers to questions concerning the Word of God. I've enjoyed our visit very much," he assured her.

Mrs. Hayes smiled and then started toward the house. "Oh, dear!" she exclaimed. "The flowers are wilted so, and we just can't spare the water. I do hope it rains soon."

Mark and his friend sat quietly for a time. Mark could hardly bear to think of what he would do when the man was gone. As though knowing Mark's exact thoughts, the man laid back on the grass. Resting the back of his head on his hands, he gazed into the heavens.

Mark knew his friend would be staying a while longer. Almost instinctively, Mark's lips were forming the words: "Thank You, God, for causing him to stay." He knew the man heard enough of his words to know what he said. He breathed a sigh and then lay back resting his head on his hands in quite the same manner as his friend had done. Mark too gazed out toward the heavens.

For Mark, the day had begun as a most frustrating and discouraging day, but it was a grand and glorious one now. Now he had a feeling he was important in the eyes of God. Lying stretched out on the grass, his thoughts were of the pleasure he relished from being in the presence of the man beside him. He had heard his mother remark on a number of occasions how she felt God was speaking to her, and quite honestly, he felt God was speaking to him through this man. Eager to learn whatever his friend could teach him, he didn't want to waste time. It was Mark who broke the silence.

"Sir," Mark said shyly, "I still kind a got a problem with what we've been talking about."

"And what's that?"

"I understand God wants us to suffer so we can get to know Him. But, sir, couldn't we get to know Him some other way?" he asked. Mark was looking for an easier way than through suffering.

"I can see you're having a lot of trouble understanding the purpose for evil. Well! By Henry! You aren't the only one having that problem. Everyone has a problem with that subject."

"I'd like to tell you a story that might help you. It's a story very dear to me. Something that happened to me when I was a boy, about your age, I suppose."

Once again, the man made the gesture Mark had become so Familiar with. He had come to recognize it as a signal he was about to hear something of particular interest.

"In the living room of our home, and setting on an end table, was a bowl. Actually, it was a candy dish, but Dad had it filled with pennies. Every time I passed by, I thought how nice it would be if I could spend them on candy. The temptation became greater each day. Finally, it just got to be more than I could handle. First, I took two pennies, slipped them into my pocket, and then when I got a chance, I bought the candy. Dad didn't seem to miss them, so I took two more and bought candy with those too. I did it a third time. The fourth time I became bolder and took five pennies."

"Well! That put me over the limit." His eyes sparkled. "Dad knew what was going on. Of course, I admitted taking the pennies. My, I got the whipping of my life." He placed a hand on his buttock and rubbed it. "It was a while before I could sit down," he said, showing a grin, "but do you know what?" He sat upright and looked directly into Mark's eyes.

"No, sir, what?" Mark asked excitedly.

"I never stole again after day, by Henry, except once a friend and I stole some watermelons," he added, as an afterthought. "It wasn't till I was grown Dad told me he planned the entire episode. He thought the best way for me to learn not to steal was to face the temptation. Then if I couldn't stand up to the test, I'd have to be punished."

"Dad loved me so much he wanted me to steal those pennies. He believed I'd learn more from the guilt for stealing than I'd learn if I hadn't been tempted at all. Dad wasn't always such a wise man, but our heavenly Father always does things with that kind of wisdom. Dad used the principle and taught me a great lesson. Our heavenly Father has used that principle since the beginning of mankind. That, Mark, is why suffering is necessary. It's through the suffering we learn the true meaning of good."

"I'll guess you didn't know it will be people like you and me who will be in charge of the affairs of the universe?" he said.

The man had made a statement Mark wasn't prepared for. "I sure didn't know that, sir."

Taking his Bible from the knapsack, he began thumbing through the pages. There were a couple of matters he wanted Mark to grasp before he would leave him. Even Mark suspected the time was near for his departure. He showed Mark scripture explaining how God made man a little lower than the messengers of heaven then brought His Own Son into the world to become a man also. He showed him how God wreathed His Son with glory and honor after He tasted death and how all humanity shall enter into salvation through His death. "God placed His Son over all creation.

When we receive faith to believe in His death, burial, and resurrection, we'll share in all He received because we are of His family. Then we'll be placed over the works of God's hands and share in the kingdom of His Son.

"You know, Mark"—with a great deal of affection, the man looked at him for he wanted to share something, something quite intimate—"when I was a lad, I used to lie on the grass in the evenings and look up into the heavens. I tried to imagine what it would be like to be out there among the stars. I wondered if perhaps in the next life, I might live on one of them. One evening, I decided to choose a star and consider it being my very own. I thought maybe I could go there someday. That was long before I knew anything about what we just talked about. I've looked for my star in the heavens time and again. I used to laugh to myself when I wondered if other people choose stars for themselves. I still like to look for it now and then."

"If I could have my own star, sir, I'd pick one right next to yours," Mark said.

The man looked at Mark for a long moment, recognizing the affection shown to him. He began to speak. "You have a great capacity for love," he said with a smile.

"I don't think I know what that word means," Mark said to him.

"It means I think you have a lot of room in your heart for loving others."

"I don't love everybody. I don't even know if I love Ben." He was trying to decide whether he did or not.

"Who's Ben?" the man questioned.

Of course, it was necessary for Mark to relate the experience of his encounter with Ben Pritchard that morning.

"Have you ever met Ben when you were out on the street, when no one else was around?" his friend asked.

"I think so," Mark said. Then he remembered such an occasion. "Once, I went into the restaurant, and we was the only ones there. Edna was at the post office, and we had to wait for her 'cause the mail train was late."

"Did Ben tease you when he met you in the restaurant?"

"Naah! He was friendly. He was nice to me, sir. And once when we was in the park, he came over and talked to me for a long time." Again, the man began to speak. "I wouldn't worry whether

Ben likes you. I suspect he likes you very much, otherwise, he probably wouldn't talk to you at all.

"Son, I think it's only fair to warn you, believing the things we've talked about today will probably cause you some difficult times in years ahead. You may even decide you don't want to follow through on these matters. People will—"

"I think people will want to know God is gonna save everybody. By Henry! I'm not gonna stop believing it," Mark said indignantly. He could only think how much better it made him feel than hearing what Reverend Harper said so often.

His friend was a bit shocked, though certainly amused, to hear Mark use his own expression. "If folks could accept the truth, I'm sure they would want to know. But most Christians believe the way your pastor wants you to believe." He smiled. "They're afraid to believe differently."

The man looked at Mark. He spoke slowly and distinctly, "Always remember—believe what the Bible says even if you don't understand it. Stay close to that rule, and it will reveal more truth to you than church doctrine will ever teach you."

"Do you know about the premonition all creation has concerning the sons of God?" the man asked. "Oh my! You may not even know what the word means," he said, thinking he would need to define it for him.

"No, sir, I don't," Mark acknowledged.

"A premonition is having a feeling something will happen but not being able to explain why we have the feeling. There doesn't seem to be a reason for it—we just feel it. Anyway, all creation has that premonition.

"Paul tells us God chose a special few from among the human race and gave them a special degree of faith to believe in Him. These are said to be sons of God. Because of those special sons, every creature on this earth has the feeling something good is also in store for them. They wait for the day when those sons of God will be revealed. They know that when it happens, they will be set free from all their troubles. That is the premonition God has given to every creature.

"When we believe scripture for what it says, we often find truths not recognized by most. If what Reverend Harper and most others teach is correct, these things couldn't be true. Those people won't allow it to be taught God will save every individual, let alone Tippy and the rest of creation, but these verses teach that He will.

"I want to show you a passage of scripture. Of all scripture, these are my favorite verses. When I get discouraged and Satan causes me to feel perhaps my understanding is in error and everyone else is correct, I turn to them for comfort." His friend was explaining as he thumbed through the pages looking for the passage. "Here are the verses, found at 1 Timothy 4:9-11: 'Faithful is the saying and worthy of all welcome (for this are we toiling and being reproached), that we rely on the living God, Who is Savior of all mankind, especially of those who believe. These things be charging and teaching.'"

"Those verses not only tell us Christ is the Savior of all mankind, we are asked to teach this truth to others.

"Do you often talk to your daddy?" he asked. Reaching into his pocket, he took something from it. It was the first time in all their conversation the man had purposely changed the subject. He had a way of getting Mark to think about things he really hadn't wanted to think about before. More than that, Mark found he liked getting things out in the open. There was a comfortable feeling in knowing he could say whatever he felt like saying. And this man always seemed to have just the right answer.

"I don't talk to Daddy much," Mark said.

"Oh my!" he exclaimed. "Don't you like to talk to him?"

"Daddy says I'm a dreamer. He says I don't listen when he tells me something, and he says I don't consecrate (sic)."

The man smiled. "He thinks you need to concentrate more on things like your schoolwork then?" he asked, pronouncing the word carefully. "Many people who have accomplished great things in life were considered dreamers when they were young. Thomas Edison had a hard time during his school years, yet he gave something pretty special to the world when he invented the light bulb. He invented many things powered by electricity. It's possible God is working out some great thing for you to accomplish for Him. Wouldn't that be wonderful?" he said, giving Mark a comforting smile.

"I suspect you think your daddy doesn't love you, but I'm sure in his own way, he loves you very much. These have been troubling times for many. Jobs are difficult to find and just as hard to keep. People have to take every advantage of work that comes along. Don't be too harsh with your daddy. People often become angry with the ones they love most, and they tend to forget even eleven-year-old sons have problems too. Try to love your daddy in spite of how you think he feels for you. You will be a happier young man."

"Have you ever seen one of these?" Mark's friend asked. He was holding a coin in his hand. As it was handed to Mark, Mark observed the coin was attached to a chain. Upon examination, he recognized the chain as being like ones he'd seen for sale in Edna's restaurant on display cards. A hole was drilled near the edge of this coin for the insertion of the chain. It was the size of a fifty-cent piece, but Mark had never seen one like this.

"That's an Indian rupee, a silver coin used in India," he explained. "I've carried it for many years. It has no real monetary value, but I kept it as a kind of reminder to me. I want always to remember money is the least of the things I look for in life. I've learned hard work provides me with all the material things I need. And I've learned what others do through love bring the greatest rewards.

"I've waited for the day I could feel confident enough to give up this coin and recognize without fear—I have no money with which to buy food. It may sound foolish, perhaps it is," he said thoughtfully. "But it's important that I put my trust in God to sustain me. I want you to take this coin and let it serve as a reminder of our visit today. Let it help you learn there are more important things in this life than money. A genuine love for God and His creation will bring the greatest rewards. Mark, I hope our visit has helped you as much as it's helped me. I've enjoyed every moment of this day with you."

Mark had grasped much of what the man said to him that day, though some of the deeper wisdom was beyond his clear understanding. His friend had given more than mere words of wisdom, for he knew the meaning of words would fade and, in time, their meeting would be little more than a vague memory. The coin would long serve as a reminder of their visit. Mark sensed how much the man wanted him to have it. An overwhelming feeling of emptiness came over him.

He realized the moment he dreaded was at hand. Their meeting was nearing an end, and he could do nothing about it. A lump in his throat kept back the words he wanted to say.

"We shall meet again, son," the man said softly, answering the question Mark was unable to ask.

He stood gazing into the man's eyes.

"I'd better be going before the rain gets here," he said.

Mark looked to the western skies and observed the dark clouds forming. He had been oblivious of the gathering storm clouds. Like a display of magic, the desperately needed rain would soon be upon them.

"God is answering his prayer. He could still remember the exact words the man spoke at lunchtime. *"And, Father, You know the need there is for rain in the area. We ask if You would end this drought, even this day if You can find it in Your will to do so."*

"God must have heard your prayer," Mark said. Hearing no reply, he turned toward the place where the man had stood. To his astonishment, his friend was not there. At some distance, the man was walking toward the railroad tracks from where he had first come. Mark stood, unable to do anything but watch as his friend walked away. He expected him to stop and wave, but he continued on until at last he reached the tracks. Only then did the man turn and look in Mark's direction. Waving briefly, he resumed his walk toward the bridge, which stood just above the dam.

It occurred to Mark that just a short distance down the right- of-way was a clearing where he would be able to see the man from the back porch steps. From the steps, Mark watched patiently until his friend appeared in the clearing. Jumping to his feet, he waved, but only too soon, it was apparent his friend was unaware Mark was within his range of vision. In a moment, the man disappeared entirely from sight.

Reality settled in. For a time, he felt nothing, a complete absence of feeling, as numbness. The same feeling he had when Tippy died was upon him. *"I don't see how it could be any worse if he died like Tippy did."* Fie was sure he would never see the man again. Flow he loved him! Flow he wished he had not gone away. *"If only I could speak to him now. If I could just wake up and find it was all a dream."* His mind was in turmoil.

But it was very real. Mark began praying silently. "Oh, God, will I ever see the man again?" he asked. "Please, God, make him come back. Please let me see him again." He sat motionless with his head resting on his knees. He thought about the entire experience. The man seemed to appear out of nowhere, and now he was gone as quickly as he arrived. "Why did he come at all? No! I don't really mean that. But it would be so wonderful if he were only just arriving now. Then I could begin the entire wonderful experience all over again."

Suddenly, a resounding clap of thunder roused Mark. At almost the same moment, his mother called from the front door. Quickly, he ran through the house to open the door for her.

"As your daddy would say, 'It sounds like the potato wagon upset!'" she exclaimed. Mrs. Hayes had purchased groceries before stopping to visit with Molly. "Molly wanted me to wait," she explained, "but I wanted to take a chance on getting home before the rain came."

"Did you have a nice visit with your friend?" she asked. The thunder became more pronounced. "Oh! I meant to ask before. What was your friend's name?"

The realization came to Mark for the first time. He didn't know the man's name. "Oh, Mama," he said sheepishly, "I forgot to ask."

Having spent the entire afternoon with his new friend, then coming to love him like he never loved anyone before, he hadn't thought to ask his name. Grasping for an explanation in his embarrassment, he could only say, "I called him sir!"

Mrs. Hayes was puzzled, hardly able to believe what she heard. Recognizing Mark's despair, she tried to remember if he had introduced himself when she met him. "Oh, dear!" she pondered. "I don't recall hearing him say, either."

It was getting darker. The welcome breeze began to intensify. Walking to the back porch and looking to the west, they saw the rain as it came sweeping toward them. Being rushed by a sudden gust of wind, it arrived quickly and sped on by.

"I hope we get a nice rain. We need it badly," his mother was saying. Mark's eyes focused upon the clearing where he had last seen his friend. "Where is he now?" he wondered.

Mark told his mother how he watched his friend until he was out of sight. She was coming to realize how much Mark missed him.

"What will he do if it rains?" he asked. "I wonder where he can go to stay dry?"

Mark was deeply concerned now, for the rain was falling heavily. Mrs. Hayes wanted to reassure him. "I'm sure he will find a place where he can stay dry. Perhaps he's sitting under a bridge somewhere down the tracks," she suggested. "Maybe he found a barn to go into. I'm sure he's all right. God will take care of him."

What his mother was saying didn't really help, for now he was sure sir was sitting under a bridge somewhere and probably not far away. Mark was sure he must have got wet before he could find a dry place, and besides, even a bridge might not keep him dry in the downpour they were having. How strange! The man prayed they would get rain. Now the very rain he prayed for was probably drenching him. "Please, God, watch over sir. Please keep him from getting rained on," he pleaded.

Mark walked into the living room. Taking a pillow from the studio couch, he laid down on the floor at the doorway. As the rain came down harder, he continued to ask God to watch over sir. The rain continued to fall in a steady manner. The words of sir's prayer suddenly came into Mark's memory—the part where he prayed for the rain. He marveled of the way in which his prayer was answered so quickly. His friend hadn't arrived until midmorning. And there was no forecast of rain so far as Mark knew of. It wasn't suppertime yet, and the rain had already arrived.

With tree branches swirling with the wind, the lightning and thunder continued for a time but soon began to abate. Mark relived conversation after conversation with his friend. How he would miss his friend, but oh, how he enjoyed thinking of the things he had learned. Interspersed with his thoughts were the flashes of lightning and the rolls of thunder as they faded into the distance. He watched as the water collected on the walk and then ran to each side where the warm, dry earth took it deep into its soil. Quietness set in. The only sound to be heard was the steady rhythmic patter of rain on the roof and on the sidewalk outside the door. It was apparent they were enjoying a welcome late-afternoon shower.

CHAPTER 4

A beautiful morning followed the rain, the most comfortably cool morning they had experienced in many days. A good-soaking rain fell and was indeed welcome. Already the grass contained traces of green. With the moisture received, it was sure to become much greener in the days ahead.

Mrs. Hayes had wanted Mark to help her clean the cave for some time. She suggested that while it was still cool would be a good time to get it over with. It wasn't a job to look forward to, but immediately the thought of having it out of the way appealed to Mark. His mother was quite pleased Mark was willing to get started. "With both of us working, it should go rather quickly," she said. The potato bin wasn't nearly as hard to clean as Mark had expected it to be, and it was quite cool inside the cave.

"I think maybe the rain came in time to help the potato crop. I sure hope so," she added, revealing a remaining concern. "From the amount of water in the can on the fence post, I'd say we got about an inch and a half of rain."

"Mama," Mark said, hoping to find a way to share his new understanding with his mother, "do you believe everything Reverent (sic) Harper says?"

His mother was puzzled by his question. Not quite knowing what he was getting at, she asked, "Do you mean as far as his understanding of the Bible?"

"Yeah, that's what I mean. There are lots of churches, and I don't think they all believe the same things. I just wonder how to know which one is right."

"Well," his mother said thoughtfully, "I suppose if I could belong to any church I wanted to, I probably wouldn't have chosen the Methodist Church. But I don't think the denomination is the most important consideration."

"Then you don't believe everything Reverent Harper believes?" He hoped she was going to agree with him.

"I wouldn't say everything. But I think we agree on the important things. I don't like the idea of being sprinkled in baptism the way they do it. I guess I feel we should be totally immersed." Mrs. Hayes laughed. "My daddy used to say, 'If you're gonna be cleansed of sin, you might as well be clean all over.' I think the important thing is in the idea of wanting to be cleansed of sin," she added. "The water doesn't really add anything."

"Did you know everybody's gonna be saved?" Mark was surprised at himself for asking his question so bluntly. He was trying to be so careful. "I-I-I mean, wouldn't it be nice if everyone would be saved?" he asked, trying to cover his mistake.

"Ma-a-rk! Of course, it would be nice to see everyone saved, but the Bible doesn't teach that."

"Oh yes, Mama, sir told me it does. He told me how we were put in the eons to adjust to God's faith and how everyone in their own time will believe like God does. Mama, I get so tired of hearing Reverent Harper talk about going down to chaos and destruction. It's scary when he says that, and I don't think God wants us to be a scared of Him. God wouldn't want that. Sir makes it seem so good, a-a-a-and I think it should be good, don't you, Mama?"

Mrs. Hayes was speechless over the things Mark said. Strangely, they made a lot of sense, and she was at a loss to give an answer. "If you pray about it, God will give you the answers."

"I know, Mama, sir said that's why we were put here on the earth to learn those things."

Mrs. Hayes was troubled. But she felt she should be silent on the matter for the time being and search for the explanation, which would be correct.

The cave was cleaned by eleven o'clock. His mother told him he could spend the rest of the day doing something he would enjoy.

"Would you look at that?" his mother asked in astonishment.

It took Mark by surprise. His first thought was she had seen the snake again. "Where, Mama! Where!"

"Down there at the bridge. Those boys are swimming naked again. Don't they have any shame? They stand up there on the diving board naked as jaybirds. The whole world can see them."

"Mama, nobody goes down there. Nobody's gonna see 'em."

"Anybody walking up and down the tracks can see them. They have no shame. You can be sure Jason isn't down there. I told him if he ever swam down there naked again, I'd tan his behind."

Mark laughed. "He's a lot bigger than you are, Mama. Besides, maybe they're just getting baptized."

"Oh! Get out of here," she said, becoming flustered. "Go get the mail."

"I'm on my way," he told her, pretending to be desperately trying to avoid her fury.

Rarely a day went by when his mother didn't need something in the way of groceries, but there was nothing she needed this day. The Hayes family couldn't afford an icebox—they couldn't afford to buy the ice even if they had one. Of course, it created the need for more frequent purchases in order to have fresh foods.

As Mark walked toward town, his hand went to the bottom of his pocket. He grasped the coin and chain the stranger had given him. Entire conversations came back to him.

"Sure a nice rain we had." Molly Patton interrupted Mark's thoughts as he walked by her house. Looking at her flowers and pulling a weed here and there, she walked along in a stooped position. The muddy ground didn't seem to bother her, and the weeds did seem to pull quite easily.

"Did your mother get home before the rain came?" she asked. "I wanted her to wait, but she insisted on going home. Wanted to beat the rain!"

"She got home just in time," Mark told her. "When we went to the back door, we saw the rain comin'."

As Mark had become accustomed to doing, he felt he must apologize for not staying to visit. He told Molly he must get to the post office before they closed for lunch. That really wasn't a stretch of the truth since it was already a few minutes past eleven-thirty.

He continued on toward town. As he reached the post office, he thought he saw Ben sitting in his usual place at the window ledge. It seemed unlikely it could be Ben at this time of the day, but he soon learned he was right. Unable to do much around the farm because of the rain, he stayed in town after picking up his mail.

"Hello, Hayes!" Ben said, as Mark entered the door.

"Hello, sir."

"Hello, Sir Ben!" Ben shouted, placing emphasis on the title "sir," as though Mark had made a grave error. "You're supposed to call me Sir Ben, remember?" he said, giving a hearty laugh. Ben had a laugh Mark thought to be most annoying, and there was rarely much humor behind it. "Did you hear about the bum they found out south of town?" he asked, directing his question to Mark.

"No, sir," Mark replied, placing no significance to his statement. At this point, John Barkley interrupted, "Ben! You've been in here since eight o'clock this morning. You must have told fifty people about that bum. Thank goodness, it's noon. You're gonna have to seat your carcass somewhere else. I'm closing up for dinner." With those words, John put his hand on Ben's shoulder, as he guided him to the door.

"There's no mail for you, Mark," he said. Mark slipped out the door ahead of them. "You know something, Ben? You're like a wart. When you get on someone, it's next to impossible to get rid of you." Ben was unruffled by John's words. He continued to pursue his remarks about the hobo. "They found a bum outside town last night along the tracks."

For the first time, Mark began to connect Ben's statement with his new friend from the day before. "What do you mean, they found him?" he asked. "Where is he now?"

"I don't know whether he's in heaven or in hell," Ben said mockingly, "but he's sure enough dead."

Mark looked at Ben hoping he might start his laughter so he could know Ben was joking. But Ben had no reason to joke about this man. He likely wouldn't have known about sir under any other circumstances.

At first, his feelings were of disbelief. Then there was fear it was probably true. As the realization moved in, there came to be little doubt in Mark's mind. He didn't want to accept it as being fact, but he realized if it was true he was going to have to face it.

"You sure he was dead, Ben?" he asked. As the truth made its impact, the tears came streaming over his cheeks. "He was my friend, Ben," Mark confided.

Ben tried in his awkward way to console Mark. "Naw!" Ben replied. "He weren't no one you knowed. He was just a bum walkin' the tracks."

"He was my friend," Mark assured him. "He told me why my puppy died. A-a-and he told me my daddy loves me. A-a-and he prayed for rain, and it rained last night," he said, running out of breath in trying to convince Ben it was true.

Ben looked at Mark in bewilderment. "You're weird, Hayes," he said, clearly not knowing what to make of him.

Desperately wanting to be understood, Mark thought of the coin in his pocket. He showed it to Ben. "See," he said, "my friend gave the coin to me. Just yesterday, he gave it to me, Ben."

Ben glanced at it and was immediately impressed. "Boy! That must be worth a lot of money," he said. "What kind a coin is it? Boy! I bet that's worth a lot!" By then the coin was in Ben's hands, and he was inspecting it carefully. He read the word rupee on the coin. Again, he exclaimed, "It must be worth a lot of money."

"He told me it don't have no real m-mon-tary (sic) value." Mark vaguely knew the meaning of the word, though he struggled to pronounce it. "He wanted me to keep it so I'd remember meeting him. I did meet him, Ben. He gave me the coin yesterday."

Ben began to question Mark. "If he was your friend, what was his name? Nobody knows what his name was."

Once again, Mark was embarrassed in not knowing the man's name. "I-I-I don't know. I called him sir! Really I did Ben," he said, when he realized how hard it must be to believe.

"You are weird, Hayes, the only thing is, I believe you. You call everybody sir."

Upon further pleading with Ben to tell him what he knew about the man's death, he told Mark where the body was found. "You know the old railroad bridge on the Hayes farm."

Mark knew well about the bridge. The name Hayes referred to Mark's grandfather who once owned the farm.

"Would you take me out there?"

"Sure," he said, "there ain't nothin' out there. Sure, I'll take ya." Ben started for his car with Mark just a step behind, and soon, they were on their way to the scene. "You want your coin back?" Ben asked, holding it out for Mark to take. "How'd you know the of guy?" Ben questioned. "Ain't nobody around here knowed him." Mark proceeded to tell Ben of the events of the day before. He told of some of the things they talked about. How much he had come to love the man, and how the man had built a go-kart for him.

They reached the railroad crossing. Having gone as far as they could by car, they set out on foot to walk down the tracks. Mark remembered what his friend had said about Ben teasing him. *"Maybe Ben will tell me if he likes me if I ask him straight out."* With little thought as to the possible reaction to his question, Mark blurted it out, "Do you like me, Ben?"

Ben looked at Mark in disbelief. "Why do you ask a dumb question like that?" His face flushed as he tried to provide an answer. "Well, what do ya s'pose? I guess I like ya. I wouldn't talk to ya if'n I didn't, would I?" he asked through embarrassment.

Mark was elated to hear Ben's response. "Sir knows the answer to everything. I told sir you teased me all the time. He said you did it because you really like me."

"That's what I said," Ben replied. "I wouldn't talk to ya if'n I didn't like ya."

It wasn't like Mark to ask such a question. He had begun to wish he hadn't asked, but now he was glad he had. It was one more of sir's statements proving to be right.

Ben was already down the embankment. "Right here's where they found 'im." He proceeded to give Mark all the details. "Cecil Cummins found 'im." Cecil was the man living on the farm at the time. "He was hayin' over yonder," he said, pointing across the tracks and farther to the south. "It was a rainin', and Cecil was hurryin' home when he seen this here guy layin' under the bridge. He stopped and hollered so's the of guy would get movin' along, an' he didn't move. Cecil went over and shook 'im, but he didn't wake up. He didn't breathe an' he didn't have no pulse, so he went home and called the coroner."

"How'd you know about it?"

"We was settin' under the bandstand down town when we saw the coroner drive by. Goin' up the hill he was. Me an' Jake, an' Tom Smith, an' Bill Dowds, an' an' Walt Daily, I think it was—

yeah, it was. We got in my car an' follered him out here. He said it looked like the of guy just went to sleep and died. Said there's one thing kind of strange though."

"What's that?" Mark interrupted.

"Well, he said it was odd the old guy carried a knapsack for his clothes an' razor an' stuff, but he didn't look like no bum. Said he was clean an' had on clean clothes, an' had a close shave. Looked like a hard worker too."

"I told you, Ben," Mark said excitedly, "he was at my house. He took a bath in the woodshed, and shaved, a-a-a-and he was wearing Grampa's clothes."

"I know! That's what I was a thinkin.' I bet the coroner would like to know about it. He kept a sayin,' 'Someone had to a seen 'im.'" As soon as Ben felt he had told Mark everything he knew about the man's death, he asked, "You ready to go now?"

"I want to stay here awhile," Mark said. "I'll go home pretty soon." Ben didn't want to leave Mark alone, but he insisted he had walked the tracks many times before. Mark convinced him he just wanted to be alone. Ben walked slowly up the embankment. Upon reaching the rails, he turned and looked at Mark. In the kindest voice Mark had ever heard Ben use, he said to him, "I do like ya, Hayes, even if'n ya are weird." He turned and began walking toward his car.

Mark walked over to the spot where Ben told him they found the body. Sitting down, he remained there for some time thinking about the previous day spent with sir. Many of the things they discussed came to memory. He thought of the way, in which the man had left him standing there in the garden. There was no chance to say goodbye, for when he turned to speak, the man was gone. *"Maybe sir didn't want to say goodbye any more than I didn't want him to leave. Oh, how I'll miss him. I'll never see him again now. "*

"I have his coin and chain in my pocket. I can remember him that way." He took them from his pocket. He didn't think he would ever need a reminder of their visit, having been placed so vividly in his mind. *"Why hadn't he tried to learn which star sir had chosen? Maybe then he could reach out to him.* "But that was useless thinking. Even if by some strange coincidence he did choose the same star, he would never know.

It was much easier to think of Tippy now. He was getting used to not having him around, even though he still loved him and missed him. He had known both sir and Tippy such a short time, but he had grown to love both of them. Now both of them were gone. *"Is God trying to teach me something?"* Sitting there on the ground, it became harder and harder to think about anything else. *"Ben was right when he said there wasn't anything out here."* Still it was the last place sir had been while he was still alive. Mark lay down on the grass placing his head on his arm and gazed off to the west. No sooner had he done so, when there, not two feet in front of his face, the edge of a book was visible to him. Mark didn't have to think twice about what he had seen. Without question, it was sir's Bible. There it was, laying on the ground under a rock.

Jumping to his feet and looking down at the stone, he knew unless having been seen from the vantage point he experienced, it most probably would have been overlooked. Lying with his face at ground level, Mark could hardly miss seeing it. One thing was sure. Those who took care of the body and gathered up his belongings hadn't found it.

It was a flat stone but not heavy. Sir could easily have lifted the stone and placed the Bible there while lying on the ground. *"Did he put it there to keep it dry?"* Mark wondered. "*Or could he have known he was going to die and left it there for me to find?"* His imagination raced wildly. *"No!"* He decided. *"He couldn't have even thought I would find his Bible, being so far away from home and hidden under a rock."*

"But God could have! Sir said God was teaching me something when Tippy died. Maybe he's teaching me something now!"

The Bible was covered with soil gathered from beneath the rock. He brushed most of the soil away and opened the book. As he thumbed through it, he discovered a number of marked passages. There were several different markings. Some verses were circled, some were underlined, and some appeared in parenthesis. In some areas, it was only a word or two being set apart. Many of his own notes were inserted.

At a place somewhere just past the middle of the book, Mark found markings, which immediately caught his attention. It was the place sir had told him were his favorite verses of scripture. He recognized it because of the way it was so carefully marked. When sir read it to him, he had noticed how each word was separately underscored, the lines drawn over a straightedge. He remembered the very words sir spoke concerning this particular passage: *"It's my favorite, and anytime I get discouraged and feel maybe my understanding is wrong and everyone else is right, I turn to it for comfort."*

"Faithful is the saying and worthy of all welcome (for this are we toiling and being reproached), that we rely on the living God, Who is Savior of all mankind, especially of believers. These things be charging and teaching' (1 Tim. 4:9-11).

Mark wondered if it could be God was speaking to him through this experience. He recalled sir saying, "*Maybe we should say God is causing us to do certain things instead of telling us."* Oh, how those words stood out in his memory.

"Maybe God caused sir to leave his Bible under the rock and then caused me to find it." His thoughts ran rampant again. *"Maybe everything happening yesterday happened by God causing it."* Mark could understand the coroner being puzzled at how neat the man appeared after his death. He was sure it would not be characteristic of a hobo.

He took consolation in knowing the man hadn't suffered, especially remembering how Tippy suffered before he died.

He sat there not knowing where to turn. He had received his own Bible, after winning second place in a contest reading Bible verses. On the page just inside the cover, his mother had inscribed the verse: "This book will keep you from sin, but beware—Sin will keep you from this book."

Just above the verse, she had written his name. Quickly, he turned there hoping to find a name to identify the man.

He read this title:

> "Concordant Version
> The Sacred scriptures
> Concordant Publishing Concern."

But there was no name.

In his disappointment, Mark closed the book and looked at it in despair. While he gazed, he brushed more of the accumulated soil from the cover. Suddenly, something in the lower right hand corner caught his attention. He could scarcely believe what his eyes revealed to him, but there in small but unmistakably clear gold letters were inscribed the initials—SIR!

It was late afternoon when Mark arrived home from visiting the place where sir died. Mrs. Hayes heard about the death of a hobo and was fearful it was the man who made such a vivid impression upon Mark. She was worried when it became late and Mark hadn't returned. She was noticeably relieved when he arrived home safely.

He wasn't hungry, but his mother insisted he try to eat something. She always kept his food in the warming oven when for some reason he was late getting home for supper. This evening was no different.

Mark showed his mother the Bible he found and some of the markings sir made in it. She was astounded by the idea of the initials Mark found, spelling out the very name he had given the man.

"It must have been by the will of God!" she exclaimed. "It's very strange, so strange you found the Bible when everyone else passed over it. Oh, dear!" she said, while shaking her head in disbelief. "I-I-I just don't know what to make of it."

They talked of things pertaining to sir all through Mark's supper hour. He told her about sir choosing a star when he was a boy, how he still liked to look for it in the heavens now and then. "He won't never get to look for it again. But maybe that's where he is now," he said, as tears filled his eyes. "I want to pick out a star tonight to call my very own," he said.

His mother puzzled over his comments concerning the star, but she felt a great sadness concerning the man's death. She knew it would help for Mark to talk about the matter. "Why do you want to choose a star?" she asked, trying to comprehend his reasoning.

He replied eagerly, "You see, if we pick out a star, where we'd like to go after we die, maybe someday, God will let us live there. We're gonna be in charge of all those stars you know, all the works of God's hands. He didn't tell me where his star is, though," he said, showing disappointment.

In the evening, Mark laid a blanket out on the grass. He spent some time looking up into the heavens, trying to determine which star he should choose. A star was chosen, and many times afterward, Mark wondered if by some remote chance he might have selected the same one as sir.

The days passed slowly following sir's death. They were lonely days. Most of the time was spent thinking of sir and of the developing relationship. Many hours were devoted to reading from sir's Bible. Each afternoon and evening, with Bible in hand, Mark went to the spot where he and sir spent those meaningful hours. Determined to find as many of the passages the man had discussed with him as he could find, he did find several of them.

During the time of searching the scriptures, he came upon a piece of paper inserted inside the first page. It was of a long narrow shape, placed to the bound side of the pages. On the paper, in what appeared to be publisher's type, was a title: *The House of Israel—Then and Now.* Noted on the paper were the penciled words, "See that Harold gets a copy."

The Stranger

Sitting alone in the garden
beneath those August skies,
I saw the man who called me,
through my sad and tear-dimmed eyes.
His clothes were soiled and disheveled,
though hunger his only strife.
He spoke with voice warm and gentle,
reflecting a peaceful life.

I met a stranger one morning,
he spoke of many things—
why children cry! Why puppies die!
Just a man with a heart filled with love.
Oh! How I loved the dear stranger
for wisdom he gave to me,
to look afar, for my own star,
in a universe filled with God's love.
There by the tracks lay the stranger,

lifeless, a cold lump of clay:
surely a vessel of honor
called by his Father that day.
Oh! How I miss the dear stranger,
for love that he gave to me.
He gave of joy, to a little boy,
and he filled up my heart with God's love.

CHAPTER 5

The days passed quickly. In less than two weeks, the summer vacation would be over. Where had the months gone? Another school year was about to begin, confining Mark to the classroom walls for the greater part of each day. Perhaps it wasn't so much a dislike for school with Mark, as it was about losing his freedom to wander the countryside. He would certainly miss walking the back roads and railroad tracks and wading in the stream searching for something new and different to investigate. He always returned home by a different route than the one by which he left. While there was little chance of anything very exciting taking place, Mark was able to turn each journey into some degree of adventure.

If there would be one of those adventures this particular day, it would have to be later. His mother had made plans for the two of them to stop at Bishop's General Store and get a pair of shoes for Mark. He would need them to begin the new school year, but he hated to even think about wearing shoes again.

"Inez told me you're doing pretty well with your piano lessons," his mother told him, as they were getting ready to go down town. "She thinks you kind of like the song you're working on now. I can't think of the name of it right off."

"Clare De Lune," Mark responded quickly. "Yeah, I kind of do like it, but I can't play it like Elaine does. She makes it sound real pretty."

As they were leaving the house by way of the front door to start down town, a car pulled up and stopped in front of the house. It was an official looking car, but they were unable to read the name on the door. A man dressed in a business suit got out of the car and descended the terrace then approached the porch where they stood waiting for him.

"Mrs. Hayes?" the man inquired, as he came near.

"Yes!" she said. Her voice revealed noticeable apprehension. "And this must be your son," he continued. "I'm Dr. Charles Waters, from Winterset," he said, introducing himself. "I'm the County Coroner."

"Oh, dear!" Mrs. Hayes exclaimed as her voice began shaking. "Is something wrong? Has something happened to Paul?" She had been extremely worried about his health because of his drinking. Her mind would only allow her to think something dreadful had happened to her husband.

"No, no!" he interrupted. "There's nothing wrong. That is not concerning your family. May I come in please, Ma'am?"

"Yes, of course! I'm sorry! You gave me such a start. I was afraid—" "I quite understand, Ma'am," he consoled. "I was talking to a man yesterday, by the name of Benjamin Pritchard. You likely know him. He lives in this community."

"Yes, we know him," Mrs. Hayes replied. Being relieved, she had regained her composure.

Benjamin! Mark thought. *Benjamin must be his real name. That sure sounds like Ben, always trying to impress someone, especially someone he thinks is important.*

"I assume you're aware of the death of a man found along the tracks a few days ago?" he asked. "Well, there are a few things making me curious, and I'd like to fill in some of the details of his death if I can. Unfortunately, he wasn't carrying identification when I arrived on the scene and no wallet. He had no money, not even pocket change. I assumed he was a hobo just passing through, since he was carrying a bundle of clothes and a razor and a razor strop. But it did seem unusual, the body being clean and his face close shaven. He was wearing freshly laundered clothes, not exactly what we expect of a hobo."

"Ben said you said that," Mark interrupted. "I told him sir was with me that afternoon. Mom gave him some of Grandpa's clothes to wear. That's why he looked nice. He took a bath in the woodshed and everything."

"That's fine, Mark. That's pretty much what Benjamin told me, but I'd like to fill in all the blank spaces I can about him. You see, I have no idea who the man is, so anything you can tell me may be helpful in identifying him. Ben said you and the gentleman became quite close friends. Did he by any chance mention his name to you?" It continued to be painful for Mark to be reminded of the fact he never asked the man's name nor had it been volunteered. "We didn't know his name, sir." Mark seemed to want his mother to share the responsibility with him. "We called him sir."

"I understand, son, but it's important you try hard to remember. Think carefully. Did he at any time mention a name, any name we might work from?" he stressed.

"We already did that, sir. There wasn't no name," Mark said with complete confidence. "All we got was his initials on the Bible," Mark added. "They spelled the name I called him."

"A Bible?" Dr. Waters questioned. "What's this about a Bible?" "The Bible I found out where sir died," Mark told him. "I found it under a rock where sir put it to keep it dry, I think."

"Could I see the Bible, son?"

Mark went to get it. Only then did it dawn upon him the Bible might be of interest to the authorities. He reasoned that it might be helpful to find out who the man was. But it also occurred to him he might be forced to give it up to them. "Can I keep the Bible, sir?" he asked, showing a great deal of concern.

Dr. Waters took the Bible from Mark as it was handed to him. He began thumbing through it. "Looks like he made good use of it. I'd say the man spent a lot of time reading this book," he said, noting the many markings it contained.

"He told me he read some passages hundreds of times, sir," Mark explained so he would understand just how much sir loved his Bible. "This was his most favorite one of all," he said, taking the book from Dr. Waters and quickly finding the passage. "Here it is," he said, as he began to read. "Faithful is the saying and worthy of all welcome (for this are we toiling and being reproached), that we rely on the living God, Who is Savior of all mankind"—Mark stressed the word all, as he read—"especially of believers. These things be charging and teaching."

"That's found at 1 Timothy 4:9-11," Mark said, as he handed the Bible back to Dr. Waters. "Sir said he read it whenever he started feeling he was wrong, and maybe everyone else was right.

But I don't think he was ever wrong, sir, not about the Bible."

Dr. Waters was patient with Mark. He smiled realizing there was a bond between Mark and the man who had died. He knew it would be difficult for Mark to give up the book, but he really had no choice. The Bible would need to be looked through carefully for any help it might offer. And certainly, the initials could be important in eliminating other missing persons from the list of possibilities—if indeed; the initials even belonged to this man.

"I'm sure you realize, I will have to keep the Bible for investigative purposes." He was directing his statement to Mrs. Hayes. "But be assured I'll try to get it back to you. There may be others with first claim to it you understand."

When the thought of finding out who the man was made its impact upon Mark, he felt differently about giving it up. Immediately, he volunteered to give him the chain and coin sir had given him. Taking them from his pocket, he handed them to Dr. Waters. "He said the coin don't have no real m-monetary value, sir. He said he wanted me to have something to remember him by. You can have those too if it'll help find out who he is," Mark said.

Dr. Waters recognized the bravery Mark exhibited. He knew it wasn't easy to give up something having so much meaning. "Hmmm! An Indian rupee," he remarked. "I'm sure it's all right if you keep it, Mark. You keep it so you'll have your reminder. But it does seem odd he would give you his very last coin. He didn't have a cent with which to buy a meal."

"That's what sir wanted, sir," Mark replied.

"What do you mean, son? You mean he wanted to be out of money? Very strange!"

"No, sir! That's not strange. Sir said he wanted to be all out of money so he couldn't even pay for a meal 'cause he wanted to put all his faith in God to provide food for him by helping him earn it."

Dr. Waters looked at Mark in amazement. But it soon gave way to a look of genuine pleasure when he recognized Mark's innocence.

"Well, Ma'am," Dr. Waters said, as he prepared to leave, "you both have been very helpful. I don't know what will happen to the Bible, but if I can, I'll get it back to you. And thank you for your cooperation," he said. He walked to the door.

When the man reached his car, he stopped, and returning a few steps, he said, “I recall you were about to leave the house when I arrived. May I drop you off somewhere?” he asked.

Mrs. Hayes was about to thank him for the offer and tell him they didn’t mind walking, when Mark volunteered the fact they were on their way to Bishop’s to buy a pair of shoes for him to wear to school.

“I insist,” Dr. Waters said. “I’m going right down Main Street anyway. I insist you let me drive you there.”

There was the usual casual conversation, mostly about the weather. When they reached the store, they thanked him for the ride.

“He’s a very nice man. I think I should have voted for Dr. Waters,” Mrs. Hayes remarked, as he drove away. “I guess it doesn’t matter much now, though, he got elected.” She shrugged.

As Mark sat in the chair being fitted for shoes, Reverend Harper happened to enter the store. He greeted both Mark and Mrs. Hayes, and they discussed the weather briefly. As the pastor was about to leave, Mrs. Hayes told him they had something to discuss with him. “It isn’t urgent,” she said, “but we would like to talk to you whenever it’s convenient.”

“Any time is good with me, Mrs. Hayes,” he said, “on your way home if you like. I haven’t anything especially pressing this morning. You can stop by on your way home. I’ll be in my office in the church.”

Mark didn’t look forward to any conversation with Reverend Harper and especially listen to his “chaos and destruction” doctrine. He was certain he would hear it before the meeting was over. His mother insisted they stop while the pastor had the time.

“I understand you have something you want to discuss,” Reverend Harper said, as Mark and his mother entered his office at the Methodist Church. He was sitting behind his desk. “I’m here to help in any way I can.”

Mrs. Hayes began to explain the problem, saying, “Mark met this friend. You may know of him. He was the man who died out south of town along the tracks just a few days ago.”

“Yes, indeed! What happened was very sad. I understand there was no identification on the body to help determine who he was. Very sad! I assumed he was a hobo just passing through, but you say he was a friend of yours?" he asked curiously.

"Only because Mark made friends with him when he stopped for a meal. Mark enjoyed being with him. He seemed like such a fine Christian man. They had a long visit, the better part of the afternoon, I guess. Mark thought a great deal of the man, and they discussed things of the Bible quite freely."

"There was one passage they discussed which disturbed Mark. It's the passage we want to discuss with you. These verses are in the eighth chapter of Romans. They talk about the suffering of creation." "Oh yes! I know of those verses. They're speaking of the new creation. Let's look at them, and I'll explain their meaning."

Mark interrupted the pastor for there seemed to be a very real misunderstanding. Mark felt he understood the passage quite clearly. He had only wanted to share it with his mother and anyone who would hear him. "I'm not disturbed about it, sir," Mark said. "I just want everyone to know what it really means."

"All right, son," he acknowledged, "but let's read the verses and see if we can determine what they're saying."

Reverend Harper read the verses from the King James Version of the scriptures. After each verse, he stopped to explain his understanding of the meaning to Mark.

> "For I reckon that the sufferings of this present time are not worthy to be compared with the glory which shall be revealed in us" (Rom. 8:18; AV).

"This verse tells us about suffering of the believers," he began, "everyone who has accepted Jesus Christ as their Savior. They are the ones having become a new creation. Their sufferings cannot compare with the glory they will receive for living righteous lives. It means the rewards for living Christian lives here on this earth will be far greater than any suffering we have to go through." He continued to read.

> "For the earnest expectation of the creature waiteth for the manifestation of the sons of God" (Rom. 8:19; AV).

"The second verse speaks of all the creatures that are waiting for the appearance of the sons of God. These are the ones who will believe in this life. They're given the ability to expect to see these sons. In God's great foreknowledge, meaning He knew ahead of time, in God's great foreknowledge, He knows who will believe and who will not. So He gives those He knows will believe, a kind of premonition they can look forward to. You see it's all quite a simple matter when you understand."

"But, sir," Mark interrupted, "I don't think it says they have to be Christians. And sir says it means all creation."

"Oh, but, son, it goes without saying if they're not believers and if they aren't going to be saved anyway, why would they even want to see the sons of God?"

"But they will be saved, and they will want to see the sons of God. Everybody will be saved," he blurted. "Even the animals!" He wanted so much for the pastor to share in his newfound truth, but it appeared the pastor only wanted Mark to understand it as he understood it.

"Where did you get such an idea, son?" he asked.

"Those verses say all creation," Mark told him, placing emphasis on the word all. "All creation has a feeling they will see the sons of God, and sir says we should always believe the Bible, whether we understand it or not. I do believe it. I do believe what the Bible says," Mark explained. "And it says all creation will be freed from sin and be like the sons of God."

"Son," Reverend Harper said in a gentle tone, "there are certain things in the scriptures that simply won't stand alone. Many times, we have to go to other places in the Bible to find the true meaning. There is much scripture telling us there will be no unbelievers in the kingdom of God so we know these verses have to be talking about believers."

Mark knew the pastor's teaching was based on his own personal views and what he had learned in seminaries. Certainly, it wasn't based on what seemed so clear to Mark, but he was unable to cope with the pastor on the matter. He thought about a statement sir had made. It pertained to another verse of scripture, but the truth he spoke was just as true in this case. "The statement is clear enough, but people won't believe it. There is much fear instilled within people by the doctrine of eternal torment."

"Sir says everyone will come to know God and Jesus 'cause that's what His plan and purpose is. Everything God created will be like God, and He had the plan before anything. That's why He sent Jesus here. So He would believe for us," Mark said, becoming quite shaken by the pastor's lack of interest in his view.

"Son," he said, "you can be sure not everyone is going to heaven and certainly not animals. Can't you imagine what it would be like to have all kinds of wild animals, and snakes, and birds, and bugs in heaven? Don't you see how silly it would be? There won't even be unbelievers there. God couldn't permit it, could He? There will come the day when countless millions of people will be thrown into the lake of fire and brimstone. They will burn there forever and ever. That's why we try to warn everyone so they will believe. It's the pastor's responsibility to warn people of that terrible end, the terrible chaos and destruction."

"I like it a lot better that everybody's gonna be saved and be with God," Mark explained.

"We would all like to believe that, son, but it just isn't so."

"But sir says it's so, and I believe he knows."

"Son!" Reverend Harper said, trying to remain calm. "The man may have meant well, but he was a very mixed up and confused individual. Obviously, Satan blinded him to cause him to believe such evil nonsense."

"He's dead," Mark said to the pastor, wanting to defend his friend.

"Oh, but God will punish him nevertheless and punish him severely. If he didn't repent in his few remaining hours of life, you may be sure he will spend eternity burning in the fires of hell. You get these ideas out of your head or the same thing will happen to you. Do you understand, Mark?"

Mrs. Hayes had become quite upset with the pastor and tried to come to Mark's defense. "Don't you think you're being unnecessarily harsh? Mark's only believing what his friend told him the verse meant," she explained.

"You must realize, Mrs. Hayes, the man has made a very deep impression on your son. He's mixed up with an extremely dangerous doctrine. That man was a heretic, and I dare say, teaching heresy was the very reason God took his life." Reverend Harper was becoming angry now, and even Mrs. Hayes was a little frightened of him. "The boy needs to be punished severely," he continued. "You know the old saying, 'spare the rod, and spoil the child.' He must be punished so he will forget such an evil doctrine. A thing like this will destroy him if we don't destroy it first."

"Reverend Harper, I'm disappointed with your conduct. I think you're overly excited about this matter. I don't think Mark has done anything terrible. We need to get to the truth and teach him what the truth is. We better talk another time, pastor," she said, as she ushered Mark to the door.

"Mark my words," he shouted as they were leaving. "The boy must be punished."

"Mama," Mark said, as they walked toward the street, "the Bible does say all creation is waiting to see the sons of God, and they do have a feeling they'll be with God. It says that real plain."

"I don't know, Mark. I'm just so confused right now, I don't know. It does seem to say every creature has a premonition, yet I just can't believe every creature will be in heaven."

Mark began thinking about what sir had said. The very thing he spoke of had just happened. It was as though sir had known exactly what would occur when he warned Mark so clearly during their visit. "Mark," he had said, "you will find it difficult, many times in life, to proclaim what you believe if you accept these truths, but it will be worthwhile in the end. God will be pleased, and you will find peace in your heart."

What a great feeling! Serenity Mark had never before experienced swept over him. His conscience was clear, and he felt completely at ease about his encounter with Reverend Harper. The words Reverend Harper spoke didn't seem to really matter, for the words of sir had given him a wonderful peace. Mark sensed a new truth was taking root in his heart. Oh, there wasn't even a vague idea of what role God had in mind for him, but he supposed the knowledge of it would come as a result of believing what scripture had to say to him. He sensed a seed had been planted, but he would have to await its development to know what fruits it would yield.

One other matter would become evident: the strain in the relationship between Mark and the pastor would continue.

One morning late in the following week, Mark made his usual trip to the post office to get the mail. In the post office box was a card-marked package. Mr. Barkley had seen Mark coming and had the package waiting for him. To Mark's great surprise, he discovered the label was addressed to him. It was rare indeed for Mark to receive mail and certainly rare to personally receive a package. The only time he got a package was when he received clothes ordered from Chicago Mail Order, or Montgomery Ward, or one of the other catalog outlets. Even those were always addressed to Mark's parents.

As Mark walked home, he discovered the name in the return address was the same as the one he had seen in the front of sir's Bible. *Why?* he wondered. *Why would I be getting a package from the Concordant Publishing Concern. Why would they be sending me anything?* He began walking faster, becoming more puzzled and even more intent on learning what was inside the wrapper.

When Mark reached home, he showed the package to his mother and quickly began removing the contents. To his further surprise, there was a Bible exactly like the one belonging to sir. Now Mark was really puzzled. Who could know how much he missed having the Bible? And why would he be getting one in the mail?

"I declare," his mother was saying, "here's a note inside the wrapper from the publishers. Let me read it to you," she said, beginning to read even before Mark could answer.

"From the publisher—this Bible has been provided for you by the compliments of Dr. Charles Waters, of Winterset, Iowa. He wants you to know he also ordered one for himself. He wishes you many happy hours of reading."

Mark closed his eyes and began thanking God for the bible. "Thank You, God, for causing Dr. Waters to send me this book, and please let him enjoy his book too."

Immediately, Mark found the verses sir had marked so carefully in his Bible. With a ruler, he underlined just as clearly and as carefully as sir had marked his, the verses at 1 Timothy 4:9-11.

CHAPTER 6

Roseman Bridge was one of about nine covered bridges still remaining in Madison County. All of Iowa's covered bridges were built in the eighteenth century. A great deal of nostalgia surrounding them still remained for those who grew up in areas where these bridges stood.

One wonders how many lovers advanced courtship while passing through by horse and buggy, not particularly caring if old "Daniel" or "Jane" stopped to rest for a few moments, while the young man exchanged kisses with his lady friend in that darkened atmosphere. So common was it, the local boys hid among the rafters while waiting for just such an event so they might heckle the lovers. Certainly, there must have been good reason for the covered bridges being so often called "kissing bridges."

Halloween would arrive in less than a week, lending authenticity to a story appearing in the Madisonian just the Friday before. That was the name of the weekly county paper. According to this story, there was something unique about Roseman Bridge. Not only was this bridge a nostalgic reminder of those by gone years, but also it was a haunted bridge, complete with legend of sorts. The facts were somewhat vague, leaving much to one's imagination as to what actually led to the events creating the legend.

Mark had just passed his fifteenth birthday by a few days. A new girl, Nancy Borden, had moved into town about two months before. So attractive, Mark was somewhat intimidated. He had seen Nancy several times. Having thought her to be quite tall, he managed to stand close to her in order to compare heights. After careful consideration, he decided half an inch difference shouldn't keep him from getting better acquainted. Anyway, he was still growing, and it was possible she was as tall as she would get. He had talked of his feelings to Allen Dawson, a good friend.

Mark always attended the Epworth League fellowship on Sunday, and that was where they were on this particular evening. The meetings began early so they would be finished before time for the church service to begin. The fellowship was mostly for young people of high school age but including those who were older if they were still unmarried. Mrs. Garvey was the Sunday school superintendent and also in charge of the fellowship classes. She was well up in years but a lady everyone loved. And she knew how to keep things interesting for the young people. There wasn't much going on in this small town, so anything such as this function would likely be the only activity around, especially on Sunday evening.

Allen Dawson poked Mark in the ribs to get his attention. "Hey, Mark! Look who just came in the door."

Nancy hadn't attended Epworth League before this evening. Mark was glad to see her but much too shy to approach her. It wasn't as though she hadn't made friends yet, for she was outgoing, having already made friends with quite a few young people.

A large portion of those attending the fellowship had made plans to have a get together after it was over, out at the bridge. The rumor was there would be a ghost storytelling session. Excitement was in the air.

"Why don't you go over and greet her?" Allen had grasped Mark's shoulder and was turning him in Nancy's direction. "You'd better talk to her before someone else asks her to be their date," Allen said, trying to prod Mark.

"Don't rush me," Mark said. "I can't just go busting—"

"What do you mean, don't rush you? You never would get around to asking her out. Looks like I'm gonna have to do it, or you'll be going alone. I'll have you two together before the night's over," Allen said in a whisper.

Allen went straight to where Nancy and her friends were seated to talk to her. Then he stopped to have a few words with his brother before returning. In five minutes time, he had made a date for Mark and arranged transportation as well.

"I asked Nancy to go with us out to Roseman Bridge," he told Mark, "but she said she can't tonight. I've got good news, though." Allen's eyes sparkled. "Mrs. Garvey told me if you wouldn't keep her out too late, she would be delighted to go with you." Allen had barely finished his punch line when he doubled over with laughter.

"I'm kidding," he said. "Carl"—Allen's older brother—"said we can go to the bridge with him. Oh yeah! Nancy's your date! I think Nancy's got a crush on you. Must be my way with the women," he said with a chuckle.

Mark was disgusted with himself for not making his own arrangements, especially after seeing how easy it was. But he was still awfully glad it was done. So much the better if she already liked him.

Nancy and the other girls had to get permission from their parents before they would go. As soon as permission was granted, the entire group was on their way. Being new to the area, Nancy hadn't heard of the legend of the haunted bridge. She was excited. As they came nearer their destination, she became apprehensive. Allen had indeed arranged for Nancy to be Mark's date, and she sat beside him as they made the trip. The more they talked about the legend, the uneasier she became. Finally, they arrived at the bridge.

A large part of the group attending the fellowship also made the trip to Roseman Bridge. Soon, it was confirmed the idea was to gather around a campfire and tell ghost stories. It was a cool crisp evening and reminded one that frost was a possibility before morning. It was a beautifully clear night. The moon looked down from its cloudless place in the sky. There was almost no breeze.

The twigs, starting to burn, ignited the dry wood, causing a crackling sound in the chilled night air. The heat from the campfire felt good. Extra logs were dragged from the creek bank to the site and placed nearby. Looming up before them was the outline of the bridge as it made a clear majestic etching across the moonlit horizon.

"We sure were lucky you had a book of matches with you, weren't we, Harold?" Harold's brother, Ralph Kale, was giving

Harold a hard time because he had started smoking and was able to furnish the matches for starting the fire. "Sure hope Dad doesn't find out," Ralph continued in an intimidating tone.

"Dad wouldn't care if I smoke. He knows I'm old enough." "Yeah! Sure, and if you'd just ask," Ralph chided, "he'd leave you a pack of cigarettes and a book of matches each morning to help you through the day."

Nancy and Mark found a place on a log where they could be close together by the fire. "Are you having fun?" Mark asked Nancy, as he turned to face her.

"Oh yes!" she exclaimed. "This is so exciting. If I were alone, I know I'd be scared to death, but I feel safe here with you."

Nancy sat where the moonlight found its way through the leaves; the shadows dancing upon her face. What a lovely girl she was, and the shadows appeared as beautiful lace enhancing her already delicate features. Oh, how Mark wanted to tell her how pretty she was, but there were too many around for that. He knew he would be teased a great deal for saying such a thing. As he sat gazing upon her face, he experienced something different than he had experienced before. It seemed much more than infatuation. Mark thought, Is this the way it feels to be in love. He wondered if Nancy was having similar feelings about him. She was enjoying herself and sitting awfully close, and she didn't seem ready to move.

Everyone sat around the fire laughing and joking, as it burned brightly. The atmosphere was comfortable and relaxed. Clearly, everyone was enjoying themselves. Harold stood up and made the announcement it was time to begin telling ghost stories. "I think we all agree this will be a lot more fun than going out destroying someone's property," he said matter-of-factly.

"And probably getting into trouble," Allen added.

"We want everyone to tell a ghost story," he continued. "The scarier the better. If you don't know one, make one up. Who wants to start?" he asked, moving to the place he had reserved for himself.

It was quiet for some time, except for the complaining from almost everyone they didn't know a ghost story. Then someone reminded them of the strange light seen out on the Farr place.

"Oh yeah! Just last summer! Did anyone ever find out what the light was?" Harold asked.

"Of course! It was a ghost, what do you think?" Tom Reed was trying to get the mood going for a good night of storytelling. Tom could often be very convincing.

"Tell us about it. Probably not everyone has even heard about it," Harold told him.

"Well," Tom said, shrugging his shoulders, "he was out by the south fence next to the woods, when he saw a light shining on a tree. It was a big light, lighting up the whole treetop. He started climbing over the fence, and when he did, the light went out. He climbed back, and the light went on again. This happened over and over. On one side, he could see the light. On the other side, the light disappeared. He swears it's true, and he said he never could find out what was causing it to happen. It must have been a ghost turning it on and off," Tom said with seeming assurance.

Diane Halsey, one of the girls meeting Nancy at the fellowship, told of an experience her mother once had. "My mother said something weird happen to her. She went up into their attic one day, in broad daylight too. Setting by the window was an old rocking chair, just rocking away, and her grandmother was sitting in it. When her grandmother saw her, the chair stopped rocking immediately, and she disappeared. Mom said her grandmother had been dead for twenty years, but she had died in the very same old rocking chair."

"I've heard the spirits of the dead often come back to the place where they lived when they were alive." It was Harold again trying to add substance to Diane's story.

One after another, the stories continued with others adding strength to each one. Finally, someone mentioned the legend concerning the bridge where they were spending the evening.

"I wondered when that subject would come up," Harold said, having made himself master of ceremonies. "There's a lot of different tales about the nature of the haunting. What have you heard, Craig?" he asked, picking out Craig to try and get a discussion going.

"Well," he began, "the story I heard was of the guy who escaped from the Madison County jail, and the posse chased him out here and then hung him. His spirit is supposed to have lived on here for about twenty years or so, but no one's seen or heard of him since right after the war."

"Randy, you look like you want to say something," he spoke to Randy Bishop, the son of one of the brothers who owned the local general store. "What do you know about the legend?"

"Some say the guy was hung all right, but his body wasn't found afterward, and a hole was found in the roof right over the rafter where he was hung. They say fisherman have heard the sounds of laughter coming from the bridge and footsteps running across the roof."

Mark felt Nancy move closer to him during the discussion of the hanging, as though wanting to feel safer. "Think of it," she exclaimed, "he was hung right here on this bridge." She grasped Mark's hand tightly. The other girls were beginning to feel less secure as well.

Harold took charge once again. "It seems," he began, "somehow the guy was able to stay in his body after he was hung 'cause some of the legends tell of him standing on the bridge and yelling for people to stay away. It seems he didn't want anybody snooping around. But he must have been separated from his body later 'cause he hasn't been heard of for more than twenty years now, as far as anyone has talked about."

"I thought maybe we could hold a seance and bring the guy's body back to him. Is everybody game to try?"

Everyone was taken by surprise, but there were no objections among the boys. The girls weren't so sure it was a good idea, but they soon consented to go along with it.

"I don't think there's anything to worry about," Nancy said, as she squeezed Mark's hand. It was obvious the other girls were hoping she was right.

"Okay! Let's get on with it. Everyone take the hand of the one next to you so we can have an unbroken circle. You have to concentrate very intensely and be very attentive to what is said."

Some were already feeling uneasy and beginning to wish they hadn't got into such a thing.

"Oh, great spirit from the other world, hear what we are saying. Oh, spirit, we beg you to speak if you can hear us. Acknowledge you are aware we are trying to reach you."

Harold asked for greater concentration toward reaching the spirit world. "Someone may be breaking the circle of concentration," he said. "We'll try again."

"Oh, great spirit from the other side," he began again, "hear us as we call to you. If you can hear us, give us a signal. Tell us if we have reached you, oh, great spirit."

It became quiet as they waited. They could almost hear the heartbeat of the one seated next to them. Then with perfect cadence, there came three sharp raps from up on Roseman Bridge.

Fear spread quickly through the entire group, and the ring was broken.

"Come on, people!" Harold shouted. "We're getting through. Don't stop now. Everyone hold hands again, quickly, while we still have contact with the spirit world."

"Oh, spirit from the other world, we know you have heard us. Oh, great spirit, give to the man his body. Give the body back to him that he lost so long ago. Oh, spirit, hear us and tell us you have heard. Oh, great spirit, we wait once again for your signal."

It was silent again for a long moment. Then there came the same rhythmic sounds as before. Rap, rap, rap came the sound, unmistakably meant to be a response to the contact. Again, fear ran rampant among the group, and everyone determined to get out of there as quickly as possible. Suddenly, a blood-chilling scream was heard coming from the area of the bridge. Then after a few moments of silence, the sound of laughter echoed out across the cool autumn air, loud laughter, as from some devilish one. With Roseman Bridge still silhouetted against the moonlit sky, they watched in disbelief as a figure appeared on top of the bridge. Leaping high into the air and screaming, the figure ran the bridge's full length. Jumping from the far end, it disappeared into the darkness.

"I think we'd better get out of here," Harold said, apparently able to keep his composure while everyone else was too frightened to think clearly. "Let's all stay together until we get to our cars and head for home. Don't anyone panic," he stressed. "Just stay together until we're all ready to leave."

Everyone did indeed stay close together. They were almost walking on one another's feet as they readied to leave. They scampered across the grader ditch and up the embankment to the road. Soon, the cars were racing down the road in getting away from the place.

For a time, everyone in the car seemed too frightened to speak. Then Diane began to sob hysterically. When her sobbing gave everyone something different to think about, the anxiety lessened, and the attention was directed to her. Certainly, no one blamed her for being frightened.

After several minutes of quiet, Carl broke the silence. "I think we were set up!" he exclaimed.

"What do you mean, set up?" Allen asked.

"I mean I think the whole thing was acted out according to a plan. Think about it. Everything went too smoothly to just happen. Harold had the whole evening going his way. If you'll remember, it was all Harold's idea we go out there in the first place. It was all Harold's idea we tell ghost stories. The seance was Harold's idea. We only heard the rapping sounds after it was real quiet, right on cue. And Harold was the only one who wasn't scared out of his gourd after we saw the ghost on top of the bridge. I never did see his car. He must have hid it somewhere."

"Yeah!" Mark interrupted. "And how did it happen we were all sitting in just the right place to see the ghost so clearly on top of the bridge in the moonlight?"

"I'll bet if we went back out there, we'd find Harold and his buddies laughing their fool heads off." Carl was pretty angry about the whole thing now.

"I don't want to go back out there," Diane began sobbing again. "I just want to go home."

Nancy came to her defense. "We should all go home and forget about the whole thing for tonight."

It didn't seem nearly as frightening once reason was given for the entire bazaar event. The boys even considered returning to the scene after they took the girls home. They were all sure it had been thoroughly staged, but they decided it might be fun to just let Harold think he had completely fooled them.

"Come to think of it," Allen said, as he gave a hardy laugh, "Harold really did put one over on us."

Mark didn't see Nancy for several days, but he thought about her almost every waking moment. He pictured the way she looked sitting with the moonlight casting lacy figures on her face through the leaves. He thought about the romantic setting at the bridge. The evening was beautiful but cool and ideal for finding love for someone. It seemed the evening had been made just for Nancy and Mark to fall in love. And shouldn't there be a song written about such a thing? With boyish words and a simple tune, Mark wrote his first song—a song conveying his innermost thoughts about Nancy.

It was on the following Saturday night Mark met Nancy again. They went to the park where they sat and talked. Mark was so set on singing his new song to her, and letting those words convey his special feelings for her, he was unaware anything was wrong with their relationship.

When I Fell in Love with You
The leaves drawing lace
through the moonlight on your face,
brought out your heavenly charms.
'Twas love at first sight
on that beautiful night,
when I held you in my arms.
The ev'ning so divine
to fall in love—
for us the stars
were twinkling high above.
When I saw you there,
it answered each and every prayer,
and I fell in love with you.

"The song was lovely," she said, when he was Finished, but still she seemed unimpressed by it. It was only then Mark realized the feelings she had for him did not match the ones he felt for her.

It remained quiet for some moments. Nancy seemed to be looking somewhere beyond him.

"What is it, Nancy? Don't you like the song? Did I do something to make you angry?" he questioned.

"It's nothing you've done, Mark. I just don't think we should be serious," she said, though not very convincingly.

Nancy got up and started walking from the park.

"I don't understand, Nancy. What did I do to make you dislike me so much?"

"You didn't do anything. I just don't want us to be serious," she protested, walking away leaving Mark to himself.

Mark stood and watched in dismay concerning what was happening. There was no real reason given for her actions. "What have I done? Wait, Nancy! Can't we talk it over? Can't we get together and talk it over? Nancy!" he called.

Nancy didn't wait. Mark couldn't believe what was taking place, let alone understand it. Talk about a bubble bursting. One moment, Mark was high up in the clouds, thinking life is really full of joy and beautiful thoughts. The next moment, the clouds are gone in one quick puff, and nothing remains, and with Mark crashing back to earth.

"Next Sunday evening is Epivorth League fellowship again. Maybe she'll talk to me then."

Mark did meet Nancy there. She was just as cool as she had been before.

He hardly opened his mouth to speak, when she shouted at him, "You just don't understand, do you? I only want us to be friends, nothing more."

"No, Nancy, I don't understand. We don't even seem like friends," Mark replied.

"You better just talk to Reverend Simmons about it," she said. Nancy walked away making it clear she intended to avoid him.

Mark had never dealt with Pastor Simmons. He was the replacement pastor for Reverend Harper and hadn't been there very long. Mark certainly wasn't aware of any problem between them. He was puzzled by her words. "Maybe I should contact him and see what's bothering him."

Mark made several attempts to set an appointment with the pastor. Each attempt was rejected with the reason given: he was too busy at the time. Only after refusing him several times did

Mark get the appointment he asked for. When they finally met, no question remained concerning bad feelings between them.

"I can't believe you're here to talk to me, Mark, after what you've done," he said, as Mark was sitting down. "Reverend Harper warned me about this situation. He told me about the horrible doctrine you're involved with, a 'universal reconciliation' heresy. I decided I would wait and judge for myself if the situation was really as bad as I was told. Well! I find it to be even worse, and I see you're still involved with it. Now I find out you're conducting seances. Reverend Harper said that situation would only escalate. He even tried to warn your mother how evil it really is."

"But, Reverend Simmons, I didn't conduct the seance. I didn't have anything to do with it. I didn't even know there'd be one."

"You don't understand do you? Evil just naturally follows those damnable doctrines. They give evil a foothold, and everything just gets worse and worse. You have no control over what happens. You simply become a slave to Satan. That's what you are, a slave to Satan." Mark had heard quite enough. Sooner or later, he would have to stand up for what he believed and right now certainly seemed to be the right time.

"I think what I believe about the salvation of all is very beautiful, pastor," he said calmly. "I could never go back to believing God would allow anyone to lay burning in fires of hell, screaming for help and mercy for an endless eternity, and then do nothing to save them.

My God is a God of love. One Who will save every creature he has ever created, otherwise, He wouldn't have created them."

"Reverend Harper was certainly right when he said you wouldn't stand correction."

"Reverend Simmons, I've learned to believe the scriptures mean what they say," Mark interrupted, "not necessarily what people say they mean."

"Good day, Mark," the pastor said, as he walked to the door and held it open for him.

Mark had thought the situation with Nancy couldn't get worse than it was, but it was certainly worse now. Why would anyone get so upset over such a minor thing? At least it seemed minor to Mark.

Once again, he remembered what sir had said about having some difficult times ahead if he chose to believe those matters. *"I wonder if it is worth it. Is believing everyone will be saved really worth having people angry with me?"*

As if placed upon his lips by some great power, Mark found himself repeating sir's favorite verses, 1 Timothy 4:9-11. And then as though part of scripture came the words sir had spoken about the verses. *"It is one of my favorites of all scripture, and anytime I get discouraged and feel maybe my understanding is in error and everyone else is right, I turn to it for comfort."*

Mark felt a wonderful sense of peace come over him, a peace becoming more familiar as time went on. Perhaps it was just an assurance from his subconscious mind helping him deal with the pastor's harsh words, but Mark preferred to think he was being given strength from God to help him through one more of the many trying experiences he would have to deal with in his lifetime.

"Thank You, Father!" Mark said silently.

Mark's first love affair had been a disaster, but he had learned a most valuable lesson on the subject of life.

CHAPTER 7

The year was 1945. Mark graduated from high school in the spring. Life in the small town never seemed to change, and virtually, no jobs were to be found. He had tied sheep's wool for his father, which consisted of folding the sheared fleeces into bundles, being careful to remove any dung found clinging to the wool and then tying the bundles. The wool buyers didn't appreciate being expected to pay for any weight added to the wool itself. Mark felt any kid could tie wool, and learning to shear sheep wasn't his idea of a satisfying career.

Mr. Hayes had gone west to shear sheep in Wyoming and the Dakotas for a number of years. Establishing a return business, he was able each spring to confirm by letter the customers requiring his services for the year. Some had been customers for more than ten years.

Mark went to Wyoming and Montana with his father the year before. It was an unhappy experience for him and one where he spent a great deal of his evening time in the bars in town, waiting for the shearers to get their fill of liquor and return to the ranch wherever they happened to be shearing at the time. He managed to do a few of the things he enjoyed. The movie houses changed their films about three times a week, giving him something to do on those evenings. He enjoyed shopping for clothes, but the money supply was extremely limited. He liked to visit the music stores where he looked through the sheet music of the popular songs at the time. For several years, Mark had made it a hobby to learn every new song he liked, which included just about every new song.

One evening, as he browsed along the music rack filling one entire side of the store, a young man and young lady walked over to a piano located near the music rack. The man began playing what was probably the number one hit song of the day, "I'll Be Seeing You." After the introduction, the young lady sang the lyrics. Mark was never quite sure whether they were extremely talented or if his loneliness make it seem so beautiful. The song made a lasting impression on him. It made him think of home and how much he would love to be there. Funny how memories and certain songs remain associated, especially when one is young.

But this year, Mr. Hayes was unable to make the trip west. His health had deteriorated every year, and now he was subject to weakness. He was unable to carry on work for more than brief periods of time. He had been building a garage for one of Mark's sisters who lived some distance away. She and her husband hadn't given him the job as a matter of charity. "We have to hire someone to do it," Elizabeth had said, "and we'd like him to have the job."

It was during that project he became too ill to continue working. While Mrs. Hayes was fearful for her husband's health, it wasn't fully realized his condition had become life-threatening. He was stricken with a heart attack one morning just after he awakened—a massive heart attack, as it was later diagnosed. He passed away quickly and without regaining consciousness. Mark's youngest sister, Edith, came after being told of his condition.

His oldest sister, Inez, was still engaged in missionary work. Her family was unable to attend the funeral. Jason was serving his country in the European War theater and hadn't yet returned, though he received his discharge the following October. Edith and Irene spent a few days with Mark and his mother.

"Paul was reading my latest *Hour of Truth* magazine just the evening before he died." His mother was telling the family what she had discovered, after they finished supper the next evening. "I found it lying on the floor on his side of the bed. Maybe the Lord spoke to him. Maybe Paul accepted Christ as his Savior before he died. That would be so wonderful," she said.

"Mama," Mark said to his mother, "you don't have to worry about Daddy. He'll be saved in his own time."

"Oh, Mark! Please don't start on that now."

It hurt Mark to be rejected by his mother, especially at such a time as this. He knew it would give her much consolation if she would accept the truth, for it certainly should remove any fear concerning the future for their loved one. He loved his father too, though he was sure, not as much as his mother did. He recognized finding the paper gave his mother the glimmer of hope she needed at the particular time.

The day of the funeral, and the time for the services arrived. Reverend Simmons was about to conclude his message to the family. "Mrs. Hayes was given hope her husband came to know the Lord just before he died, and we ask each of you to join the family in prayer concerning this matter."

Mark was disappointed at the importance placed upon one such faint glimmer of hope, for without that glimmer of hope, there seemed to be no hope at all in the pastor's view.

"May the Lord be with this family in their time of bereavement. Amen!"

The pastor finished the service with those words. The friends of the family of the deceased began filing past the casket, and last to view the body would be the immediate family members. As two ladies had stood before the casket, Mark clearly overheard their whispered conversation.

"The nerve of Reverend Simmons offering hope to Mrs. Hayes her husband was saved and is going to heaven."

"Indeed!" her sister replied, showing equally as much contempt for the matter. "If the pastor had heard some of the things he said to us, believe you me, he'd feel a lot differently. I don't know how God could save such a wretched person," she concluded.

"I certainly can't believe God would permit the likes of him to enter the gates of heaven. He gave us so much trouble when we tried to witness to him down at the tavern."

Mark was greatly disturbed with them. The two ladies were sisters and often did missionary work in connection with temperance

Sunday for the church. The ladies likely went well beyond the scope of church principles, as they conducted their not-so Christian duties. Mark knew his father had several encounters with them as they tried to reprehend him for his drinking problem, and they were anything but diplomatic as they carried out their work.

After the graveside services were complete and his father had been laid in his final resting place, Mark saw them walking toward their car. He was finding it extremely difficult to keep from letting them know he heard their words spoken near the casket. But even if they deserved to be reprimanded, this was neither the time nor the place for it.

"Good morning, ladies," Mark said, as he approached them from behind. "Mama was real glad you could come to the funeral. She said it's comforting to know there are people who have so much love for their friends."

"Well thank you, Mark," Mrs. Brimsley said. "Sally and I feel it's our Christian duty to support our friends in times of need, especially when there has been the death of a loved one."

"Oh my yes!" Sally interrupted. "I was just saying to Gretta when you stopped, 'Your daddy was such a fine man.' And we so hope he found the Lord in those last few moments," she said, placing her hand upon Mark's in a gesture of comfort. "It's possible," she added. "God will also bring fruits of reward for our witness to him."

Graduation came and went. Mark was a worried young man during the next few days. *At least guys in the big cities have a chance of finding jobs,* he thought. He wasn't at all sure what going to Des Moines to get a job would entail, and he had hardly spent a night away from home. He hoped he could stay with Irene who lived there. The only solution seemed to be to get a job in the big city. "But what about Mama? How can I leave Mama here alone?"

On one of those mornings, Mark sat on the back steps pondering what to do. It rained the night before. The morning was cool, and all indications pointed toward a beautiful day.

When Mark was a small boy and the family went for a Sunday

afternoon drive, they often traveled the road atop the rim of the valley stretching from east to west just south of town. From the side window of the back seat of their 1931 Model A Ford, he always watched with anticipation for the appearance of the clearing among the trees. From there, he would catch a fleeting glimpse of the valley below, always thinking how he would like to stop and find out just what could be observed from there. When Mark did later stop on one of his walks through the countryside, he was intrigued by what he saw. Many times afterward, he made special visits to the place just to sit and marvel at the spectacular view. It was especially comforting for him when he was lonely or faced with some problem.

Well, today, he was faced with a problem of real proportions: the biggest problem of his young life. He always felt better after visiting the place. Maybe that would be the case on this particular day.

As Mark walked the road along the rim of the hill, he began walking a little faster as he approached the clearing. He passed the place where he remembered the fragrance of lilacs being overpowering with their aroma. Even though it was not the season for them, Mark could almost smell their beautiful fragrance as he passed the yard where an old house once stood. The house became victim of the tragedy of an overheated stove on one of the colder winter nights. As so often happened, the house burned to the ground because of the inadequacy of the dilapidated firefighting equipment. The volunteers always had to resort to the bucket brigade, and when the well was pumped dry, there was nothing to do but watch the house burn. The lilac tree remained along the edge of the fenced in yard.

He climbed the gate at the clearing. As he stood straddling the top rail, the keen smell of catnip came riding the gentle breeze, stinging his nose with a minty-cool sensation. A robin nearby tugged at a struggling earthworm eager to remain in the moist, cool soil.

Mark thought about the wonders of nature as he stood there. The worm had the intelligence to know there was moisture above, brought by the recent rain. At the same time, the robin knew the worms would soon be surfacing to take it in. Since the day his friend visited him, he had become increasingly aware of those wonders.

A short descent of the hillside revealed a rocky ledge jutting from the smoothly sloping terrain. As he sat on the ledge, the view was unveiled before him. With one panoramic sweep, from city limit to city limit, the entire community stretched out in a single view.

At the base of the hill below where he sat, the little stream formed a border for the beautiful field of corn covering the bottomland. A flawless green carpet covered the entire floor. On the distant side of the valley, houses and outbuildings made fascinating designs on what appeared as a deeper shade of a green drapery background. The streets resembled plumb lines descended from a ceiling of blue.

Meticulously centered on the green backdrop stood the old Methodist Church building. Its broad sweeping stairways, descending in two directions, accented the structure and enhanced its grandeur. The large stained-glass windows reflected the sunlight, changing them to a rainbow of colors.

To the right and at the bottom of the hill was the business district. Every building stood out clearly. There was the hotel with its wrap-around porch, the lumberyard and the sprawling stockyards, reminiscent of a more active livestock-shipping era. Mark could almost see the flag waving over the post office.

A wisp of smoke at the northeast end of the valley appeared as a blemish on the canvas of a beautiful painting. A hush prevailed as it drifted lazily on the cool breeze. In the distance, the lonesome wail of a train whistle echoed between the hills and down through the valley, breaking the strange silence. *Clickity clack*, the sound of wheels thumping over gaps between the rail sections, grew louder. Then the rhythmic sounds began to slow. From out of the distance, the winding train found its way around curves and over bridges. The seemingly endless flow of cars continued to appear from beyond his range of vision. The engine rolled gracefully into town as it slowly passed the depot, then with one great thud, the train stopped with the water car directly beneath the drain from the huge water tank. After taking in what seemed an endless supply of water, it started on its way. Finally, the last car disappeared from view, and once again, the serenity of the small-town atmosphere returned.

Mark placed his chin on his hands, his elbows on his knees, and then looked toward the stream lying at the bottom of the hill. A small herd of cattle stood grazing along the bank. They stood in a shady area, perfectly content.

All of God's creatures do what He created them to do, he thought, as he pondered the things he observed of nature. *Surely, they express God's faith in whatever they do. Animals don't even have to think of doing things by faith. Why is it so hard for me to do what I should do?* He continued to reason in his mind. *God gave His other creatures faith so we can observe them and learn from them. That's what the Bible means when it says people see the truth but then change it into a lie. Even knowing it doesn't seem to make things any easier.*

Life Is Quickly Passing By

Why do I keep chasing after rainbows?
Looking for my pot of gold?
Someday, I'll find I can have peace of mind—
all I ever do is dream.
I think good fortune soon will overtake me,
maybe then my luck will change:
I'll surely win if my ship will come in,
but life is quickly passing by.
I look for a star!
The first star I see tonight—
I wish on that star!
Oh! How I wish, and wish,
and wish, and wish with all my might.
I guess I want the world to make me happy—
fill my life with joy and bliss,
pastures of greens are in all of my dreams,
but life is quickly passing by.
Yes, life is quickly passing by.

Out of frustration, Mark closed his eyes to ask God to direct him in the way he should go. "Oh, Father!" he said aloud. "Everything is so mixed up right now. I don't know what's best for Mama and me. Oh, God," he said again, "I don't think Em ready to leave this town, but if I must, give me the necessary strength. Please, Father, if You can find it in Your will to do so, let me stay here until Em ready to leave. I ask it all in the name of Jesus Christ, Amen!"

For quite some time, Mark sat quietly, half expecting to hear a voice instructing him on what to do and half convinced God may not have heard his prayer at all. Finally, he arose from his position on the ledge, gazed out over the valley for one last view, and then walked slowly toward the road.

All the way home, Mark thought about what he had prayed for. "It's one thing to pray for the solution to some problem, but it's something else to have the faith to believe it will be answered. What is faith? I know it's the substance of something expected," he remembered. "We see truth everywhere around us, but we can only realize it is truth when we have the faith to believe it." Mark continued to contemplate the matter. "Maybe that's what God is—faith. God is everywhere, they say, but no one's ever seen Him. They say God is in nature, but we're not able to look at Him." Fie remembered sir saying, "The creation we see is the substance of God's faith, and that's how God is teaching us during the eons. For all the long eternity," Mark pondered, "God was saying, let there be this created thing, and let there be that created thing, all out of His faith. Then one day, the substance of God's faith became tangible for us, and everything He had created took shape. It became what God expected. That's why it was faith. God and faith may not be the same, but they sure must be closely associated with one another.

"So when I pray for something and the prayer gets answered, that's faith. When I pray, the substance of my faith is the answered prayer because it's what I expected. I guess if it doesn't get answered, then it wasn't faith.

"Wait a minute," he said to himself. *"What if I pray for something God doesn't want to happen I It can't be a lack of faith when it doesn't*

get answered. ''The matter was becoming confusing. It seemed like he'd been on to something, but now it was suddenly lost.

"Maybe our prayers somehow have to be the same as God's will in order for Him to answer them. It makes sense. That's probably how God becomes everything to His creatures—-by the will of creation becoming the same as God's will." It seemed to make a great deal of logic, and it didn't seem so difficult. Mark had already prayed in that manner quite often mainly because everyone else did. Even sir prayed it would be according to God's will, but now there seemed to be good reason for praying that way.

Mark began again to pray silently. "Oh, Father, help me to know what to do about finding a job, and may You direct me in the way You want me to search. May Your will be done, Father. May Your will become my will. Amen!"

The journey home was almost complete, but Mark hardly remembered having walked the mile and a half or so distance. The morning had been a good experience. Being out in nature for such a long time wasn't unusual for Mark, but he had never felt such close association with the things of God. *"I wish I could feel close to God all the time, instead of just when I need His help about something."*

As Mark entered the kitchen door, his mother told him Harve Finch had stopped to see him. "Didn't say much as to what he wanted to see you about. It did sound like it was a job of some kind. When I asked him if he needed help on the farm, he said, 'No, it hasn't anything to do with the farm.' You know Harve, he doesn't tell you any more than he has to. He asked if maybe you could stop in the store this afternoon if you got home in time. Wouldn't think he'd be in need of any more help in the store. Doesn't seem to be busy to me," she said, trying to find a logical explanation for wanting to see Mark. "I sure think you ought to go and see him, though. It may be something will work out real well."

There couldn't have been better agreement with his mother. He would have to find out right away what Mr. Finch had in mind. And a job in the store didn't seem even remotely possible. Amos James had been the clerk there for as long as Mark could remember, and he would likely work there until the day he died. The thought crossed his mind. *''Maybe Amos died. No! I saw Amos just the other day when I walked by the place,''* he said to himself.

No time was wasted. Mark went directly to the store. Upon entering, he saw Amos standing behind the counter.

"I'll bet you're looking for Harve, aren't you?" Amos said.

"Yeah, he left word with my mother I should stop in and see him." "Hello, Mark," Harve said, as he walked from the back room. "I'm glad you could stop in so soon."

At Mr. Finch's invitation, Mark sat down across from his desk. He quickly came to the point of the meeting. "Amos told me he's quitting his job as grocery clerk, and so I'm going to need a replacement. Amos tells me he'll stay on as long as I need him, but he'd like to leave as soon as possible. He's been with me sixteen years, and I know it'll be hard to find someone as reliable as Amos."

Mark was already feeling uncomfortable listening to Mr. Finch. He sensed he was being measured against Amos.

"You know I could leave for two or three days at a time, and things would run as smooth as if I had been here all the time. It's pretty reassuring to know one is leaving the place in good hands. Your pa used to charge groceries during the winter, but come spring, he never failed to clear the books. I admired him for that, and if you're as honest as your pa, we'll get along just fine."

Mr. Finch stood up as though the meeting was concluded. "You can let me know what you think in a day or so."

"But, sir," Mark said apologetically, "I don't believe we talked about what the job pays yet." He felt the same skeptical eye he had felt before.

"Oh yeah, it pays fifteen dollars a week. The hours are 8:00 to 6:00, Monday through Saturday, and we stay open 'til 10:00 on Wednesday and Saturday nights, sometimes later on Saturday nights.

I suppose if you're doing well, I can raise you to eighteen dollars in six months or so. You let me know what you decide," he said, as he took his hat from the shelf at the end of his desk.

Mr. Finch went on out the door ahead of Mark, giving him a chance to stop and chat with Amos. "You rather like working here, don't you, Amos?" Mark said to him, as he approached where Amos was sitting on the edge of the counter.

"Well! I never really felt like I had much choice, Mark," he responded. "It gave me the opportunity to stay with my mother and help take care of her. That was about the only good part. Oh, I guess I liked being able to talk to people. I enjoy chatting with people. Mostly, though, it was a matter of too many hours and not much time to myself. That's pretty important you know.

"Mark," he said, showing he wanted to be confidential, "I was the one who suggested to Harve, he hire you. I probably haven't done you any great favor, it just seems to me you have a similar situation to the one I had. I mean, with your dad passing away and all. I thought maybe it would help you along until you can arrange something better. It sure isn't any picnic working for Harve, I can tell you that.

"What do you think of the arrangement he offered?" Amos hopped down from the counter and walked to the refrigerator, not giving Mark much of a chance to think about an answer. "What kind of pop do you drink?" he asked, as he opened the door. "We got orange, cream—"

"Cream—cream is just fine," Mark interrupted.

"This is one of the few fringe benefits to this job. I think you should know right up front whatever you agree to now is about the way it's gonna be from now on. Least ways, it will be a lot harder to change later on. I couldn't help overhearing the offer Harve made you, and if you don't mind, I'd like to give you some advice. Of course, I know you didn't ask for it." He stopped long enough to get a response from Mark.

"I'm beginning to think I need a whole lot of advice, my friend. This sure is something new to me. Mr. Finch didn't give me much chance to say anything really," Mark said.

"Cause that's the way he wants it. The less you demand, the more he likes it. Once you're hired, he's got you over a barrel. Least ways, he sees it that way."

Mark was finding matters becoming interesting, but he wasn't sure he liked what he was hearing. "He sounds like a tyrant," Mark said.

"No, he's not all bad, but you have to know where you stand with him. Tell him you want one week's paid vacation after one year and two weeks after two years, if that's what you want, of course. It took me two years to get any vacation at all, and then he pushed me to the point of quitting before I got it. That's what I mean, whatever you agree to will be okay, just make sure you know what you're agreeing to. Tell him you want to be raised to eighteen dollars a week after the first month. That way, you'll probably get it in three months instead of six. Oh, and another thing, today was the first time he ever said things ran as well when he wasn't here as they did when he was here. It was likely so much baloney. I never felt he trusted me to run the place alone."

"Wow! I didn't know there was so much involved in getting a job. I thought you have to take what they offer and like it," Mark said with a grin.

"Well, you still might, but it sure won't hurt to let him know where you stand. For whatever it's worth, Mark, I know he's hoping you take the job."

"Amos"—this time, it was Mark speaking in a confidential tone—"you didn't say what you were leaving your job to do. Is that a secret?"

"No! It's no secret. Least ways not since I gave my notice. I've got an uncle living down in Westerville. He bought a 290-acre farm and asked me to come and work for him. Said it will be easier for me to take care of Mother there too, and there will be others to help make her comfortable."

A customer came into the store. Mark could see Amos didn't want to discuss their business in front of anyone. "See you in the morning," Mark said as he left the store.

Mrs. Hayes was delighted when Mark told her what the meeting was about. "My, it would be wonderful if you could get the job," she said to him.

"Well, Mama," he said, trying to sound casual, "I don't have the job yet. There are some things we have to work out, like vacations and holidays. I have to establish some rate of promotion. I don't want to work for nothing forever. I think it's best to have those things arranged ahead of time. Don't you agree, Mama?"

Mark did negotiate his conditions the next morning. He was surprised at how smoothly the meeting went. Mark got all his points across, and Mr. Finch even agreed to give him the raise after two months, instead of three. Of course, it depended on whether he did a satisfactory job. Mark had an odd feeling Mr. Finch wanted him to talk to Amos about the job the day before.

Mark couldn't wait to get home to tell his mother about getting the job. A little quick arithmetic showed him he would be earning about twenty-four cents an hour. "It doesn't sound like much money," he said, "but Don Tobin went to work in Des Moines in a mattress factory at eighty cents an hour. He has to pay five dollars a week for a room, and he has to eat all his meals in restaurants. And he has to ride a bus everywhere he goes. Besides, he pays a job service four dollars and eighty cents a week for getting him the job. My hours aren't too good, but I guess it will be all right for a while," he concluded.

Mark sat down in a rocking chair, feeling pleased with the way things had turned out.

"I'm so pleased you got the job, Mark. I think it has been an answer to prayer," his mother said.

"Yeah, Mama, it does seem to be an answer to prayer." He walked over to his mother and kissed her on the cheek.

CHAPTER 8

Once, the small town was a busy and important part of Midwest society. Today, the small towns are disappearing at an alarming rate— alarming that is to someone like Mark who regretfully watches from a distance as the place of his childhood memories withers and dies.

The year Mark graduated from the public school was the last year high school was taught in his hometown. He remained there for fifteen months, working in the grocery store. His salary had only increased to twenty-five dollars a week, with practically no hope of reaching any higher and putting in nearly sixty hours a week to earn it. It became apparent the time had arrived to put down roots somewhere else.

Tom Reed already lived in Davenport, a city at the other end of the state, so Mark boarded a bus and headed east. It was an uneasy and trying time for him. The very decision to make the change had been difficult, and it was not going to get easier until the change was complete. He prayed often for everything to work out according to God's will.

Even greater was his concern for his mother. Mark had persuaded her to move to Colorado to live with her daughter Inez, and he couldn't help but wonder if he had done what was best for her. Perhaps arranging for her welfare was only a way for him to ease his own conscience. As the bus pulled away from the station, night was closing in. Many and mixed were the emotions filling his mind.

Mark remembered many times having seen a Trailways bus pull

into the depot to pick up or discharge passengers or just watched as it sped down the highway and wishing he was a passenger going to some faraway place. He thought of the romantic feelings he had so often fantasized, of racing into the night with the cool breeze blowing across his face, caring not what was in store as he headed for some unknown destination. He was indeed doing what he had long dreamed of doing, but somehow, the romanticism was missing. The trip was enjoyable enough, but the unknown was far more vivid than the fantasy.

With the window open just enough for him to feel the breeze gently rushing over him, he sat back to enjoy the quiet and the privacy. It was like being alone, not knowing anyone on the bus. He thought of sir, the stranger he had grown to know and love so long ago, more than eight years now, but for some reason, the man came into his thoughts as the bus sped through the night. *"Why hasn't someone sought to find out what happened to the man? How could such a fine gentleman as he not have some friend or relative curious enough to try to locate him?"*

During the first year or so after the man's death, Mark inquired a number of times at the police station as to any progress in the matter. Each time, the answer was the same: "There has been no report of a man missing, which answers this individual's description." They always seemed genuinely concerned, not only for the man's identity but also for Mark when they realized his attachment to the man. *"It's been about five years since I inquired. Perhaps I can pursue the matter from my new location,"* he assured himself. *"The larger cities may get more up-to-date information on such things and perhaps more details. It will certainly be worth a try."*

When Mark arrived at his destination, his friend was waiting for him at the bus station. Tom Reed and Mark had been good friends since before they started school in the first grade. It was late when Mark reached the depot, but they went for a leisurely drive around the city. As they toured the city, they stopped at an all-night restaurant for a sandwich and fries and a cold drink.

Mark was indeed impressed with what he saw and fell in love

with the town almost immediately. It soon became home to him and remained such Irom then on. Probably, no place can quite take the place of one's hometown, but the attachment is the difference. For the small town, the attachment is mostly sentimental and, in Mark's case, childhood memories, bur he loved Davenport almost as much.

Tom had been busy making arrangements for Mark and had certainly made things a lot easier for him. He had already set it up for them to room together until Mark decided what he wanted to do. "You can bunk in with me, or they have an empty room available right now if you want it," Tom said. "Thought you might want to save your pennies for a while."

"You sure are right there," Mark said with concern. "The grocery clerk jobs aren't very lucrative back home these days. I'll have to find a job real quick," he added.

"Might have a solution for that one too." Tom looked at Mark and grinned. "You may be able to get my job. I've been working in a print shop down on Fourth Street for about six months. The work just isn't my cup of tea. Mr. Dickins owns the shop. He's a real fine man. You couldn't want to know a nicer guy than he is. I just don't care for the kind of work it involves. To me, it's boring. Well, you always liked those subjects in school, English and stuff. I thought you might want to go for it. I told Mr. Dickins I'd bring you in. I'll take you in, but you'll have to make your own impression," he said with a chuckle.

Mark was curious as to what Tom was going to do. "Do you already have a job lined up?" he asked.

"I've got a job at a factory making radios and victrolas. I start in two weeks. You might be able to get on there too. It's up to you, but I think you have a real good chance of getting work at the print shop. It doesn't pay very good to start, but I'm sure there's a future for someone who likes the work."

It seemed Tom had thought of everything. He told Mark the buses stopped just a block from the room and he could get on the bus right in front of the print shop. "The buses run until midnight," he said.

Before many days passed, Mark paid a visit to the police station hoping to find more information concerning "sir." He felt a bit uncomfortable entering the station. *"They probably wonder what I've done."* Everyone looked so busy, like each one had been assigned a job having to be done immediately. He could only guess how a police station was run, but just to see an officer in uniform gave him the feeling they were concerned with duty and responsibility.

"May I help you, son?" a man asked, as Mark came near.

"Well, sir, I-I-I don't quite know where to begin," he stammered. "I want to check about a missing person."

"You want to report a person missing?" the officer asked, without taking his eyes from his paperwork.

"No! No, sir, I just want to check on someone who died," Mark tried to explain. "I mean he's not missing, but it's because nobody reported him missing, a-and I just think they should have."

"You have me confused, son," he said, as he turned from the paper he had been studying. "You say he hasn't been reported missing, but he should have been."

The man tried to summarize what Mark had said, and it didn't make much sense even to Mark. "Sir," he said apologetically, "do you have a few minutes? I can tell you the whole story."

"That's what I get paid to do, son—listen to people's stories." He grinned at Mark. "You go right ahead."

"Well, sir," Mark began, "I only knew the man a few hours, but we became real good friends."

"All right, son, just begin at the beginning and tell me all about the man. What was his name?" the officer asked.

"Well, that's a problem. I don't know his name, sir. I called him sir.

"Now you really have me confused. You don't know his name, but you were good friends?" The officer lowered his head and looked at Mark over the rim of his glasses. "All right, when did you meet him?" he asked.

"About eight years ago, in my hometown in southwest Iowa. I used to inquire in Winterset, but they never had reports of anyone missing. I just thought you might have more information in the big city. Anyway, I was only eleven then, and I was out in the garden when this stranger came walking up from the railroad tracks."

Mark was amazed how readily the events of the day came to memory. He could still see the stranger standing there as though it had just happened. "He was such a wise man," Mark told the officer, "And he taught me many things. It doesn't seem right no one ever tried to find out what happened to him."

"I suspect someone did try to find him, son, but you don't have much to go on. It's hard enough to identify bodies even when there is a name," the officer explained.

"Sir, I did find a Bible I assume was his. It had the initials on the front in gold letters—S-I-R. That's what seemed so strange. They were the initials spelling the name I called him and remembered him by. I told the coroner about the Bible and the initials, in fact, they took the Bible and still have it," he added thoughtfully.

"S-I-R," the man repeated. He seemed to be pondering something. "Those initials, they sound familiar. I can't think why or where I heard them. Well, I doubt we have any more information than they had in your hometown. We can see if something may have come in during those years since you last checked. Say! Wait a minute. I think we got something just three or four months ago. I think I know where I saw those initials. Wait here, I'll be back in a few minutes." This was the first ray of hope Mark had concerning the identity of the stranger. *Wouldn't it be great if I could find out where he lived, what he did, who he was? I wonder if he had a family.* His imagination raced wildly as he considered the limitless possibilities. His mind was miles away when the officer returned carrying a form he obtained from the file.

"Here's the report I told you about, son. Let's see. It was filed on June 20, 1947, only about four months ago. And a man filed it in Waterford, Michigan, by the name of Harold Mason, 2730 Rosewood Avenue. Yes, here it is, Sidney I. Rawlings. The I. is for Ivan. There are the initials you told me about."

"Couldn't it be coincidence?" Mark cautioned.

"There's more, son. It says he was last seen in Waterford, in about June of 1939. He hasn't been heard of since then. That would be just about eight years now. Here's a description of him.

Male, Caucasian, about 5'8" tall, 170 pounds, 55 years of age when last seen, blue eyes, brown hair, had a long scar along his right arm. A friend made the report."

Mark was elated with this information. "Would it be all right if I wrote it down?" he asked, realizing it was much more than mere coincidence. "Maybe I can go and talk to this, a-a Harold Mason. I'd like to do that."

"Sure," the officer complied. "Let's find a map and locate Waterford. Now it's your turn to help me. I need information as to where all this occurred eight years ago so we can follow up on the investigation of the matter. For now, just give me the name of the town where the original report was filed. I think you spoke of Winterset, Iowa? We'll check out the autopsy report and whatever else they may have," he said, as he took Mark to the map in the next room.

"Now according to the index, Q2, it should be somewhere near Detroit. Let's see if we can find it. Says the population is something around ten thousand. Oh yes, there it is. Looks like about forty miles northwest of Detroit. Practically a suburb."

After Mark gave the information he had, the officer thanked him for stopping by and wished him good luck in finding the man in Michigan. Mark felt extremely confident much would come from the information he learned. For the first time in all those years, there seemed good reason to believe the stranger would be identified. Mark was already trying to determine in his mind how he could make the trip to Waterford, and he never swayed from his intent to go there.

Thanksgiving weekend is coming soon. He had only been working at the print shop less than two months and realized it might be hard to get time off so soon. He decided to offer to make a trade of working the holiday instead of Friday, thus giving him a three-day weekend to make the trip. While the idea did not particularly appeal to Mr. Dickins, when he heard the entire story about Mark's friend, and since he had work he needed to catch up on, he quite willingly allowed him to make the change. Tom had certainly been right about Mr. Dickins being a fine man, and Mark could now attest to the fact he was also a fine employer.

In addition, there was the matter of contacting the man in Michigan to know if he would even see him if he did make the trip.

With the name and address he had obtained from the policeman at the station, he wrote a long letter to Mr. Harold Mason, giving him the complete details of what he had come to know about their mutual acquaintance, and to arrange a meeting. In less than a week, he was in receipt of the answer he hoped for.

"I cannot express my relief when receiving your letter" was the response. "I was much grieved at hearing of Sidney's death but must confess I already knew in my heart he was gone from this world. Sidney and I were friends since we were old enough to have a friend. I look forward to meeting you and hearing more about your visit with Sidney. Please don't let me down. Sincerely Yours, Harold Mason."

The days passed slowly as Mark looked forward to the time he would visit the man, but of course, the day did arrive. He could hardly get home quickly enough to get ready and be on his way, though his bus wasn't scheduled to depart until 8:15 p.m. He should reach Waterford at 8:15 a.m. the following morning. At 8:30 the next morning, Mark's cab was parked at 2730 Rosewood Avenue. To his surprise, upon arrival, Mr. Mason was sitting on the porch wearing a light jacket. The air was filled with the cool of autumn, but Mr. Mason didn't seem to mind.

The man watched the cab stop in front of his house. When Mark stepped out and looked toward the porch, Mr. Mason was on his way to greet him. There was little question in the man's mind concerning who Mark was. "Mark Hayes, I presume!" he called as Mark came near. He appeared to be in his early sixties, quite active and energetic. He seemed a happy person and very friendly. He had just retired during the summer after working thirty years in a factory, as Mark was about to find out during the first few minutes of their meeting. He had enjoyed his job all those years, but he had looked forward to his freedom, as he called it, for a long time. "Now I want to live long enough to enjoy my freedom." Pretending to speak as a tottery old man out on his last walk, he said, "I figure I've got a year or two to go yet."

"Did you enjoy your trip last night, Mark?" he asked, giving Mark his first opportunity to speak since he arrived.

Mark didn't mind at all. The man had a wonderful personality, was good-natured, and had a warm and friendly smile. After just a few minutes, Mark knew he would become fond of the man. It wasn't at all difficult to understand why he and Sidney had been such close friends.

"I slept part of the trip," Mark explained, "but I have to say, there isn't much I enjoy more than racing through the night riding on a bus."

"You must be getting pretty hungry, I'll guess."

"Yes, in fact, I did wait, hoping you'd let me take you out for breakfast this morning," Mark said.

"Nonsense! You're my guest, and I'm taking you out for breakfast," he interrupted. There was no question as to who the guest would be.

"You live on a beautiful street, Mr. Mason," Mark said, as they were getting into the man's car to leave for the diner.

"Harold!" he quipped. "The name's Harold. There's only one Mr. Mason. That's my father," he said, placing emphasis on the mister.

"We're proud of our street. I lived right there in the same house for sixty-three years. Yep! I was born there. When we get back, I'll show you where Sidney lived. He was born just across the street. He spent his whole life there too, until eight years ago. I'll introduce you to Sidney's father. My but we do have a lot to talk about," he said.

"Right now, I want to get started with breakfast so we can get down to some serious business of hearing about your meeting with Sidney. And don't leave out a single word," he said.

There was still the problem Mark had with the entire matter concerning Harold's lack of effort, or seeming lack of effort, in trying to find his missing friend. He felt awkward asking the reason but decided it was not something he needed to apologize for. If it caused anyone embarrassment, it surely would be Harold's rather than his.

"Sir," Mark said, trying to be as casual as possible, "there's something puzzling me a great deal. If you don't want to answer my question, I won't be offended, but I've been wondering about the fact that, well, sir, I mean Sidney, had been missing for about eight years, but you didn't make a missing person's report until, well, this summer. I mean, didn't you know all the time he was missing?" Mark asked, relieved he had finally completed his question.

"Son," he began, "I appreciate your concern in the matter, and I certainly understand why you would be so mystified. There really is a very sad story behind it."

Harold wanted to go into the diner and get seated and order breakfast. "Then I have quite a tale for you to hear," he said to Mark. They found a booth and then placed their orders.

The man, who had appeared so jovial and enthusiastic a few minutes before, suddenly seemed a very troubled man. His eyes reddened as he paused in search of the right words to relate to Mark. "I suppose I'll need to start a way back in order to give the whole picture." He began slowly. "Sidney Ivan—I used to call him that sometimes when we were being confidential with one another. Sidney and I were born in 1884. Sidney was two weeks older than I was, two weeks to the day. We became more like brothers than any brothers I've ever known. In fact, we were better friends than I think it's possible for brothers to be. But then I never had a real brother, nor did Sidney. We went to school together, all the way through. It was rare for us to have an argument, and never was there a serious quarrel of any sort. We were virtually inseparable during those years while growing up. That's why it hurts me so much when I think of the way the last eight years turned out."

Mark's new friend was visibly shaken as he struggled with his emotions to keep from breaking down. Mark felt helpless in knowing how to console him, but the man soon regained his composure and continued speaking.

"Sidney was only eight years old when his mother died. I think we loved each other's parents as much as we loved our own. I know I missed Sidney's mother terribly. Ivan, that's Sidney's father's name, was a good father I'm sure. But he was strict, a Pentecostal minister, had a church just a few streets over from where we live. My father was never a very religious man, but he allowed me to attend services with Sidney. Sidney, of course, didn't have a choice in the matter. I remember a time Ivan reprimanded Sidney before the entire congregation for causing some ruckus. He believed in setting examples, and Sidney paid the price all too often, I think. I guess it must have all worked out well, though. I gave my life to Jesus Christ one evening at a revival meeting. The following night, Sidney went forward at the altar call. I used to joke with him about it. I told him he couldn't stand me having something he didn't have. We were sixteen then, old enough to know what we wanted, an easy date to remember, being the year 1900.

"Am I boring you, Mark?" he asked apologetically.

"Not at all, sir," Mark answered quickly. "I find it very interesting. I loved Sidney a great deal, and I find your story fascinating. I'm sure no one knew him quite the way you knew him."

"Well, we were both active in Ivan's church for many years, about thirty years in fact. I married and raised two daughters. Sidney never married, much more of a Bible student than I, pretty well devoted all his spare time to Bible studies. I enjoyed studying and learned with Sidney, but I couldn't devote the time he did. Of course, I wasn't the student he was either.

"He was always learning and spent a great deal of time at the library. He could go into a library he had never visited before and spend hours looking through their literature. One day, right here in Waterford, he found a Concordant Version of the scriptures and several volumes of Concordant writings someone had donated. There was a particular rendering of the words 'ever and ever' in that Bible, which gained his attention. It started him on an exhaustive study of the eons and eventually into a whole new premise of Bible understanding."

Harold paused for a moment while staring at the table and then continued. "Sidney was very devoted to these studies. He tried to discuss some of the matters with his father, but his father wanted no part of it. Sidney then stopped all discussions with him along those lines. After a time, Sidney felt he should make a commitment to his beliefs. He began making it clear to all his friends in the church, just what his convictions were. He knew very well he might be asked to leave the church because of them. It was indeed upsetting to many of the members, but his own father took the initiative to oust him from membership. When Ivan fully realized his son was making a stand for his convictions, he ordered him out of the church. He then refused to even speak to his own son.

"Of course, it deeply hurt Sidney, though he rather expected how it would turn out. Sidney thought it would be a good idea for him to go away for a time and be away from his father. That was in late June of 1939. When Sidney left here, he looked for all the world like a common hobo. He made a blue denim bag with a drawstring, and tied it to a shortened hoe handle, and placed it over his shoulder. He said, I want to be wholly dependent on the Lord. I want to become as close to God as I can possibly become.' Sidney was already close to God.

"Anyway, I expected to hear from Sidney as soon as he became established somewhere. Time went by, and I didn't hear. After about two months, I knew something was wrong, or I would have heard from him. I talked to Ivan, and he informed me Sidney was dead. He wouldn't discuss the matter with me, but I assumed what he told me was true. I didn't even think to doubt him. All those years I was of the persuasion Sidney was dead."

Tears were welling in Harold's eyes as he brushed them with the back of his hand. "It wasn't until late this spring Ivan came to me with tears in his eyes. He told me he really didn't know what had happened to Sidney. He told me in anger he had written him off as no longer being a son of his, and as far as he was concerned, Sidney was dead. Ivan also suspected his son had died since he hadn't heard from him in so many years. Ivan felt badly for the way he treated Sidney and said he would like to try to find him, on the chance he was still alive somewhere. It was then I put out the missing person's report. I really didn't expect to hear anything, but when I received your letter, I was sure I was about to learn the truth about Sidney. Then we were soon notified through the police department."

"I'm sorry," Mark said to Harold. "I'm sorry I doubted your sincerity. I had no idea the extent of your friendship."

"No need for an apology, Mark, I quite understand your perplexity. We were indeed the best of friends," he said weakly.

All the time the man talked, the same questions had been arising having been present from the day Mark met Sidney so long before. What kind of work did he do? Did he have a steady job somewhere along the way? Why didn't he carry identification on his person? Harold was eager to answer any questions he could. Mark learned Sidney was a handyman who did repair jobs around the neighborhood. He did lawn and garden work, taking care of flowers, and shrubbery and trimming trees. He was a hard worker, Harold stressed, but he really only made a living. "He didn't charge enough for the work he did," he told Mark. "During the fall and winter seasons, he cut wood for people in the area for heating their homes and firing their cookstoves. Almost as many people heated with wood as with coal," he told him.

Harold loved talking about his dear friend. Mark watched his expressions as they reflected the love he had for him. Pride was evident as Harold told him his neighborhood was as beautiful as any neighborhood in Waterford. And that was because of the care and joy Sidney put into his work and his love for all God's creation. "He said he wanted to keep it as God intended when He made it," he said softly.

Mark watched Harold's expression sadden as he told how Sidney seemed always only to get by on his income and then suddenly brighten when he spoke of the happiness Sidney felt in everything he did for the Lord. "Sidney was at peace with God and the world," he said. Harold seemed to be lost somewhere back in time, obviously reminiscing some of his most happy moments, doing what was nearest to his heart, talking about his lifelong friend and savoring every moment of it.

"It isn't difficult to know why he was penniless," he said, with a faraway look in his eyes. "Sidney was never very far from poverty. I don't know, though, why he wouldn't have a form of identification with him, unless his wallet was lost or stolen. That might provide the answer. I guess we'll probably never know," he said thoughtfully.

They had finished breakfast and were still visiting, when they realized the diner was filled to capacity and people were standing as they waited to be seated in booths.

"What do you say we retreat to my home so we can continue our visit?" he said, as he slid to the end of the booth. "A big pot of coffee ought to keep us going for a few more hours."

CHAPTER 9

The sun shone brightly as Mark and Harold returned from the diner. The air was still crisp but warming as the morning wore on. While walking in the sunshine, it was tempting for them to remove their jackets, but when entering the shade, they were quickly reminded of the lateness into the autumn season. Never could Mark remember having seen such a high sky, scarcely a cloud to be seen anywhere. It was like viewing into endless depths of clear blue heavens above.

"Would you like to take that walk through the neighborhood now?" Harold asked. The look in his eyes seemed to beg for an affirmative reply. "It's a great day to be out and about," he said.

Mark knew Harold fully expected to show him some of the places Sidney had taken care of, and he did indeed look forward to seeing the kind of work Sidney had been so capable of doing. Harold was proud of the neighborhood in which he lived and mainly because of the meticulous care Sidney had provided it.

But there was something noticeably different about this part of Waterford. Oh, it was quite true more than eight years had passed since Sidney had done any work there, so there was much evidence of neglect in keeping up the gardening chores—the pruning and trimming—but this was much more than attractive lawns and trimmed shrubs. Long rows of grape arbors and blueberry shrubs graced the backyards along the alleyways. Almost every residence exhibited a few rose bushes or climbers, but many contained large rose gardens. Vine-covered overhead latticework was commonplace, lending a dimension of intrigue everywhere he looked.

"Sidney was responsible for most everything you see," Harold told him, showing a great deal of pride in the entire area.

"There's someone I want you to meet, Mark," he said, catching a glimpse of an elderly lady at the rear of the house nearby. "She never ceases to sing the praises of Sidney's work. Mrs. Price!" he called. "Oh, it's you, Harold," she said, recognizing him immediately. "Yes, Mrs. Price," he replied, "I brought along the friend I told you I heard from—the young man who came to know Sidney before he passed on." They neared the place where Mrs. Price stood. "I'd like you to meet Mark Hayes. Mark came all the way from Iowa to learn more about Sidney."

"My, how wonderful," she exclaimed. "I've looked forward to meeting you, and we want so much to hear all about your meeting with Sidney. We miss him so."

Mrs. Price wouldn't allow Mark to stop talking until she had learned everything about his relationship with Sidney. She was a slender woman, standing straight and tall. Her silvery white hair glistened in the bright sunlight. The rims of her glasses also reflected the rays of the sun. She was eager to hear all the details of their visit so long ago. Mark learned also her husband had been deceased for almost four years. She and her late husband had taken care of the property all those years, but Sidney had helped with the planning and getting it established so they could keep up with the work. Obviously, it had been well cared for since her husband's death, even though the growing season was well passed for the year.

They walked along a cobblestone path surrounded by plants, forming, what would be in the spring, a lush ground cover. All this was beneath an ivy-covered lattice ceiling. Pots for flowers and foliage hung in abundance. A self-supporting swing neatly painted a brilliant red, set cozily along the lattice wall.

"This was Tim's favorite spot," she said quietly. "We used to sit there together on those warm summer evenings listening to the birds and crickets, just enjoying the wonders of nature. We remained there many evenings well after dark watching the flashes of light made by the fireflies. Tim would say, when another light flashed in the grass, 'There's his lady friend responding to his courting.' How Tim loved this yard. We never would have had it without Sidney's help, though," she spoke with a note of melancholy in her voice.

"Sidney put up all this lattice work and all the posts and framework for it. He built the swing you saw. He was a superb carpenter. He even built my kitchen cabinets. Tim and I worked right along with him, but it was Sidney's genius, which designed it all. We laid the cobblestone all through the yard, being careful to place each one in just the right place so we could have the best view of each plant and figurine. He built this wishing well and filled it with moss roses. See the cobblestones breaking away from the main path and leading up to the well?" she said through a pleased expression on her face.

Mrs. Price relished every moment as she reflected the joy of her memories. "I'm seventy-five years old, but I still enjoy the things Sidney did. He made it possible for Tim and me to enjoy the happiest years of our lives. I shall always treasure every moment." Tears welled in her eyes.

"See the shrubbery along the picket fence?" she said, as she pointed toward the back of the yard. "Those are blueberry shrubs. Sidney planted those. We get the nicest big juicy blueberries you ever tasted. The nursery over on Marlin Avenue used to buy the foliage from these shrubs. They called it huckleberry greens. They used it in their flower arrangements. Mrs. Thomas, across the alley, has blackberry shrubs along her fence. Sidney said they were the only cultivated blackberry shrubs he knew of. I guess they're still quite rare."

Harold enjoyed Mrs. Price as much as Mark did. They let her go on talking, not so much as adding one unnecessary word.

"And here is the rose garden," she said, not even trying to hide her pride for the bushes. "You can see everything has been wrapped up for the cold winter ahead. My! I dread the long cold winters. But I wouldn't move away from here for the world. The beautiful springs make the worst winters worthwhile." She hastened to tell them.

Mrs. Price was a remarkable woman. It was hard to leave her company. In just those few brief minutes, her love for God's handiwork made Mark appreciate life a little more than he had before. Indeed, in her own way, she was living life to its fullest, for she made every moment count.

She thanked Mark profusely for telling her of his brief meeting with Sidney and the experience of visiting with him. But Mark knew from those few fleeting moments spent with her in Waterford, he came out the richer one.

It was quiet as they walked to the sidewalk from the Price residence, and it was Harold who broke the silence. "The Prices probably put more of themselves into the care of their property than any other neighbor," Harold said. They continued on their walk. "But most of the properties looked very much as nice as this one at one time. It's hard to realize how beautiful they can be when viewing them in November. You should see them in the spring when the richness of color breaks out in its entire splendor. Perhaps you'll return in the spring. You will always be welcome, son."

"You've already made me feel welcome."

"I remember the week Sidney laid that sidewalk over there," Harold interrupted, pointing across the street. "It goes all the way around the corner lot. Folks still miss Sidney. He probably replaced every sidewalk in this part of town at one time or another, built his own forms, mixed his own cement, and poured it all himself."

"This is where the Waltons live, next door to where Sidney lived all his life. His father still lives there. Homer has a gorgeous arbor. I wish you could see it in full bloom, but of course, it has to be seen in the summer to be appreciated. It's an especially well-developed Clematis panniculitis." Harold smiled as he pronounced the words. "I only remember the name because Sidney talked about it so much. It provided a lot of satisfaction for him. He told me a number of times he'd like to plant one on his father's property, but he didn't want to detract anything from Homer's arbor."

It was indeed a fully developed perennial vine. Harold told Mark it was virtually a solid white with flowered forms when in bloom.

"I don't believe they take as much care in Iowa to protect from the freezing weather," Mark said, as he turned, expecting to find

Harold beside him. Instead, Harold was walking toward the Rawlings residence some short distance away.

"Come, I'll introduce you to Ivan," he called to Mark.

Mr. Rawlings was carrying a bag of leaves toward the backyard. Mark walked to where Harold had joined him.

"Our friend from Iowa, is it not?" Mr. Rawlings asked. There was a tremor in his voice.

It came as a shock when Mark realized this man was Sidney's father. It hadn't occurred to him the man would be so elderly. But after all, Sidney would have been sixty-three, the same age as Harold. Mr. Rawlings was quite frail, pale of color, and spoke softly. Harold took the bag from him and carried it to the rose garden where Mr. Rawlings intended to cover the rose bushes.

Mr. Rawlings listened intently to every word of Mark's visit with his son. Not until Mark was finished did he express his sentiments in any way. "I don't know how Sidney got mixed up in the universal reconciliation nonsense. I'm sorry he involved you in it." His voice shook slightly as he spoke.

"Oh, but I don't think of it as nonsense at all, Mr. Rawlings," Mark replied respectfully. "I found it quite refreshing and revealing. It's a beautiful thing to know we have a God who is interested in everyone, rather than merely those who happen to believe in Him."

"Of course, He's interested in everyone. Do you think everyone isn't given a chance at salvation?" Mr. Rawlings face flushed with anger, but he quickly regained his composure. The subject obviously was a sore spot with him, but he seemed determined to keep his emotions under control.

Harold was concerned for Mr. Rawlings. Because of his years and with his health failing as it was, Harold didn't like to see him getting so excited. "Don't you think you should accept Sidney's beliefs as being of his freedom of choice?" Harold asked, trying to calm him down. "You know, Sidney believed the things that really matter—the death, burial, and resurrection of Christ. He died for all of us."

"Oh!" Mr. Rawlings interrupted. "But Sidney's view was if you don't believe in the salvation of all men, then you have the spirit of antichrist. And he said not to believe in the salvation of all was to deny Christ was able to save all. And if He failed to save all, then

He failed to accomplish what God sent Him here to accomplish in the first place."

The words he spoke struck Mark with tremendous force. What a magnificent statement! Mark thought. Obviously, Mr. Rawlings quoted Sidney quite accurately, yet he didn't seem to be at all impressed with the statement. Mark looked at Harold, who had seen his astonishment, but not wanting the conversation to get away, he winked at Mark and continued speaking.

"You know, Ivan," Harold spoke affectionately and deliberately, "in the second chapter of first Timothy, Paul tells us we should pray for all mankind. He says, 'For this is ideal and welcome in the sight of our Savior, God, Who wills that all mankind be saved and come into a realization of the truth' (1 Tim. 2:3-4). It's pretty hard to argue those words," he said.

Not wanting to give Mr. Rawlings a chance to escape the issue, Harold continued, "And in the tenth chapter of Hebrews, the Lord is quoted as saying, 'Lo! I am arriving to do thy will, O God'" (Heb. 10:7). Again, he stressed the word will.

"Yes! Yes! Yes! You've referred to those verses before." Mr. Rawlings tried to avoid further discussion along the lines Harold was pursuing.

Mark stood wondering how he might get a good discussion started, which would illuminate his own understanding. It did seem like the perfect opportunity to hear both sides of the argument. He didn't want to put Harold on the spot, yet he felt sure if the things he believed were true, they would reveal themselves. He thought about the words he might use and then carefully put them together in the form of a question.

"I understand the value of verses and passages in speaking truth to us," Mark said thoughtfully. "But while many of them speak clearly and unmistakably, many others seem to be a matter for interpretation. How can I know for sure what the truth is?"

Mark could almost see the thought processes being set in motion. Both Mr. Rawlings and Harold seemed ready to present their views. It was Mr. Rawlings, however, who spoke first. Immediately, he began quoting scripture verses, one after another in rapid order. It was as though he was standing at the podium of his church shouting forth his sermon.

> "Then shall he say also unto them on the left hand, Depart from me, ye cursed, into everlasting fire prepared for the devil and his angels" (Mat. 25:41; AV).

> "And these shall go into everlasting punishment: but the righteous into life eternal" (Matt. 25:46; AV).

> "But he that shall blaspheme against the Holy Ghost hath never forgiveness, but is in danger of eternal damnation" (Mk. 3:29; AV).

"Any argument against what those verses say isn't worth an engineer's toot." Mr. Rawlings wasn't about to let anyone interrupt his argument..

> "And the smoke of their torment ascendeth up forever and ever" (Rev. 14:11; AV).

"Son—" Mr. Rawlings had hardly taken a deep breath after he began quoting Bible verses. He appeared to be getting much weaker, but still he continued. "Son, there are many verses telling us what happens to those who do not accept Jesus Christ as their personal Savior in this life. They teach us that those people will spend the rest of eternity apart from God. Imagine never having another opportunity to know God. They will lie there in the fires of hell and brimstone, screaming and writhing in pain and begging God to have mercy on them. But God will say to them, 'I do not know you, you will burn forever and ever and ever.' That, my friend, is what happens to those who ignore the gospel in this life."

Mr. Rawlings appeared exhausted, but just when Mark thought the man was finished speaking, he began anew with rejuvenated energy.

> "There are countless scripture passages telling us salvation is for eternity. Sometimes, it says ever, or forever, or forever and ever. One of the clearest verses of the entire Bible is John 3:16: 'For God so loved the world that he gave his only begotten Son, that whosoever believeth in him should not perish, but have everlasting life' (John 3:16; AV).

"How could any verse make it plainer than this one, pray tell?"

Mr. Rawlings had become very excited. While he had been slowly working his way toward the picnic bench in the yard, he was almost on a run now. He seated himself to catch his breath. It was necessary the discussion should end, for it was clear any further pursuit would only endanger the old man's health.

Mark's heart ached for Sidney. How hard it must have been for him to hear his father deny and argue so forcefully against what he believed to be such beautiful truth. How Mark wished he could see the truth as Sidney had seen it.

"Mr. Rawlings certainly has a single mind concerning that subject," Mark said, as they began walking toward his house across the street.

"Oh yes, but he has changed a great deal over the past few years. He used to be much worse," he said with a chuckle. "I sometimes get very annoyed with Ivan because of his narrow-mindedness." He became serious once again. "But I still love him, and I have a great deal of respect for him. Perhaps it's the respect I have for Sidney, though, which allows me to remain patient with him," he said, as his expression saddened.

They entered Harold's home where he invited Mark to be seated in the living room. "I'll get the pot of coffee going that we talked about awhile ago," he said. "My, would you believe it was well over two hours ago?" he said, disappearing to the kitchen.

It was a modest home but nicely furnished and very clean. *I've heard of floors being clean enough to eat off of but I think these really are,* he thought. Several neatly framed family portraits arranged on the table in front of the picture window caught Mark's eye as he looked about the room.

"Well, the coffee's a brewing," Harold announced jovially as he entered the living room. "I see you discovered the pictures of my lovely family—lovely, except the goat with the beautiful lady there," he said, pointing to a picture of himself and his wife. "This gentleman here is my father. He's the only Mr. Mason I recognize, and those are my two daughters and their families," he said proudly. "Marsha is our youngest and lives here in Waterford. Jose, that's short for Josephine, lives in Detroit. My wife, Marjorie, is there now for the weekend. She's spending Thanksgiving with Jose and a few extra days. I'll go there later this weekend. Then we'll return home together."

"Well, Mark!" Harold slid a chair closer to where Mark sat and seated himself. "Mark, you asked a while ago how all humanity can be saved while many will be cast into the lake of fire. Isn't that about what you asked?"

Mark positioned himself squarely in front of Harold. "As for Mr. Rawlings's view, if men go on dying forever and never get to see God, as Mr. Rawlings says, then how can death ever be abolished? In other words, if death is abolished, how can death continue for eternity?"

Harold's face beamed as Mark reasoned aloud. "I'm proud of you, Mark, for being able to think the matter through."

"I have to confess, Harold, I have a rather serious problem with the death aspect. I must be missing something in the meaning of death. We won't have these fleshly bodies in heaven."

"Mark, I think you are confusing the kind of death we are talking about, and I assure you, you are not the first to do so. There is physical death, and there is death of the soul. When Adam sinned, the Bible says he began to die. We can be sure Adam did not die a physical death the day he sinned. It is the same with all of us—we do not suddenly experience an end of physical life at the moment of our birth, yet we do enter into a 'dying state' of our soul on the day of our birth. That's why God brought His creation into the eons—we enter the 'dying state,' and when we have come to know God, our soul becomes a new creation. Mark, it comes down to this. It is the 'dying state' of the soul that is the last enemy to be abolished.

"Mark! There is something I must make clear to you. When Jesus died on the cross, was buried and resurrected, He completely nullified the dying state one inherited from Adam, but the problem was to continue because the Law of Moses has entered the picture. When any individual reaches the age of accountability, the law causes them to sin, and so the dying state begins all over again. There is a big difference though; whether they die because of salvation, or by physical death, sin no longer has control over the body. Now Mark, this is very important. Those who are cast into the lake of fire will be chastised for their sin and be cleansed. So at the consummation of the eons they too shall be incorruptible and also become immortal."

"I get it," Mark said excitedly. "The souls of those who do not believe continue to perish for as long as the 'dying state' holds its power over them. And when the dying state has been abolished, they are vivified, and they also cease to perish, right? And the souls that continue to perish are the ones that are cast into the lake of fire."

Mark continued his reasoning, "All the word perishing means is those who do not have eonian life, remain in the perishing state until death has been destroyed. Those who have eonian life have already ceased to perish. But all humanity shall one day cease to perish when they receive the faith of Christ. Then Christ will hand that kingdom over to His Father, and then God will become all in all to every creature."

Extreme happiness appeared upon Mark's face. "Paul must also have been speaking of the dying state' when he said:

'Swallowed up was death by victory.
Where, 0 Death, is your victory?
Where, 0 Death, is your sting?'"

Mark looked at Harold. "Those eternal tormentors, they would place victory in the grips of the death of the soul and make the sting of death the final blow for millions of people."

"No man has the faith to live righteously, Mark, so if Jesus hadn't died for us, then Mr. Rawlings idea of eternal torment would be absolutely correct. But it would be for every man, woman, and child. If God had not given Mr. Rawlings the faith to believe, he would not believe today. It is by the grace of God coming through His Son that all creation will be restored to Him. But, Mark," he said pointedly, "it is more than these few years each of us spend in these fleshly bodies—the entire period of the eons is required to accomplish His objective.

"I'm pleased you have seen the truth about the salvation of all, Mark. I can assure you, Sidney would have been elated to know you have seen it too. Sidney once said, 'It's so discouraging to talk to people and know they don't really hear.' I know you have heard, and Sidney would be very happy."

"It's a beautiful thing, and I know scripture will become more and more clear as I study," Mark said. "So many verses have been a puzzle to me. I feel I've just overcome a great obstacle, as though I've conquered in some great victory."

Harold smiled. "You, my son, have experienced something many Christians never experience—the joy of knowing the Holy Spirit has revealed a great truth to you." Harold became very serious. "It's a mystery to me why God allows these matters to remain so confusing to the many who profess salvation. Perhaps in good time, He will unveil His reason. Perhaps," he said, looking intently into Mark's eyes, "perhaps God will even reveal the solution of that mystery to you." When Mark told Harold of the feelings he was experiencing, Harold was more than receptive. "I've sensed God has been dealing with you today, Mark. It's very likely God has spoken to you."

"I remember the day I spent with Sidney," Mark said. His thoughts raced back to the conversation of that day. "I remember him saying so clearly, 'God doesn't usually speak to us as I'm speaking to you now, but you'll know when He has spoken'. Sir, I'm sure God has spoken to me today through you."

Mark remained in Waterford the rest of the day, but by the following morning, he knew it was time for him to leave. Sensing Harold's desire to be with his daughter, Mark decided to leave early. And after all, he experienced one of the most enjoyable days of his adult life the day before. It was a day he would remember as long as he lived. The Holy Spirit had spoken and the message had been received. The specifics of God's calling perhaps weren't vividly clear, but the goal had been established. Mark was heading in a new direction with his scriptural understanding.

As the bus sped on its way back to Davenport, Mark's thoughts had turned once again to the day of his visit with the stranger he met in the garden. What an enlightening experience that was! He needed assurance then that God had a purpose for involving him in the death of his puppy. He had never heard of such a thing as animals going to heaven, but hearing the words brought him much peace of mind. There was no doubt in his mind now that the things he learned that day had established the way he was following now. And the visit with Harold gave him the confidence he needed to know he was following in the will of God. The premonition he had ever since he could remember was taking shape just as he often imagined it would.

Mark often pictured an elderly man in the congregation saying he believed that in the last days God would give understanding to all the difficult passages of the scriptures. Each time Mark heard those words, he wondered if God was speaking directly to him. He had to admit he was never positively sure his ego wasn't getting in the way or if God really was speaking to him. One thing he knew for sure was that when the ego concept moved in to cloud the picture, the Holy Spirit revealed some difficult passage of scripture to renew his confidence. Mark had never been as confident as he was at that very moment. Maybe God really did have some wonderful role for him to fulfill.

CHAPTER 10

"For every man there's a woman, they say. So why is it we can't meet any girls, at least not the kind we'd like to meet?" Mark sat in the passenger seat moving the station selector over the radio dial. Tom had come directly from work at the factory where he had taken his new job and met Mark standing in front of the print shop waiting for his bus. They usually went out to eat after work but more often after they had gone home and changed clothes. "Too hungry to take time to change!" Tom said, as Mark opened the door.

Tom's 1936 Plymouth coupe was headed up Brady Street toward the Maid-Rite stand. "Maybe we should go to a different place to eat. We might find some girls just getting off work," he said.

"It's a lot more likely we'll find some girls whose boy friends are just taking them home from a date," Mark said dejectedly. "I had my mouth set on some of Berney's red-hot chili myself."

"How about the Maid-Rite stand across the river then? At least it's a different place to eat. Wanta give it a try?"

"Oh, oh!" Tom exclaimed. As he slowed in order to make a U-turn in the street, there was a car stalled in their lane of traffic. He pulled to a stop. "What do you think we should do? Shall we see if they need help or play it safe and get out of here real quick?"

Immediately, two young men stepped to the rear of their vehicle and called out, "Can you help us out? We ran out of gas. We sure could use—"

"No problem," Tom said. "Got an empty gas can?"

It was apparent they were not prepared for such an emergency. "We'll get one at the station. Be right back," Tom said, as he swung his car into the passing lane. "I think I just got a great idea for getting us some dates. I'll tell you about it as soon as we get the gas."

Soon, Mark and Tom returned with the gasoline and emptied it into the gas tank. After collecting the cost of the gasoline and for the deposit on the can, they returned to their car.

"We sure do appreciate what you did." It was the driver who spoke. "My dad gave me this car for graduation. I couldn't leave it parked on the street while we went to get gas. We sat here forty-five minutes before you stopped. My dad would scalp me if anything happened to it. Thanks again."

When they were sure the boy's car was running, Tom made the U-turn and headed his car toward the other side of the river.

"You might know, those two are barely out of high school, and they have girl friends," Mark said.

"That's not so strange. We had plenty of girls in high school too," Tom reminded him. "We're just too far away from where the girls are."

"About the idea you had for finding some dates."

"Oh, you remembered. I wasn't sure you heard me," Tom said with a chuckle. "Do you remember Yvonne Towns?"

Mark did indeed remember the girl. She had come from Davenport to visit her grandmother in their hometown a couple of summers during the war years. Mark remembered her as being a great dancer and doing the jitterbug in Edna's restaurant. "You're not thinking of getting a date with her, are you? She's about the same age as Jason. In fact, they went together a few times."

"No! No, I wasn't thinking of dating Yvonne. Anyway, she's married now. Her name is Green," he spoke with a bit of sarcasm. "I was thinking of dating her younger sister, though, only I haven't seen her in about four years. She was pretty young then, but I'm sure she's grown up now. I think her name was Brenda. I'm right, it was Brenda," he added with assurance.

"So there's a date for you. What about me, or am I not part of the idea?" Mark was hoping for a few more details.

"The plan is if, of course, you're still interested. Brenda gets a date for you."

"Aren't you taking a lot for granted? You haven't seen the girl in four years. She could be married and have children by now. I doubt if she'll be real eager to find a date for me if that's the case." Mark wasn't very excited about the plan, but he did want to find out how Tom expected to work it out.

"Very simple," he said. "I know where Yvonne lives. We'll stop by to visit her tomorrow afternoon and ask her all about Brenda. What could be more simple?

The news learned the following day was good news. Brenda was not married and was not dating at the time. She still lived on the farm where Tom had seen her. Yvonne called her on the phone, which gave Tom the opportunity to speak to her.

As he talked, Mark could clearly hear one side of the conversation. After hearing Tom explain that he was asking for a date, Mark listened closely to the part, which was to involve him. "Do you know a girl you could ask to be Mark's date? We'd like for this to be a double date for Saturday night." Tom winked at Mark as he spoke.

It was silent for some time, then looking in Mark's direction, he questioned, "You say, ask 'Vonne about Claire? Who's Vonne, oh, Yvonne. She'll know who we're talking about, I take it? Good! I'll call you Saturday morning to see if you could arrange something."

With those words, Tom hung up the phone. Turning to Yvonne, he said, "She says ask you if you think Claire would go on a blind date. So what do you think?"

"Who knows," she said as she shrugged her shoulders, "with a little convincing from me, she might consider it. But how do I know what your intentions are?" she said, directing her question to Mark. "Claire's a nice girl, and I sure—"

"And I'm a nice boy." Mark became flustered with his response. "I mean, I don't have any intentions—I mean, I have good—I don't know what my intentions are," he said, grasping his head with both hands, trying to hide his embarrassment. "I just want to meet a girl." Mark was finally able to regain his composure.

"Well, I knew your brother pretty well. You couldn't be too

bad, with a brother like Jason. Her name is Claire McDonald," she said, indicating she had given her own personal approval of Mark. "I can tell you one thing for sure, though—you'll never go on a blind date with her without Old McDonald's approval."

"Old McDonald!" Mark could hardly believe what he heard. "How did you come up with that one?"

Yvonne began to laugh. "It's a name I came up with, but it really was in self-defense."

"You would have to know Will, that's her father's name, to appreciate it. He's a hotheaded Irishman. I swear he's only happy when he's having an argument with someone. He deliberately started an argument with me every time I set foot in their house. I think I hated him at one time. He would argue something was green if you told him it was blue, just for the sake of arguing. I know because that's exactly what happened to me." Yvonne chuckled as she continued her story. "I bought a pair of teal blue shoes, and one day, I went over to show them to Claire and Alice. He insisted the shoes were not blue—they were green. I always got upset with him, but this time, I was furious. I said to him, 'What difference does it make what color you say they are? They go with my blue outfit, and besides, it says right on the box they're teal blue.' Then I said, 'You would argue black was white just to be arguing.' He told me that was the dumbest thing he ever heard. 'Any idiot,' he said, 'could take one look at those shoes and know they were green.' I was so angry. I turned and ran through their front doorway, slamming the screen door behind me.

"Claire and Alice told me quite often, Will liked to get that kind of response. For some reason, he likes to see the ladies become angry. When I got to thinking about it, I realized I had responded exactly the way he wanted me to. The angrier I became, the more he seemed to enjoy it. I made up my mind right then I would do something to get even. I went back to their front door and looked inside. He was still sitting in the same chair. I opened the screen door and yelled, 'Why don't you go back to the farm where you belong, you old goat.' He asked, 'What are you talking about? What farm?' I said, 'I'm talking about the farm you must have left when you came here.'

I sang, 'Old McDonald had a farm, E-I-E-I-O.' Then I shut the door and ran for home. Alice said he laughed about it for a solid week. I think he truly enjoys it when people talk back to him. He still loves to argue with me, but I always call him Old McDonald and tell him he's an old goat and to get back to the farm where he belongs.'"

As they were leaving, Yvonne said to Mark, "Just you remember, Claire's a nice girl. If you do anything to hurt her, I'll personally come looking for you."

"I won't forget." Mark wasn't quite sure how to take someone as outspoken as she was. He grinned as he closed the door.

As they left the Green's residence, Mark stopped short. "Look at the boy heading for that car. He's the same boy we got the gas for the other night. And it's the same car. He must live pretty close around here." "Yeah," Tom agreed. "Sure is a small world, isn't it?"

Mark was uneasy about the situation he had put himself in. Second thoughts were making him doubt the wisdom of the entire decision to carry out a blind date. When he began comparing the possibilities with girls he already knew, he realized there was really no way to know what to expect. The closer it came to Saturday, the uneasier he became. He found himself relying on the slim hope Brenda would be unable to arrange anything. But when Saturday morning came, Tom brought him what should have been good news. Everything was according to plan.

"You're supposed to meet Claire at her home at seven o'clock sharp," Tom told him, concerning the plans for the evening. "Then the two of you are to go to Yvonne's where Brenda and I will be." The time for the date came all too quickly for Mark, but he knew he had to carry through on his commitment. He reasoned if he didn't like the girl, there was nothing saying he had to date her again. With that in mind, he got up the courage to follow through.

"Good evening," Mark said to the young lady who answered the door. "I'm Mark Hayes. Is this the McDonald residence?" he asked.

Mark was quite sure of the address, but after all, he should try to make a favorable first impression.

"Well! Isn't this the cute one?" The young lady's actions took

Mark completely off stride.

"Ask the young man in. Don't keep him standing outside," said a voice from the living room. Mark assumed the man to be the girl's father.

When Mark had entered the room, the man motioned toward the couch. "Have a seat, Mark. We've heard quite a lot about you from our neighbor." He sat for some time just looking at Mark. Mark was sure the man must have been evaluating him in order to determine whether to allow him to date his daughter. "How old are you, Mark?" the man asked. "I'd guess you to be about twenty years old."

Mark decided the girl's father was concerned about the obvious difference in their ages.

But before he could respond, the girl had seated herself next to him. She sat squarely on his jacket where it lay open beside him. "Look at the suit and the pretty red tie," the girl teased. He was virtually unable to move.

"Oh, boy!" he said to himself. Mark was beginning to perspire.

"Uh no, sir!" Mark tried to pull away from the girl, but he was unable to move. "No, sir, I'm only nineteen, a-a-and I won't even be twenty until my next birthday, a-sir."

"Hmmm, it figures out about right," he said, looking at Mark over the rims of his reading glasses. "Claire is only seventeen, but she'll be eighteen on her next birthday."

"Oh, boy!" Mark continued to fidget.

"How come your face is almost the color of your tie, Mark?" the girl said to him. She grinned as she spoke.

"Kitty," her father said to her, "why don't you go upstairs and tell Claire, Mark is here. Tell her to give us about fifteen or twenty minutes, though, so Mark and I can get acquainted."

"Are you all right, Mark?" Kitty said to him as she stood up to go upstairs. "You look so pale."

Just then, Mrs. McDonald arrived in the room. "Claire will be down in just a moment, Mark. I'm her mother. I guess you've already met the rest of the family."

Mark rose quickly to his feet only to have his knees nearly collapse from under him. "Oh yes, Ma'am, I-I-I have, and I-I-I'm very glad to meet you too, Ma'am. Boy, I sure am."

At the same moment, a young lady appeared at the foot of the stairs. Her mother quickly went to her and whispered something.

She walked to the door, taking Mark by the arm with one hand and opening the door with the other. "We gotta go, Daddy, we're already late. Be home early."

"Hey! Come back here, I want to talk to you two," her father shouted.

"Sorry, Daddy. We're late. Be home by midnight, promise."

She waved at her father and blew him a kiss. Closing the door, she burst into laughter then hurried from the porch, still clutching Mark's arm.

"Hey! Hold on a minute," Mark said, trying to catch his breath. "I thought the other girl was my date. How do I know who you are?" "I'm sorry, Mark," she said, becoming more serious. "I'm the one who's supposed to be your date. I'm sorry for all the rush, but from what my mother told me, I thought it was urgent we leave quickly." "Yeah," Mark said, "I saw her saying something to you. I'm curious 'cause it sure did make things happen."

Claire laughed again. "Mama whispered to me, 'You had better get Mark out of here fast. He's a wreck.'"

"It was pretty bad, I guess," Mark sighed.

"Probably a lot worse. I know my family, so I didn't have to ask her what she meant," she said with a chuckle.

"Oh yeah, about your family. You've got to do something about your little sister."

"I guess Kate's a lot like Daddy—a lot of fun, but harmless fun." "Harmless!" Mark shouted. "What she did to me wasn't harmless! That little flirt destroyed me in there. I don't think I can ever face your family again."

"Oh, Mark," she apologized, "I am sorry. It really was bad, wasn't it? Kate does get a little carried away sometimes. But I promise that if another boy ever comes calling on me, I'll make sure she doesn't embarrass him," she said with a grin.

"How kind of you," he said, giving a fake smile. "You Irish people sure have some different ways about you. It just occurred to me maybe, if you would promise me a date for each of the next, say five Friday evenings, I just might be able to overlook what happened and get through the devastating experience with your sister."

"Oh, but I'm not all that sorry," she replied, sticking out her chin and gently shaking her head from side to side.

"What's this Kitty and Kate business?" Mark asked.

"Her name's Katherine, but Daddy gave her the nickname, Kitty. We all call her by that name most of the time. I'm not going to tell you what he calls me, though," she said.

"I guess you've met most of my family now."

"What do you mean, most?" he interrupted. "Surely, there are no more McDonalds in your house?" Mark pretended to be in shock.

"Just one more," she replied. "I have an older brother you haven't met. Mike just graduated from high school last June."

"Oh, boy. The world keeps getting smaller, I think, " Mark said to himself.

They reached the landing above the terrace in front of the Green's house. At arm's length, they stood just looking into each other's eyes. For the first time, Mark realized what a beautiful girl she was. She tilted her head back and gently shook her head. Each lovely blonde lock fell perfectly into place around her shoulders, except for one, which came mischievously close to her deep blue eyes. By design, the light blue suit she wore was beautifully accented by her deep blue eyes. Her lips were like delicate rose petals. Her skin was soft and clear.

"Hello." Mark didn't take his eyes from her. "I'm Mark Hayes, and if I'm not mistaken, your name is Claire McDonald. I believe plans have been made for us lor the remainder of the evening. Shall we get on with them?"

"We should," she said. Taking Mark's arm, they walked to the door of the Green's residence. Mark rang the doorbell.

It was an evening Mark would remember as long as he lived. They went to the Eagle's Perch, where they had a breathtaking view of the river. Raymond White, his orchestra, and the musical stars were playing there. Mark had never danced before. He knew he was all feet while he groped around the floor, but with Claire's patience, he was able to learn a few simple steps. It had never occurred to him he might enjoy dancing.

To make an already perfect evening even more perfect, well,

after he met Claire, that is, she quickly accepted when he asked for a date for the following Saturday night.

That night, there seemed to be no way Mark would be sleeping. For what proved to be hours, he lay there on his bed, reliving in minute detail the events of the entire evening. Over and over, each situation was reenacted in his thoughts: the embarrassing moments, how he might have reacted differently, the rewarding moments, meeting Claire for the first time and hearing her accept when he asked for another date, and how beautiful and poised she was. The longer he laid there the more wide awake he became.

Suddenly, it occurred to him, he was constantly asking God for favors, and now when something wonderful happened, he hadn't given thought to thank Him. After all, it must have been God Who arranged such a grand experience.

"Father," he began to pray, *"thank Yon for giving me the most wonderful evening of my life. I know you must have arranged it all, Father, for I never could have planned a time to compare with this. I would like to ask one thing of You, Father. Please give her the same kind of feelings for me that I have for her. Amen!"*

The longer Mark knew Claire, the more he came to love her. Her still being in high school bothered him a little while he had been out of school two full years. He did graduate at the age of seventeen—he chose to remember—but he was painfully aware Claire, in many ways, was more mature than he was, in spite of the age difference. There was a gnawing awareness he tended to be insecure of himself, and it became even more difficult to deal with when he was forced to observe the positive way she always presented herself.

Because she was still in high school, her father had put down strict limits on her dating. He stipulated Claire should date only one night a week and only on Friday or Saturday nights.

Mark had known Claire only slightly more than a month. During the week, he asked her to wear the same blue suit she wore the night they met. "Good evening, Mr. McDonald," Mark said, as her father came to the door. "I've come to take Claire to the dance. She's expecting me."

"Come in, Mark. Peggy isn't quite ready, but she'll be down soon." Her mother came into the room just as Mark walked to the couch to be seated. "Good evening, Mrs. McDonald," he said.

"Claire's a working girl as of today," she said to him. "She got a job at the dime store working Saturdays. It seems the girl who was scheduled to come on at five o'clock didn't show up, so they asked Claire to work until six-thirty. It made her a little late, but I think she'll be ready soon."

"I'm a little confused, sir." Mark directed his question to Mr. McDonald. "You said Peggy, but didn't you mean Claire?"

"Oh!" her mother interrupted. "That's just a name Will has for her. It's just a family thing between Will and Claire. He's the only one who calls her by that name."

"If you could have seen her," Mr. McDonald said as he gave out a hearty laugh. "Claire was only three years old at the time. We had just said grace after sitting down to Thanksgiving dinner. Claire looked at me with those big blue eyes and said, 'Can I have a chickie leg, Daddy?' Well, what she called chickie legs were turkey legs, and they were almost as big as she was."

"Will!" Mrs. McDonald interrupted. "You're going to embarrass Claire."

"I put one on her plate," he said, ignoring Mrs. McDonald's advice, "and within two minutes, she was turkey leg from the top of her head to the bottom of her shoes and so was everything else within reach. I said to her, 'Daddy's girl looks more like a little piggy.' She looked at me and said, 'I'm not a little piggy, I'm a little girl.'"

"Daddy!" Claire, upon descending the steps, heard her father telling the story. "Why must you tell that awful story? It's so embarrassing." "I can't stop now, Peggy. Anyway, there's nothing embarrassing about the rest of it," he said apologetically.

"There is when you tell it. But you're right, you can't leave it where it is now."

"I called her Piggy for several years. I guess no one else thought it was appropriate. Then one day, she crawled up on my lap, and again, with those big blue eyes, she said, 'Daddy, please don't call me Piggy anymore. Everybody laughs when you call me that.'

"I told her I was sorry and asked if it would it be all right if I called her Peggy. She thought about it for a while then sat up and grinned. 'Yeah,' she said, 'I like Peggy.' So it just became habit." There was a most satisfying smile on his face.

Mark got to his feet. "It makes me feel good to know I'm not the only one who can be embarrassed while in the presence of this family. I brought you something to go with your pretty blue suit. Perhaps I should have chose something in a shade of red," he said as he grinned.

She opened the box and took the corsage from it. "Oh, Mark! What beautiful white roses! Pin them on me, would you please."

Hours flew by like minutes. The evening was nearing an end. Mark and Claire got into his car to start for home.

"I wish the evening didn't have to end," she said to Mark.

"We have some time before you have to be home. Why not sit here for a while? I enjoyed the story your father told tonight."

"Oh, Mark, it was so embarrassing. Let's not—"

Mark interrupted her plea not to talk about it. "It was beautiful. If I could have an experience like that with a little girl of mine, I think it would be wonderful. You should never allow anyone to share the name with your father. It should be between you and him." Mark stole a kiss as he looked into her eyes while they sat in the dimly lit parking area. "Aren't you the philosophical one?" She drew away from his lips. "I just never felt real close to my father. I thought it was a beautiful experience." Mark placed his hand on her right shoulder and started to kiss her again.

Once more, she pulled away from him. "I wish you would wait until we say good night, Mark."

"It's your fault, you know," he whispered softly.

"Oh, Mark!" she said, as she pushed away from him. "I'm sorry if you think I led you on. I didn't mean for it to happen. Please, Mark, I think you should take me home! Please, Mark!"

"But, Claire, I didn't mean it that way. I just meant it was you who made me love you the way I do. Oh, boy! I didn't mean it the way you took it, really, I didn't," Mark pleaded. "I love you. I would never hurt you. I'm sorry, Claire! Don't let the evening end this way. I love you, and I think you love me too. Please forgive me!"

Slowly, Claire moved across the seat to where Mark sat.

"Mark, I have a confession to make. That exchange of words, I knew what you meant. I just had to stop any advances." Claire gently laid her head upon Mark's shoulder. "I feel very strongly we should wait until after marriage, and it must be that way," she said.

"I love you, Claire. I just hope marriage doesn't take too long."

"Why, Mark! That sounded an awfully lot like a proposal to me."

"I never thought about marriage in my whole life 'til now," he said. "I'm not sure I'm ready to call a minister, though."

"I really do have to get home, or Daddy will be out looking for us—both of us! I love you, Mark," she said softly.

Mark felt good as they drove to Claire's home, especially when he thought of the way the evening might have ended.

As they stood on the porch about to say good night, Mark said to her, "I felt so smug to think I was mature enough to recognize the

beautiful experience between you and your father. Then I ended up getting the lesson on maturity."

"We really do need to move slow with our plans. You probably don't even know I'm Catholic, do you?"

"Oh, boy."

"But then I see no reason why two reasonably mature people shouldn't be able to work something out. Good night, Mark."

Mark was speechless, but then there was no one to talk to anyway. He walked slowly to his car.

He was about to start the engine, when the door of the car parked across the street opened and a young man got out. Mark recognized both him and his car.

The young man approached Mark. "I'm Mike, Claire's brother. I've been keeping an eye on you two. Just make real sure you take care of my sister. Hey," he said, suddenly placing Mark in his mind, "I know you."

"Yeah, I recognized you too. Oh! I'm Mark Hayes," he said, holding out his hand in friendship. "Glad to know you, Mike."

"We sure did appreciate your helping us out that night," Mike said, as he accepted Mark's gesture. "I was really in a pickle. Well, see you around."

"Yeah, nice seeing you too," Mark acknowledged.

Mark sat watching Mike as he walked to the house. He watched him open the door and disappear inside. Finally, he reached for the ignition key he had already inserted into place. “I may never understand the Irish,” he said aloud.

CHAPTER 11

"How did you know I was Protestant?" Mark asked Claire, as they sat at the dining room table in her home. Claire's parents were visiting relatives, and Mark was spending the afternoon with Claire.

"You gave it away," she replied.

"And when did I give it away?" Mark asked. "We've never discussed religion."

"You made a very clear statement, and I'll bet you'll never remember when it happened."

It was obvious to Mark Claire was enjoying his quandary. "Give me a clue. Every good mystery needs clues to be solved."

"All right, I'll give you an excellent clue, and you still won't figure it out. Remember what you said when I told you your comment sounded an awfully lot like a proposal?"

"Sure, I remember," Mark said smugly. "I said I never thought about marriage before in my life until right then."

"And then what did you say?"

Mark had to think about it. "Oh, let me see. I think I said something like, a, 'I'm not ready to call a minister, though.' That's all I remember."

"I told you. You found the clue, and you still haven't solved the puzzle."

Mark was bewildered. "Okay, I give up. How did telling you I wasn't ready to call a minister give away the fact I was Protestant?" "Elementary, my dear Watson," she said, imitating the master sleuth from the radio series. "If I was planning a wedding and wanted to contact someone about conducting the ceremony, I wouldn't call a minister, I would call a priest."

The realization of Claire being Catholic was finally dawning upon Mark. The strong possibility of problems arising didn't really occur to him when she mentioned it on their last date. Mark sat looking into Claire's eyes, desperately trying to find something appropriate to say. "I guess I have a mystery for you too," he said.

"And precisely, what is your mystery, Mr. Watson?" she asked. "How are two reasonably mature people going to overcome the problem they have before them?"

Looking away from Mark, she said hesitatingly, "I don't know, but you're scaring me with this concern about our religious differences."

"Claire, look at me!" Mark said. "I'm sorry! I know I should have considered what was happening." Mark was even more alarmed because of Claire's lack of concern about the issues likely to arise later on. "I think you're completely unaware we have a problem."

"I don't see why we can't simply go on believing as we choose. I mean, you believe what you want to believe, and I'll believe what I want to believe. It should be quite simple," she explained.

"Oh, Claire, there's more to it. There are many things about your church I couldn't accept, and you don't know what I believe. And you may have problems with my beliefs." Reaching for her hand, he said, "I don't know why I couldn't have expected this. I've been confronted with religious obstacles for years, but none were ever as important as this. I'm sorry. What are we going to do?"

"We were going to approach this as two reasonably mature people. Now suddenly, I don't feel very mature." She placed her other hand upon Mark's. "There's something I cannot understand. Please tell me why my solution won't work."

"Claire, we love each other so much. I think I could accept you any way you came to me, and I think you feel the same way about me, but it would be pure selfishness for us to marry on that basis alone."

Mark had developed strong convictions for his beliefs. He had read enough about the Catholic Church to know it would not be a belief he could accept. It wasn't a matter of singling out one particular church, for he could say the same about five hundred Protestant denominations. The fact was he had no problem with Claire believing as she wanted. But Mark knew the possibilities of having children were great. How could he stand by and allow his children to be taught something he didn't believe? Could he, in all good conscience, give his consent based on the mere hope there might not be children to be concerned about? No, Mark realized any existing differences must be worked out before going any further.

Mark did his best to convey his deep concern to Claire.

"I must be progressing," she said. "At least I recognize the problem now. Oh, Mark!" she said, squeezing his hand. "Why must things be so complicated?"

"Maybe we should present to each other the things we can't accept," Mark said, "and see how big the problems really are."

"Make a list of the things you can't accept about my church," she said.

"You make me sound like a bully."

"Not at all! Wait 'til you see my list." She grinned as she spoke.

"All right! How do you defend your church for believing the pope is infallible?" he asked. "Your church feels the pope has the right to intercede for God in making important doctrinal decisions. I don't believe God has given anyone the right to make decisions on His behalf.

"Another thing! The authorities of your church believe their parishioners may pray to people they have declared saints, even to Jesus's mother. I don't believe the Bible teaches we should pray to any being, except God, Himself, and only through Jesus Christ.

"And what about the crucifix? The people carry Jesus nailed to the cross. Jesus Christ isn't hanging on a cross anymore. He lives. Jesus Christ is alive. It was two thousand years ago when He died. He died then for every one of us. He doesn't need to die over and over again. He died once, and once was sufficient.

"And about the God in three person's doctrine."

"Stop!" she said. "You're not being fair. I don't think about those things. The priest understands those matters. That's why they're priests. They're trained to know those things," she said.

"Tell me, would you go with me to see your priest and ask him to answer those questions? Could we ask him plainly and then decide for ourselves if we can accept his explanations? I would listen to his answers."

"No, Mark," Claire answered quickly. "I believe he has the right understanding, or he wouldn't be a priest. And besides, it would break Mama's heart a-a-and Daddy's too."

Mark looked into her eyes. There was the look of a subdued and shocked little girl.

"It's obvious we have a problem we can't work out," she said stoically but revealing the deepness of the hurt.

"You're angry with me, and you're hurt. I'm sorry, Claire, I didn't mean it to happen. I didn't mean it at all. I just thought I had such a good argument, you couldn't help but accept it." Mark was unable to comfort her.

"It's like we said before, we're two mature people. We simply faced an insurmountable problem."

"Please, Claire, what are we going to do?" Mark was very worried now.

"I'm going to admit defeat," she said. Tears began to well in her eyes. "Please leave!"

"Claire, I'm sorry!"

Claire burst into tears and then went running up the steps.

Slowly, Mark walked to the door. He didn't want to leave, but there was no other choice.

Mark went to his car and sat staring into the steering wheel. What a disappointment! "Could it be it was all over?" Closing his eyes, he directed his thoughts toward God.

"Oh, God," he prayed, *"I feel so bad for Claire. I didn't mean to hurt her, Father. Please help her to understand. Please make it all right, and somehow, let her know I didn't mean to hurt her this way. Please, Father, make it all work out for good."*

He sat for some time just wondering what he could have done differently. Silently, he contemplated the things having taken place. Suddenly, a feeling of peace swept over him. The meaning was not clear, but the assurance all would be well filled his entire being. *"Thank You, Father. Now help me to leave it in your hands. Amen!"*

The same evening, Mark called Claire. Her response was short. "We must realize the only solution is for us to end our relationship. Please don't call me again, Mark." Then she hung up the receiver. For a week, he called each evening, but she wouldn't talk to him. Finally, he stopped calling. Had he been wrong about the feeling of assurance he thought he received? Had he misinterpreted something else God had intended for him? Christmas came, but still she would have no conversation with him. He took a gift to the house. She had left instructions for it not to be accepted.

Days passed. Days turned into weeks. The weeks became months. Mark was a confused and disturbed young man.

On a Friday morning, about the middle of February, Mr. Dickins approached Mark at his workstation. "There's someone in the office who would like to speak with you. It's about ten minutes until twelve now. Why don't you include the time as part of your lunch hour?"

"Thanks, Mr. Dickins, I appreciate it," he said, as he stood up. Quickly, he removed his apron and hung it over the back of his chair.

Could it be Claire, he wondered. His heart began to pound. "Please let it be Claire," he said aloud. He walked into the office. "Oh, hello, Mrs. McDonald. It's good to see you. I've missed seeing you."

"I hope I'm not causing trouble by coming here. The proprietor said it was all right," she said apologetically. "I thought he was a little boy until I saw his gray hair."

"Yes." Mark laughed. "I know what you mean. He's about five foot three and about two and a half pounds heavier than a racehorse jockey. But he has a lot of ways of showing he's a big man."

"How's Claire? Is she all right?" he asked. Evidence of his deep concern was apparent.

"That's what I want to talk to you about. Can we get you lunch? It's my treat. I want to talk. Wherever you usually eat is just fine." She wanted Mark to feel comfortable.

Mrs. McDonald wasn't really hungry, but she ordered a sandwich and a cup of coffee for herself. After the order was placed, it became quiet.

"What's wrong with Claire?" he asked in uneasy tone. "Something is wrong, or you wouldn't be here."

She reached for Mark's hand and grasped it between her own hands. "Mark," she began, "I would never, ever purposely interfere in Claire's life, and certainly not in yours, but there's something I must know. I must have the answer before another word is said."

"Sure, Mrs. McDonald, if I—"

"Do you love Claire? Do you really love her?"

"Oh, Mrs. McDonald! You don't understand. We have this, this religious problem. We have, well—"

"That isn't what I asked you, Mark! I asked you if you love Claire."

Mark sat staring at Claire's mother. Without the hint of a change in expression, the tears came flooding over his cheeks. Slowly, words came expressing his warmest feelings for her. "More than anything else in this world, I love her. I've tried to face the prospect of spending the rest of my life without her. I can't even imagine what it would be like. But I don't know what to do." He blotted his eyes with his handkerchief.

"That's what I wanted to know. I'm not sure what to do either, but I know something has to be done."

She grasped his hand tightly. "One of Will's brothers has some snowmobiles up north on his farm. I asked him to call and casually invite Will to come up for the weekend. Now I'm going to ask if you will come to the house for supper tonight."

"Oh, I don't know," he began to plead. "I don't know if Claire would want it. You, you, you've got to realize we have this big obstacle."

"You're talking about this mature approach thing, aren't you? You haven't seen Claire lately. If you had, you would know something has to be done. She's lost about twenty pounds, just a little slip of a thing anyway. She's missed at least ten days from school because she was too sick to get out of bed. Her eyes look like two holes in her head, a-a-and that's only a very slight exaggeration."

"I'll be there, Mrs. McDonald. Just tell me what time."

"We'll be ready to sit down to the table at six o'clock sharp. I want you to arrive then. Somehow, we've got to get some sense into her head."

Mark found it virtually impossible to concentrate on his work the rest of the afternoon. One moment, his emotions reached a peak where he imagined the problem to be entirely solved, only to suddenly reach a low when discovering the situation had completely deteriorated and Claire might be gone forever.

Many times over the past few months, he thought of the wonderful feeling of peace he experienced. But an eternity had passed. He realized his faith had not endured the test of time very well. Perhaps God was testing his faith. More likely, God was strengthening him so he could accept a greater capacity for faith. After all, Mark was strongly opposed to the belief in developing faith from within.

He wanted so much to have a stronger understanding of the subject. Faith is such an elusive matter. He began to reason he had truly lost Claire, and he might as well face the truth. Indeed, that was not evidence of faith. But now he was feeling confident of renewed relations with the girl he loved so much. True, Mrs. McDonald displayed very positive vibrations of solving the problem, but on the other hand, as far as Mark could tell, it was out of sheer desperation rather than any concrete assurance on her part. Whatever the explanation, he was feeling more and more the way he felt on the day he reached out to God and received the overwhelming sense of peace.

The afternoon was nearing an end. Mark was feeling rather good about the entire matter. He had faced the situation squarely.

He had analyzed it in a constructive way. He realized one important matter, however, he had failed to address before. It was all well and good God had strengthened him through the experience. But where did Claire fit into the picture? It would be sheer foolishness, even pure selfishness, to believe God was putting her through this ordeal, only to make him a stronger person.

One look at Claire and Mark's breath failed him for a moment. Even Mrs. McDonald's description hadn't prepared him for what he saw. "Claire!" He was unable to utter another word. To describe to her how she looked would surely frighten her. He wanted to take her in his arms.

Mrs. McDonald asked them to be seated at the table. She returned thanks for the blessings they had received, after which she formed the cross over her breasts.

Before a dish was passed, Claire said to her mother, "Mama, why are we doing this?"

"I'm not going to lie to you. And I'm not going to pretend there isn't a problem. There is something very wrong, but we're going to get to the bottom of it here and now. All I hear is about how mature you two are about this thing."

"Mama, we recognize the problem we have, and we have faced it. If we could find a solution, we would have found it before now. We are two mature people who have faced our differences and recognize there is no solution."

"There's that word mature again," her mother interrupted, purposely placing an overemphasis on the pronunciation of the word. "It seems to me, most people who love each other fight about their differences. They have a big fight, and then they kiss each other and make up. I never heard this mature before you two."

"Mama," she pleaded with her mother, "it's just plain childishness for two people to fight. Besides, the differences we have are insurmountable," she explained calmly.

"Oh my!" her mother exclaimed. "In, in, oh, such a big word insurmountable. That must be what mature means. Why don't you forget mature and fight. Get this thing out where you can see what it looks like."

Claire reached for her mother's hand. "Mama, let me tell you exactly the problem we face."

"To that I'm listening."

"It's simply a matter where Mark has told me I must give up my church if there's a chance for us to marry. He's made it perfectly clear he will not allow his children to be raised in the Catholic Church. It didn't occur to him he should tell me, until after I had fallen in love with him." Sarcasm became more pronounced with each word.

Mark's feelings were hurt, but he couldn't be angry with her. "I'm sorry, Claire. I didn't know you felt that way."

"Does Claire have to do all the fighting?" Mrs. McDonald said. "Fight with her. Tell her your side of this thing."

"Oh, Mark," Claire apologized, "I know you didn't realize what was happening. It's like you said then. I was angry, and I was hurt. I still am. But we're really no nearer a solution than we were then."

"Claire," her mother said, "I don't want you to be angry with Kitty because I twisted her arm a little, but I know you went to visit Father Murphy, and I know you visited Pastor Miller. What I don't know is what you decided as a result of your visits."

"You wouldn't like what I decided, Mama. But I can't bear the thought of hurting Daddy and you by leaving the church."

"It's better you leave the church than die of a broken heart. My baby, you have to do what your heart tells you to do, not what you think will please us. Besides, if you don't tell your daddy, he probably will never know anyway."

A smile crossed Claire's face. A tremendous weight had been lifted from her. "Can it be so simple, Mama?"

"There will be a lot of adjustments to make, but you can do it. I see no reason why two people learning to fight couldn't work out a solution even to the problem you have." Her mother returned the smile. "I think I would suggest you find out what Mark believes, though, right away."

It was a spur of the moment thing, but it occurred to Mark he might never have a more opportune moment to at least mention his viewpoints. "The only thing I believe might be considered a little unusual," he said with a look of concern, looking first to one then the other, "is I believe God will save all mankind and give all humanity rule over His creation."

"Oh, dear!" Mrs. McDonald exclaimed. Then as though giving the matter some serious thought, she said, "That might have its good points, I suppose. About once a month, after Will loses part of his paycheck at the gambling table, he says to me, 'I'm going straight to hell, Alice, and I know it.' Maybe you can convince him that won't be necessary."

The food was cold, but neither Mark nor Claire minded. Mrs.

McDonald offered to warm the food, but they were already filling their plates.

The following days were happy days once again. Love continued to blossom. Claire's health was restored. Plans for wedding bells filled the air. June 23 seemed just the right day. Claire would graduate from high school in early June. She hoped to find a job so she could help them save for a down payment on a home and purchase the furnishings to get started in it.

Soon, even Mark's employer was informed of their wedding plans.

One day, Mr. Dickins approached Mark in his work area. Pulling up a chair beside him, he asked, "I've been wondering if you've made any plans concerning where you'll be living."

"No, sir, we really haven't looked yet. Since we won't be getting married until late June, we thought it was too soon to start paying rent.

"Wouldn't you rather buy a property? Wouldn't it be better than paying rent to someone else?"

Mark knew Mr. Dickins always looked at things from the practical point of view, being a businessman. "I wish such a thing were possible, Mr. Dickins, but we don't have that kind of money saved. I mean, we can't afford a down payment on a home."

"Suppose," Mr. Dickins spoke slowly and deliberately, "suppose you and your lovely bride-to-be stop by and have a look at a property, which might be of interest to you. I might make you an offer you can't refuse."

Mark was quite sure nothing good could come out of the matter, but he agreed to take Claire and go see the property at the address Mr. Dickins gave him.

Mark and Claire arrived even ahead of Mr. Dickins. "Oh! Look at the screened in porch." Claire couldn't contain her excitement. She looked inside the door. "There's a swing. We could spend our evenings right there. Oh, Mark, the house is beautiful."

It was a one-and-a-half-story home, setting on a corner lot. A shallow terrace surrounded the street sides of the house. Painted on the top of the two-step incline were the numbers 2040.

Claire found nothing undesirable about the place. "Even the paint seems different. Why do you suppose it looks much whiter than the other houses?"

Mr. Dickins arrived while they were looking the house over from the outside. "That's my little secret, Claire, but I'll let you in on it," he said, answering the question she asked Mark. "I had the painters mix a trace of deep blue pigment into the paint. It not only looks whiter when it's put on—it stays white much longer. What do you think, Mark? Does it meet with your idea of what you're looking for?"

"I'm awfully sorry, Mr. Dickins, but we're really just wasting your time. You see, we already know we can't afford anything as nice as this. I truly am sorry," he apologized again.

"Don't say no until you've seen the inside. I seem to be having a difficult time showing this house," he said. He continued to unlock the door and then invited them in.

"What a beautiful place," Claire gasped. They looked about the room. A large picture window was located at the point where the porch swing hung. On the Euclid Avenue side of the property, a fireplace graced the wall. "The fireplace was my pet project when the house was built," he told them. "It was the nicest part of the entire place when we moved in. Still is I guess. I'm still very proud of it. It's real marble, just in case you're wondering, both the fireplace and the floor surrounding it. We were told it was all taken from a home being demolished in Illinois. The shovels and tongs stay with the house."

A stairway took up most of the south wall of the living room. Turning to the left at the top of the steps was the door opening to a hallway separating the dorm-style bedrooms. The rooms were large. Sliding doors separated the living room from the dining room and the dining room from the kitchen. Mark loved the place as much as Claire did, but he couldn't help feeling a little sick to his stomach just thinking of the likelihood they probably would not be its new owners.

"Mr. Dickins." Mark was about to continue pleading with his employer but realized he wasn't getting anywhere.

"You're a hard man to sell. Why don't you and Claire leisurely look the place over? Take as long as you like. Be sure you lock up before you leave. Bring the key to the office. If you're interested, maybe we can work out a deal.

"By the way, the front porch has combination storm windows and screens. All the windows are stored in the basement by the steps. You will have excellent shade throughout the yard. The trees are young, but well developed. If Mother Nature's good to you, you shouldn't have to worry about planting trees for many years."

They looked the place over very carefully. The question was never whether they liked it.

"We might as well listen to what he has to say," Mark conceded. "What do we have to lose? Shall we go to the office?"

"So," Mr. Dickins said, as he sat down behind his desk. Mark and Claire were already facing him. "Danielle and I had the house built just before the war. We lived in it until three years ago and then rented it out. The people were good renters and took excellent care of it, but renters are never quite the caretakers homeowners are. Anyway, the house is vacant. After some necessary repairs, I plan to put it on the market."

He sat briefly studying the two of them. "I think you once told me, Mark, you pay six dollars a week for your room. I calculate that to be twenty-six dollars a month. Eating all your meals in restaurants is surely more expensive than cooking your meals at home. Keep in mind that's for one person. There will be two of you now. On the other hand, I'm sure you could rent a very nice furnished apartment for twenty-six dollars a month. But the thing you must consider is after each month of paying your rent, you still only have a place to live for the duration of the rent period. Then it's money gone forever."

"Here is my offer. I will rent the house to you for fifty-five dollars a month for five years, guaranteed. Then you will have the option to allow the rent you've paid to become a down payment on the purchase of the property. The asking price is 13,200 dollars. The down payment you will have accrued will be thirty-three-hundred dollars. That's twenty-five percent down. We'll draw up the papers necessary to make the contract legally binding.

"You want to ask, 'What's the rub,' don't you? You're right. I'm not making the offer just to be one of the good old boys. There's one stipulation you must adhere to in order for the arrangement to be carried out."

Mr. Dickins spoke slowly, choosing his words carefully. "You have been an excellent employee. Your attendance record is flawless. You were late once, some concocted story about a flat tire or some such thing." He winked at Claire. "Your work has been excellent, and your efficiency improves each day. The simple truth is, I want you around for a long time. This will require you to stay for at least five years to be eligible for the purchase.

"That, Mark, is my offer. Let me know of your decision within the next two months. If you decide you're interested soon enough, you can choose the interior decorative colors.

"Oh, one other thing! Your wages will increase to fifty-eight dollars a week, as of the first of June."

CHAPTER 12

Mr. Dickins had the papers drawn up within a week after he discussed the offer with Mark and Claire. The papers were signed, and the only matter remaining was for the house to be repaired as he had promised. The old paint was stripped off and the house repainted with the deep blue pigment added, as Claire requested. "Let's call it 'The White House.' That would be neat," she said. "Then I must refer to you as the 'first lady,'" Mark replied.

A number of times the two of them sat in their car across the street just to look at the house. They discussed marriage plans, which seemed to be more enjoyable in that atmosphere.

"It appears our neighbor-to-be is a wheelchair invalid," Mark said, on one of those evenings. "I wonder why he's been sitting at his step for such a long time. Maybe we should check and see."

They walked across the street to the house next door to the one they were about to occupy. "May we help you Sir," Mark asked? He hoped to be of assistance in some way.

"It's all right. Abbie went to find a neighbor to pull my chair onto the porch. It's too heavy for her." The long wait had brought signs of stress for having to intrude into the lives of others to help with his needs. "I hate having to depend on neighbors to do it for us. It's all so senseless— dang drunken drivers. Sometimes I think I'd like to—"

"I'll lift you onto the porch," Mark interrupted. "Tell me what I should do."

"Hey," the young man apologized, "I'm sorry for the outburst. I just feel so helpless sometimes. It really gets to me! Here's my neighbor now. He's pretty used to wheeling me around. I know it's not easy, but I never hear Harry complain."

"Just glad I can be of help, Vic." Harry seemed happy to oblige.

Mark moved in close to observe how Harry worked. He was sure in having done it many times he would have learned the most efficient way. "I'm going to watch so I can help one of these days. I'm Mark Hayes, and this is my fiancée, Claire McDonald. We'll be renting the house next door. Be married June 23rd and moving in after our honeymoon."

"Seems like we've learned the most important things about you two already. I'm Victor Britton. This is Abigail, my wife. Everybody calls her Abbie. This is Harry Downing—Lives next door the other way."

"Glad to know both of you."

"Nice meeting you, too, Harry. No doubt we'll be seeing you a lot in the days to come," Mark said.

The Brittons were an attractive couple, and young. Abigail was a lovely girl, and vibrant. Victor seemed bitter about his condition, but Abigail seemed exactly what he would need in the way of encouragement.

"How did you manage to find a house like this to rent," Victor asked? "Most people would give their right arm for something so nice to live in."

"I was able to keep both arms in the deal," Mark joked. He told them the whole story and about the option to buy as well.

"That's wonderful," Abigail said, directing her words toward Claire. "It just couldn't be nicer. I'm happy for you. I have a feeling we'll become very good friends."

"Probably not until long after the honeymoon, Abbie. Right Mark?" He winked mischievously at Mark, as he spoke, and reached out and slapped him on the knee.

They left their neighbors-to-be, and started toward their future home. "Abbie seems like such a nice person—so bubbly and full of life. I think I'm going to like her very much."

"What about Vic," Mark asked, wondering what she was thinking?

"I think he got rather personal, since you asked. I don't think what we do on our honeymoon, or after it, is any of his business," she said, readily showing her annoyance.

"I have a feeling it's a subject he'll be bringing up quite often," Mark said. "Seriously, I think we need to try hard to understand Vic. It must be terribly difficult for him."

There was much discussion of wedding plans over the following days and weeks. Claire was noticeably pleased to hear Mark's suggestion they carry out the marriage instructions required by the church when a member planned to marry a non-Catholic. They would do so out of respect for her parents. They would be married in her church, making arrangements early to insure reservations for the day of their choice. The instructions began soon because of the busy schedule of the priest. They agreed any children born would not be raised in the Catholic Church.

They gave the priest no problems concerning the matters they discussed. Rather, they discussed privately their own personal opinions. Claire was disturbed at the priest's insistence contraceptives should not be used. "I think whether we want to have children or not, is our business," she told Mark. "And if we want to use preventive measures, it's our business too. What difference does it make whether people abstain, or use contraceptives," she added, showing her displeasure?

Most of all, Mark was pleased they could talk freely on any subject, and try to find answers according to how they would understand Bible teaching. Certainly they weren't very adept at Bible study yet, but Claire was more than willing to learn.

Claire chose her sister to be the maid-of-honor, and three of her closest friends were to be her brides-maids. Mark's brother, Jason would be the best man. Tom Reed would be an usher, even though he would be moving to Oregon in a few weeks. Some of Mark's family attended the wedding and the reception: some couldn't attend. His mother couldn't make the trip, but Mark and Claire decided to shorten their honeymoon by two days, and spend those days with her in Colorado. It wasn't very far out of their way.

The choice of colors for the ceremony was decided upon. The gowns were purchased, and the order for flower arrangements was placed. They worked out a desirable arrangement for the wedding announcements. Deciding upon the wording, they made them up in the print shop where Mark worked: on Mark's own time after hours. They even made up their own thank you cards to send out after the wedding gifts had been received. "You're taking a lot for granted aren't you?" Mark had asked, "What if we don't get any gifts?"

Mr. and Mrs. William L. McDonald
Request your presence at
the wedding ceremony
Of their daughter
Claire Louise McDonald
To
Mark Christopher Hayes
On
June 23, 1949
2:00 p.m.
St. Martha's Catholic Church
A reception will follow
At the home of
Mr. and Mrs. Charles D. McDonald
4212 Lancaster Road

In buying all the house furnishings at one store, the store manager was more than happy to allow them to make the purchase with a ten per cent down payment. Mark was also quite sure giving Mr. Dickens, as a personal reference, hadn't hampered their chances for credit in any way. The furnishings were moved in on the 16th of June, giving ample time to get things arranged, and curtains up. There would be no payment due until the first of August. Mrs. McDonald insisted they should not buy small appliances or linen, any dishes or silverware, and no cooking utensils until after the wedding showers were over and the wedding gifts opened.

The evening was spent arranging furniture. They were eager as well, to hang some pictures they had purchased. Mark found it necessary to go to the car for some nails he forgot to bring in with him. His neighbor had just arrived home, and Mark offered to help him onto the porch.

"I see you're ready to set up housekeeping, Mark. I think I can guess where you two will be staying tonight! Hey Mark," he said, in an accusing manner?

"No Vic, that issue was settled a long time ago," he said, clearly hoping to set the matter straight once and for all.

"Sure Mark," he said, "whatever you say." Victor revealed a skeptical approach. "Just remember this. If a man and a woman are right for each other, they don't have to wait for the wedding vows to be read."

"I can assure you, Vic," Mark explained, "our situation isn't like that at all. I have the utmost respect for Claire and I mean to make sure it remains so."

Mark returned to the living room and removed the cover surrounding the large picture intended for the area over the couch. He sat down on the couch, instead. "I feel so guilty—like I don't deserve any of this. Look at us; we'll be making a twenty five percent down payment on a home in five years without having to save a penny of it. Most people have to pay rent and try to save for a down payment, besides. It's like someone's handing us a gift."

"And you feel you're not earning it," she said? "Is that it?"

"I guess you're right," he admitted.

"Let me tell you something, Mr. Hayes." She sat down beside him. Grasping his chin, she turned his head toward her. "You have given Mr. Dickens almost three years of solid effort, and he appreciates it. He offered it to you as a further incentive for good work. But if you don't think your effort is good enough, I can inform him he's overestimating your value to him. I could tell him he should get rid of you, and hire someone more competent." Claire stood up and turned to walk away.

Mark reached for her hand, and grasping it, he pulled her to him.

"You are earning the down-payment, Mark. Believe me, if you weren't, Mr. Dickins would know it. Sure, maybe it is a fortunate break for us, but you're no less a man because it worked out this way." She placed a kiss on Mark's lips.

"Speaking of being a man, I got some friendly advice - I think it was supposed to be friendly advice—from Victor just a little while ago. He told me if a man and woman are right for each other, it isn't necessary to wait for the marriage ceremony."

Claire started to stand up, but Mark pulled her close. "You don't have to change the subject. I just want you to know how much I respect you, and I don't want it to ever change."

"What really bothers me is the way Victor seems to be so obsessed with the subject. I know a lot of guys seem to make a habit of talking that way, but I just wonder if he doesn't have a serious problem of some kind."

The wedding went without a flaw. Even the weather cooperated. It was a beautiful day: more like mid-spring than a day in early summer. Mrs. McDonald was quite right in thinking they should not purchase the miscellaneous things. It appeared nothing in the way of usual needs had been overlooked. They would have to return a few items. "After all, we don't need three toasters," Claire joked. She decided to keep all nine tablecloths they received, however. Besides she wouldn't be able to choose which ones to return anyway.

They spent their honeymoon in the Black Hills National Forest, returning by way of Colorado. It had been almost three years since Mark left his mother back in their hometown. What a comfort it had been for him, knowing she would be staying with his older sister, and not having to live alone. Mark wasn't sure if he could have left her had that been the case.

As they drove the miles between Colorado and home, Mark took the opportunity to discuss more in detail the experience with Sidney Rawlings having taken place so many years before. He told her of his great affection for the man, and how he learned so much concerning God's plan and purpose. He showed her the Indian rupee and chain which he still carried. He told her about meeting the man who had been Sidney's lifelong friend, and how much he enjoyed his visit with him in Michigan. "I'd like to visit with him again some time," he told her. "He seemed to understand so clearly when I told him of my premonition."

"It was from Sidney I learned to believe in the salvation of all mankind. Harold told me Sidney's understanding began from a study of the eons. I think I'd like to write to him, and find out where to get a copy of the study," he said, at the same time, determining to follow through on the idea.

"I want to study with you." Claire laid her head on Mark's shoulder as they rode down the highway. "I won't be relying on the priest now to tell me how to believe. We'll have to learn these things on our own. I do want us to study together," she said.

Having had a wonderful time, they returned home, and the days they had yet to look forward to were every bit as wonderful. They had a beautiful home to live in. It was filled with all the essential furnishings. Claire's mother had filled the kitchen cabinets with a considerable amount of the most staple grocery items. Most of all, they would have each other in complete privacy, and for five more days.

"Through the door of The White House, 'my lovely first lady,'" he said, making a bow and a sweeping gesture toward the interior. "May your term as first lady last at least fifty years."

"Aren't you going to carry the bride across the threshold," she asked?

"Indeed I am." Sweeping his bride into his arms he entered through the doorway. After crossing the threshold, he put her down.

"According to the custom, there should be a very meaningful kiss at this time," he said. "You see, the longer this particular kiss lasts the longer we will be together."

"I never heard of the custom."

"That's because I just made it up," he said, looking into her eyes.

"I love you Mark/Claire." They laughed when they realized they had said it at the same time.

Claire was to start her job, the job she hoped to get, and on the same day Mark was to return to work. It just happened to be the starting day they had in mind all along, and the reason Claire had been hopeful of getting it.

Five days of total bliss, and another two weeks of dedicated love for each other passed. Mark sat at the kitchen table while Claire prepared the evening meal. In full view of Britton's front steps, he saw Victor sitting in his wheelchair, much as they had observed the day they met him.

"I'm going to help Vic onto the porch," he said. "I'll be right back." He stopped for a moment. "How about me inviting them over some evening? Maybe this evening," he said, hoping Claire would agree.

"Do it!" Claire said eagerly. "I'd love to get acquainted with Abbie."

Mark arrived as Abigail was about to go to find a neighbor to help. "We'd like to invite you over sometime soon." Mark spoke casually. "Tonight, if you don't have other plans."

"Let's go tonight, Vic! Please? I'm dying to see Claire's house." Abigail had obviously been waiting for an invitation.

"Did you catch that, Mark? Claire's house!" He grinned at Mark. "What time? Seven-thirty okay?"

"Be there!" was the reply.

Claire washed the dishes and Mark dried and put them away. No sooner had they finished than a knock came at the front door. Mark pulled the wheelchair up the steps and into the house. He was finding it easier after having done it a few times.

"I'm sorry Vic! It didn't occur to me I should give you a hand getting out of your house," Mark apologized.

"That's no problem. We have no trouble getting down the steps. Abbie just gives me a push, and away we go."

"Oh, cut it out, Vic," Abigail said, showing a degree of impatience with him.

"What's that on the table? Looks like a Bible. Don't tell me you're studying to be a preacher."

"It's a Bible my mother gave us. We keep it on the end table. The Bible we use is on the kitchen table right now. We just want to study the scriptures and try to understand them our way... I mean, instead of letting other people tell us what everything means. Mark found himself apologizing for their lack of attention to the matter of study. "We haven't been studying like we want to...guess we've been too busy lately," he said.

Victor gave a hearty laugh. "I didn't think you wanted to discuss that subject, Mark."

Mark was embarrassed upon recognizing the innuendo. He was about to try to change the subject to something more enlightening when Victor began to apologize.

"I do admire you, Mark, for waiting until after you were married."

"I think it's time to take up another subject, Vic," Abigail said coolly.

"Hey! I happen to know; the Bible says if two people can't contain themselves, then it's okay, as long as they marry. Now, if it's in the Bible, it must be all right to talk about it." He looked at Mark. "You're a Bible student. Isn't that right?"

"I just hadn't given it much thought, I guess, Vic."

"Well!" Claire interrupted the conversation. "I've thought about it and you totally miss the point. It says, 'if' they cannot contain themselves, let them marry. The truth is when two people are in love; they have a responsibility to refrain. I believe it's more difficult for the man, nevertheless they still have the responsibility to act like one."

"What's that supposed to mean," Victor asked, though realizing he had been verbally chastised.

"It means, shut up," Abigail said. "Claire just has a nicer way of saying it than I do."

"I believe you have something you want to say to Mark, Vic," Abigail said? There was noticeable sarcasm in her voice.

"Yeah, Abbie, you're right," he said. Victor became serious. "I know I've been much too vulgar in my talk around you two. I want to apologize to both of you. I really am sorry and I'm going to watch my conversation better."

"There's something else I'd like to say to you if you're willing to listen," Victor said. "But if you don't want-"

"We're listening, Vic," Mark interrupted.

"I know there really isn't any excuse for my actions, but maybe you can understand a little better where I'm coming from- Anyway, three and a half years ago, Abbie and I were enjoying the good times you two are enjoying right now. We loved each other very much, and we had a good marriage.

"Then one day this happened." He spread out his hands and swept them over his lower extremities. I worked late one night - till about ten-thirty. On my way home a drunk driver came speeding through a stop sign on my left, hitting me broadside. I didn't have time to think. The drunk didn't get a scratch, but he was so wiped out from the liquor he didn't even know what he'd done."

"Anyway, I'm not able to carry on the responsibilities of a husband, as a result. Those days are far in the past for me. I look at you Mark, and I remember when I was a whole person like you. I guess making those silly comments help me think people won't know I have a problem."

Mark wanted to be of comfort even knowing anything he could say would be pretty feeble. "I know it probably seems trite to you, Vic, but there's a lot more to being a man than the way you're looking at it.

It was quiet for a short time. No one seemed to be able to think of an appropriate comment.

"Vic," Mark said, breaking the silence, "I really am sorry, and I don't have any idea what to say, but I wish someone could give you more help than you seem to have. I just can't think it's as hopeless as you seem to believe."

Abigail broke into the conversation. "Dr. Carne did offer some hope, Mark, but Vic doesn't want to pursue the matter."

"She's talking about what he said about people with injuries like mine, being able to enjoy each other in other ways. Abbie doesn't realize how kinky the whole mess is. Dr. Carne told me a little about it. I just said thanks, but I don't think it's an option."

"See what I'm up against," Abigail asked? She reflected her feelings that she had been defeated in her suggestion. "He won't even talk about it!"

Mark didn't feel comfortable in pressing the matter in the company of both Victor and Abigail. He tried to appear casual as he changed the subject. "Did you ever think about building a ramp up to your front door, Vic?"

"Oh sure! I just didn't want to ask anyone to do it. I know I can't do it myself. Don't know if I could afford to pay to have it done anyway," he said.

"What do you say we figure out just how much lumber it would take, and how much it would cost? I'm not much of a carpenter, but I'll bet we could get one built somehow. I'll bet Harry would be willing to help, too."

"He'd probably welcome the opportunity so he wouldn't have to be bothered all the time. I don't mean that, Mark," he apologized. "Harry has never shown signs of feeling it's a bother. I just feel I'm putting a burden on others by depending on them."

Mark walked to the window and looked out to the back part of Victor's house. He stood studying the situation for a time. "Vic," he said, "Had you thought about building a ramp up to the back door instead?" He motioned for Victor to come to the window.

From Mark's window they were given a good vantage point for viewing the entire area. Starting back toward the alley they would have almost a level plain all the way to the back door. "It would take a little more lumber, but look how easy it would be for you." Mark said, as he pointed it out.

Victor was surprised at what he saw, and quite pleased.

The next evening Mark went to the library and found a book showing various plans for building just such type ramps. After viewing plans together for some time, Victor chose one seeming to best suit their particular need. They priced the material at the lumber yard, and then placed the order being promised an early Saturday morning delivery. Of no surprise to Mark, several of the men in the neighborhood were eager to help with the construction. No sooner was the delivery made than the men appeared and the project was under way.

By eleven thirty the wives began arriving carrying card tables and folding chairs, table clothes, covered dishes and silverware. The entire event had turned out to be a very enjoyable one and a social affair as well.

Mark felt good about the project done for Victor. He couldn't help but think of the other problem Victor and Abigail had briefly discussed with them. He was curious as to what Dr. Carne had meant when suggesting there was hope for Victor. He was even more curious why Victor would think of it as being kinky.

"It might be there are films made on the subject, which are in good taste," Mark said to Claire, almost thinking out loud. "Maybe that's what he considers being kinky. It doesn't seem he would need arousing emotionally. Still Abbie said the doctor mentioned the possibility he didn't want relations. Didn't you tell me that?"

Claire wanted Mark to pursue the subject of Victor's problem with him. "You know, if it was only a problem for Vic, I would probably say, 'That's the way he wants it,' and then let it go. But it has to be awful for Abbie too, and she deserves so much more."

"You think I should question Vic as to what Dr. Carne had in mind, don't you," he said?

"There might be a way you could help him. I think it would have to come from you, since he doesn't want to discuss it with Abbie, and apparently, he refuses to get professional help. Wouldn't it be worth a try?"

CHAPTER 13

After finishing their morning meal, Mark and Claire stayed seated for a time. "I'm going to write to Harold Mason about the study of the eons when I get home from work," Mark said. He had considered several times the decision made at the time he told Claire of their visit but kept putting it off. "It would give our study a lot more direction," he added. "We can take that study and still check it out for ourselves."

"Have you thought about what you're going to say to Victor?" Claire asked, being reminded he wanted to get Victor and Abigail involved in their studies. "Whenever you want privacy, Abbie and I will arrange it. We'll find something to do so we can be out of your way.

"By the way, I talked to Abbie about what Dr. Came said to Victor. You won't believe this, but he said they could find no reason at all why Vic and Abbie shouldn't be able to have successful relations. She said the doctor is convinced it's purely psychological with him."

"What about all the paralysis? Certainly, that's a handicap!"

"They realize the limitations," she said. "They're well aware there's no motor function in his left leg, and well over half is gone from his right leg. But according to every test they've given him, they're convinced his ability to have intimate relations is quite intact. They tell Abbie it's only a matter of his believing he can't or he doesn't want to."

"They think he doesn't want to?" Mark asked in dismay. "It's hard to believe."

"It's because he made such a big thing about it being kinky. You heard him say it. They think maybe because he knows an alternate method would be required, he objects because he views anything not quite orthodox as being unacceptable, kinky, as he puts it." Recognizing some frustration with Mark, she said, "I don't know, I'm only telling you what Abbie told me."

Mark sat staring out the window across the room. His thoughts were considerations of the idea they might be interfering more than helping. "Getting into psychology is scary stuff. Maybe we should just stay out of it entirely."

In the evening, upon reaching home and getting comfortable, Mark wrote the letter to Harold. He requested, either he send him the material for study or the name of someone to contact so he could order it himself. He was sure Harold would respond quickly. When the dishes were washed, dried, and put away, Claire informed him she and Abbie wanted to go shopping and would he go over and keep Victor company.

"Sure," he said. "Be glad to."

Claire was gone when it occurred to him he had been set up for the opportunity to talk to Victor. Mark became uneasy about approaching him concerning the subject. What if he messed things up and made matters even worse? On the other hand, he reasoned if it became too much for him to handle, he could simply back away and let it drop.

"Somebody's buying new clothes, I'd say," Mark said, as he entered the living room of the Britton home.

"Probably both of them," Victor replied.

There was very little conversation between them as the evening progressed. About an hour had passed when Victor asked, "What's troubling you? You're awfully quiet tonight. Got a problem?"

Mark felt he had better make his decision soon. There was no good point to what had gone on already. "Vic," he said, "I'm concerned about something you said about intimate relations. You said it would be kinky for you. Would you tell me what you meant?"

Victor took immediate offense. "No, Mark, I won't tell you

what I meant. And just so there'll be no misunderstanding, I don't want to discuss the matter in any way or to any degree, ever. So let's drop it now and for always." He stared at Mark. "Is that why you've been so quiet this evening? Wondering how you were going to approach the subject? You've approached it, now drop it!" he shouted.

Mark remained patient. "I'd like to help you if I can. You must have something mighty heavy weighing on you to make you feel so defeated. Abbie told Claire the tests you've had don't show you having nerve damage concerning—"

"I don't care what their tests show. I know my capabilities. And Abbie had no right to tell you anything. She knows where we stand on the matter. Please, let's drop the whole subject once and for all."

Mark had no allusions it was going to be easy. He knew it would be hard to break through, and he was determined to give it at least one very good try. "Vic, I'm your friend, I want to help."

"For crying out loud, Mark! If you're a friend, then knock it off and mind your own business?"

"You are my business."

"Get out of here! If I were a man, I'd get out of this chair and bust you in the mouth! Now get out!"

In his anger, Victor had thrashed his way to the edge of his chair and was slipping to the floor. Mark ran to him. Grasping him around the waist, he lifted him back into his chair. As Mark withdrew his arm from around Victor's waist, he remained standing over him in a stooped position. With his face only a few inches away, Mark said quietly, "I'm not going to give up. If it will make you feel better, hit me. Hit me right in the mouth, Vic, but I'm not going to give up." Mark didn't move. He looked into Victor's eyes waiting for some kind of response.

Victor's eyes filled with tears. "I've had enough. Leave me alone," he said.

"I've known you only a short time, Vic, but you're already like a brother to me. Please don't shut me out. I want to help. I have a feeling there's something you need only to talk about. I think you're well aware of what it is. You just won't face it head on. You are my business, Vic. You're like a brother to me."

"You have no idea the terrible thing I've done," Victor said, as the tears came streaming over his cheeks. "It was so terrible. God planned for nine whole years to punish me. That's why I'm in this chair. Surely, you can see why I can't talk about it." His face was buried in his hands as he sobbed.

"You're telling me God punished you for something you did nine years ago? God doesn't do that. There's judgment where everyone will be disciplined for sin, but God doesn't punish anyone today." He looked squarely into Victor's eyes. "Tell me about it. How old were you? You couldn't have been more than ten or so at the time?" "I was ten. I even found stuff in the Bible about it. Mark, those people in the Bible was supposed to be stoned to death for doing what I did. I didn't know I was doing a terrible thing. It was kid stuff, I mean, real innocent. You know how ten-year-old kids are. But I know God punished me. Look at me!" he said, pointing to himself as though he was positive proof God did such things.

"Every boy does things he's not particularly proud of. It is innocent. Nothing more! You just grow out of it."

"But this was different. This was something really terrible." Mark was becoming more concerned now, but he couldn't allow the opportunity to slip away. "Describe what happened. You don't even have to say the words if it will help," he said.

"Why do you insist on opening this whole thing up?" Victor sat in his wheelchair a short distance from where Mark was seated on the couch facing him. Mark remained silent, watching Victor's expression and waiting for some kind of positive response from him. After a long pause, Victor began relating the experience to Mark. "I was a farm boy," he said, "born and raised on the farm, lived there until Abbie and I were married. About a quarter of a mile down the road was the farmhouse where Clarence Jasper lived, sort of a-a part-time minister in a little country church—lay preacher, they called him.

He had a son, David. David was twelve at the time. Well, David had invited me over on this particular day. We were out in, in the barn lot." Suddenly, the tears came rushing once again, and Victor began sobbing uncontrollably. "Mark! Please don't make me go through this, please, Mark." Victor's face became paler with each word. He turned his wheelchair so he wouldn't be looking at Mark.

"What happened, Vic? The day out in the barn lot, what happened? If you face it now, it will never be a problem again, I promise. That's when it happened, wasn't it?"

With wheelchair turned and Victor looking in the opposite direction from Mark, he spoke slowly and in barely audible words. "David had relations with his Shetland pony." Victor was silent for a time, as though waiting to see what the response would be from Mark.

Mark wasn't prepared for what he heard. Never had he heard of such a thing before. The shock was taking its time for allowing Mark to regain his composure. He was keenly aware how glad he was Victor hadn't seen the shock he knew he must have displayed. "Don't stop now," Mark was able to respond.

Slowly, Victor turned his wheelchair around and faced Mark once again. Mark knew the worst was over for Victor. He had faced what he had to face, and now the rest should be easier.

Victor looked down at his hands as he began to speak once again. "Afterward, he talked me into doing it, and I did. And David even did it again. "He told me, 'We do this all the time.' I asked him who he meant by we, and he said, All my friends. I bring all my friends out here, and they do it too,"' he said. Victor glanced in Mark's direction, then he said, "Oh, I had a bad feeling, you know, like I wouldn't want Mom and Dad to know, but it didn't really seem so terrible.

"Then I happened to turn around, and there stood David's father watching him. I didn't know how long he'd been watching, but I was just sure he'd seen me too. He yelled at David and said, 'You did a wicked thing, David.' I still remember his exact words. 'God will surely strike you down,' he said. 'He'll not let this go unpunished.' He grabbed David by the hair, half dragging him to the house, David continuing to scream all the way." Victor sat quietly for a few moments just gazing at his hands, not being at all sure he even wanted to continue.

The entire concept was beginning to come into focus for Mark. He was already able to understand how innocent the experience should have been looked upon. "I think you should continue," he said. "Tell me how you responded."

It was beginning to be apparent Victor felt more at ease. He was truly anxious to get the matter into the open. "I was so scared! I stood there and wet my pants. I couldn't help it. I watched them all the way into the house. Then I started running as hard as I could go, all the way home. I ran straight to the barn and climbed the ladder to the haymow a-and laid down on the hay. It wasn't until then I realized how out of breath I was. My heart pounded so hard I thought it was coming out of my chest. I was scared I was going to stop breathing. I actually thought God was striking me down at that very moment.

"Well, I stayed in the haymow all afternoon expecting Mr. Jasper to call on my folks anytime. I knew Mom was looking for me 'cause she was outside calling my name, but I stayed hid until dark. I couldn't eat supper. I couldn't look at Mom or Dad. To a ten-year- old, moms and dads are supposed to know almost everything, so I was sure if they should see my eyes, they would know exactly what I'd done. I simply couldn't allow it to happen. Well, Mom thought I was sick, and I'm sure I was. They sent me to bed, which was just fine 'cause it meant I didn't have to face them. I remember thinking I hadn't realized how long nights could be. Night hours had always seemed to go so much faster than day hours. I know how crazy it sounds, but everything was like that, like a dream when nothing really adds up right. Anyway, I never told another person what happened. When I went back to school, every time a boy got hurt, no matter how slight, I always wondered if it was one of those boys who had done what I did. It didn't get any better in high school. Then it was basketball injuries and broken arms, always wondering if God was punishing them. One boy I knew then even died later in a car accident. I became very certain he had to have been one of those boys.

"God waited nine years before He struck me down. He finally had a drunkard ram into me. But He didn't let me die. He'd rather I remember what a kinky thing I did. He's been punishing me for three years now. I figure if I don't get involved in any more kinky stuff, maybe He'll eventually stop punishing me."

Something tremendously heavy was lifted from Victor's shoulders. For the first time since he began relating the story to Mark, he was able to look him in the eyes. It was obvious he still believed he was being punished, but a great step had been taken.

"Thanks, Vic. Thanks for telling me everything. You would only tell it to a friend. Now I know that's the way you look to me, as a friend. I hope you soon realize how easy it will be to resolve this whole thing."

Victor took offense to Mark's words. "I don't know why you think the problem will go away. The fact remains I did a terrible thing. It was something God will not allow to go unpunished."

"That's exactly where the problem lies. Think about it. What you did was a perfectly innocent response for a ten-year-old boy. It was innocent in every way. You said yourself, it didn't seem such a bad thing at the time. You were ten years old. You probably never had a true sexual experience before in your life. At the age you were, every boy is curious. It was the first time you had been confronted with such a situation, and that's how you responded. It's just that simple!" "I know," Vic interrupted. "I know it was innocent. I'm sure had I been twenty, or sixteen, even maybe thirteen, I wouldn't have done it."

"Then put it in perspective. Ask yourself, does it make any sense for God to be out to punish someone for doing something they didn't even know was wrong?"

"You're saying what I did really was wrong."

"I'm saying that's what determines whether it's sin. Let's take this one step at a time. What is sin? If we knew having relations with an animal was wrong, but did it anyway, it would be sin, because we couldn't do it in good faith. Now if a ten-year-old boy sees it happening and becomes curious enough to want to experiment with it as something entirely new, it's a matter of innocence, not a lack of faith. Faith didn't even enter into the situation, so it can't be a matter of sin."

Victor was pretty much in agreement with Mark, but he felt the most important fact hadn't been dealt with. "You're not recognizing the fact the Bible says a sin like that has to be dealt with."

"We have to get back to perspective again. Let's not even consider for a moment what the law said about the degree of the punishment. We have to decide whether a sin had even been committed. And that's my point right now.

Vic, I realize what you are saying and I know people were put to death for what they did, but I also want you to know something else about sin. All those living from Adam to Moses did sin, but their sins were not counted against them because the Law of Moses hadn't yet been given. They were held guilty only for the sin inherited from Adam—the dying state. But when Jesus died, was buried and resurrected, the sin inherited from Adam was forgiven for all humanity. Do you realize what I'm saying? That sin inherited from Adam was forgiven for every human being.

But then the law came along. Most people don't realize the law did not come to condemn. It came to teach people what righteousness is, until we reach the age of accountability we do not sin. So if you didn't know you were doing something wrong, you did not sin. But Vic, even if you did sin, the blood of Jesus covers you. If you ask Him to forgive you, you are free from all guilt.

Now, let's carry this even further. Suppose you didn't receive forgiveness in this life, and you are cast into the lake of fire to be chastised? You would suffer agony and regret for what you did, and it certainly would not be a pleasant experience. But at the consummation of the eons you would have been cleansed of all sin and be roused up incorruptible to meet those incorruptible ones on earth. Together we shall all become immortal. That's when all death is swallowed up by victory.

"Maybe you oughta be a preacher, Mark," he said with a grin. "I don't know if I'm quite sure about all the things you said, but you are convincing."

"Claire and I are going to have Bible study, just the two of us. If you and Abbie would like to be a part of it, we sure would be glad to have you join in. Anyway, you can talk to me anytime you want to about these things. I don't want to meddle in your personal affairs, but I want you to know you can talk to me about anything you desire."

"I might want to talk to you about some of the kinky things sometimes," he said with a grin.

"I don't think you have to worry about doing anything kinky in your home, Vic, especially with the handicaps you have. I just want you to be as happy as I am."

Mark looked at the clock. He knew it was getting late, but he had no idea it was nearly midnight.

"I think the girls decided to let us talk as long as it was going to take. They're probably waiting for you to come home." Victor was relaxed and noticeably in a better frame of mind. "I'm not sure where I stand in all this, but I know I feel a whole lot better now."

"I'll be praying for you, Vic."

"Oh! Please don't say anything to Abby about what I told you, not even to Claire. I know you don't like to keep secrets from her, but this is awfully important, and it is different."

"I understand." Mark formed a circle with his thumb and forefinger and held it up for Victor to see. "See you tomorrow. I'll send Abbie home right away."

Mark went straight home. When he opened the kitchen door, Claire and Abbie were sitting at the table waiting for his return.

Abbie looked anxiously at him. "Either you two had a good nap, or you had a long talk."

Mark observed the look of concern on her face.

"Abbie," Mark said, choosing his words carefully, "Vic asked me not to relate anything concerning our conversation, and I want it to be confidential. I honestly feel Vic is going to see things differently now, but you will need to be very patient with him. I invited him to join us in Bible study, along with you. I think it would be good for him."

"You've given me the best news I've had in nearly three years." She gave Mark a kiss on the cheek and then hurried out the door.

"I hope I never have to go through anything like that again as long as I live." He sat for a moment reflecting on the entire episode. "I guess if he comes out of it the way I think he's going to, though, it will be well worthwhile."

In just about one week from the day Mark wrote to his friend in Waterford, Michigan, a large envelope came in the mail. He could hardly wait to get it opened and view the contents. On the top was a personal letter from Harold, written in his own handwriting.

> Dear Mark:
>
> What a pleasure it was to receive your letter. I have made it a point over the years to keep plenty of copies of the studies you will find enclosed. Please accept them as my ministry to you.
>
> A lot has happened in the two and one half years since we met on that

lovely autumn day.

Both Mr. Rawlings and Mrs. Price have since passed on, just three days apart, as a matter of fact. I don't give the fact any particular significance. I'm sure their mission was accomplished, and God's purpose for them on earth was fulfilled.

I also have a beautiful little great granddaughter and a great-grandson to give me joy.

The flowers wither and die, and new buds come to take their places. Even in my little circle, time comes ever racing toward me, bringing the glorious consummation of His purpose nearer.

Mark, I hope you are vigorously pursuing the matter we discussed when you were here. You were so sure God was revealing His will for your life. You felt God was giving you concern for the reason He allows the doctrine of eternal torment to continue in the world. May God bless you richly, and keep leading you toward His objective for you.

Won't you come and visit again and bring your lovely bride.

Your friend in Christ
Harold Mason

"What a beautiful letter!" Mark said aloud. He never before considered time as coming out of the future. The idea was intriguing.

Mark and Claire had invited Victor and Abbie to their home for Bible study on the approaching Friday evening. "Shall we use this material for our study?" he asked Claire. "We'll have to look it over a little to find out more about it. But I have a feeling it will make an excellent beginning study."

"You said Mr. Mason told you this was what interested your friend in the Concordant teaching," Claire said to him. "I would think if it was good for Sidney, it would surely be good for us."

After reading the material, Mark was more excited than ever. He was eager to get the group into a study of the eons. They all agreed this would be where they should begin.

"We think of all the various divisions of time as having their own measured duration," Mark began. "We consider seconds, minutes, hours, weeks, months, seasons, years, decades, centuries, and even millennia. Every one of those time periods has a predetermined beginning and end. We may find ourselves at the beginning of any one of them and looking toward its consummation. Most of those periods of time are short enough we can live through the entire duration. But even of the ones longer than our own life spans, we are still aware of their exact length and can visualize their consummation in relation to historical events.

"We never look back to some event and anticipate its arrival for it has already passed. There is never a thought as to what yesterday may bring, for it has already delivered what it had for us. Time comes from out of the future. We anticipate what tomorrow may bring, or the day after, or next year, then tomorrow, or the next day, or next year arrives, and the anticipation is over.

"The point of it all is, all time comes out of the future. In all the time periods we discuss, we know at all times how far into the future they reach and when they will end.

"But when it comes to the total time God requires to carry out His plan and purpose, theologians discard that idea of understanding. They push the point of consummation further and further into the future, never allowing the end to arrive. If all other time periods come to an end, then why shouldn't the period of the ages also come to an end? The only difference in the ages and all the other segments of time is God keeps the exact end moment a secret from us until each particular eon runs its course."

Mark wanted to stop for a moment to give the material time to be digested. He knew Bible study in any group form was probably quite new for Victor and Abigail. "Are there any questions? Is there anything you want to discuss?" he asked.

Victor spoke up, "I think it's pretty clear, I mean, clear what you're saying. I'm just anxious to find where the Bible actually shows these things to be true."

Mark was pleased with Victor's response. "That's good, Vic. Can you briefly summarize what we just talked about?"

"Sure! You said all time periods have a beginning and an end. You said they all come out of the future, like the year we're living in. It began, and then it continues on by, until now in just a few weeks 1949 will be behind us. You said the overall period of time it takes for God's plan and purpose to be carried out would also come to an end, just like all the other periods. That's my understanding of what you said." Victor sat back in his chair.

They spent some time following through on the references listed; however, they kept the study brief in order to let the concept of time and its many divisions make their impression. Mark was pleased with the findings of the evening. What they discussed hadn't taken them into any great depths of study, yet it was an excellent beginning into a very enlightening one. Learning the eons are also periods of time, though extended ones, had introduced them to an all-new approach to understanding scripture. It had supplied a new premise upon which to build their learning.

CHAPTER 14

On the day following the first group Bible study with Victor and Abigail, Mark and Claire discussed the letter they received from Harold Mason. "Something puzzles me," Claire said. "I have never met Mr. Mason, so why would he refer to me as a lovely bride?"

Mark put on his best "puzzled face" look. "I can't imagine! Someone must have tipped him off. I suppose it was probably me who let it slip. That must be it!" He grinned at Claire. "You know, I've decided I don't want to call you the 'First Lady' anymore. That makes it sound like there might be a second or a third. But I have no problem thinking of you as my 'lovely lady.' It doesn't mean I want to shorten the fifty-year term, though."

Claire drew the water for the dishes and then poured in the liquid soap. She placed the silverware, plates, cups, and glasses in it to begin soaking. "Mark, what did he mean about God directing you in the matter of the eternal torment doctrine?"

"Well," Mark said thoughtfully, "it all goes back to a premonition I've had for so long. I don't really know when I began to feel it. Sometimes, I think I was born with it. One thing's sure, though—-it's been a strong feeling since I met Sidney in the garden. I came to know Jesus Christ and believed in Him, quite a while before, maybe two or three years before. So I guess it could have begun anytime after that.

"Every time the idea began to fade, I started thinking it was all in my imagination, or it was merely coincidence. Then the Holy Spirit seemed to give me comfort in some difficult situation, and those same old feelings would return.

"I went to visit Harold in Michigan. It appeared God was giving me direction. Until then, it was all only a gnawing feeling. That day, it became so positive. I felt God was instructing me to seek guidance into the matter of why He allows the doctrine to be so much a part of the Christian teaching. It presents such a paradox. The doctrine is a grave error as to truth, yet it seems to be God's will for it to go unchecked. It appeared God wanted to unveil the reason to me. My premonition and the eternal torment doctrine seemed to become closely aligned, yet I still haven't received further enlightenment. But always when the matter starts to fade, something comes along to renew the feeling all over again. I hadn't thought about it in a long time. Now Harold reminds me of it again in his letter. I pray about it a lot, but it's still no more than just a feeling I have." "Hey!" Mark exclaimed. "I was going to wash those dishes." "It's all right. You can wash and dry them tomorrow night. Oh, on second thought, I won't hold you to it since you called me your 'lovely lady.'"

"You are my lovely lady," he said with affection. "I know talking about the premonition, if it is a premonition, probably makes me sound self-centered or even worse, but I hope you don't think that's what it is. I can't explain it any better than I have. It's just a feeling, which doesn't go away. It sort of keeps crowding me but never quite enough to be annoying."

"You said the man died the very day you met him. Do you think it's possible his mission in life was finished after his visit with you? I don't know! I'm just suggesting it as something to think about. Maybe God was laying the groundwork in him then passed the role on for you to complete." With a look of much assurance, she said, "I haven't the slightest doubt—if God plans to reveal something to you, His will shall be carried out. Maybe that's God's very plan, to keep you aware He's chosen you but not meaning to reveal what it is until the proper time."

Mark continued preparation for study of the works his friend sent him. It was designed to bring all scripture references of both the Old and New Testaments together, those concerning the matter so much in question. It was meant to supply the student with the necessary tools to allow him to discover the truth for himself.

The study was divided into two quite natural parts. The word olam, being the Hebrew form, was found in the Old Testament scriptures. In the New Testament, the Greek word was aion, and its adjective, aionian. He discovered the entire "eternal torment" concept was contingent upon the meaning of those two words. Mark had decided to approach the Old Testament study first, discovering the word olam occurred 448 times in those scriptures. They would simply begin a systematic study of any or all those references.

Victor sat looking at the selections of words the King James Version had used as English equivalents for the Hebrew word *olam.* Mark had made a copy for each member of the class to refer to. Even before the study began, Victor was counting: three, four, five. One by one, he counted the different renderings used—twenty-six, twenty-seven. Can you believe what those translators did? They thought twenty-seven English equivalents were required to give the accurate meaning for one Hebrew word—*olam?*

"That's not unusual," Mark said. Some Hebrew words are given forty or more English equivalents. What's even more interesting is nearly every English word they used involves the meaning of time. Look at them: old, of old, ancient, old time, always, ever, any more, long, world, continuous, long time, any time, eternal. And every one of them is meant to convey the meaning of the word olam, as eternal."

"Here's another interesting point," Mark continued. "Many of them were translated in a way to indicate a limited period of time. Then they also use forever and ever together, which suggests there is something yet following eternity. That's pretty hard to conceive of, don't you think?"

Going about the study of each reference, they found many more items of interest.

"Look at this one," Mark pointed out. "In the forty-ninth chapter of Genesis, it speaks about the everlasting hills. We should expect it to mean the hills shall last for all eternity. But look in the fortieth chapter of Isaiah. It says every mountain and hill shall be made low. And in the fifty-forth chapter of Isaiah, it says the mountains shall depart and the hills moved."

Example after example was found to discredit the value for the concepts used in translating the word. The four of them marveled at what was discovered as they checked out scripture verse after scripture verse and found virtually the same results at every reference. Like countless others, they had understood scripture the way the church leaders insisted it should be understood.

The conclusion they reached indicated to them the entire Old Testament writings were concerned with the time element. All of them were confined to a prescribed period, having a beginning and an end. Had the translators been as conscientious when considering all instances, the errors should have been obvious to them.

"Many of the doctrines of today"—now Mark was adding some of his own thoughts to the study—"find their origin dating back to the early centuries after Christ's time. Most of the Bibles in use today are only minor variations of what was contained in the Latin Vulgate, coming out of the very early centuries since the time of Christ. What is said to be translations is little more than revisions of the Latin Vulgate, or revisions of other revisions of it.

"It seems to me church leaders everywhere are much less concerned about truth than they are with promoting their own pet doctrines. They tend only to press forward the same tired doctrines having contained error from the beginning of those concepts. Look at the denominations of today. It's often some peculiar belief fostering their beginning, while they continue to stay in the same narrow area of difference. They continue to seek converts to their strange concepts. They care little for testing any matter for truth or even to test their own beliefs very far for error."

"Don't you suppose that's the reason there are so many different denominations today?" Victor asked. "I mean, they just get stuck in those differences."

Abigail interjected her thoughts. "Obviously, every denomination can't be correct, and sometimes, they are in absolute contradiction to one another."

"The Catholic Church believes infants should be baptized," Claire suggested, "but I know some churches say it should only be done by persons old enough to know right from wrong."

Mark reminded them churches are even in disagreement as to

the method of baptism. "The church I grew up in believes sprinkling is the correct way, while others believe one must be totally immersed. Some even feel it can only properly be done their way. And then some believe we are baptized, not into water but only into the death of Christ."

"So what should we do? Have everyone baptized four different ways so we can cover all bases?" Victor asked, drawing a round of laughter from the group.

After the brief exchange, Mark spoke out once again, "That's why I wanted to have a Bible class of our own. I found out quite a long time ago, there's no room in most churches for anyone who departs from their established doctrines. They've reached a niche where they're comfortable with the status quo, and that's precisely where they want to stay, and heaven help anyone who attempts to clear the waters with elements of truth."

"So!" Victor asked. "What's the direction of our class going to be? If we take off on a doctrine based on what the works we're looking at now teach, won't we be doing the same thing?"

"That's an excellent point, Vic," Mark exclaimed, "and you're absolutely right. We could easily take off on whatever else these people teach and wind up in some other error. We'd be no better off than the denominations then."

"I want to make something clear, though. There's a very big difference in the premise upon which most of the doctrines of today are based and the premise this doctrine is built upon. Probably more than ninety-five percent of Christians today hold to the concept the great majority of humanity is doomed to eternal torment. But the time factor we've been discussing proves the program as referred to throughout the entire Bible comes to an end. That would mean the judgment God brings upon all unbelievers is for a limited time only. It appears we are building on the correct premise while it is likely the other ninety-five percent have built their doctrine upon a basic error."

By common agreement, the group had decided to hold their study to one hour's duration. It had already gone something over an hour and a half. "Maybe we'd better continue our study next week," Mark said, taking a quick glance at his watch.

"Mark!" Victor said. "Before we get into other things, I have something to discuss with you. A Reverend Holliday stopped by the house this afternoon. He saw the ramp in the backyard. That's why he stopped in the first place. His church has this program where they help people like me—you know, the wheelchair. Well, they take people to church services. See, they have this new bus. They had someone build a hydraulic system at the side door so they can take in wheelchairs. I thought maybe it would be a good way for me to get to his church."

Signs of disappointment registered on Mark's face, but he didn't want to discourage Victor in any way. "I think that's fine, Vic, if that's what you want."

"Don't misunderstand. I'm not looking for a church. I like what we're doing just fine. You know after we talked that evening?" He referred to the discussion on the evening Victor had opened his thoughts to Mark concerning his problem. "Well, since then, I decided I wanted to believe God has forgiven me, to believe Jesus Christ covered the sins I committed. A-a-and I sort of thought He did."

"That's all that's required. All you have to do is believe. God has already forgiven you."

"Well," Victor explained, "Reverend Holliday says it should be done publicly. He says we need to have witnesses knowing we have accepted Christ. He says the best way is to go before an entire church so there will be lots of witnesses. Well, I just got to thinking, maybe you would go with me?"

"If that's what you want, I'll go with you. But I wonder if you're sure it's necessary," Mark said.

"Reverend Holliday says where two or three are gathered together in Jesus's name, He will be there also. Then I'll know I'm saved, he says."

Mark was skeptical that perhaps the minister had other reasons for Victor making a public confession, but he didn't want to create a problem.

"He wants me to come to their services next Sunday evening. I think I want to go, Mark."

The two of them did attend the service the following Sunday evening. They went to the rear pew of one of the outside sections so Victor could remain seated in his wheelchair. One of the church members promptly brought Mark a chair, and he seated himself. Soon, Reverend Holliday greeted them as he approached, welcoming them to the service.

"It's good to see you in our service tonight, Mr. Britton!"

"Victor," he interrupted, "just call me Victor. And this is Mark Hayes, my neighbor and close friend."

"Oh yes, Victor, and it's good to meet you, Mark."

Mark noted a degree of coolness in his greeting. The thought even crossed his mind Victor had discussed their beliefs with him.

"Now here's what I want you to do, Victor," the pastor said. "At the end of the service, I'll make the altar call. This is where Victor will need the help of a friend." He looked at Mark, indicating he was the one he had in mind. "On the third altar call, I want you to push the wheelchair down the aisle to the front of the church. That's all you'll have to do, Mark." He asked if they had any questions then walked to the podium.

Victor whispered to Mark, "I don't think I liked the sound of that. What do you make of it? Doesn't it sound phony to you?" he enquired.

"I'd have to agree with you. If you don't want to go forward after the service, just stay where you are. There's nothing saying you have to do it. It's up to you," he whispered back to Victor.

It was only at this point they learned this particular evening was the beginning of a ten-day evangelistic crusade. Mark was getting the picture quite clearly. He was sure Victor didn't recognize it. He felt a great deal of sorrow for Victor, for he knew he had chosen to go forward thinking it was the right thing to do. He also felt embarrassment for him for being set up and, in fact, taken advantage of. He hoped Victor would choose not to go forward, but he would leave it entirely to him.

The sermon was one of creating much fear and unrest in the hearts and minds of those in attendance. Indeed, it was quite typical of most of the evangelical services, using the element of fear as the tool for bringing sinners to the altar. He warned, in gravest of terms, the consequences of refusing to accept Christ after hearing the truth presented to them so vividly. The organist had already begun playing the hymn, "Just as I Am." The first altar call was made with no response coming from the congregation. He began again to warn of the terrible consequences of shunning such an opportunity. The second call was made. Still there was no response.

Mark felt the eyes of the minister upon him. He was sure Victor could feel the tension as well. He waited for some signal from Victor before going forward. The minister went through his third altar call, and then the plea for sinners to come forward was made again. There was no indication Victor wanted to respond. The meeting ended without one single person coming forward to publicly accept Christ.

The congregation filed out. Mark and Victor held back to allow most of the people to leave before trying to make their exit.

The minister approached them as they waited. "I have to say I was quite disappointed in you fellows tonight. It seems you rather let the Lord down too. Why did you not come forward when the altar call was made? It could have been such a wonderful evening of souls giving their lives to Jesus Christ."

Mark was angry, but just as he was about to speak, it was Victor who began talking.

"I think you let me down, pastor. God has already forgiven me for my sins. You led me to believe I was only making a public confession before witnesses. Instead, you wanted it to appear as though it was your sermon bringing me to the altar. You wanted credit and then use me as bait to get others to follow. I think those were insensitive tactics you used in your service tonight. I simply chose not to be a part of them."

The pastor was shaken. He hadn't expected the response he received. "Can it be the two of you feel you know the mind of God better than me, a man who is trained to know the mind of God? As a matter of fact, I'm quite sure the Lord was going to heal your crippled body tonight," he said quickly. "He was about to allow the Holy Spirit to show His great power in front of this assembly tonight." "Heal my body?" Victor interrupted in surprise.

"Yes, indeed, you would have been healed, my son. The Spirit was with me tonight. Yes, I could feel the very presence of the Holy Spirit. It was just waiting for you to come forward," he said.

Mark did interrupt at this point. "Reverend Holliday," he said, "what would keep the Holy Spirit from healing Victor right now if you have the power?"

"I'm afraid the willingness of the Holy Spirit has passed. One doesn't delay when those opportunities arise. You must realize those circumstances may never arise again," he stressed.

"If I would come back again tomorrow night, could you heal me?" Victor sounded desperate.

"Vic, please don't let him hurt you any more than he already has. If the Holy Spirit was with him so strong tonight, other people would have come to the altar. It didn't have to depend on you? Ask him about that, Vic."

"Victor," the pastor said to him, "I suspect the unhealthy doctrine you have become involved with is at the root of this apparent belligerence toward God."

Victor was not particularly listening to the words of Reverend Holliday, only grasping upon the hope he would be given opportunity to be healed. He could hardly be blamed for that.

Victor turned his conversation toward Mark at this point. "If there's a chance I can be healed of this, I want to take the chance. You don't know what it's like to know you'll be confined to a wheelchair for the rest of your life? Don't deny me the opportunity to get out of this thing once and for all?"

There was deep disappointment. Mark was sure it would only end in disappointment for Victor as well. "I don't deny God could heal your body in a moment of time, if it was His desire to do so. We know God is not limited in what He can do. But He doesn't perform miracles just to make some minister look good in the eyes of his church members. God has a plan and purpose for all creation. He does things only according to His Own counsel. I'm saying God would only heal your body if it were according to His overall plan and purpose. Reverend Holliday doesn't know what God's will is in this matter."

"Come tomorrow night, Victor, we'll see if God is willing to heal you." Immediately after the pastor spoke, he disappeared among the remaining church members, making it quite obvious he had become not a little upset.

"Don't say a word," Victor said to Mark. "I have to find out if God will heal my body."

"I just don't want to see you hurt, Vic. You're too much of a friend for me to let that happen." Mark wanted so much to spare Victor the pain he likely was letting himself in for.

"Don't try to stop me, Mark. I have to find out if God is going to help me. I think now that He's forgiven me as a sinner, He'll take away this awful condition as well.

"Can you imagine what it will be like for me to be able to walk and run again? I can hardly believe this is happening to me. Mark, I know it's going to turn out to be a wonderful experience. I know God wants me to be free from this contraption."

The anticipated time arrived. Victor was like a child waiting for Christmas morning. As he sat at the rear of the church, his enthusiasm neared the point of impatience. The difference in Victor's excitement and Mark's concern was a contrast of great proportion. Mark felt sure Victor was riding much too high and was letting himself in for disappointment. The healing experiences he had witnessed in this type of service was never well substantiated. There was always the element of doubt of anything very convincing taking place, and it was always questionable whether a "miracle" had happened. It had never been a question of whether God could heal. In fact, Mark was confident God had answered many prayers by speeding the healing beyond what nature alone would accomplish. He believed prayer would, in many instances, be part of the process of God working things according to His will and through His Own council. In fact, Mark was sure any number of people's lives had been extended as a result of the "power of prayer," but this was different. "Of course, this is not a situation beyond the power of God," Mark assured himself.

"What shall I do? Victor probably won't be healed, yet if I try to prepare him for disappointment, I'll be blamed for failure. "Mark didn't mind being blamed. But he would mind seeing Victor hurt again, and besides, there was the outside possibility it was God's will he should be healed. Mark prayed silently God would direct both Victor, and himself, and especially himself, as to how to become prepared.

When the altar call was offered, Victor was eager to go forward. Mark pushed the wheelchair to the front of the church and waited before the platform. A young woman, whom Mark estimated to be in her early thirties, also came forward. The call continued to be offered. It did seem quite evident to Mark their presence had given others the courage to follow, for soon, a number of people had come forward.

The minister praised God for touching the hearts of so many in response to his message. Victor was required to sit patiently in his wheelchair with Mark standing behind him all the while, for Mark was not about to leave him alone. All those who had come forward were dealt with individually, while members of the church came to minister to them. This was a lengthy ceremony, and all of it was taken care of before the healing ceremony began.

When the ones who had expressed desire to give their lives to Jesus Christ had been ministered to, they took their seats once again in the place of worship. A new call was issued to those who wished to be healed of some physical affliction. An emotional plea was made by the pastor, telling the people he could feel the mighty power of the Holy Spirit in their presence and they need only come and lay claim to the works the Spirit was about to manifest in their midst.

Mark continued to keep his feelings inside, not wanting to prevent Victor from receiving any healing God might desire to accomplish. A woman came to the platform and stood beside Mark. She was a middle-aged woman but every whit in excess of two hundred pounds above what her ideal weight should be. As she struggled to reach the altar, she gasped for breath and was perspiring profusely.

When Reverend Holliday's plea was complete, he walked first to the woman and inquired as to her needs. When told of the serious heart condition, he placed his hand upon her shoulder and then began to pray for her. Suddenly, he removed his hand from her shoulder, and holding it in front of her forehead, he shouted, "Come out of this woman at once, in the name of Jesus of Nazareth, so she may be healed." Then with the palm of his hand, he struck the woman on the forehead. In spite of her obese condition, she was jolted backward into Mark as he stood a short distance behind her.

The woman began praising God and waving her arms in jubilance. After some time of rejoicing and the pastor claiming a great victory over the demons of illness, the woman returned to her seat.

But Mark noticed the excitement had made her even worse than when she came to the altar. She sat in her seat gasping for breath, but the pastor failed to recognize her present condition.

At long last, the time Victor had waited for arrived. The procedure followed by the pastor was the same as with the obese woman. He prayed longer, perhaps because of the obviousness of the condition, Mark thought. With the same theatrics, he thrust the palm of his hand into Victor's forehead, causing the wheelchair to rock backward and repeating the words: "In the name of Jesus of Nazareth, come out of this man."

Victor was visibly given to his emotions. With his elbows on the arms of his wheelchair, he worked his way to the edge of the chair. He tried to stretch his legs out to reach the floor, but they failed to respond. The pastor repeated the words: "In the name of Jesus of Nazareth, I command you to come out of this man." Again, there was no response.

After a time, Reverend Holliday apologized for what he said appeared to be failure. "We can only assume," he said, "when the Holy Spirit fails to heal, it's because the subject doesn't have the necessary faith. Perhaps another time, he will be healed."

The congregation was dismissed and began to disperse. Victor sat bewildered and unable to comment on what had happened. Soon, he began to realize nothing had taken place and it was not going to. There was the look of utter helplessness. Tears began to stream down his cheeks. At that moment, the pastor arrived to speak to them.

"You said I would be healed! You said you were sure the Holy Spirit would heal me!

I'm sorry, Victor," the pastor said. "There was obviously a lack of faith involved here tonight. Perhaps it was the lack of faith of your friend preventing the healing. I strongly suggest you reconsider your idea God will see everyone being saved. Why don't you come back again? Perhaps the Holy Spirit will heal you then."

"Reverend Holliday," Mark interrupted, "I believe I have as much respect for God and love for His Son, Jesus Christ, as anyone in your congregation. It disappoints me your love appears to be so superficial. It seems to me you are only interested in making yourself look good in the eyes of your church members."

It occurred to Mark the obese woman was a good example of what he was saying. "That woman," he said, "the woman you tried to heal of the heart condition—you say you have the gift of healing. Why didn't you recognize the real problem in her condition and help her to lose those excess pounds? You would have witnessed to every person in this congregation had she suddenly lost two hundred pounds of weight right in front of their eyes. Perhaps it would even have healed her heart problem.

"Instead, you put the blame on Vic and me, when it became apparent you had failed to make good on your claims. I'm afraid as long as you believe men can have the kind of faith salvation requires, you will never understand the source of men's faith."

CHAPTER 15

They found three references stating the earth abideth forever, then eight passages saying the earth passes away to make room for a new heaven and earth. So it went all through the Old Testament.

Three weeks passed since the little class began pursuing the study of the eons. Victor remained quite upset over his ordeal with Reverend Holliday. Mark felt badly about the incident, but he honestly believed he had done all he could to prevent it from happening, short of interfering. It wasn't difficult to put himself in Victor's situation, imagining how he would have felt in being given the hope he might soon discard the wheelchair. Tears came to his eyes whenever he gave it serious thought. He had given the matter much prayer as it continued to weigh heavily upon him. But now Victor was getting back to being able to accept his condition for what it really was and eager to resume study.

"It's hard to imagine a doctrine, such as we have always known, could have survived for all these centuries," Victor said, marveling at the fact most of Christianity wouldn't consider the possibility of their own view being wrong.

"It's more than a matter of centuries too. This teaching was already vigorously taught as early as the third and fourth century after the time of Christ. Most people don't question the common versions of scripture because they believe every word, just as we find it, was inspired by God," Mark continued. "Someone once said, the clergy would like us to believe all the prophets spoke in Shakespearean English."

Everyone sat trying to justify such a doctrine being taught. It was Abigail who expressed her feelings first. "I just can't comprehend how the Bible scholars wouldn't have recognized many of the contradictions this study reveals. I mean, they seem so obvious when they're pointed out to us."

"I suspect most Bible students were looking at the quality of the matter rather than the time factor." Mark was speculating now, but he felt he had a rather good explanation.

"What do you mean?" Claire asked.

"Like the Law of Moses being an 'everlasting' covenant. They may have thought of it as being God's Law continuing in heaven, even though it would end on earth. In other words, maybe they thought the principle of the law would endure, even if the law reached a time of fulfillment on earth. It seems pretty feeble, I know, but it's hard to explain it any other way. I admit it's a mystery."

Victor had been sitting quietly for some time. Mark wanted him to be a part of the study.

"What are you contemplating, Vic?" he asked.

"I'm just thinking. We haven't even studied the word in the New Testament—aion, I think it was, but we can already see how questionable it should be to consider these things as being never-ending in duration." Victor was deep in thought while at the same time trying to put his thoughts into words. "I'm not sure where you get the idea— the idea of faith having to be given by God. But you say we can't have faith originating within ourselves, even suggesting to Reverend Holliday he didn't understand where faith comes from. Well, the point is, if most Christians believe the masses will spend eternity in never-ending torment, maybe that's why they feel justified in making people responsible for their own faith."

Abigail interrupted, "I see what you're saying. If they thought faith had to be given from God, then they would be unable to blame God for tormenting men for an endless eternity."

Claire put her thoughts into the discussion. "I see! They can feel justified for teaching the doctrine of eternal torment as long as they can place the blame on man for failing to believe."

Mark was excited about Victor's comments. "Let's summarize what you just said. It appears the eternal torment doctrine goes hand in hand with teaching salvation depends upon man's ability to find Faith from within himself to believe."

"I think there's even more," Victor said. "It appears they have no choice but to put the responsibility upon man. Otherwise, there are no grounds for believing in eternal torment at all because they know God wouldn't cause it to happen. See then if God didn't give them faith, it would be God's fault, and they could never blame God for it."

Victor paused for a moment and then continued, "Do you remember how quickly Reverend Holliday put the blame on me when I wasn't healed? He said I didn't have enough faith to believe for healing. Well, he certainly couldn't blame God for not healing me. Of course, he wasn't accepting any of the blame either." Victor chuckled.

"If you recall, he was putting quite a little of it on me too, Vicie boy." They all had a good laugh.

"It must be the power of Satan keeping the truth from people." Claire was supporting Abigail in her comment.

"Well, I don't think we've found many solutions tonight, but I think we've sure focused in on some important questions," Victor said with a hearty laugh.

Mark spoke up quickly, "Maybe we've come a lot closer to some solutions than we think, and Claire just may have put her finger on the reason, about Satan keeping the truth from the people." Mark suddenly became excited. "There are some verses in 2 Thessalonians about the matter."

Quickly, he went to those verses and began reading: "For the secret of lawlessness is already operating. Only when the present detainer may be coming to be out of the midst, then will be unveiled the lawless one" (2 Thess. 2:7-8). Then they read the entire paragraph in which those verses were found.

"Do you folks realize the significance? Christ came to the earth and died for all mankind. It's a matter of each individual coming to believe the truth. Satan has been convincing people faith comes from within. He has been able to deceive the masses for nearly six thousand years, but he has been able to keep secret the fact they have been deceived. At the same time, God has purposely allowed the deception to continue while He quietly goes on giving faith to those whom He chooses."

"Thanks for your views, Vic. We did get a little off the track tonight, but I don't think anyone will mind when we touch on things as important as this. I think you opened up a tremendous area for truth. It's an indication we're positively in the end times, and seeing a most significant truth being brought to light. I think we are in for some interesting times of study. I appreciate your views more than you know, Vic. For years, I've prayed for the answer to why God has allowed the deception to continue. It may also be the way God has kept the Jewish people blind to the secret of grace. We know it is God's will they not understand grace at this time. At the same time, I can't imagine a Jew believing the eternal torment doctrine."

The Bible classes were becoming very enjoyable to Mark, and he felt the rest of them were getting a great deal from them as well. Actually, it was the group participation, which uncovered the remarkable truths. This group had discovered a far more rewarding form of enjoyment and much different than attending a dance or movie. This made him feel closer to God, as though having communication with Him. He hoped they all felt the same way.

As they sat at the supper table a few evenings later, Mark said to Claire, "Do you remember the time we broke up soon after we met?" Claire pretended to be trying hard to recall the time. "No, I can't say I remember anything like that."

"You've got to be kidding! You don't remember?"

"I believe you're the one who's got to be kidding if you think I could forget something so devastating," she said, not entirely joking.

Mark was taken aback somewhat by her quick response. "I'm sorry. I guess I really didn't mean it quite like that. I was just trying to get us focused in on the event. I wanted to discuss something that happened because of it, something I've thought about many times since. I'd like to know your answer to something."

Claire held out her hand to Mark. "I was kidding about me forgetting. I didn't think either of us would ever forget, but I don't know what you're referring to."

"When you became angry and went running upstairs, you left

me standing in the dining room. I didn't have much choice but to leave. Anyway, you used the word devastated. Devastated is exactly what I was too. I left your house and went out and sat in the car for a long time. After a while, I began praying about the situation. I pleaded to God to cause you to know I didn't mean to hurt you. I asked God to make it all turn out for good. Then while I sat there, the most wonderful feeling of peace I had ever experienced came over me."

He reached out and grasped Claire's hand. "I felt perfectly confident God would make everything turn out right. But over the next three months or so, my complete faith turned to a complete lack of it. I decided I must have totally misunderstood what God was saying to me. Anyway, after we got back together, I realized I was being tutored in some way toward a better understanding of faith. I had been brought to the point of giving up and then was given answer to my prayer.

"That's where my question for you comes in. I've always known God was working out something for you too and not just for me. I wonder if you have come to understand God's purpose for you, as a result of what happened. I guess I learned from Sidney, all things, which happen, do so for a reason, according to God's will. We certainly know all things work together for good for those who love God."

Claire's mind was already reviewing some of the events taking place after the experience. "I've thought about it many times. Maybe not the way you're saying it, but I feel the things happening would never have come about in any other way."

"Like what, what do you mean?" Mark questioned.

"Well, I'm sure I never would have gone to see Pastor Miller for any other reason. I doubt if I would have talked to Father Murphy about the things you mentioned, you know, the infallibility of the pope, the crucifix, and praying to 'saints.' I asked Father Murphy to show me scripture to support those matters, and he more or less told me the church determines those things. He said the church has been granted the authority to make those kinds of decisions. He assured me they only use their authority in very important matters.

"He didn't really try to discourage me from marrying you, but he made it clear I should remain Catholic. I soon got the idea he wasn't really concerned about me being a Christian, but the thing I should guard against at all costs was giving up being Catholic. To be honest, I didn't care for the way he answered the questions you asked me."

"What about your visit with Pastor Miller? Did he give you any assurance?" Mark asked.

Claire smiled as she thought about it. "I really didn't see any humor in it at the time, but when I think of it since then, it seems rather funny. It seems Father Murphy was afraid I might give up being Catholic and Pastor Miller was afraid you might become one."

Claire smiled broadly. "At any rate, I was able to make a decision as to what was right for me. The problem was I couldn't bear to think of hurting Mama and Daddy. I don't know how long it would have taken for me to get the courage to tell them. Not seeing you helped a little to ease the pain. I don't know what I would have done if I had been seeing you. I know I was awfully glad when Mama suggested I give up the church.

"So!" she exclaimed. "I guess to answer your question. Did I ever come to understand the reason for it happening? I am very happy with my decision. I love studying the Bible for myself. I feel like a free person and no longer chained to a lot of ritual I can't find reason for in the Bible."

Mark and Claire finished the dishes at about the time the conversation ended. Mark went into the living room and began reading the newspaper. Claire brought a box in from the bedroom, getting his attention as she entered. She opened the box, took a dress from it, and held it up for Mark to see.

"Wow!" Mark exclaimed. "It looks expensive!"

"A little," Claire answered, hoping cost wasn't going to be the main issue. "Isn't it beautiful? I just love the color."

"I like it too," Mark said. "But I still think it looks expensive. How much did you pay for it?"

"Maaark! The price isn't everything." She was trying to prepare him for the shock.

"It just might be, if the rent was due, and there wasn't much money in the bank," he said. They both knew the rent was due. "What did you pay for it?" he asked again.

"Twenty-nine dollars. But isn't it the most beautiful fuchsia you ever saw?"

"Twenty-nine dollars!" he gasped. "That's equal to half the amount of the rent."

"I'm sorry, Mark. I didn't think you would mind. I think there's money in the bank. I'm sure there's money in the—why are you grinning?" Tears were flooding over her cheeks.

Mark was angry with himself. He hadn't meant it to turn out this way. "I'm sorry, Claire! I was joking. I didn't mean for it to get out of hand." He brushed the tears from her face with his hand. "I'm sorry for being such a clod. Forgive me?" he pleaded. He placed a kiss on her cheek.

"It seemed funny a minute ago. I was thinking of what your mother said. 'Does Claire have to do all the fighting, Mark? Tell her how you feel about it.' I just remembered we've never had a real quarrel, and I thought maybe we shouldn't forget how. I was joking, but I'm sorry."

"The funny thing is now I know you were right. It is entirely too much money. We can't afford it, and I'm taking it back tomorrow night. It isn't really very pretty anyway," she said, as she placed it back in the box.

"You're not taking it back. And it is so a pretty dress. It's exactly what you should wear to the dance next Saturday night."

"When did you make reservations to the dance?" she asked.

Mark stood up and then walked to the telephone. "Right now," he said, as he looked up the number. He made the reservations and then turned to Claire. "Guess who's playing at the Eagle's Perch, Saturday night!"

"From the way you're smiling, it would have to be the one we liked so well, what's his name, a-a-Raymond White?"

He gave her a little shove on the arm. "I like that! The most important night of our lives, and you call him, 'What's His Name.'"

"I was still trying to remember your name that night," she said, giving him a shove in return.

"Claire," he said, pulling her close to him. "You're lovely anyway, but in this dress, you will be the most beautiful lady at the dance. I couldn't get a table providing a view of the river on such short notice, but I'll still have the most beautiful view in the place, just sitting across the table from you, admiring my 'lovely lady.'"

"I just finished a song I wrote for you." This had taken place in those few days following the making of the reservations at the Eagle's Perch.

Claire looked surprised. "You wrote a song for me? Where is it?" "What do you mean, where is it?"

"Well, doesn't it have to be written down somewhere to be a song?" she questioned.

Mark was surprised at Claire's lack of comprehension of the subject. "I guess the only place it's written down is in my head."

"I don't understand. You mean you have all those notes and letters, and all those funny little marks printed out in your mind, and all you have to do is play them. I don't understand that at all."

He hadn't realized he was going to have to explain something like this to Claire. "Well, maybe I shouldn't say I wrote it. I just have the words and melody stored in my head."

"I understand," she said, showing signs of becoming impatient. "It's all the other notes going with the tune. How do you ever know what they should be?"

Mark tried to be patient. "It's only the tune, you have in your head. You play all the other notes by ear." One look at Claire and he was sorry he tried to explain, but he didn't know she was teasing now.

"You have all those notes in your head, but you have to play them with your ear?" she said. Then she burst into laughter.

"You knew what I meant all the time, didn't you?"

"No! Not until now, Mark. And I still don't understand how you can have a whole arrangement stored in your head." She was more serious now. "Are you telling me if you had a piano, you could play the whole thing just like you would if it really was a song?"

Mark's expression was one of bewilderment. "Yeah! Something like that, I guess," he said in exasperation. "I wish I had a piano. I guess you'll never hear the song if I have nothing to play it on."

Mark had talked with Claire a number of times about purchasing a piano. It always seemed rather expensive when considering it wasn't a necessity. Both of them knew how much Mark would like to own one.

On the following Saturday morning, the day on which they had reservations for the dance at the Eagle's Perch, Claire had a surprise for Mark.

"Mark," she said, wanting to be sure she had his full attention. "I think I found a piano you might like. I followed up on some ads in the newspaper."

"Oh, I don't know, Claire. It might be pretty expensive, and we can't afford to pay out much cash all at once."

"It's only fifty dollars, and you don't have to pay for it all at once. When I told the man where you worked, he called Mr. Dickins for a personal reference, with my permission, of course. He's willing to set up a note where you can pay ten dollars a month, and he won't even charge interest."

It seemed too good to be true. "Are you sure it's in good condition? I mean, are you sure it's worth what he's asking?"

"I only know it's a beautiful piece of furniture, and it looks like brand new. I suppose it could be broke or something. You can look at it yourself. I want you to look at it. You know more about pianos than I do. I guess I'd have to admit he does want to get rid of it awfully bad, but I think I believe him."

"What do you mean, you think you believe him?"

"He said his wife was the only piano player in the house and she passed away a few months ago. He said, 'I dearly loved my wife, but frankly, I hate to be reminded how bad she played. The sooner it's out of this house, the better.' He even said if you have a way to haul it, he'll help you load it at his house and unload it here, just to get rid of it."

"Guess we'd better get over there before he sells it to someone else." Mark was excited.

"I told him how much you would want it, and he said he'd hold on to it until noon today."

Mark was even more excited when he saw the piano setting in the man's living room. There was no question it was in excellent condition. It had only been a few months since it was tuned. It was a better one of the upright Baldwin models and not very many years old. The man was indeed grateful to get rid of it, and Mark was just as happy to have it.

When it was placed it their home, Mark asked Claire if she would give him a little time to practice. After all, it had been a long time since he had a chance to play, and he did want it to sound as good as possible the first time she heard it.

"Believe it or not, the words of the introduction came to me just after we first met. The rest took a little longer," he said with a laugh. "In fact, it was since we made the reservations at the Eagle's Perch the other night when I finished it."

When Claire returned, she was anxious to hear the song. Mark was eager and waiting for her return.

Claire

I think the Irish folks
prefer the death of me,
a family determined I should go:
I'll spite with them—and fight with them,
then conquer every foe.
And I declare, my love for Claire
will ever grow—oh!
Dance once more,
and as we glide across the floor,
we'll capture joys we knew the night we met:
for the deep blue of the skies
still linger in your eyes,
since the night I first declared
my love for you.
Love me true,
for while I say these things to you,
you'll know they're just because I love you so:
let me hold you in my arms
remembering the charms,
of the night that I declared
my love for you.
There at the window, caught in a spell,
beneath the moon above:
it wasn't the moon casting the spell,
it was the glow of our love.
Stay with me
Throughout the rest of time to be,
my "lovely lady" while you share my dream:

though our love has just begun,
we'll always be as one,
every day, I shall declare this love for you.

"That was beautiful, Mark." Claire leaned over and kissed him on the cheek. "I guess there's not much doubt whether it's a song or not," she said with a loving smile. "I still don't know how you can have it all in your head. And the words were lovely."

"It was easy. It was inspired by a very 'lovely lady,'" he whispered softly.

The following week, the Bible class members studied in the works of Vladimir Gelesnoff, in quest of a better understanding of the eons. This man was Russian born, a count, and had to a degree spearheaded the study, and his work dated back to about 1911 or 1912. Dying as a relatively young man in 1922, the life of an extremely talented student of scripture and a prolific writer had been cut short.

It was Mark's desire they should read directly from the words of Mr. Gelesnoff's conclusions made as a result of his studies. "Let's take turns reading and ponder these words written nearly forty years ago," he said, asking Victor to begin the reading. "Why don't each of you read two paragraphs. Vic, we'll begin with you."

Here are the words by Vladimir Gelesnoff.

"Salvation and Punishment are inseparably bound up with the ages and have no reference to the time before their commencement or after their conclusion. There is no such thing as 'endless punishment' taught in the Word. Instead of that, we have the 'punishment of the ages' and at the same time the 'redemption of the ages.' Where no sin exists, there can neither be punishment or redemption.

"If we see the truth that the ages are to come to a conclusion, then we must likewise perceive that evil also is destined to come to an end; and that the dogma of endless suffering and endless sin is wholly without scriptural support. It is a relic of Manicheism, a survival of pagan myths. The so-called fathers transferred them bodily into Christianity; their successors have made them an article of Christian faith and a test of 'soundness' as to truth; translators imported them into the versions of the Bible by translating the original scriptures into the terms of their theologies and creeds."

At this point, Abigail took over the reading chores.

"The ringing declaration, the 'last' enemy that shall be destroyed is death (1 Cor. 15:26), overthrows the whole structure of accepted, but unproved, theology. When the 'last' enemy is abolished, it is self-evident that none remains. Sin was allowed for wise ends, and when these are secured, it must cease to exist.

"The current evangelical theology involves in its system belief in the deathlessness of sin, the indescribability of error, and the permanence of evil. That though there was a time in the history of the universe when sin in any shape or form did not exist, when no cry of pain or sense of guilt darkened the all-extensive bliss and holiness of creation, yet since sin has once effected an entrance into such a scene, it has come in never to go out again, indestructible, unconquerable, ineradicable, endless. Absolute happiness and sinlessness have forever vanished like the phantom of a dream. Pristine perfectness is never again to be regained. The 'eternal state' is a universe endlessly finding room for myriads of souls rolling and writhing in the burning agonies of ceaseless flame, eternally sinful, vile, and morally hideous. It pictures the final perfection yet to be attained, as having room for a vast cesspool of immoral and degraded beings, continually existing in opposition to God.

"And now, Claire, you read the rest of it."

"This system of doctrine, though as old as man, as venerable as the tradition, as hoary as the pyramids, as orthodox as anything in ancient or modern theology, is a misconception, a travesty of God's character, a caricature of His wisdom, and must be relegated to the scrap heap of ancestral errors.

"Gladly do we turn from this figment of natural reason to the grand, simple statements of the bare unadorned Word of God. It looks forward to a time when God shall be all in all, when heaven and earth shall be purged from every stain of sin's pollution. It anticipates that glad occasion when every heart shall beat in unison with the heart of God, every mind and will shall coalesce and harmonize with the divine wisdom and purpose, every knee shall bow and every tongue confess that Jesus Christ is Lord. The second death shall be swallowed up in victory, and the victims of its rule shall come forth in resurrection glory—the redeemed of the Lord."

CHAPTER 16

In the following few weeks, the Bible group concluded the study of the eons. The breakdown showed the word eon and the word eonian occurred 199 times in the Greek scriptures. The word eon broke down as showing the Authorized Version giving it seven different variations of meaning. It was rendered ages, two times; course, once; world, forty times; ever, seventy-two times; never, seven; evermore, four; and eternal, twice. The word eonian broke down as showing this version rendering it everlasting, twenty-five times; eternal, forty-two times; world, three; and ever, once, for a total of four variations of meaning.

There were New Testament scriptures showing the eons to have a beginning: Hebrew 1:2 (God made the eons), 1 Corinthians 2:7 (before the eons), and 2 Timothy 1:9 (before eonian times). There were scriptures proving the eons will come to an end: Hebrew 9:26 (the end of the eons, plural), 1 Corinthians 10:11 (the ends of the eons, both plural), and Matthew 24:3 (the end of the eon, both singular).

There were scriptures proving there are at least five eons in all: Colossians 1:26 (hid from eons), past, at least two; Luke 20:34 (this eon), present, one; and Ephesians 2:7 (eons to come) future, at least two.

All agreed it had been the finest and most revealing study they could have endeavored, especially for a group just entering into Bible study. Mark would be reminded many times during his lifetime: this was the single most enlightening and fascinating truth he had learned in all his years of Bible study. They were unanimous in their opinion the intent could not be to convey the meaning of eternal or everlasting.

Basically, the class remained composed of just the four of them. It never was a matter of not wanting more members, only that others didn't remain for very long. Some moved away to other places, but mostly, it was people wanting to return to their regular churches where there was more activity. It usually didn't take long for them to realize the things this little class stood for weren't very popular and were shunned by the denominations.

Growth continued in grace and knowledge of the Lord, Jesus Christ. Mark had incorporated into his own thinking, many of the things he learned as a boy of only eleven from Sidney Rawlings on the day they met in the garden. His relentless pursuit toward believing scripture for what it says, rather than what others wanted him to think it means, had been a rewarding practice and had taught him things he never would have known had he accepted the more traditional concepts.

Many had been the difficult times when he stood up for his beliefs, but it was just as Sidney had promised him: he was much the happier person for it now. Mark grew in maturity in the Word. He became surer of his convictions as he became older, becoming less and less ruffled by those who disagreed with him. Teaching the class had been good for him and no doubt contributed greatly to his maturing. While he encouraged others in the group to teach, they all preferred Mark to be the teacher. And so it was.

Victor's attitude had changed dramatically after he accepted Christ. He was no longer bitter about his condition, or if there was any remaining bitterness, he concealed it well. He no longer felt sorry for himself, and he soon realized he needed to get a job. Mark suspected he was running low on funds to keep the household going. They had received a fair settlement for all the expenses they incurred, and it had provided for them quite adequately. But now as Victor so succinctly stated it, it was "Time to pick up the pieces and move ahead."

There was a number of things Victor would be capable of doing. He had a high school education. He had two strong arms and hands. He had a good head on his shoulders. Mark was well aware of his sharp mind in mathematics and probably his strong suit. He suggested bookkeeping as a possible career to look into. Going to the employment office, he underwent a battery of tests for dexterity and thought processing—all directed toward allowing him to choose from a variety of occupations. Bookkeeping fit nicely into those findings, and it greatly appealed to Victor. An interview was set up with the auditor's office where he was promptly accepted. And so Victor became a workingman once again, and Abigail also successfully sought employment. Victor became well-adjusted to his job, and they were both happier than they had been in many months.

Months passed. Months turned into years. The five-year waiting period for becoming homeowners was almost upon Mark and Claire. It was a Sunday morning, and they were finishing their last cup of coffee after breakfast. Mark folded up the newspaper.

"Do you suppose we could take a nice vacation this summer to celebrate the signing of our contract on the house?" Claire asked. She sounded quite deliberate with her question.

"Where do you want to go?" he asked. "Sounds like you have something specific in mind."

"No, really I don't. Well, a suggestion maybe, but that's not important." She hesitated for a moment then continued. "We haven't taken a vacation since our honeymoon."

"And?" Mark asked.

"Well, Abbie and Vic have never had a vacation together. We enjoy their company so much anyway." There was more than a hint of a plea in her voice.

"Go on, Claire! I already think I'll like what I'm going to hear. Vic's got so he loves getting out and away. Seems like a great idea."

"I think they'll love the idea. Abbie has sort of hinted she needs to get away. I don't think she's feeling well lately. Maybe a nice trip is just what she needs."

"Oh! There's something else," she said with a laugh. "Mama and Daddy are coming for dinner. What are you going to tell Daddy now?" She gave Mark a quizzical look.

"What does that mean? Is there something I should prepare

myself for?"

"You know how he often asks when we're going to have children? He's been pretty determined to get an answer lately. I can just hear him now—'When am I going to see some little Claires and Marks running around this house?'"

"I really am sorry we haven't had children, but—"

She interrupted Mark, looking at him as she spoke, "I'm not sorry!"

"What do you mean?" he asked in astonishment. "You were the one who always wanted children. Well, I did too, but I mean you used to talk about it so much."

"Sure, I'd love to have children," she said matter-of-factly. "I just don't worry about it anymore. I figure if God wants us to have children, we'll have children. If He doesn't want us to have children, we won't have them. See how easy it is? I'm not trying to be funny, I simply decided to leave it with God and allow Him to work it out. I think of all the things that can be wrong with a child, like deformities and crippling diseases, I want to leave the decision with God."

"I love you, Claire," Mark said softly. "You always were the mature one. But I'm not so sure your dad will accept your explanation."

When getting together with Abigail and Victor later in the week, the idea of a vacation was discussed. Victor was extremely pleased with the suggestion. Surprisingly, Abigail was the one who was reluctant to heartily embrace the invitation.

"I-I-I think I'll have to check with my doctor. I'm not sure it would be all right with him." She was beaming from ear to ear by the time she finished speaking.

"Looks like I'm going to be a father before you are, Mark. What do you think of that?" Victor asked proudly.

Mark and Claire were both bursting with excitement. They couldn't have been happier had it been them making the announcement for themselves.

"Surely, you're not very far along, are you?" Claire asked.

"I went to the doctor on Wednesday. He said I'm about six

weeks along."

"Doc says everything is set for January fifteenth," Victor added. "I like the idea of taking a trip, but it will have to be with the doctor's blessing." She looked at both Mark and Claire, hoping it would be something she could join in.

"Congratulations, Vicie boy. I knew you'd have a family someday."

Abigail sat, still beaming, leaving no doubt as to her extreme happiness. "We have a girl's name already picked out, Claire."

Victor interrupted her, "You know, honey, if it should turn out to be a boy, people will still expect you to keep it."

"You can be sure if it's a boy, we'll keep it, but I'm still hoping it will be a girl," she said, turning once again to Claire.

"We're going to name her Deanna Claire after you, Claire, because you're such a special friend."

Both Claire and Mark were visibly moved when hearing of the honor she had given Claire.

"Where did you have in mind going?" Victor asked. "Abbie can ask the doctor and let him decide if it's okay."

"I don't know," Mark said, "but I think Claire had somewhere in mind. Where were you thinking of going?" he asked.

"I just thought it might be nice to visit Mr. Mason up in Michigan. He was the one who sort of directed us into our Bible study, and he did invite us up to see him. I thought we could stop for a day or so as part of a longer trip, like Niagara Falls, maybe." She raised her eyebrows and looked around to see if she could observe an objection.

"Sounds pretty exciting to me," Mark exclaimed. "What do the rest of you think? The Thousand Islands are quite an attraction this time of year, I'm told, wouldn't be much further."

All were in agreement the first obstacle to get around would be to find out when vacations were available for each. There were four different job schedules to be coordinated. The end of July proved to be the best time for all. The doctor felt a time early in the second trimester of the fetus was the most advisable time for her to travel.

The usual writing for information concerning travel routes, lodging, and sightseeing brochures were done, especially information about Niagara Falls and the Thousand Islands. In general, all the plans were made for what they hoped would be the most enjoyable trip they could arrange on such short notice. They dropped a line to the Masons to let them know their plans and make sure it met with their schedule.

Harold Mason wrote to express his pleasure with their plans to visit him and his family. He looked forward to meeting the "lovely bride," even though it had been five years since the wedding. He hoped they could stay long enough to take in a Tiger's baseball game, but he informed them the team wasn't even playing five hundred ball. "We can still see some fine baseball, and there's no end to the things of interest in this area," he said.

Mark was excited about the trip, and he was sure everyone else was excited too. Half the fun of a vacation was in looking forward to it. If anyone deserved a vacation, it surely was Abigail and Victor, and he wanted them to have a good time.

Their first stop was Waterford, Michigan. They reached Waterford the evening before they planned to visit the Masons, spending the night in a motel. It allowed them to be fresh when they arrived at the Mason's home about midmorning on Monday. The day was beautiful and clear, and even though it was late July, the weather couldn't have been more ideal.

Mark had asked Harold if it would be possible for him to arrange for them to see the yard where Mrs. Price had lived. He realized Mrs. Price had passed away, but he thought perhaps the new tenants would allow them a visit. It was so arranged, and Harold was eager to take them on the tour. He was as proud as ever of his neighborhood and quite willing to share it with them. When asked about taking pictures, the new tenants insisted they take all the pictures they wished. Claire was as fascinated with what she saw as Mark had been. They indeed would use many of the ideas they observed.

Harold gave them much the same tour he had given Mark when he visited with him. Mark well remembered Harold's assurance his neighborhood was a beautiful place in the summer. The plant life, having become dormant or covered from sight, had come out in all its fullness of color. It was indeed a beautiful place, and Mark could readily appreciate the loving care Sidney put into it.

Victor was absorbed with the gorgeous snow-white clematis plant Sidney had been so proud of. "Wouldn't it be pretty between your house and ours? That would be a great spot for one of those!"

Mr. Mason had made plans for the next day, having purchased tickets for the double header at Tiger Stadium. It would be about an hour's drive to Detroit. After arriving there, they would have lunch and then go on to the games.

"You told me you were going to try to get reservations to stay in the Wixley Motel. I happen to know that's right on the road to Windsor. Assuming, of course, that's what you did arrange, it should work out quite conveniently." It was clear Mr. Mason wanted them to enjoy themselves while they were in Michigan.

After lunch, they sat visiting. Mrs. Mason was much like Mark had pictured her: quite attractive, pleasant, and cheerful. Mark had formed a rather accurate mental image of her from the portrait he saw. Mr. Mason was the same jovial individual as always, constantly making sure everyone was comfortable and having a good time.

He hadn't lost his desire to talk about his lifelong friend, Sidney. He told of many of their boyhood experiences together. "Perhaps," he said, as a smile crossed his face. Then directing his remarks to Mark, he continued, "Perhaps you remember seeing a scar on his upper arm. I think it faded considerably as he got older, but it used to be a nasty-looking thing." He smiled sheepishly. "I suppose it's just another of those tired old stories about kids stealing watermelons. I'm not especially proud of it, even if we were just kids. But Dave Hatfield just naturally set up a challenge for every boy who was a daredevil at heart. He had never actually shot anyone before, but we didn't know it at the time. We heard the shotgun blast and the pellets flying over our heads. Anyway, as we went flying across the patch toward the street, Sidney tripped over something and went sprawling right through a barbed wire fence. It cut a gash on Sidney's arm about fifteen inches long."

Harold was still grinning as he continued. "I can smile about it a little now, but it sure wasn't funny then. When I went to him, I felt the blood on his arm and on my hand. I thought he had been shot.

When I got to the streetlight and saw blood all over me, I ran to the closest house and had them call an ambulance for Sidney."

"I thought he was dying, and I let everyone know it. Well, it turned out he needed the special attention all right, but it wasn't from being shot. Everyone got a severe tongue-lashing, especially Dave Hatfield. As you might well imagine, it was our last attempt at watermelon stealing."

"Mark, I hope you don't mind me telling that story." Harold sounded as though he was apologizing for telling it. "I've given it some thought. It seems like I've been making Sidney sound like some kind of a saint. I realize your entire experience in meeting him was one greatly exemplifying his character. And even our visit concerning him here in Waterford when you were here tended to bring out only his best qualities. At the risk of damaging any of your fond memories of him, you probably should remember he was a man just as we are. Believe me, we grew up together, so I know. Don't misunderstand, Sidney was a fine person and a devoted Christian, as devoted as any man I've ever known. The point is he was just a man. As boys growing up, we stole watermelons, fibbed once in a while to our parents, and even smoked a pack of cigarettes one afternoon while we hid in the creek bottom over by Farley's grocery store. Oh, we paid for the cigarettes. We took the lawn mower along and rang every doorbell along the way until we found someone who would pay us for cutting their grass."

"I guess maybe you're right," Mark said, as he pondered the matter. "You're absolutely right in thinking I had him placed on a pedestal. I hadn't thought about it before, but it does seem difficult to think of him in any way but as a perfect gentleman." Mark looked at Harold in appreciation. "I'm glad you brought it to my attention. I guess it was obvious to everyone but me."

"How many members do you have in your class?" Mrs. Mason asked.

Mark lowered his head and peered at her, as though in shame. "I'm afraid there are only the four of us, Mrs. Mason. We occasionally invite others, ones who seem to show an interest in what we believe, but it never takes very long until we're back to a class of four. Maybe we're not persuasive enough in our discussions. I'm not sure what the reason is."

Harold spoke up quickly, as though coming to their defense, "My experience over the years has shown me the closer we get to the truth, the smaller the study groups become. It's a sad thing, but it seems to me, professing Christians simply don't want the responsibility of deciding upon making a change in their beliefs. Can't say I understand why that's the case. I wouldn't think they would feel comfortable in blaming their teachers if what they believed turned out to be wrong. I really don't know."

Mark was pleased when Victor thanked Harold for sending them the study pertaining to the eons. He told him how much he personally had enjoyed them. Harold was equally pleased they had been appreciated. He told them he had given out more than thirty copies of the study. "Some have enjoyed them, some I'll probably never know if they were even read. We just keep trying to be a witness to the truth," he said.

It was obvious Harold would like to get some kind of a discussion going with the young men who were his guests. He had the same kind of problem finding people wanting to discuss the distinctive message of Paul's writings, which anyone seems to have who strikes out in that direction. Most assume Paul merely takes a different approach to what they feel should be considered the same evangel as the rest of the apostles teach. "You know," he said, "it puzzles me a great deal why Paul seems to carefully distinguish between the uses of the pronouns, especially in the book of Ephesians. Have you ever given it any thought, Mark?"

Mark had not been aware of it before, and so it was an entirely new thought to him.

"The most obvious matter to me is those whom he speaks to as 'you' are a different group of people than those whom he refers to as 'we' and 'us.' I suppose the usual understanding is that it distinguishes between Paul and the other apostles and those to whom they are speaking, but it seems to me it's much more than that. If either of you ever come to an understanding, let me know what you discover."

It was a most enjoyable day of Bible study for all. Harold was a good teacher and obviously had spent many years in his pursuit for knowledge in the Word of God. The four of them received many good ideas for subjects to think about, and they looked forward to doing so. It was a fine experience to share their study with someone so knowledgeable and someone who based their study on the same premise as themselves. The time spent with Harold and his wife was refreshing indeed.

Mark told the Masons of their discovery of the possibility the eternal torment doctrine might be the solution to the matter of the secret of lawlessness. "We haven't fully substantiated that as yet," he said, "but we certainly like the way things are piecing together."

"That does seem interesting, Mark. Yes, indeed, very interesting." Giving a most satisfying look, he told Mark, "You must keep me informed on the matter. I'll be looking at it too, I assure you."

The next day proved to be a long day of baseball. Mark wondered if sitting through two games in one day was a very wise decision, especially for someone who had only been to one major league game in his lifetime before this evening. None of the rest of them had ever been to a major league ballpark. The Tigers split the two games with Philadelphia—the Tigers winning the first game, three to two, on a single in the ninth inning by Bill Tuttle driving in the decisive run. Mark read the Wednesday morning Detroit paper, which informed them the win was the twelfth of the season for Virgil Trucks.

"It says Willie Mays is running eight days ahead of Babe Ruth's home run record. Oh, oh, seven of those home runs were off Cardinal pitching. What do you think of this, Vicie boy? Stan, our man, hit his twenty eighth home run of the year, yesterday." Both Victor and Mark were Cardinal fans, and quite naturally, they thought highly of Stan Musial. "They beat the Giants, seven to four. Hey! Wally Moon got four hits."

After spending the night at the Wixley Motel and finishing their breakfast, it was just a short straight drive to where they crossed over into Ontario, Canada. Harold had certainly been right when he told them of the unique experience of driving under the Detroit River, when traveling through the Detroit Windsor Tunnel.

"Can you believe there could be an ocean liner steaming over our heads?" Victor said, as they drove through. "Harold said the United States and Canada have agreed to a major development of the Saint Lawrence Seaway. He said by 1960, the entire waterway would be open to ocean going vessels. I can certainly see why the Detroit River would be such an important part of the Seaway," he said, as he studied the map he held in his hands. "It appears to be the only access to the other Great Lakes. Otherwise, Lakes Huron, Michigan, and Superior would be completely cut off from the whole navigation system. Can you imagine seeing ocean liners in Chicago and Duluth? I guess Harold was sure right. What I haven't figured out is how they will ever get those big ships over Niagara Falls, especially those going upstream," Victor said dryly.

They followed highway number 3 across the southern portion of Ontario until they reached Port Colborne. From there, it was only a short distance to Niagara Falls. They reached the city early in the afternoon, having gotten an early start in the morning.

The tour sheet having been prepared for them, suggested they plan to spend at least one entire day taking in the various points of interest. Those events were a major part of their plans, and so they wanted to make the most of the visit. They sought as much advice as possible to ensure an enjoyable day and then set out on their own to see the sights. The lighting setup for after-dark viewing gave a spectacular display of the falls. They were told the view from the Canadian side, where the American Falls could be seen, was even more spectacular.

After the evening meal, Victor suggested they go to a drugstore to get something for Abigail's indigestion. It seemed she had been experiencing discomfort for some time but considered it a further stage of the morning sickness.

"I'm not so sure it is a normal symptom, Abbie. Maybe you should see a doctor about it," Claire suggested.

"I don't think it's anything to worry about. I just need to get some Alka-Seltzer or something. I'm sure it will do, at least until we get home. I can see my doctor then." She hadn't complained before because she didn't want to spoil anyone's good time.

"I'm sure there's a hospital in this city. We'll take you to the emergency ward, and then we'll know you'll be all right." Victor had thought she was more pale than usual but decided she was tired from all the traveling and just needed a good night's sleep. But if she was concerned, there probably was good reason.

It was decided she would visit the emergency ward and undergo an examination. If necessary, they could return home the next morning after she got some rest. At the hospital, a blood test was made. It was determined she was anemic and should have more extensive tests made when she reached home. But for the present, she was given a prescription for the anemia. Abigail did feel better after resting, and it was decided to spend the day at Niagara Falls. The medication seemed to help considerably, so they decided to continue their trip but allow enough time for a leisurely journey home.

An appointment was made for her to be examined by her own doctor as soon as possible. More tests were made, and when the results were fully known, her condition was diagnosed as pernicious anemia. Dr. Moore assured her, though it was at one time considered a very dangerous condition, it was no longer measured as a menace. "In fact, with the newer medications, it's relatively easy to control," he assured her.

They were all quite concerned about her health, especially because she had been so tired all the time. Victor had coached Abigail to ask for a careful explanation of her condition. When she related that to Dr. Moore, he was very cooperative with her and even drew a picture of the normal body function concerning her problem.

Abigail tried her best to remember the things the doctor told her in explaining her condition but relied heavily upon the picture he had drawn. She had gone through the explanation with Victor but explained it again for Mark and Claire because of their great concern.

"He said this drawing represents the castle factor. The intrinsic factor is a substance found in the gastric juices from the stomach lining. The extrinsic factor is in the food we eat. These combine, resulting in the formation of a third factor called the anti-anemic factor." She grinned as she continued. "If all this gets too technical, be sure and let me know. He said the purpose for the anti-anemic factor is to bring about the maturity of the red blood cells of the body. This third factor is taken by the blood stream to the liver where it is stored until needed. The red blood cells are manufactured in the bone marrow. See, that's a picture of a bone. As they are produced, these factors are called upon to cause them to mature. They are again dumped into the blood stream and taken to the bones to do their job.

"That's what's supposed to happen. He says a deficiency of any one of those factors can be the cause of pernicious anemia, but pernicious anemia happens as a result of the deficiency.

"Dr. Moore says the walls of the stomach receive a poor blood supply, either not enough blood, or a deficiency of properties producing the intrinsic factor. I think pernicious anemia occurs when the anti-anemic factor is unable to cause the red blood cells to do their work. Now if you want to know any more about my condition, you'll have to ask Dr. Moore."

"It all sounds clear to me," Mark said, with a casual shrug of his shoulders.

"He says we should have nothing to worry about, and he hopes you will all understand my explanation," she said with a laugh. "Now when I think about it, he laughed too when he said it."

CHAPTER 17

After a few days of liver and stomach preparations prescribed by her doctor, Abigail began feeling much better. Her color improved rapidly. She regained her energy level over the next few weeks, and even the rapid heartbeat slowed to a more normal count.

While all this was encouraging to the doctor, the gastritis returned causing her a great deal of apprehension. Because of its recurrence, it was diagnosed as chronic gastritis. However, the blood cell count returned to normal, removing cause of concern for the anemic condition.

Late September rolled around. It was a beautiful autumn day, and Mark had just got off work and was making the most of it by working in the garage.

"What are you up to, Buddy?" came the sound of a voice from behind him.

Mark turned to see Victor sitting in his wheelchair at the garage entrance. "Hey, I didn't hear you coming. Nice day to be outside," he said. "Good idea, getting some of this sunshine."

"Just oiled my wheelchair," Victor said with a laugh. "That's why you didn't hear me. Abbie and I were just going out to get a bite to eat," he explained.

"How is Abbie? Is her gastritis any better?"

"I don't think so, Mark. She seems to be about the same. I don't know if there's anything to worry about or not, but I think Abbie's rather concerned. She doesn't say much. She sits around a lot, sort of daydreaming. Either she's daydreaming, or she doesn't feel good. Doc says the baby's doing fine."

"Maybe she needs a change of scenery," Mark suggested. "It might help get her mind off the baby."

"What are you thinking about? Got something in mind?" Victor asked.

"Nothing in particular," he answered. "I just heard the weather forecast on the radio. They said it should be like this all weekend. Maybe we should take a little weekend trip to somewhere."

"Sounds great. Is it on the map?" Victor asked.

Mark gave a hearty laugh. "We'll get a map and see if we can find it."

Claire and Abigail were in the yard where Claire was digging around some flowers. The idea immediately appealed to them.

"Do you want to leave early in the morning?" Abigail asked.

"I have a feeling he means right now," Claire explained, directing her remark to Abigail.

"Sure! Why wait 'til morning?" Mark was excited. "Looks to me like you and Vic are ready to go. Claire and I can get ready in no time. We'll toss some clothes in a suitcase and be on our way. Okay with you, Claire?"

Claire began laughing. "I think we're all crazy, but it sounds like fun. We don't even know where we're going."

"Sure, we do," Victor interrupted. "We're on our way to somewhere, so get moving while I find it on the map."

They were approaching the intersection with Brady Street. "We have to make a decision," Mark said. "Shall we go north, or shall we go south?"

Claire spoke up quickly, "Let's go south along the Mississippi. We'll make our decisions as we go along."

"Why don't we just keep following the river," Mark suggested. "We'll make sure we only go as far as we can comfortably drive back on Sunday. Let's just head down sixty-one."

No one was enjoying the drive more than Abigail was. It seemed to be the best therapy she could have had. "I just love letting the wind blow through my hair. There's nothing like it. Of course, there's nothing like combing the tangles out, either," she said with a girlish laugh. "I feel so, so irresponsible, and it's kind of fun too. It's nice to leave your worries behind and enjoy life."

Victor registered concern in Abigail's last comment, but he didn't want to diminish her enthusiasm. Both Mark and Claire noticed, but neither had any intentions of responding.

Somethings wrong, Mark thought. *Something is very wrong.* But he knew the answer would have to wait the course. Right now, they were going to enjoy the weekend.

For quite some time, they enjoyed the rush of air as they drove along, but as the evening wore on, the cool of autumn made too much of its presence.

After crossing the Des Moines River, they stopped to fill the gas tank, and while there, they picked up a road map of the state of Missouri. When paying for their purchase, Mark saw a holder containing pamphlets placed there by the Hannibal Chamber of Commerce. "How far to Hannibal?" he asked the attendant.

"Between fifty and fifty-five miles" came the answer. "If you need reservations, I'd suggest you make them now. The motels fill up about every night during the tourist season. Most of the good motels are listed in the brochure."

"Thanks, sounds like a good idea," Mark said to him.

After discussing the matter with the rest of the group, Mark completed reservations on the first call, but they were the last available rooms at that motel. The cashier would hold the rooms until 11:00 p.m., which would give them adequate time to arrive and make arrangements. Once they were settled in, they would find a restaurant.

"Thank you, sir," Mark said to the attendant, as they were about to leave. He thanked him again for being so helpful. "I think you may have saved us a lot of grief later on."

The customers had cleared out of the station, and the attendant seemed to want to visit. "Are you familiar with the city of Hannibal?" he asked.

"Never been there before in my life!"

"I probably sound like the chamber of commerce, but I was born and raised there. There's a lot to see if you have some extra time."

"We have all day tomorrow," Mark said. "What do you suggest that's entertaining?"

"Well, as you probably know, Hannibal was the hometown of

Samuel Clemens. Under the penname of Mark Twain, he wrote many books. I suppose the best-known book he wrote was *The Adventures of Huckleberry Finn.* The residential area where he grew up has been preserved as it was in his day. There are several buildings you can go through, including his boyhood home. There's a real nice museum containing things from the era.

"Let's see, you can take the 'Twainland Tour.' It takes you to most of the places of interest. There's the lighthouse on Cardiff Hill. I wouldn't suggest a pregnant lady should climb it, though. There's Lover's Leap. I wouldn't suggest any of you become too adventurous at that one," he said with a chuckle.

"And then there's the caves. They're open to public tours. They had a part in Mark Twain's story. I'd say there's enough to keep you busy for most of the day.

"Oh yes! There's a couple of mansions, which are well worth the time it takes to go through," he said, as an afterthought.

Obviously, the young man was proud of his town's attraction to tourist trade. "Hope you have a good time, sir," he said, as Mark turned to leave.

"Thanks again."

The evening before had been one filled with fun for all of them. They arose early and enjoyed a hearty breakfast and were set to take in whatever good things the day might offer.

While everyone enjoyed the day's events, it was Abigail who had the time of her life, and they all felt that was the way it should be. After all, she was the reason for the little jaunt in the first place. "What a day!" she exclaimed, as the afternoon wore on. "I've never had so much fun."

"Maybe we should stop trying to plan vacations and just have more of these spur-of-the-moment trips," Claire said, at the same time observing everyone's cheerfulness.

Mark laughed. "There's one thing wrong with that idea. What if we want to go to the Grand Canyon or Yellowstone Park? We can't very well drive there after supper some evening."

Abigail wasn't the only one having the time of their life. Mark felt a sentimental attachment to the town and was feeling that, in a sense, this was his town too. He was thinking of many of the things written in the various brochures he had read. He wondered if a song had been written about the town or at least about the things the local people cherished about Mark Twain. There should be enough material contained in the brochures to write a knowledgeable song. He remembered from the "Twainland Tour," the quaint-looking lighthouse near the top of Cardiff Hill, and then seeing it up close. Also the beautiful scene of the river they had observed from the ridge of the hill where the statue stood. He suggested returning to the spot. They were able to observe it all at leisure then.

A cluster of barges was seen in the far distance to the north going upstream. Mark had seen many barges traveling up and down the Mississippi, but never had he seen such an enchanting view of river life as this one afforded. *Perhaps some things just don't change,* he thought. In the days of Samuel Clemens, river traffic was a way of travel for many and certainly an important way of transporting goods. Although not many paying fares traveled the river anymore, there was still a great deal of barge traffic, especially hauling coal and grain. Mark had seen farm equipment being shipped that way.

He couldn't help thinking just about everyone ought to appreciate the events they experienced. In his thoughts, the names Tom, Huck, and Becky replaced the names in the old saying, every Tom, Dick, and Harry. When he made his thoughts known, Victor seized upon the idea of calling Abigail, Becky, in view of the way she had been drawn into the mood of it all. For the rest of the trip, her name was "Becky."

The consensus of opinion was, no amount of planning could have provided a more entertaining and exhilarating experience than they had enjoyed this day. While everyone knew Abigail's spirits were high, they also understood the reality of it: whatever was causing her to worry would likely return in a short time. But for the moment, she was happy, and everyone was happy for her.

Mark and Claire and Victor and Abigail held their weekly Bible studies during the pregnancy. Abigail became more apprehensive and uneasy with each passing week. Early November arrived, and Claire was no longer able to contain her anxiety.

"What's wrong, Abbie?" Claire asked one evening following

Bible study. "Something's wrong and you're not telling us what it is." At first, she denied anything was troubling her, but she soon realized she hadn't been very adept at hiding her concern, even denying it to Victor who was becoming frustrated with her for not confiding in him.

"Oh, Claire, I don't know what's wrong. I just feel something is terribly wrong, and I don't know what to do about it." She was expressing all the fear she had been trying to avoid showing. "I don't know if I can have my baby. It doesn't seem like I can possibly carry it much longer, and it's still six weeks to the due date. Dr. Moore thinks the gastritis has me worried. He says they can run tests to try to determine if something is wrong. He suggested we do it right away so I'll have peace of mind."

"Then that's what we will do," Victor said. "All this worry could do harm to the baby, not to mention what it's already doing to you. We want both you and the baby to be well."

"I know we should run tests, and that's what has me really worried now 'cause I think they'll reveal something awful." Abigail was sobbing now. "I think I have more than just a chronic case of gastritis. I think there's something, which might be a problem for my baby. I want my baby more than anything else in this world."

Victor was usually quite passive in his approach to serious matters, but this time, he spoke with authority. "We'll have the doctor arrange for the tests to be run as soon as they can be scheduled," he said. "There's no need for you to be so worried."

"Claire, there's something I want to ask of you and Mark." Abigail held her head down as she spoke. "I know it's asking an awfully lot, but it would take such a burden off me if you would agree to it."

"If it's something we can do, Abbie, you know we'll do our best to carry out your wishes."

"If something should happen to me, I'd like you and Mark to help Victor keep our baby."

Mark spoke up immediately, "Now wait a minute, Abbie, you're getting all worked up without knowing if you have a problem to worry about." Mark wanted to be reassuring but wondered if he was doing so. He realized nothing was very clear about the entire situation. "Why don't you wait until the tests are run and more is known about it?"

"Please, Mark," she pleaded, "tell me if you will help Victor care for the child. And if anything should ever happen to Victor, would you adopt the baby as your own?"

Both Mark and Claire were speechless for a moment. "Oh, Abbie, you know we would. But nothing is going to happen to you or Vic," Claire said, trying just as hard to be reassuring. "Now you just stop all the nonsense and get on with having your baby—the baby girl we all hope you have."

"I'm afraid, Claire. I-I-I'm just so afraid."

The tests were scheduled and made as requested by Victor and Abigail. More tests were made. None of the fears, which plagued Abigail, were worse than the truth proved to be. X-rays revealed a large tumor attached to the lining of the stomach and surrounding part of the liver. It was highly probable the tumor was malignant. Tests of the actual tissue would have to be made before knowing for sure. Whatever the type of tumor, it would be an extremely serious matter to operate for its removal while being so far along in her pregnancy.

The days were difficult ones for all. Even the doctors were unable to agree on what was best in this situation. It had come down to a matter of whether to save Abigail's life, or the life of the baby, in all probability. Whether it would be surgery to remove the tumor, or a cesarean section to deliver the baby, either one would seriously complicate the other. But perhaps the most serious complication of all was from the insistence the baby be the first consideration no matter what. It was determined the baby should be taken as soon as possible, but they were equally sure it must not be taken too early.

Many evenings were spent together on those days bringing them nearer the time for delivery. Abigail still had a month to go before the end of the full term. Mark and Claire had been a great comfort to them both, especially to Abigail.

On the evening before she was scheduled to enter the hospital, just as they had done every evening for some time, they sat in the living room in Mark and Claire's home.

"Do you guys remember on our trip to Hannibal, I mentioned

wanting to write a song about the town and about Mark Twain's association with it?" Mark asked.

"I meant to ask you about it!" Abigail exclaimed. "Did you write it? Did you really write a song about Hannibal?"

Mark was pleased she was interested in his song and was eager to play it for her and for everybody. "Sure, would you like to hear it?" he asked. He was already on his way to seat himself on the piano bench.

"No, I don't think anybody wants to hear it," Victor said dryly. "Why are you sitting on the piano bench, Mark?" he asked. "You never sit on the piano bench."

"Shut up, Vic!" Abigail exclaimed. "Give it one of your introductions with the big flourish," she said with almost childish glee.

Here on the Hannibal Shore

On the Mississippi banks
there stands a small town—
the most famous small town anywhere.
This is called Twainland—
the cherished Mark Twainland,
here on the Hannibal shore.
Every Tom, and Huck and Becky,
will be dreaming
of the days that were so long ago;
just be a kid then,
and do what they did then
here on the Hannibal shore.
I gaze across the waters just flowing by,
there's riverboats I can see,
and there stands the lighthouse
way up on Cardiff Hill—
looks like it's beckoning me.
Let's go searching for the treasure
in the caverns—
climb the hill that stands above the town:
wherever your own town,
come make this your hometown,
here on the Hannibal shore!
Here on the Hannibal shore!

"I love it! I remember how everyone was calling me Becky that day. What a fun day it was," she exclaimed. She seemed to forget her worries for a time. "It's a beautiful song, Mark. Vic, Claire, Mark"—Abigail's eyes met Victor's as the tears began streaming over her cheeks—"I will remember that weekend as long as I live. I can't recall a time I enjoyed more than I did that weekend."

The excitement was wearing on Abigail, and she was well aware of it. "I think I should get some sleep now," she said weakly. "Tomorrow will be a big day."

"Just remember all of us will be in the waiting room when you come out of your surgery," Claire assured her. "And our prayers will be with you, tonight and tomorrow."

The next morning, Mark and Claire were suddenly awakened by the sounds of sirens screaming as they approached their street.

"They're coming this way," Claire shouted, quickly getting out of bed.

Mark was already at the window, looking out into the early morning dawn. "They're stopping at Vic's," he said. "Oh no! It must be Abbie. Something must have happened to Abbie."

He went racing toward the Britton home. With both of them in their pajamas, Claire ran to catch up. They arrived even before the ambulance attendants reached the front door. The resuscitation equipment was just arriving in case it was needed.

"What is it, Vic?" Claire asked while entering the living room. His face a ghostly white, Victor was gripped with fear of losing Abigail. With a great deal of difficulty, he managed to say, "I think Abbie's dying! She woke me up g-g-gasping for breath. Then she just went limp. She wouldn't talk. I think she's dying."

Victor regained his composure, somewhat. "Help her," he pleaded with the attendants. "Don't let anything happen to her." The resuscitation equipment was being hooked up so they could administer needed oxygen. Her face was pale. There were no signs of life visible to Mark and Claire. They immediately took her on a stretcher to the ambulance, with the equipment still attached. Because of Victor being confined to a wheelchair, they were unable to take the time of allowing him to ride in the ambulance.

Victor gave the attendants the name of her doctor. Apologizing to Victor, they quickly went on their way toward getting her to the hospital.

Neighbors from as far as two blocks away had congregated. All wanted to be of help if there was something they could do. Mrs. Walters volunteered to call Abigail's mother to let her know.

"Mrs. Lane will probably still be at home before leaving for work," Claire told her. "She's listed under Harry G. Lane."

"Vic," Mark said to him, "Claire and I will get dressed and be right back to get you. We'll take you to the hospital right away."

Quickly, they returned home, taking time only to change to their street clothes so they could get back to Victor. Just as they were about to leave the house, the sound of a gunshot rang out.

"Oh, dear God!" Mark shouted. "It came from Vic's house. Dear God, don't let it be what I think it is," he muttered, as they went running toward the Britton house. Claire was close behind.

Mark arrived ahead of Claire, entering through the front door. They went straight to the kitchen, and there, still in his wheelchair, was Victor's body, limp and lifeless.

"Don't look, Claire," he shouted. But it was too late. Claire had entered directly behind him. Victor had pointed the barrel of his shotgun to his head and then pulled the trigger.

A number of neighbors hadn't yet returned to their homes when this happened, some even followed them inside.

Claire stood, sobbing hysterically. "Why! Why would he do such a thing?" she cried. "Oh, why, Vic?" she said, looking once again at his shattered face and skull.

They were the first to reach the scene, and so Mark felt they should call the police and report the incident. It was difficult to call it a suicide, although there was no doubt in anyone's mind. They reported it as an accident, further explaining how it appeared he had taken his own life. Because of the great number of witnesses to the sound of the shot, the police allowed them to go on to the hospital. They offered to make a police report later in the day if necessary.

At the hospital, they met Mrs. Lane. She had just arrived a few minutes ahead of them. "They can't tell me anything about Abbie's condition yet. I think she's still alive though because they took her into surgery immediately." Mrs. Lane was shaking from the shock, and it had been so sudden.

There was no further word on her condition, and they were informed there probably would be none for some time. "If you'll remain in the waiting room, the doctor will talk to you as soon as he's available," one of the nurses told them, trying to be helpful. "Dr. Moore is with her now. It just happened he was already in the hospital when Mrs. Britton was admitted."

Mark and Claire took Mrs. Lane to the waiting room, knowing they must tell her of Victor's death. It was extremely difficult for her. She had stood by them all through Victor's ordeal brought about by the accident, the surgery, the long recovery, and the disappointment in learning Victor would remain in a wheelchair for the rest of his life.

"I called Harry at work," Mrs. Lane told them. "He was out somewhere, but they'll send him here as soon as they contact him." Mrs. Lane was concerned for Mr. Britton, knowing it would be a tragic thing for him. "I don't suppose anyone has informed Ray about Victor's death," she said. "It will be so hard on him. He's had such a struggle getting over Cecelia's death. Victor's accident just about put him in the mental hospital. Victor was their only child. Ray loved Abbie as much as he did Victor. He used to tell Abbie, 'Now we have the daughter we always wanted.' Oh, dear!" she exclaimed. "I'm just chattering away. I'm sorry, don't pay any attention to me."

"That's all right, Mrs. Lane, just be as comfortable as you can," Claire told her, hoping she could relax while waiting for the doctor to give them a report. "Abbie and Vic mentioned his parents some, but they really didn't tell us much about them. Mr. Britton was a fine-looking gentleman, and Victor certainly did take after his father. We only met him once."

After a time, Dr. Moore appeared in the doorway of the waiting room asking for Mrs. Lane. "Mrs. Lane," he said when they were seated together, "we did everything we could possibly do to save Mrs. Britton's life and the life of her baby. I'm sorry to have to tell you this, but your daughter died on the operating table. I must say she had an extraordinary will to deliver her baby alive. She gave up only when the baby was in our hands. The baby is small, of course, but it appears to be normal and healthy. We will naturally watch it closely for a few weeks, but there seems to be no problem, at least for now. I can't tell you how sorry I am, but I hope there is consolation in knowing you have a beautiful little granddaughter. I was just informed about Mr. Britton's death. I truly am sorry, and I want to offer my condolences to you. I know it has to be extremely difficult."

Claire offered to contact Victor's father, but Mrs. Lane felt perhaps she should do it herself and felt also she was up to the task. "Harry should be here any time, so we'll probably go over together."

"I had no idea they could save the baby's life," Claire said, as she and Mark were leaving the building.

"Oh my!" Mark exclaimed. "It just occurred to me—the promise we made to Abbie, I mean. We told her we would adopt her baby if anything happened to her and Vic."

"Oh, dear! Well, we have to do it, don't we?" Claire said, more as an assertion than a question. "I can't believe what's happened and all in just a few short hours. What are we going to do, Mark?"

"I don't know. I don't know if any legal action will be necessary. If it comes to that, there's no one on earth knowing about Abbie asking us to adopt her baby. It would be our word against the world." "And what if Mrs. Lane decides she wants the baby?" Claire asked. "It's her granddaughter, and she's such a lovely person."

Mark sat quietly for some time, then he said softly; "Claire, remember what you said to me one day about us having children?" Without waiting for her reply, he said, "You told me if God wants us to have children, we'll have them. And if God doesn't want us to have children, we won't have them. Maybe we should continue to look at it in the same way," he added comfortingly.

CHAPTER 18

Deanna Claire Britton was a healthy baby girl. Tipping the scales at a mere four pounds at birth and losing a few ounces in the days following, she began gaining weight. All the nurses thought her to be special partly because of the tragic way in which she became orphaned immediately after birth. But she was a beautiful little girl and in their words, "She hardly ever cries, and she sleeps most of the time."

Mark and Claire decided at first only to suggest their desire to adopt the baby. They spoke with both Mr. and Mrs. Lane about it. On the one hand, the Lanes couldn't bear to give up their grandchild to adoption. They felt a strong sense of responsibility to see the child retaining its family ties, especially keeping the name. On the other hand, the Lanes were well aware of the close friendship between the two couples. Abigail had told her mother what she would name the baby if it was a girl, and they had in turn told the doctor the name their daughter chose. They deeply appreciated the overtures Mark and Claire made, but they decided they should make every effort to raise the child. Neither Mark nor Claire could gather the courage to inform the Lanes of their daughter's expressed desire for them to claim the baby as their own.

"I suppose we were wrong," Claire said, as they walked to their car after the conversation with Mr. and Mrs. Lane. "I just don't have the heart to tell them. What are we going to do?"

"We're certainly finding ourselves in the middle of a bad situation," Mark agreed. "I don't think the problem will just go away, but let's wait a few days before we do anything. We can talk to the doctor and see what he suggests. We probably haven't a leg to stand on.

Apparently, neither Abbie nor Vic said anything about their desire to anyone else."

"Maybe we should speak with Mr. Britton. Oh, dear! It would make it look as though we want him to take sides in the issue. I'm sure there's no way he could take custody of the poor little thing," she said as an afterthought.

"I think we'd better let God work out whatever is right for everyone concerned. We do have the faith to do that, don't we, Claire?"

Claire's thoughts were far away, but she was aware of what Mark had said. "You're right! You're absolutely right! Why do we feel we have to solve every problem ourselves? I feel much better about it already."

"It's good to know we have a God with Whom we can leave all our worries," Mark said.

As the days passed, there was no change in the Lanes' approach to the matter. There seemed to be no considerations other than taking the child home when it was ready to leave the hospital.

Mark was concerned as to what was best for the child. The Lanes had raised their family. He felt they should desire their lives be free from further responsibility. He and Claire had wanted a child for years and seemed to be unable to have one of their own. It could be the perfect solution. And there was still the best reason of all: they had been Abigail's choice since she first realized things weren't progressing, as they should.

They decided to approach Dr. Moore about the problem and get his opinion. "I quite understand your dilemma," he said to them. "I think situations like this are usually decided by a judge. As far as I know, he'll decide who will be given custody in raising the little girl. I suppose his most important consideration will be of the age of the grandparents, both now and by the time the child is grown, also whether or not they are enjoying reasonably good health now."

It was the doctor's further opinion, if the situation should prove untenable to the judge, then an orphan's home and the adoption process would likely be the alternative. "I honestly don't know what his feelings would be."

"I quite understand what you're saying, Doctor, but it seems terribly unfair," Claire said to him. "I realize it is our word against everyone else's, but Abbie was so sincere in her request for us to adopt her baby. We simply didn't realize there would be reason for so much concern. It seems obvious now Abbie had some sort of premonition and wanted to cover all her fears. Oh, dear! I wish we had followed up on the matter then."

"I indeed sympathize with you in your problem," the doctor said to her. "But you could not have anticipated things turning out as they have, and you certainly can't blame yourselves. Let me talk to Mr. and Mrs. Lane. I'm assuming you haven't discussed Abbie's request with them."

"No, sir, we haven't," Mark began to explain. "We just thought if they would give the baby to us because they wanted to, it would be much better than appearing to put pressure on them, and there would be much less room for regrets later. Frankly," he added, "I honestly thought they would welcome the offer, but it certainly isn't the case."

"I'll try to put it to them as plainly as you've stated it to me. I can't promise anything, but it seems to me it surely won't hurt to let them know. Maybe it will help later on, even if it doesn't convince them now." The doctor gave them a reassuring smile as he left them.

One evening later in the week, Mark stood looking out the window viewing the area lying between their property and where the Brittons had lived. "Do you remember?" Mark turned to see precisely where Claire was. "Oh, there you are. I had the strange feeling I was talking to myself."

"Don't feel bad," she replied. "I've felt the same way for days. Mark, I want her so bad I can hardly stand it. And it doesn't seem like anyone cares."

Mark placed his arm around her and kissed her on the cheek. "I have a feeling it will turn out very good, Claire. Don't ask me why. I just feel God is very much in this matter, and He's working it out for the good of everyone. I wish I could be more reassuring."

"That's all the reassurance I need. I didn't know you felt so strongly about it. If you have faith, then I'll try to believe it too. What were you going to ask me if I remembered?" she asked.

"Oh! Do you remember when we were in Michigan looking at the clematis plant? It bloomed in the yard next door to where the Rawlings lived. Remember how Vic remarked about how beautiful one of those would be, standing between their house and ours? What do you think of the idea of us planting one? A clematis panniculitis I believe was the name of it. We can plant it in the spring. We'll let it be a memorial to both Vic and Abbie. It would give us something special to remember them by for as long as we live here. We should make sure we plant it on our side of the property line so there will never be trouble from the neighbors. Though, I don't know why anyone should complain. I can hardly wait for spring so we can do some landscaping in the yard. We'll put some of those great ideas we saw in Michigan to good use."

Mark felt Claire grip his hand as they continued to stand gazing out the window. "You have Vic and Abbie on your mind, don't you?" he asked.

"Yes, yes, I do. They're on my mind most of the time these days. I was thinking about the night you talked to Vic about the problem he had—you know, the problem."

"Yes, I know," Mark interrupted. "I remember it well."

"I've often wondered what the problem was about," she said. "Vic thanked me at least twenty times for helping him. He would tell me everything was great, yet he never told me any more than that, and I never asked. I figured I wouldn't pry."

"Since Vic is gone, do you still feel obligated to keep it confidential?" she asked. "I happen to know he never discussed it with Abbie, at least not up until a few weeks before he died."

Mark no longer felt it necessary to keep the truth from Claire, especially since it was obvious she was still curious. He related the experience to her, much the way Victor had stated it, for it had been an experience so vividly placed in his memory he might well never forget it. "It's hard to comprehend things like that, I mean things affecting a child so deeply, and place it so indelibly in its memory. What the minister did seems cruel, even unchristian, yet I know he was sincere, and he no doubt thought he was doing what scripture taught as being right. I have to confess I've spent many hours trying to figure out what can be the good coming from it. I know all things happen for a reason, but I still need reassurance sometimes."

"Well, it's a problem for me too. I was already having difficulty with his suicide, now you tell me this. It makes me angry, Mark. I have a hard time dealing with anyone committing suicide, but why! Why would he take his life when a child is going to be left without a parent? It-it-it seems like pure selfishness he wouldn't think about the poor little baby and want everything good for it."

"Claire!" Mark interrupted, hardly able to believe what she was saying. "Claire, don't you realize Vic probably never had the slightest notion the baby would survive the tragedy? Think about it, Claire! The baby wasn't due for another month. When they took Abbie to the hospital in the ambulance, there seemed no hope for her to even live long enough to get there. I doubt Vic had any hope at all for the baby. In fact, I would wager, the thought of a child being born alive never even crossed his mind. Quite frankly, it never occurred to me." Claire felt guilty for her response. "Oh, Mark! I admit I was wrong. I remember I was just as surprised as anyone to learn of the baby being alive, not to mention being strong and healthy. I guess I just want to blame Vic for taking his life. It still makes me angry. Now I don't know who to be angry with. I don't like being angry with God, yet I can't understand why He would allow such a terrible thing to happen."

"We all become angry with God sometimes, Claire, but it's always out of frustration."

Claire was finding it hard to contain her anger. "It wasn't Vic's fault in the matter happening to him when he was a boy, either," she said. "What a torture it must have been, always thinking God was just waiting for the opportunity to strike him down. And all those kids being hurt, and thinking it was God out to punish them. I'm glad Vic and Abbie had those five years of happiness together. They were happy, don't you think?"

"There's no question about that," Mark said to her after a brief pause. He had been deep in thought when she asked her question.

"Perhaps, Claire, if we must be angry with someone, we should be angry with ourselves."

"That's a strange thing to say," she said, giving a quizzical look. "How could this possibly be our fault?"

"That's not quite what I mean. It just occurs to me, all the things happening are according to God's will. God works all things out according to His Own counsel. Instead of looking for someone to blame for things happening, maybe we should just accept the fact God allows it. It may be we already have the solution, if we would just put things together in our minds. I guess what I'm saying is, in the final analysis, maybe it was God's will for Vic to take his own life." Mark spent a great deal of his spare time thinking on those matters he and Claire had discussed. He followed through on the study of terms, which seemed deeply involved in the subject, such as sin, evil, and even Satan himself. He found a number of articles written by A.E. Knoch and printed in the Unsearchable Riches periodical. The more he searched, the more convinced he was, the origin of those matters had to be traced back to God in one way or another. Of course, it couldn't be said God directly created sin, yet the creation of Satan and evil could have no other possible origin than coming from God. And it seemed quite plain, if God created Satan and evil, then ultimately, it must be acknowledged the entrance of sin into His plan and purpose had to be according to His Own counsel. When all was considered, it came down to the fact God did not create sin, yet it was according to His will for every creature to be put in the position where they cannot avoid sinning.

Mark was realizing one more experience of coming to grips with the deeper things of God. How the church fathers must have fought to keep truths such as this from undermining the strange doctrines of the centuries. Apparently, it was one more of the dogmas retained from the pagan philosophies of the period following the time of Christ, which hold there are at least two gods in control of the universe: one in control of good, the other in control of evil. Each was fighting desperately to gain total victory over the other. The question Mark was asking himself was of how any rational person could believe such nonsense. Yet he soon came to the recognition it was no worse than believing in eternal torment as he once believed. But wasn't it essentially what he had been taught or at least what he was forced to conclude from what he was taught?

Mark realized it would be extremely difficult to make an appointment with the judge to discuss any plans for adopting the Britton infant. He had contacted an attorney to act on their behalf. They sat in the reception room of his office waiting to be called. The two of them discussed the subject of the origin of sin and evil. Only one other person was in the room: a man reading a magazine and sitting a couple of seats away from them.

Their conversation continued as they sat in the waiting room, and Mark was anxious to relate some of the things he had learned to the subject at hand. They had discussed those matters in considerable depth, when Mark said softly, "In a way, it is our fault we don't understand why God allows all these terrible things to happen mostly because we don't need to understand. The only thing we really need to know is, God has a reason for it and no matter how bad it may seem, it will turn out good simply because it occurs because of His counsel. I was reading in the book of Job about all the evil coming upon him. He said to his wife something like this, 'We accept the good God gives us, shouldn't we also accept the evil?' The Bible says Job was perfect and upright in the eyes of God. Yet when Satan told God it was because of a hedge placed around Job and all his possessions that he remained perfect, the Lord gave Satan power over him. Now whatever else we learn from the book of Job, we learn Satan had power over him only because God gave it to him. It doesn't exactly sound like Satan's power is in any way equal with God's power. We also know the Lord set limits on the control Satan would have."

"You know," Claire said to him, "it seems to me, it's just one more of those matters the church won't allow to be taught because it goes against the eternal torment doctrine."

"That's right, just like Victor pointed out to us. They can't allow any of those things to be associated with God, for it would make Him responsible for them. They simply can't allow God to be responsible for creating evil or even Satan. That's one instance where they have to teach another error in order to support the error of their hellfire and damnation theory."

"Pardon me," said the man seated nearby. "I couldn't help overhearing your conversation, and I do apologize for eavesdropping, but I was very interested in your comments. I'm sorry. My name is Leland Bartholomew. I'm a radio announcer on station KLA.D. I have a program airing each Saturday morning called *Viewpoint.* I must tell you, I find your ideas quite refreshing."

This was certainly a different response than Mark had grown accustomed to, and he did appreciate Mr. Bartholomew's comment. "Thank you, sir. My name is Mark Hayes, and this is my wife, Claire. We were just waiting to see Attorney Chad Worthington. I guess I got a little loud with our discussion. I'm glad we didn't offend you. It seems most people are offended with our approach to scriptural discussion."

"I don't believe you're a pastor, are you? I thought I knew all the pastors in this community," he said.

"We had a small Bible study class meeting once a week, but we're down to just my wife and I now. Our classes never seem to grow very large," Mark said with a laugh. "And no, I'm not a pastor."

"I wonder," Mr. Bartholomew said, trying to sound casual. "I wonder if you might consider taking part in a debate some Saturday soon? It seems to me a debate about evil should stir up a healthy interest for our listeners."

"Sir"—Mark became serious as he spoke—"I can assure you, my views indeed would stir up an interest, but I'm afraid it wouldn't be a very healthy one. It's my observation these matters are, almost without exception, viewed with extreme disdain. You see we believe all humanity is being reconciled to God and all creation will come to know God at the consummation of this physical realm, as we now know it. I can state unequivocally, there is not likely one pastor in this entire community who would allow it to go unchallenged, at least not publicly. What they believe, in their private studies, might be another matter. I think, sir, and I say this with all due respect to you, you would be letting yourself in for all kinds of attack from the local ministry. I've been verbally attacked by ministers ever since I came to believe as I do, so you see, I'm well aware of the cruelty they can exhibit when their stand on eternal torment is challenged. Sometimes, I wonder how they can call themselves Christians, to say nothing of being ministers entrusted with God's Word."

"Well, Mark, if what you say is true, then I guess you'd have to admit, if you were going to defend your viewpoint, it wouldn't be hard to find someone to challenge it. Isn't that about what you were telling me?" "We have no disagreement there," Mark said with a laugh.

Mr. Bartholomew became quite serious. "Mark, I'm impressed with your interest in scripture. I'm impressed with your self-styled approach to study. And I'm impressed with the confidence you exude. Frankly, I think the things I hear you say contain a great deal of logic. It seems to me there should be many of our listeners willing to learn more about these matters."

Mark was quite hesitant about following through. It was never his desire to speak out simply to cause controversy. Controversy never promotes truth in a positive way, and he had too much respect for the Word to do anything, which might be construed as mockery. If he thought there was the slightest chance, he would refuse immediately.

Leland Bartholomew sensed Mark's reluctance. "I note a feeling of reservation in your expression," he said to Mark. "I think we feel somewhat the same about how we treat the things of scripture. I also assure you, I won't permit ridicule between participants on my program. I have always been able to keep close reigns on the flow of things. Even when there seems to be a lack of preparation, I try to help them express their position. But I will not allow them to belittle the Bible, or one another, even if I feel the other one is totally wrong. I think if someone were to look bad, it would be as much a reflection on me as it would be on them."

"Mark," he said, still expressing himself quite seriously, "I would like you to debate one of the local pastors concerning the things you spoke of in your conversation with Mrs. Hayes. You mentioned the creation of sin, evil, and Satan."

"Hold on!" Mark interrupted. "I didn't say sin was created. Evil and Satan were created by God but not sin."

"I'm sorry! I didn't mean to imply something you didn't say. Can we say God originated sin or allowed it to begin? Am I using acceptable terms now?" he asked, obviously wanting to build a workable platform for a debate.

"Actually, Leland—" Mark wanted the matter to be perfectly clear. "Actually, I believe scripture plainly indicates God did create Satan and evil, but as for sin, it came about as a predictable consequence of the entrance of evil. In other words, sin was the unavoidable result of evil. But we must acknowledge God had good reason for its entrance and did so according to His counsel."

They discussed the matter of a debate for some time. Finally, Mark was able to convince Leland a debate probably was not the best way to serve as a means of showing both sides of a matter as controversial as this one. It was decided both Mark and the pastor to be selected to oppose him would give their position on different weeks. The idea being there would be less opportunity for hostility between guests. It was really the only basis acceptable with Mark because of his past experiences. When Mark heard the name of the pastor Leland had chosen to oppose him, he was doubly glad he had insisted it be done his way. The pastor Leland had in mind was none other than Reverend Holliday, the man for whom neither Mark nor Victor had retained much respect.

"May I ask why you particularly want Reverend Holliday to be a part of this?" Mark asked, smiling as he spoke.

Leland Bartholomew grinned sheepishly. "I think you see right through me." His smile changed to a bit of a frown. "That minister has embarrassed me more times than I can count. Somehow, I think you have what it takes to keep him in line. Mark, my desire isn't to get even with him—well, maybe it is, come to think of it. I hope you will forgive me for setting you up like this, but it would be worth a lot to see him get his comeuppance. Believe me, there are a lot of listeners who feel the same way."

"Be sure you understand I won't go out of my way to draw discord from him, but I do know what you're saying. He did his best to annoy me, I feel. He seems bent on putting himself in the best possible light with others, at least with the ones who can profit him." Mark became quite serious. "I really only want the truth of the Word of God to show through, whatever happens."

Saturday morning arrived. The stage was set for the beginning arguments of the opposing view. Reverend Holliday wanted, in the worst way, for Mark to take the first session so he would be given the last opportunity. "It's my program," Leland told Mark when they discussed it on the telephone. "So we'll be doing it my way." Mark would be opposing him on the following Saturday morning.

Mark not only prepared to listen to the program, but also he taped it so he could refer to it again and again. Both he and Claire listened to Leland Bartholomew's introduction of Reverend Holliday and the format on how the opposing views would be carried out.

"The problem in understanding the origin of evil lies in the fact it must first be realized there are two forms of evil," Reverend Holliday began. "We are plainly told at Isaiah 45:7, 'I form the light, and create darkness: I make peace, and create evil: I the Lord do all these things' (AV). We are also told God brought evil upon the Israelites many times. This was the first form of evil, and it applies to catastrophes of nature, such as tornadoes, earthquakes, forest fires, and the like. These are the evils with which God is associated.

"There is also a second form, which is termed 'moral evil.' That is a form of evil, which God did not create, for God could never be associated with immorality and immorality is what moral evil is. It would be utterly unthinkable to believe God created that kind of evil, for it can have no other origin than from Satan himself. Keep it in mind, only Satan can be responsible for that kind of evil."

Reverend Holliday continued, "Satan too was created by God, but he was created perfect in every way. Satan remained perfect until one day he became greedy and determined to take over the heavenly realm. It wasn't God's fault Satan fell from the great position he once held. Satan could hardly blame anyone but himself for such foolishness. The angels of God overthrew him and cast him from the heavens. It probably took place just before he approached Adam to tempt him in the garden of Eden."

As many times as Mark had heard those explanations, he could still hardly believe what he was hearing. He did listen to the rest of the presentation, but he had already determined what his approach would be. Mark had heard pretty much what he expected to hear as far as this man's viewpoint was concerned, but he was not prepared for the personal attack with which the pastor closed his message.

"Friends in the radio listening audience," he said, "I feel compelled to warn each and every one of you, concerning what you may hear next week from the man who will be opposing me on my viewpoint. This man beyond any shadow of a doubt is a heretic."

There was silence for a moment, and then Leland Bartholomew spoke, "I must apologize to our listeners and especially to our next week's guest, if he is listening, for the shameful and inexcusable outburst we just heard. I do not allow such things to be said on this program, for it is our practice to air opposing viewpoints even if they may be somewhat controversial. Reverend Holliday may speak as he chooses from his pulpit, but he may not attempt to open anyone to ridicule on this program. I am going to leave it to the discretion of our next week's guest, whether he wants to give a message following those unkind words. Again, I apologize for this unfortunate experience of today. I hope you will all be back again next week. This is Leland Bartholomew, with today's segment of Viewpoint."

Mark sat looking at Claire. He wouldn't have thought much about it had it been a private conversation. In fact, it would not have been unusual, but coming as it did threw Mark for a loss. "I didn't think Leland would allow it to happen," he said.

The telephone rang. Claire answered. "Right now, he's quite speechless," she said to the caller. "I'll let you talk to him," she said, handing the receiver to Mark.

Leland hadn't wasted any time calling Mark. He apologized profusely and tried to explain. By the time he suspected what was coming, he couldn't get to the microphone quickly enough. "Mark, he did it to me again, and I wasn't alert enough to stop him. I don't know how I can make it up to you, but I sure want to try. If you don't want to be on the program for a while and want to give it time to pass—"

"I want to be on next Saturday," Mark interrupted. "I want to be on before he has time to stir up the whole town against me, and I believe he could do it. Would you do me the favor of not announcing I'll be on until at least next Friday? It will give you some time to let your listeners know but not enough time for him to stir up his followers."

"Thanks, Mark," came the reply. "See you Saturday morning."

CHAPTER 19

During the week following the presentation of Rev. Holiday's message, Leland Bartholomew called Mark no less than three times. Each time it was to express concern, Mark might be upset with him, and insisting if he preferred to wait a few weeks, he would understand. "If there is any way I can make it up to you for what happened, don't hesitate to ask," he insisted. "I'll do whatever it takes. I can't tell you how sorry I am I let it happen, and I certainly do accept all the blame."

Mark was apprehensive as he sat in the waiting room, waiting for the time to begin his response to Reverend Holliday's message of the week before. Silently, he opened his heart to God, asking for strength to get through his radio message. "Father, I ask for Your blessing on this ministry. Help me not to be antagonistic toward Reverend Holliday. Help me to speak the truth, and then leave the burden of the responsibility with You. And now, Father, may much good come from this message. I ask it all in the name of Your Son, Jesus Christ. Amen."

As he finished his prayer, he heard Leland speaking.

"Good morning. This is Leland Bartholomew speaking to you on this day's *Viewpoint*. Last Saturday, Reverend Holliday spoke to you on the subject of how sin, evil, and Satan came into being. Are sin and evil to be associated in any way with God? Or as Reverend Holliday has suggested, was sin, and a part of evil, created by Satan? It's his opinion, we must not in any way cast a reflection upon God, of the terrible stigma sin and evil would bring to Him. Now other than to tell you the viewpoint of today's guest is quite different from Reverend Holliday's, I will leave everything to our guest. It's my pleasure to introduce today's speaker. He is not a minister, but I have heard some of his concepts concerning scripture, and I find them quite stimulating. I trust you too, will appreciate what he has to say. Here now is our guest, Mr. Mark Hayes."

"Thank you, Leland, for your fine introduction."

"It is a basic truth of biblical revelation, all things are of God. Romans 11:36 reads, 'Seeing that out of Him, (Jesus Christ), and through Him and for Him is all: to Him be the glory for the eons! Amen!' There is a similar thought expressed in the first chapter of Colossians (Col. 1:16-17). Those verses read, 'For in Him (Jesus Christ) is all created, that in the heavens and that on the earth, the visible and the invisible, whether thrones, or lordships, or sovereignties, or authorities, all is created through Him and for Him, and He is before all, and all has its cohesion in Him.' And when John speaks concerning the Word of God, at John 1:3, he says, 'All came into being through it, and apart from it not even one thing came into being which has come into being.' Yet when it comes to the subject of evil, men are diverted from truth, and make the Devil the source of much evil. At the same time, they fail to explain how the enemy could originate it, without the Creator giving Satan the power to bring it about. The verses just referred to will soon dispel their theory.

"Reverend Holliday observed Isaiah 45:7 as proof God is creator of evil, to which I heartily agree, but I am unable to find scriptural evidence indicating evil has more than one origin. This is not an unusual stand, but I suggest any valid attempt to prove such a position will be a futile one. The reason for this faulty conclusion lays in the fact their conception of evil and sin makes it necessary to change the truth to fit the misconception.

"Who of us chose to come to this earth to be born? Who of us chose the era of history in which we would enter into this life? Who of us wanted to take the form of these frail human bodies to be short instead of tall, to have dark hair instead of blond, or light skin instead of dark? We breathe air already put here for us. We eat food provided for us, and our bodies assimilate it apart from our direction. Who of us would have volunteered to suffer in these bodies to be subjected to pain and hardship and to mental anguish and torment? Who would have volunteered for hard work to make a livelihood or suffer the pain of child bearing?

"Truth will force us to conclude evil, as well as good, had its source in God. Only God can originate. From where then did the suffering of creation come? Paul tells us creation was not subjected to vanity voluntarily. He further says creation was subjected to it because of the One Who subjected it. It surely appears God created evil then subjected his creation to its effects. God created evil for a very good reason, and it will not help for us to try to remove the supposed awful blemish from God's unimpeachable character by placing the blame upon Satan. It may seem a noble gesture, but even God has not attempted to do that.

"Sin means to miss the mark, nothing more. Sin is the failure to accomplish what is expected of us in order to maintain perfection. Whether we eat a second helping of desert because we can't resist or if we murder a brother as Cain slew Abel, all have missed the mark and sinned in doing so. The human appraisal of the degree of sin has nothing to do with the matter. Failure to fully realize the high standard of holiness and glory God has set is sin.

"Since all things are of God, yet God cannot sin, how did sin originate, and where did it come from? And why did it come upon us? In finding this source, it won't help to suggest sin entered into the world through Adam. Nor is it enough to trace its origin to Satan, for like Adam, Satan is only a creature created by God. We must recognize this truth, as 1 John 3:8 states it: 'From the beginning is the Adversary sinning.'

"Now the question we must answer is this: if God created Satan as Satan, did God sin in creating him? The answer depends upon the object God had in view. Did God really intend for sin to enter into this universe, or did He fail in what He wanted to achieve? Was the entrance of sin into the universe a mistake? If so, then God sinned. Did God fail to hit the same mark He demands from every one of His creatures? If God created Satan to be perfect, and his failure to maintain perfection came as a surprise and a disappointment to God, then there is no other explanation except God sinned. For if any of God's creatures became flawed or bad, God would be a failure. Forbid the thought. God cannot fail. God could never miss the mark, at which He aimed when creating the adversary. God fully intended the role, which Satan must carry out. The Lord states at Isaiah 54:16: 'I have created the waster to destroy.' God created Satan to cause creatures to sin. Reverend Holliday would have us believe Satan was created perfect, but then something went awry with God's plan, causing Satan to desire to deceive. Men have twisted the truths of scripture to suit their own particular doctrines for centuries, and this is surely a case in point.

"When Adam and Eve were placed in the garden of Eden, they were told by God, concerning the trees in the garden, they could eat the fruit of all the trees except one, the tree of the knowledge of good and evil. They were explicitly warned not to eat its fruit for it would bring death: 'To die shall you be dying' (Gen. 2:17). The one, who was a sinner from his beginning, tempted them, telling them they surely would not die, but rather God did not want them to become as He is: knowing good and evil.

"Adam did miss the mark God set for him. The day Adam sinned his soul began to die. It was not sin, which humanity inherited from Adam. It was Adam's dying state as it entered the human race. And thus death passed through into all mankind, on which all sinned' (Rom. 5:12-13). It is this dying state, which makes us vulnerable to sin for, 'Sin reigns in death' (Rom. 5:21).

"God did not hope even for a moment Adam could in any way resist the temptation placed before him. God made His physical creatures in such a way, once they were subjected to the cunning of Satan, they would have no choice but to submit to his craftiness. Having once entered the death state they could do nothing less than continue to sin. Furthermore, God did want man to know both good and evil, and that is the reason He intended they should partake of evil. This is precisely why God created the adversary to carry out the role for which he was so well fitted.

"Now we must consider the details of the operation in connection with the individual sinner. The sinner, you and me, experience evil so we may ultimately come to know good. We come to know good so we shall love God. The result of our dealing with evil is made more intense by revealing sin in our lives. This is not merely calamities and misfortunes, which mankind cannot control but all evil. Then the law hedges us in, making it a transgression against God, thus giving sin a quality, which offends Him.

"We must ask now, how did sin enter into the world? God created evil, and He created Satan. God then allowed Satan to use evil to tempt Adam and Eve to cause them to miss the mark, which He set for them. When they failed to live up to the high standard, death entered their bodies. It is because of the dying soul, which all of us inherit, we sin and are sinners. It was according to the plan and purpose of God, purely and accurately stated.

"But God justifies every sin ever committed. However, few people believe God actually justifies sinners. They determine God only alters the records, so the proof of guilt can no longer be used against them. Or God simply forgives us of our offenses toward Him when we become believers. That is not true. Every sin ever committed is absolutely necessary for the promotion of our spiritual growth. But the death, burial, and resurrection of Christ were equally necessary for the justification of those sins.

"God did not create sin, but He created us in such a way as to make us vulnerable to sinning when tempted by evil. It is the evil causing us to sin. Even under the law, God required a sin offering from His people to cover transgressions against the law. When His Son Jesus Christ came into the world, God did not cause man to sin in putting His Son to death. Yet a perfect and sinless figure was required to justify our sins. Through the evil placed before man, God allowed man to make the most perfect, and only adequate, sacrifice possible to be made. God kept the secret from man, knowing they would never have crucified Him had they realized. Unbeknown to man, they were presenting the perfect sacrifice for sin. As in the days of Abraham, when God, according to the parable, required the death of his own seed, Isaac, God provided the sacrifice by placing a ram in the thicket for Abraham to offer. And so when the whole world needed a sacrifice for their sins, God also made provision by providing the sacrifice of His only begotten Son, Jesus Christ, for this too was God's intention all along.

"In the beginning when the Word was toward God, God saw the Word there before him as a sacrificial Lamb, a propitiatory shelter for the sins every creature would ever commit. Through faith in the then future shed blood of His Son, every sin, every miss, evil would be responsible for, would be justified. From the very beginning, the perfect sacrifice had already been established. The Word stood before God in the form of a perfect sacrifice, just waiting to be offered according to God's plan and purpose.

"We need never apologize for placing the responsibility for sin upon God. The entrance of evil did not make God a sinner, nor did God cause us to be sinners. Man was placed in the garden of Eden for the express purpose of knowing good and evil. It was God's intention all along for man to become sinful. That's why Adam was tempted to eat of the tree of knowledge of good and evil. But it was also God's intentions every sin would be justified. We are plainly saying every sin ever committed was necessary, but the death, burial, and resurrection of His Son justified every need for those sins. It was justified because sin was a necessary experience in order for us to learn good.

"I want to thank all the audience of *Viewpoint* for listening to this message. May God give each one of you the desire to pursue a study of scripture along these lines. Thank you."

Leland was elated over the message Mark had delivered. "What a great message, Mark. It sure ought to give our listeners something to think about."

"Thank you, Leland," he said with a hint of caution noted in his voice. "I think many people will take it to heart and try to search it out, but most of the pastors and teachers will probably try to put it to silence. This kind of study doesn't harmonize with the doctrines of eternal torment. I'll be very surprised if you don't receive a lot of criticism over what was said today. I do hope, however, I am one hundred percent wrong," Mark said.

"Mark," Leland said to him, appearing as though he didn't quite know how to approach the subject he had in mind, "I'm not aware of how much you know about this program. Viewpoint was already on KIAD when I took it over three years ago. It wasn't very popular at the time. Through hard work and perseverance, it reached the point of having a good following, considering the fact it was a religious program." He looked at Mark with sheepish expression. "I wasn't a Christian. I never claimed to be. Frankly, in my position, I think it would have been unrealistic to think I would even become a Christian. Most of the ministers were only interested in promoting their own ideas. I was subjected to their bickering and to their criticism of one another. There was a great many times when one had to wonder how 'Christian' many of them really were."

There was evidence of sincerity in Leland's eyes. "What you said this morning, Mark, made more sense than all the hellfire and damnation theology I've been listening to all these years put together. You presented God to me, as being a loving God not a God Who is out to destroy anyone who doesn't yield to His demands for being saved. I think I'd like to know your God."

"I think maybe you do know Him, Leland. It seems to me you have already allowed God into your life. The blood of His Son, Jesus Christ, has already justified the sins of the world. It's just a matter of receiving the faith to believe it. I'm anxious to begin a new Bible study. If you think you might be interested, I'd like to have you join us. You'll be most welcome."

When Mark reached home, Claire, bubbling with excitement, greeted him. She had listened carefully to his message and was greatly impressed. "Mark, you provided answers I had never even thought of before. It all made so much sense. It gives good sound reasoning for the purpose God has for all the evil in the world. I sure think I can accept the situation with Abbie and Vic now. God has to have good reason for evil, or else the things going on wouldn't make any sense at all."

"Most importantly, Claire, it isn't merely common sense. The eternal torment doctrine is clouded with unscriptural statements to hide the truth and promote the evil doctrine. Ours is backed up with scriptural evidence."

Mark sat deeply entrenched in thought. After a while, he said slowly, "I think God has made it clear to us what His role is for sin and evil and even the role Satan has in making them effective. And maybe it's God's secret program for keeping the truth hushed until He's ready to reveal it to us. It almost seems God is saying, 'Of course, the doctrine is wrong, but I'm not ready for the world to know.' I'm sure it must remain a secret until it has accomplished His objective, only to be unveiled when the proper time arrives.

"Remember the evening the four of us began to get into this area of study? I was excited about it then, and it seems exciting now to think we may be uncovering a great truth for the end times. Is it possible the doctrine of eternal torment is the method God is using to keep Israel blinded? I can see they would never accept such a doctrine. Israel is still looking for their Messiah to come and reign over them. They're not expecting never-ending suffering and hardship. They've already gone through nothing but suffering and hardship since they became God's chosen people. Can it be, what we're learning now, is the evangel God will take to His people at the end of this eon, when God has removed the blindness from their eyes? Perhaps only then will God let it be known lest Israel should learn before He is ready. And perhaps the time is near." His words were a mixture of skepticism and of intrigue. "Can it be God is about to reveal His program to all the world?"

Mark continued to mull the thoughts over in his mind. Finally, with a degree of resignation, he said, "We'll have to give the matter a great deal of prayer. I've been contemplating these things for most of a lifetime. I guess a while longer won't be so difficult."

The telephone rang. After answering, Claire announced, "It's Leland, he wants to speak with you."

Leland wanted to let Mark know Reverend Holliday had called the station manager to register a complaint about him allowing the message to go on the air. "I don't think it will do him any good, but I wanted to let you know you were right about some of the pastors and teachers wanting to silence these things. He sounded pretty hostile, I'm told," he said with a chuckle. "Just thought I'd let you know. Take care of yourself, Mark."

The following ten days brought a deluge of phone calls from the local ministers. Many were almost as hostile as Reverend Holliday had been, and all were greatly "disturbed" by the message Mark had delivered. They were virtually unanimous in thinking some form of heresy was being taught, and it was demanded such messages be discontinued at once. When Leland talked to Mark at the end of the week, he said, "The really bad news is, the station manager says we will have to abide by their wishes. 'After all,' he says, 'the ministry is what keeps the program going.' I guess he's right. I suppose what makes me the angriest is knowing Reverend

Holliday has had the last word again."

Mark was sensitive to Leland's feelings. "I don't know what it will do concerning your job, but I'm convinced a great deal of good can come from this experience. God works all things for the good of those who love Him, and we do both love Him. Let's just leave it all in God's hands, and let Him work it out for us."

"Speaking of good things," Leland said, "there must have been at least fifteen people calling in, or writing, asking about you. Most of them wanted to know how to get in contact with you. They all seemed quite interested in what you were saying. Tell you what! Drop by the studio, and we'll decide what to do about them."

This was the best news Mark could have had. He had been eager to start another Bible class, but now there were possibilities for a class large enough to require renting a hall. "That's great news, Leland. A large group study might make a real impact. Can't thank you enough! And by all means, I think you should go along with the management. You can still be a witness to the truth off the air, and I have a feeling you will be," Mark said with a laugh, "especially to Reverend Holliday."

Mark arranged to meet Leland at the studio to take a look at the letters coming in. Counting the letters and the telephone calls, seventeen inquiries had been received. Some requested they be forwarded to Mark—those, Leland gave to him. Others were more vague in their approach.

Leland suggested he could call them himself and tell them about Mark's ministry and inform them how to contact Mark if they so desired.

Both of them went to work making contacts and having a great deal of success. A number of them expressed the desire to join the class, and the letters continued to trickle in to the studio. They determined to follow up on those who were reluctant to join at the time. Perhaps with time to think about it and a casual phone call now and then, they might still be receptive to the idea. Arrangements were made to rent a room at the Family House meeting center, established for just such purposes. Mark decided since it was the message he gave over the air creating the interest, he would print the message and put it in booklet form. He would keep these available for the future as well as the present.

Mark was pleasantly surprised at how interested Leland had become, concerning the class. Nearly all those whom he contacted were eager to attend. Those whom Leland approached outnumbered those for Mark, even though his hadn't shown nearly the interest at the outset. It didn't take long to realize Leland was a great organizer. He worked smoothly and efficiently. He prepared an introductory letter to be sent out to each prospective member. Mark set the sermon in attractive form and printed copies. The class was scheduled to begin the following Thursday evening.

Leland acted as master of ceremonies, doing a superb job. Some even looked to him as a celebrity, having known him for some period of years through his work in radio. It took much of the pressure off Mark and gave him time to devote to his presentation. The biggest problem arose from those who wanted to discuss the more obvious differences from the orthodox views. Leland explained they would be happy to explain those matters but separate from class time. "We feel those are basic truths, which the members have already become well acquainted with." This was explained at the beginning of each study period.

A collection was taken only as often as was required to pay for renting the hall and for the purchase of enough literature from the Concordant Publishing Concern to begin and maintain an adequate supply. The first offering provided for what appeared to be enough funds to carry them for two and maybe even three weeks.

It was an experience Mark thoroughly enjoyed. They had numerous run-ins with various pastors, but those were largely due to Leland's need to "witness" to them. He was never antagonistic. He had a fine sense of humor and sometimes even provoked them to laugh with him. But he often said to them, "Why don't you drop by sometime and hear the evangel of God? We present it every Thursday evening." Some took offense to his innuendo.

Mark never ceased to thank God for giving him the class to teach. Not only did it give him the opportunity to do what he liked doing most, but also it forced him to go deeper into the Word and delight in it even more.

Claire realized how much he enjoyed it, and she attended right along with him. The group treated her much as a pastor's wife, though she tried to discourage it.

Mark and Claire went through all the legal procedures, which seemed at all helpful toward adopting Abigail and Victor's child. There seemed little hope anything would deter the Lanes from following through on their decision to raise her themselves. Mark and Claire did well in leaving the situation in God's hands. But isn't that always true?

Deanna Britton had lived her entire young life in the hospital, most of the time in an incubator. She was doing well and had already gained enough weight for the doctors to feel she could safely go home, but there suddenly arose the problem of establishing where home would be.

They had received a telephone call from Chad Worthington, their attorney, requesting they attend, with him, a meeting with the judge in his chambers at ten o'clock the next morning. "Don't be late, it could be a very important meeting," he had told them—nothing more than that.

Upon arrival, they not only found the judge was present, but both Mr. and Mrs. Lane as well. The moment Mrs. Lane saw Claire the tears began streaming down her cheeks. "Oh, Claire, I'm sorry I've been so difficult about this whole matter of the baby."

"Ahem!" came the sound of the judge clearing his throat in an effort to gain everyone's attention, especially of Mrs. Lane. "Something quite important has come to my attention," he said soberly. "It was my understanding Mr. and Mrs. Lane had decided to take the baby and raise her as their child, to which I gave my approval. Under all the known circumstances at the time, it seemed the proper thing to do. I think it's befitting to inform you, Mr. and Mrs. Hayes, only out of a sense of fairness on the part of the Lanes have this latest development come to my attention. I have here a diary, owned and maintained by Abigail Britton, the mother of the infant child whose welfare is being considered right now. Mrs. Lane gave this diary to me. On the twenty-third day of July 1954, the mother of this child expressed the desire, if the situation ever should arise that Mr. Britton would be unable to care for the child, Mr. and Mrs. Hayes should be allowed to adopt her. No less than twenty-three times, later references were made to that decision. There is no doubt the handwriting is of Mrs. Britton. Mrs. Lane has confirmed it as well. I have checked out a number of character references and have determined you are worthy individuals and quite capable of accepting this responsibility.

"There is one other important thing before we close the matter. I've heard it from all other accounts, now I need to hear it from you as well. Is it your desire to legally adopt this child, Deanna Britton?" "It is, Your Honor. It's very much our desire," Mark replied. "There is a matter of a hospital bill," the judge further explained. "The Brittons had arranged for the entire payment in advance, but they were unable to anticipate the additional time the infant would be required to remain there. There is the amount of 422 dollars and 38 cents above the figure to clear the records. If this should be a problem, the Lanes have generously offered to meet this expense."

Mark looked at Claire for quick approval and then informed the judge they were more than happy to pay the balance.

Claire quickly spoke up, "I want Mr. and Mrs. Lane to know they are welcome in our home anytime they wish to visit." Turning to the Lanes, she said, "You are Deanna's grandparents, and we will always honor your relationship. Thank you, Mrs. Lane and Mr. Lane. Thank you very much."

The day Mark and Claire entered their home—Mark carrying the baby in his arms—was one of the happiest days of their lives. Deanna Claire Hayes was their little girl. She had some of the features of her mother, but Victor had been a handsome young man, and the resemblance between her and her father was remarkable.

"I'm certainly glad I decided to change your title from the 'first lady' to 'my lovely lady,'" Mark said to Claire. "You will always be first, but now we don't have to explain anything to our little girl," he said, giving her a kiss on the cheek. "And besides, now I'll have two lovely ladies," he added.

CHAPTER 20

A beautiful child and a marvelous time of joy had arrived for Claire and Mark. Their own child couldn't have been more welcome than this one had become. As much as they had hoped and prayed for the right to adopt her, it still came as a surprise when they were told they could have her as their own. Born on the fifteenth day of December 1954, she went home to stay with the Hayes on January the fifteenth, which coincidentally was the original due date set by Abigail's doctor.

There was no question in the mind of Mark or Claire, whether Claire would quit her job immediately. Arrangements were made to hire a day nurse to care for Deanna until Claire could work out a two- week notice with her employer. Claire was torn between thoughts of the tragic circumstances for her coming to them and those of how desperately she had hoped for a child but thinking she might never have one of her own. Secretly, she had yearned for a little girl, though she would have been happy to have a child of either gender.

"I feel guilty for being this happy," she said to Mark on the first day after leaving her job. "I rather feel like I'm betraying Abbie because I'm so happy to have Deanna as my own little girl. Oh, Mark, I don't like feeling this way. I would give anything if Vic and Abbie could be living next door and planning their lives around little Deanna."

"Don't think that way, Claire. You have no reason to feel you're betraying anyone, and it's important to Deanna you feel comfortable in being her mother." Mark had never felt more love for Claire than he did at that moment. "God works all things according to His Own council. You should be keenly aware this is according to His will, and don't you ever forget it. God had His reasons for wanting us to have this particular child, and I'm sure I will always believe that. I too miss them very much, but I count it a great privilege to be given the opportunity to have this little girl as my daughter.

"Claire, I have as much problem accepting the circumstances of Victor's death as you do, but one thing I'm sure of is God looks upon the matter much differently than we do." Mark was very serious now. "Claire, I'm strongly drawn to the likelihood there are two ways of viewing everything—whether it's life as we experience it all around us, and the events of every day, or the understanding of scripture—all scripture from Genesis to Revelation. It seems very likely to me God wants mankind to observe everything from this fleshly point of view but to gradually come to see it from His viewpoint. God expects to become all in all His creatures. It seems to me these earthly experiences are what will bring about the goal."

"I'm not sure I follow you, Mark."

"Look at it this way. When we think of someone committing suicide, there's no question it's wrong from the human standpoint. Yet, even Paul says, some accuse him of saying he is teaching men should do evil in order for good to come from it. He quickly adds, 'May it not be coming to that.' However, he also acclaims this assessment is a fair judgment to make. What it all means is this—however great the number of transgressions against God may be, the more the grace of God, through the cross, multiplies to cover the transgressions. The effect then is the more transgressions abound the more grace abounds through Christ to justify them. The law was given to Israel's fathers in order for them to understand God's righteousness. They recognized they were sinning, but they would never purposely sin. Nor should we. The whole point is, no matter how wrong we may feel Vic's act of suicide is, God has fully justified its happening. We may never know the reason for it, but the fact God has a reason is the only thing, which matters.

"It seems to me we should view all sins of men in the same way. The drunk, the drug addict, the rapist, the murderer, the liar, and the false accuser—whatever the act—shouldn't we view it in the same way this thought teaches us? It should teach us, of course, it's wrong but they do not sin in order to make grace abound. They sin so they will learn good from the evil occurring in their lives. And the Lambkin as God's perfect sacrifice will justify the most outlandish sin ever committed and every sin ever committed. Through the knowledge of law, sin abounds! Through the cross, grace abounds!

"I know that's easier to say than it is to live out. But wouldn't it make us more tolerant of other's shortcomings if we would view it that same way? Perhaps the more we practice accepting it, the easier it will be to believe. More than just making us more tolerant of other's shortcomings, I think we might be recognizing a tremendous truth. It might be we would be learning to view things as God views them, and isn't that what happens as God becomes all in all?"

The Lanes had already stopped to see their granddaughter several times, and Victor's father had even stopped to see the baby. His face beamed when Claire told him Deanna shared a strong resemblance to both him and Victor.

Will and Alice were pleased to have a granddaughter. It was their first since Mike had three sons but no daughters and Kate was not yet a mother. "Now Dad will be happy we have a little Claire running around the house," Claire had said.

The days passed quickly. They hardly noticed the drudgery of the cold winter weather. It was warm inside where they spent every possible moment with Deanna. She brought unmeasured happiness to them and grew rapidly into a strong, healthy little girl.

In the spring, Mark spent much of his available time in the yard. Claire enjoyed working with him but only when Deanna wasn't demanding her attention. Mark had always loved the springtime, and now Deanna made it even more enjoyable. A chain-link fence had already been installed around the entire property. They planted Virginia creeper, the American ivy, of the grape family along the length of the fence. Taking up the cement sidewalk running from the back door to the garage, they put down a cobblestone surface of closely placed stones. Overhead and considerably wider than the walk, they erected a sturdy wooden framework and covered it with a lattice network. Here they planted more American ivy vines, heavily interlacing them with climbing red roses. Mark placed a wishing well near a corner of the backyard. Because of the link fence, they had to place the Clematis plant inside the property line, but they put it as near the spot where Victor had suggested as possible. The man who sold it to them assured them it would contain beautiful white blooms whenever the plant reached maturity. Both Mark and Claire were pleased with what they had done although much of it would take several years to develop into what they envisioned it to be. They would continue to add to their horticultural endeavors as new ideas came to them and as they could afford them.

Early autumn arrived before the Britton's estate was settled. Their home furnishings had been sold at auction, as was their automobile. The bank put the property in the hands of a realtor who readily found a prospective buyer. Barely two weeks had passed when the "For Sale" sign was removed. The purchase hinged only upon the closing being finalized. There wasn't much left for inheritance by the time the estate was probated. What did remain went to Deanna. The money was placed in a trust fund for her to be applied toward her college education.

Mark and Claire waited with a great deal of interest to find who their new neighbors would be. They hoped it would be someone who would be as fine neighbors as Abigail and Victor had been, although they realized it was a lot to expect.

What did develop proved to be a bit of a mystery. A moving van unloaded some household furnishings, and then it was another week before anyone appeared around the house. Not even a light was seen in any of the rooms. After seeing someone enter the house one evening, Mark decided to make an effort to get acquainted with them. After knocking on both the back door and the front, just in case the bells might not be working, he returned home. "That's strange," he said to Claire. "I saw the man go in the back door, but when I rang the doorbell, he didn't answer. Do you suppose he's deaf and didn't hear? I haven't seen anyone else around."

Over the course of the next several weeks, Mark saw the man occasionally but no more than for a few fleeting moments at a time. Hurrying from his garage to the back door, he always disappeared inside until perhaps the next morning when he might again be seen quickly walking to his garage, presumably to leave for work. Mark was eager to meet his new neighbor, but it was appearing more and more he simply did not want to get acquainted with his neighbors.

One evening as Mark walked from his back door, his neighbor was walking to the house. Mark called out to him and waved. "Hello there, feels like old man winter is trying to make an early impression on us. Don't think I'm ready." Continuing the conversation wasn't necessary. The man, upon hearing Mark speak, virtually broke into a run to get to his house and away from him.

"I may be a glutton for punishment," he said to Claire after entering the house, "but he's going to introduce himself to me, or I'm going to know the reason why."

"I can't tell you the reason why, but it sure seems obvious he doesn't want to be bothered. It's hard to fathom people like that, but I suppose he has his reasons. He must feel he has reasons why he doesn't want to be sociable." She looked at Mark and grinned. "I also know you will find out why."

When supper was over and Mark had dried the dishes, he told Claire he was going to see Harry for a few minutes. "Would you like to go along?" he asked.

"Yes I would like very much," she replied, "but Deanna is asleep, I need to call Elly and see if she will watch her for me."

"What do you make of our new neighbor?" Mark asked when the conversation had reached a lull. "Don't know about you, but I feel I'm very near the top on his list of people he wants to avoid." Harry became quite serious. "That seems strange. We invited him over for supper last night. He was a barrel of laughs, the life of the party, you might say."

Mark looked at Harry in amazement. "You've got to be kidding. He won't even speak to me."

"You're right, I'm kidding. But I'll have to admit he has spoken to me. I followed him to his back door the other evening. I was trying to make conversation when he let me know, in no uncertain terms, he did not want to visit with his neighbors. He told me if I wanted to wave from across our yards, he would go along with that. I was about to tell him what to do with his idea when he went inside and shut the door. I figure if he wants to be—"

"Harrrry! Neither Mark nor Claire particularly want to hear your description of the man." His wife Sally had interrupted him before he could finish his sentence. "I'm never sure what Harry's going to say. He uses such colorful expressions," she said, showing a degree of discomfort.

"He doesn't have to worry about me invading his privacy. I'm more than eager to leave the man alone. In fact, I prefer it."

Mark found out what he wanted to know. He hadn't really thought it was anything personal, but now he was quite sure it wasn't. "Apparently, he wants to be left alone by everyone. The question now is, why?" he said to Claire as they returned home.

"Don't you think you should leave well enough alone and not bother the man? Oh, oh! I should have known better than to say that," she said, taking hold of his arm with both hands and placing her cheek against it as they walked.

"Isn't it pretty obvious the man has some problem that's bothering him? I mean, it would take a big problem to cause someone to hide from everybody. That's what he's doing!" Mark said.

Mark did leave the man to himself as far as not wanting to seem to be interfering. He determined to wait for the right opportunity for approaching him. Over the course of the winter, he waved from a distance, and the man waved back to him, but there was no further overture made.

It was late March before Mark was given the chance he needed, although it all developed quite beyond anyone's control, certainly of Mark's control. Upon removing the mail from the mailbox one evening, one particular letter caught his immediate attention. His first thought was the mail deliveryman had simply given him a neighbor's mail by mistake. Upon closer examination, he found the address was correct, only the name was wrong—Jozef E. Rydz, 2040 Cleveland Ave.

"Collect, sir," the words sounded from behind Mark. "Could I collect for two weeks, Mr. Hayes? You weren't home last week when I stopped."

"Yeah, sure. Say, you wouldn't happen to have a Jozef E. Rydz on your paper route would you?" It occurred to Mark he might take a paper, and it sure wouldn't hurt to inquire.

"No, Mr. Hayes, but I have an Edward Rydz," he said.

"Where does he live?" Mark asked.

"You're fooling me! You don't know where Edward Rydz lives? You ought to know him, he lives right there," he said, pointing to the house next door.

"You know him?" Mark asked with interest. "You've talked with the man?"

"No, Mr. Hayes, he pays for his paper in advance at the office. I've never seen him. Hey, the initial E could stand for Edward, couldn't it?"

"Yeah, thanks, Craig, you've been a big help."

Thinking upon the matter, Mark decided it would not be out of order for him to deliver the letter in person. After all, the postal department probably couldn't deliver it anyway.

Mark deliberated on the matter for a long time, trying to think of some way whereby he could unobtrusively establish grounds for a conversation with the man next door. Maybe he could inquire why he went by different names in different situations, instead of always using the same arrangement. He could stress the point of having to make sure the right person received the letter so it wouldn't get lost. He wasn't sure they were the same person, but it was worth a try he decided. He didn't know if the man would even answer his door. It wouldn't be the first time if he didn't.

Later in the evening, Mark went next door in an attempt to deliver the letter. As he walked onto the porch, he heard voices coming from inside the house. Mark had never seen or heard of a second person being on the premises. He pressed the bell and could clearly hear it ring. He stood waiting, wondering what to expect.

Someone did come to the door. Opening it just wide enough to get a view of the caller, the man asked, "What I should do for you?" He spoke in halting English, not being sure where to place the accent on his words, obviously a foreigner. He was a young man, about mid-thirties Mark guessed, a fine-looking gentleman, but his face was drawn. He noticed an obvious scar on his right ear. In all the time they had been neighbors, Mark hadn't been close enough to actually know what he looked like.

"Well, sir," Mark began, "this letter came in the mail today. It had my address on the envelope, but it didn't have my name. You see it's addressed to a Jozef E. Rydz."

The man reached for the letter, but Mark withdrew it from him. "I just want to be very sure I'm giving it to the right person. One can't be too sure about something coming through the mail. You understand don't you, sir?"

"Please give me letter, please! It is mine." There was a look of fear on the face of the man standing before him. Mark felt badly for him and a bit guilty, but he wanted to develop the best opportunity possible for talking to him.

"Sir, the boy who delivers our newspaper, he told me your name is Rydz, but your name is Edward and not Jozef. I really don't understand why the difference of names if it belongs to you. Sir! I just want to be sure! You understand?" Mark questioned.

With those words, Mark was greeted by a second person, one who had apparently heard the entire conversation and one of the people Mark heard talking when he walked onto the porch.

"I can vouch for this man's identity," he said to Mark. "This man is Jozef Edward Rydz. He is my nephew, and he come here from Poland just recently. You!" He stepped back out of surprise. "You are Mark Hayes! We know each other well!"

Mark did indeed know the man well. His name was Joseph Heimann, and he was the owner of Heimann Industries, a successful business in town. Dickins Print Shop had done a considerable amount of work for the man and over quite a few years. He was Jewish and of Polish descent. Mark thought him to be a fine man and very reliable in all their dealings.

"Come in, Mark. You obviously haven't met my nephew. I understand you live right next door? Edward hasn't spoken much about his neighbors. I don't think he has done well in getting acquainted in his neighborhood." He gave a quick glance toward Edward.

Mark began trying to smooth over the situation by taking the blame for not introducing himself to Edward sooner. "There really is no excuse for not having called on him before since I live so close," he explained. He didn't really know what to say, finding himself not being altogether truthful and making himself feel quite uncomfortable. "Guess we tend to get carried away with our own routines."

"Mark, you do not need to make excuse for Edward." This man also talked with broken English, much like Edward, though he was easier to understand. "I know in Edward's life what has been going on. As fact, this is reason I be with him tonight." He sat quietly for a moment looking first to Mark, then to Edward, then back to Mark again. "Mark, Edward has been through more suffering and through more bitter heartbreak than most entire families will go through in all their lifetimes. I feel for him very much. You too will feel badly for thing he go through. I hope with my whole heart Edward will confide those things with you. I say it because I know what friend you would be to Edward. And knowing you as I do know, there is no question you make every effort to get acquainted with my Edward.

"I am not aware what you know or what you read about Jewish ghettos, the concentration camps too, even exterminating camps. They began before 1938, all the way to 1945. Edward, he go through more than one think it possible for a human person to go through. Oh yes, he go through it all, short of the death. I think there are times many he prefer death to what he go through.

"You see, I was in position to have somewhat an idea what was coming on my Jewish people. It was early as 1935. I determined then to take my family and leave Poland. I make arrangements to immigrate to these United States. A sister and two brothers I had living in Poland. Lodz was name of my city. The rest of my family, they live in Wroclaw, maybe hundred twenty mile away. I was unable to convince family of the danger to remain there. In all letters I receive, always say same thing, 'If situation become too desperate, we will leave at first signs.' My only sister, Von, had a husband and a handsome son and two beautiful young daughters. Each of my two brothers had a wife and four children. Because they wait too long to leave their homeland, Edward here is only member of all my family to survive terrible affliction coming upon my people. I bring Edward here, here to this wonderful land of America, where he make new life. He live with me for one year before he move to this house. He work in my factory. He learn to speak English good now."

Mr. Heimann looked at his nephew, displaying a great deal of affection. "But now after saying all that," he continued, "I try to be persuasive to Edward it be time to stop looking back. He must put past behind him. If he be unable to do that, he can only continue to live on in bitterness and be buried inside himself. I love my people. There is nothing I would not do for them if they be here today. Edward is alive, at least in body." Once again, he cast a glance in the direction of Edward. "But there is nothing I can do for him if he not want to help himself."

"I have the means to set something up for him, some kind of business, when he decide what he will be doing. Money is no problem within reason. There is young lady in Poland who would wish to be his wife. Edward, he is uncertain about her. I think it is out of the fear of seeing another of his loved ones getting badly hurt. I will not interfere in that. The truth is Edward can make a new start if he will only let something happen, something good. And I know he can, if he only begin looking forward instead of dwelling in the past.

"I suspect the letter you deliver here tonight, it is from his lady. Many letter like this come to my house before. Maybe I suspect too he be eager to read it. Edward, he is only one of all my nephews to be given my namesake. As you know, my name is Joseph. I change spelling to make it more American. I suggest to Edward he go by name, Edward, to stop confusing with our identity."

Through it all, Edward had sat quietly, offering no words of conversation. He sat holding the letter Mark had given him, hardly taking his eyes off of it. Mark marveled at the fact Edward had not given in to his desire to find out what it might contain. Without even knowing what Edward had gone through in the past years, Mark felt a deep sorrow for him. What a tragic thing it must be to feel there is no one to trust or turn to. What terrible things could have transpired to cause such deep hurt? How is it possible to help someone in such a state? Should he even dare to try?

As Mark sat not knowing what to say or do, Mr. Heimann rose from his chair then picked up his hat and started for the door. What should he do? Mr. Heimann had invited him in, but now he was leaving. An awkward situation, to say the least, Mark was facing a man who had clearly shown he did not wish to be bothered by anyone. After Edward's uncle left, the two of them sat looking at one another. Mark couldn't recall experiencing a more uncomfortable feeling.

"Sir, I would like to be your friend," Mark said to him. Edward sat in complete silence. Extreme fear was evidenced in his eyes, but there was no indication he even wanted to trust Mark.

"Sir" —Mark approached the man again—"if you should ever like to talk to someone about your experiences, I would be honored to have you confide in me. Perhaps it would help more than you can possibly know. Often, the most helpful thing is to bring your thoughts out and talk about them. Edward, I know your uncle well. He is a fine man. I am sure you are a fine man just like him. I want to be your friend."

Still Edward sat quietly. Mark felt it might be mere wishful thinking, but he detected a look from Edward as possibly being a cry for help. Then as though thinking better of it, he said to Mark, "Maybe you go now. Yes, I want you should go."

As Mark stood up, Edward rose quickly and began backing away from him. Again, he said, while pointing to the door, "Please go. Please." His voice was near the point of trembling.

Mark walked straight for the door, but with one last plea for understanding, he said, "Please let me be your friend, Edward." He slowly opened the door to go outside. "Oh, I do hope you enjoy the letter from your lady friend," Mark said with a smile.

There was a faint smile on Edward's face as Mark closed the door. *Maybe the smile was really because I was leaving,* he thought.

On the day following the strange experience, Mark was pleasantly surprised when Edward approached him as he reached home from work. Edward had been standing at his back door and then walked toward him as Mark started for his house. "Mr. Mark," he called, "you like visit, like you say last night and be good friends?" "Yes, Eddy, of course, I would like it very much. What do you have in mind?"

"You come over after we eat, all right?" he said.

"Would about seven be all right?" Mark asked. "You can tell me all about your experiences during the war."

There was a quick nod in the affirmative, and Edward turned

and walked to his door.

When Mark approached the front door of Edward's house, he was again surprised to see Joseph waiting on the porch with him.

"Good evening, Mark, it is nice seeing you again so soon," he said in greeting.

It was rather plain to deduce Edward had invited his uncle to be present while he "visited" with Mark. Mark too was quite relieved when he found Joseph there. He was concerned whether he would be able to instill any degree of confidence in Edward, whom he truly wanted as a friend. He immediately decided he would let Mr. Heimann carry the conversation. The small talk was soon out of the way, for Mr. Heimann was quick to get to the heart of the matter.

Looking squarely at Mark, he said, "You may notice an urgency from Edward he get to know you. I tell him today I put up with his nonsense already too long, a year already. I tell him his next-door neighbor is best friend he can know. I tell him he should get to know you, or I lose my patience. I tell him I mean it too."

"Edward told me he would like to visit and become friends," Mark said, directing his response to both Edward and Joseph. "I suggested if he would like, he could tell me of his experiences taking place during the war years. I've read a little about the treatment your Jewish people endured and of the extreme anti-Semitism prevailing all over Europe."

"It is more right to say, the treatment most Jewish people were not able to endure. Did you know, Mark, six million Jews did not live through the Holocaust? Someone say, 'The number almost equals number of people in New York City.'" The pain from the memories of the loss of his family was evidenced in the expression on his face.

"Edward—he was born in little town outside Wroclaw, Poland. All my people live there. They were truck farmers and managed to make a fair living. Evon's family is fine family, as were all of them. Ersel was eight then, Naomi was ten, and Eddy was eleven. Eddy was a fine-looking boy even when he was only eleven. I lived much too far away from my people. I not able to influence them to leave Poland. They have to do what they think best. I not change people's minds. Since 1939, everybody have to wear white armband with blue Star of David. Everybody know who Jews are. I leave in first of 1939, but my family does not leave with me. In the fall of 1940, the Jews from the area surrounding the larger cities, they was forced to move into places designated as ghettos. Leaving work tools, machines, workshops—people move to where Gentiles were evacuated to make room for Jewish population. All roads was cut off, trapping everybody in ghettos. In 1941, secure fences be put up to form prisons. Only men who work in war plant was allowed to leave and only alone. Nobody leave family and not come back."

From this point, the story centered upon Edward, and the series of events taking place in the years following were extraordinary to say the least. One is forced to wonder how any person could endure experience after experience of brushes with death the way this young man had and yet survive. It would have to be considered luck or good fortune or a dedicated life of prayer and fellowship with their personal God, and Father, or by the mere intentions of God, depending upon how one chooses to look upon such matters. Mr. Heimann was quick to point out that it was a very small percentage of the European Jews who survived the war at all. Every survival story was of a sequence of events, relating chilling details of one close encounter with death after another. Millions no doubt could have told unusual tales of torture, of watching murders taking place in great numbers, of watching people starve to death right before their eyes, had they been able to live to tell their stories. Millions could have told of the people herded into gas chambers, but not one of those was around to describe the horror of the experience. When one looks upon Edward's story properly, it is possible to believe anything, for mere survival was the exceptional experience for the European Jew of the years of World War II, and each experience consisted of a unique set of circumstances.

It was a long, very long evening for Mark, listening to the story as it progressed through the war years. It was indeed not boredom making the evening seem long but rather the incredulity of the nature of event after event taking place. The small amount of reading Mark had done on the subject of the Jews during the Holocaust years had provided little preparation for what he was hearing. The story itself seemed incomprehensible, but getting through the language barrier made it doubly hard. Joseph Heimann told the story, but many interruptions occurred, as Edward wanted to make sure of every fact. When the "visit" was over, Mark returned home totally exhausted.

CHAPTER 21

When Mark returned home the night before, Claire could see he was exhausted and insisted he go straight to bed. It was plain to Mark, Claire was eager to hear about the visit.

The next evening, after the dishes were done and they were seated comfortably in the living room, Claire asked, "Is it confidential, or can you tell me about your visit last night?"

Mark was glad Edward hadn't asked him not to divulge the facts. He certainly had no intentions of telling anyone else, but it made him feel uncomfortable, as in the case with Victor, not to be able to share his thoughts with Claire. It was a rare matter indeed they couldn't share completely. Mark had thought about it all day and had a difficult time getting through his workday. Now he was relaxed and able to concentrate on the matter.

"Claire," he said, "if you thought Victor's story was bizarre, you'll think it was mild compared with this one. What the kid went through almost defies description, and he was nothing more than a kid through most of it."

Mark told the story as he had heard it.

During the summer of 1942, the evacuation of the Polish ghettos was underway and carried out by the Secret Service men of the German government. Jewish people were told sixty thousand workers were needed to fill production jobs in war plants in the "east." They watched as people were herded away from the ghettos in great numbers. Rumors were soon circulating saying their people were being taken to the railroad stations and forced into cattle cars and securely locked inside. Though they knew not where the people were being taken, rumors also abounded saying they were being exterminated in some manner. Both Joseph's brothers and their families were forced to leave during the days, which followed. The Jewish population was disappearing rapidly. Panic became the rule of the ghetto.

Realizing their turn was coming at any moment, Edward's father approached the SS guard who was on duty in their area on one particular evening. Edward's parents had managed to keep some of his mother's jewelry hidden for when the war was over. They were still in possession of a valuable wedding band and a brooch having belonged to his father's mother. Edward's father first offered to give him the brooch. The soldier pretended not to be interested then asked if he had anything else to offer. The wedding band was then offered. The soldier rejected this also. It was only a ruse to learn of their entire stock of possessions so he could demand everything. When he learned these were the extent of their possessions, the man demanded both the brooch and the ring. "Give me the jewelry, and consider yourself lucky to still be alive," he said. Mr. Rydz pleaded for him to let them go. "Take the jewelry, but please, let my family go. You may have the jewelry, and I will stay if you will let my wife and children leave."

Afraid he would have to give up part of his newly acquired treasure if the conversation was overheard, the SS man agreed to let him and his family leave the ghetto. "Five minutes is what you have to gather your family and belongings. That gate will be unlocked," he said, pointing to the gate nearby. They understood enough German to know what he had said. "If I see anyone when I make my trip back by here, there will be one of these through their head," he said tersely. He pointed to the clip on his belt to make clear what he meant. "It's not one of my responsibilities to be nice to Jew scum. You stinking Jews better be wearing your patches. If you get caught without those, they'll shoot first and then ask what you're up to. You'll probably be shot either way. I'll bet a wedding band and a brooch you don't get out of Wroclaw alive," he said with a sneer. Then he left to make his rounds.

They chose to walk casually toward the railroad tracks, thinking it would be the least congested area of town and they should attract as little attention as possible. Approaching the station, they observed a crowd of people. Realizing these people were from the ghetto, they watched in horror as they were literally driven into cattle cars by men using whips and screaming obscenities. One of the men yelled out, "Three more days of this, and we'll be rid of all you filthy scum." Then came another vicious crack from his whip. Many were struck by the whips and then hit again and again if they cowered or even flinched too obviously.

It occurred to them the SS men were probably being kept too busy to be looking for runaways. Quietly, they proceeded on down the tracks. Keeping to the ditches, they walked until they came to the Oder River. Following in close proximity of the river, they cautiously made their way southward toward the country of Czechoslovakia.

It was a depressing experience to see the water flowing toward them. Perhaps those muddy waters anticipated freedom awaiting them far to the north, where they would finally sweep well out into the Baltic Sea and away from the strife and the torture and slaughter Edward and his family had come to recognize. Only that could explain the reason for the waters being in such a hurry to flow farther into Poland, knowing they would be beyond the land and free forever in a little while.

The distance to what they hoped would be their freedom was about one hundred miles. Walking the terrain was difficult. Making headway along the hilly region of the valley was slow indeed. It was in the spring of the year, and the tributaries lying in their pathways were sometimes a problem. Edward and his father were excellent swimmers and had to help his mother and sisters. They were not accustomed to so much walking, and there was not a comfortable pair of shoes among them. When crossing streams, it was difficult to keep those few belongings dry. On more than one occasion, the muddy water soaked entirely through their rucksacks.

Even so, the family had never felt so close to one another as they did during those days they spent fleeing the country of Poland. The nights were cool, and their blankets were damp. Mrs. Rydz was near having pneumonia, and everyone was nursing bad colds. But they were experiencing the first degree of freedom they had known in many months.

On one of those comfortably cool spring mornings, they were given some vegetables from a garden along the way and allowed to cook them over a fire provided by the farmer. Edward and his sisters playfully scuffled out on the grass. Only then could they fully appreciate the freedom they were experiencing. Their mother watched with fond affection and noted it carefully.

"My sisters are the two most beautiful young women in all of Poland," Edward said to them when they finally stopped and could take cognizance of their situation.

"There's nothing beautiful about freckles," Naomi, the older of the two, said to him regretfully.

"Oh, but there is, and those are what make you beautiful. God promised me He would make you the loveliest ladies in the land, and those freckles were to be my assurance He would keep His promise."

"You lie, Joey!" Joey was the name he went by before coming to America. "God never said no such thing," she shouted, pushing him backward onto the grass.

"I solemnly swear it," he said with a laugh.

Ersel sat gazing at him wondering if perhaps she should believe what he said.

"I know I have the most handsome big brother in all the world," Naomi said, leaning down and placing a kiss on his forehead.

They knew they had been seen on numerous occasions, but either their observers hadn't cared, or they chose to look the other way. They knew full well if men from the Gestapo should see them, they were not likely to look the other way.

It was mainly vegetables from truck gardens sustaining them. Occasionally, the farmers would be good enough to give them the food. The rest of the time, it was a matter of eating anything that appeared edible. One farmer had taken them in for a day. He told them the river water probably would not harm them, but it was turbid from the spring rains and should be filtered through scarves or handkerchiefs. They were able to identify some edible plants for food whenever there were no vegetable gardens along the way.

At last, they reached the border and crossed over into

Czechoslovakia. Because of the Polish Jews being sent to the "east" and realizing it probably meant going to a concentration camp and just as likely to an extermination camp, they felt safer now. They were to learn they would be treated much the same way in most any European country.

Near the city limits of Ostrau, local gendarmes confronted them. There, their days of running came to an end. The SS headquarters were contacted to pick them up. The gendarmes were harsh, but it was nothing compared with the Gestapo. Upon interrogation, it quickly became known they were of Polish nationality, and they were without passport and without reason to be in Czechoslovakia. With no regard for gender, both Edward and his father were severely beaten, and his mother and sisters were knocked to the ground several times. The thought of having a stroke of good fortune was far from their minds at the time, but there was a train being loaded to go to Prague at that very moment. "Get this filth out of here and on to the train before I vomit," the captain ordered.

"You will at least have a chance there," one of the gendarmes said softly, as he walked by. They were literally forced to run all the way to the station, which was a number of blocks from where they had been detained.

No different from what they had seen in Wroclaw: men, women, and children were herded into the cattle cars by men wielding whips; men who proved they knew how to handle them most proficiently. But now they were among those people and getting firsthand experience. When as many were packed into a car as they could get in, the door was closed and secured. Moving to the next car, they filled it also to capacity with people from the local ghetto.

The trip took more than a day. Travel was slow and tedious. Stench from unwashed bodies was almost unbearable, but helpfully, it was not an extremely hot day. If one's body had not been infested with lice, it would have been after this trip. One bucket setting in a corner served as the only toilet facility, used by everyone and providing no privacy.

Finally, the train came to a halt. They had arrived at Bauschowitz, a switching station a short distance north of Prague. Apparently, this had been the point of their destination, for the door to their car was unlocked, and they were ordered outside where they would at least catch a breath of fresh air for the first time in what seemed like many hours. The military men began wielding their whips, as they seemed obliged to do, as though being the most basic part of their training. The people became accustomed to the yelling and the shouted obscenities, as they were made to walk from the station to the ghetto.

Upon arrival, they were sent to the sleuse (the route where SS men relieved them of their possessions). They were led to an underground barracks. On the way, they were told to present their rucksacks to be "processed." A greater part of their belongings were dumped into a pile. Perhaps they would be allowed to reclaim as much as a third of their belongings later. They found their rucksacks, still carefully labeled with their names and departure numbers. Of the sleusen (the stolen property), the SS men took anything of value, which they chose to keep. Other valuables disappeared entirely. However, things of lesser value were kept for local use. What was left things such as partially used toothpaste tubes, ointments, flashlights without batteries, mouthwash, pencils, erasers, mostly worthless items—-was taken to the ghetto store where they could be purchased with fake money. This was meant to impress the Red Cross Commission.

In the room where they awaited the time, they could reclaim their belongings, a few young men, including Edward, were detained. An SS officer ordered the men to be strip-searched in the guise of believing them to possess stolen jewelry. Their clothing was carefully inspected for any possible hiding place. While the ghetto officers inspected their clothing, the SS officer was strangely but intently observing their nude bodies. At length, he told them to dress and rejoin their families. The officer immediately turned and left the room.

On being taken to their living quarters, the ghetto rules were explained to them. Everyone would be required to work, but the men could go to the women's quarters to visit with their families. Each person would be given one-half loaf of black bread and a cup of black coffee for breakfast. For lunch, there was soup having little nutritional value, occasionally having flour added for thickening. Once in a while, they were given lentil soup, but it was no more nutritional. In the evening, it was more soup and another cup of coffee. All in all, it was a virtual starvation diet.

It was soon known only those who were able to work received those food rations. The old people were given only soup and then stood in lines asking for the soup of those who refused to eat theirs because it was so tasteless. They took potato peelings from the refuse pile, eating them uncooked, and often contracting infections and enteritis from the putrefaction it had undergone. Those who didn't die of starvation often died of the diarrhea they could not overcome.

Even so, for those who could work, the living conditions were no worse than they had been in the ghetto in Wroclaw. By the time this family had arrived, the men were allowed to visit the women in their barracks and even go into the park. Every newcomer, however, soon heard of the "selections" made periodically. Depending on the degree of overcrowding in the camp, lists were posted containing the names of those who would be deported. It wasn't generally disclosed where they were taken, but it was understood they were going somewhere to be exterminated. Those who were on the list were gone from the premises within a few days. They lived in fear until the next "selection" to know only they hadn't been chosen yet and were exempt until some later rime.

The SS officer, who had ordered the strip search upon Edward, allowed enough time for Edward and his family to learn their way concerning the rules and even to escape one of those dreaded "selections." It had required only a few weeks to have a good picture of all they had in store. Edward was ordered into the office of the SS headquarters. "I have just discovered you and your family have been placed on the list of those next to be deported. I would like to do all I can to prevent it from happening. As you may know, the bakery has some of the most desirable job opportunities in the entire compound. It just so happens there is an opening there for some young man to learn a valuable trade. The best part is, not only you, but also your entire family will be placed on the 'protectorate' list. It means both you and your family will be forever exempt from being deported."

Edward's heart began to pound with excitement. "My family and I will be together?" he asked.

"No!" the officer replied. "But you will be given private quarters. You will be able to take food to them at any time. You will have access to all the warehouses to supply their needs. And most importantly, they will become permanent residents at Theresienstadt and have no fear of being deported. However," he said with raised voice and gaining Edward's close attention, "there will be one thing required of you."

"*Oh no*!" Edward thought, as the meaning of the man's once strange behavior began to come into focus.

"We'll be sort of like roommates. Therefore, I will have free access to your quarters. Not all the time, only as I need your company." He had made his meaning perfectly clear. Upon observing the sudden display of anger showing on Edward's face, the man said to him, "I suggest before you give your answer, you be aware your entire family has been placed on the 'selection' list. Unless their names are removed, they will be on the next deportation. I have one more thought for you to consider carefully. The only way out of the place where they're going is through the chimney."

Edward's heart sank. What a choice he had been given! Anger was his first and only response. Only the degree of his anger varied. The SS officer was well aware of Edward's feelings. The sinister smile spreading over the man's face revealed to Edward how extensively he delighted in placing such pressure on unwilling individuals. He was defying Edward to accept the alternative, which made him even angrier. The man was overweight by at least thirty pounds, and all was distributed around his waist. To think of him being a glutton, while food was such a rare commodity to all the prisoners, seemed to depict the selfish qualities of the strange breed. The man didn't look much like Adolph Hitler, but the mustache he wore indicated to Edward his desire was to emulate his Fuhrer as much as possible. The mustache did present a fair likeness.

What a life confronted him! What a dilemma! If he didn't submit to this man's request, his family would surely die. Could he allow it if there was any way at all to prevent it?

Edward sat quietly for a time but then agreed to the request. "Yes, I will do as you ask."

"I knew you would see it clearly. It is a wise decision, I assure you," the officer spoke behind an evil grin. "Go now and tell your family of your good fortune. They will be relieved to know their names are no longer on the selection list and be extremely happy for you."

As Edward sat with his family, he tried not to even think on the matter. He wanted to have one last memory of their being together without the feeling of guilt for what he would become involved in.

After a time, as they continued to sit and talk on the subject of the days when they fled Poland, pleasant thoughts came into their conversation. They recalled the sense of freedom they experienced.

"Do you suppose we will ever again have the opportunity to walk along the riverbanks and watch the ripples of the water flowing by?" Naomi asked in deep repose. "Will we be allowed ever again to breathe the fresh air of springtime and enjoy the smell of the flowers drifting on the breeze? Maybe someday, my freckles will be gone, and I will be a beautiful woman," she said, giving her brother a loving smile.

Edward choked back the tears. "I-I will be able to help all of you," he said. He had to say something to hide his feelings.

He told them of the opportunity he had been given to learn the bakery business and of the favor he would be able to show them. Extreme joy filled the hearts of the little group.

"My little Joey," his mother cried, "I am so proud of my little Joey. This is not a time for sadness, Joey," she said as she observed the tears in his eyes. "This is a time to rejoice. Be happy! It is a wonderful thing you do!"

Edward's father sat quietly. Edward had told his father of the SS officer's special interest in him upon their arrival. He said nothing, but Edward sensed his father had put things together in his mind.

The torture within continued, and the feelings for Heinrich (he told Edward his name once the relationship had begun) had not changed in the slightest. If his father suspected anything and Edward was sure he had, he never mentioned it. His mother never failed to tell him how proud she was of him for saving their lives. The guilt became unbearable over time. If it had not been for the nutritional food he had access to and the hospital facilities being readily available and, above all, the help he could give his family, he well might have broken under the pressure. The situation continued for nearly a year and a half.

One morning while Edward was still sleeping, two SS men pounded on the door of his quarters. Without waiting for a response, they burst through the door demanding he dress immediately and come with them. He was taken to the SS headquarters where he was promptly charged with first-degree theft. The charge stated he had blatantly stolen an expensive diamond ring from the chief baker for whom he worked.

Edward sat in bewilderment, not knowing what had prompted the entire episode. Then Heinrich Himmel came into the room.

"Heinrich, tell these men I didn't steal the ring. Tell them they have the wrong man,'' he pleaded.

"Allow this man four hours to produce the missing ring," Heinrich bellowed. "Don't let him out of arm's reach. If he cannot produce the ring, take him to the Little Fortress. You will let him know clearly the chances of him leaving the place alive. Soon, he will know what happens to thieves at Theresienstadt." He turned and stomped out of the room.

His denial of having done anything wrong brought one severe beating after another. Hardly a place on his body missed the onslaught, which the men passed on to him. It appeared to Edward the four hours had been allowed for their brutality. They kicked him again and again as he lay on the floor writhing in pain. The next thing he was aware of was the splashing of water in his face. Then he was kicked again.

Finally, one of the officers said, "That's enough. He must not be allowed to die before he tastes of the real punishment." Having made sure Edward was still alive, he said, "We will take him to the dungeon."

As dazed as Edward was, his heart sank. He had heard of the Little Fortress and of some of the horrors taking place there. The thing everyone tried to impress upon their minds was, over the years of its existence, very few imprisoned there had emerged alive. How many had been sent there who were innocent of any crime was impossible to know. But clearly, the charges against him had been manufactured to suit the whim of Heinrich Himmel, for he had noticed a decided cooling of their relationship. Edward then fell into a state of unconsciousness.

How long Edward remained unconscious, he had no idea. Neither had he any idea how he had reached the place he was in now. Still lying where he was when he first awakened, he became aware of the surrounding area. It was dark and damp. Moisture dripped from the ceiling. He was lying on the floor on what he assumed to be a straw mattress covered with a blanket. Directly in line with his vision stood a huge iron gate, secured with a heavy bar from the outside. He started to turn over to look to other parts of the cell, when an excruciating pain gripped him in his chest area. He again fell into unconsciousness.

Edward was indeed imprisoned in the Little Fortress. It was a centuries old structure, built during the reign of Empress Maria Theresa of Austria in the days when they warred frequently with Fredrick II of Prussia. The Austrian government later used it to house the most hardened, long-term criminals. The Czechoslovakian government kept it as a maximum-security prison. The Nazis had changed it into a most dreaded, cruel, and sadistic prison. It was a subterranean arrangement of tunnel-like dark, smelly, lice-and-flea- infested, casemate cells, laid out in twos, facing each of four courts.

Every window and door was barred heavily. It was situated about one mile from the main fortress, across the stone bridge spanning the Eger River.

When Edward awoke, Heinrich was standing a short distance away from him. When he was aware Edward was rousing, he waited for a sign of recognition from him. "I see you are awakening from your rest," he said with sarcasm. "I wanted to let you know the baker found his ring—most careless of him for mislaying it in his quarters. Unfortunately, however, there seems to be nothing I can do to get you out of here. Once you're locked in these cells, there seems to be no way out." Making it appear as a simple afterthought, he said to Edward, "Oh yes, I almost forgot to tell you. I was unable to remove the names of your father and mother and your sisters from the deportation list. But I did have the opportunity to wave goodbye to them as the train pulled out."

Even in Edward's weakness, he felt the little strength he had left drain from him. Then anger filled his body. "You filthy Nazi swine! I hope you and your dirty Fuhrer die the way you have made my people die." He could feel new adrenaline surging through him. He sat up and tried to get to his feet, but there wasn't enough strength for that.

Heinrich Himmel began shouting obscenities at him. In a furious, uncontrolled rage, he ran toward Edward with every intention of killing him with his bare hands.

When Edward had been brought into his cell, a "fresh" uniform had been tossed inside his cell to be put on after he regained consciousness (fresh, meant only it had been thoroughly fumigated and sterilized).

As he came racing toward Edward, his feet became entangled in the uniform lying in his path. Heinrich went sprawling across the floor coming to a stop near where Edward lay. Momentarily dazed, it allowed Edward enough time to grasp his own thigh just above the knee with his right hand. With every ounce of strength he could gather, both in his leg and in his arm, he thrust his knee toward the outstretched chin of Heinrich. A short, painful outcry was heard, followed immediately by a deadly cracking sound of a breaking bone echoing through the chamber. Heinrich lay lifeless beside him.

Incredible fear took over in Edward's mind. He had just escaped certain death, and now he was just as surely faced with death again. An SS man had reached the cell. He stooped over the body knowing with one look the officer's neck was broken. "You are in big trouble now," he said. Then he turned and ran to the inner court calling the chief officer to come to his aid.

Not knowing what would happen, Edward was very much surprised with the conversation, which followed.

"It appears Hiney must have met with an unfortunate accident." Turning to the young officer who had reported the incident, he said, "Make out a report explaining the accident, and bring it to me." "What accident?" the young man asked.

"The accident he had causing him to fall and catch his chin on the side of the mining car and break his neck," the officer explained. "But there's no mining cars in operation."

"Then think of something else," the officer shouted impatiently. "This boy's a hero. We'll never again have to put up with Hiney bringing his boys in through the forest. Sooner or later, he was going to have us in more trouble than we could handle anyway. Take this man back through the forest, and drop him at the infirmary. And don't answer any questions while you're there."

CHAPTER 22

"I never imagined the Jews were treated so horribly during the war with Germany," Claire said, as Mark paused long enough to get a drink of water.

"Everyone was kept in the dark about the extermination of so many people. Literally, millions of Jews were annihilated. It was one extremely successful effort to deceive the world. It seems some preferred not to believe what they strongly suspected, though. That's probably why it was so successful." Mark was ready to continue his story. "Anyway, Eddy's worries were still far from over after his disheartening experience."

Edward had a number of broken ribs, a broken collarbone, a broken nose, he recalled mention of some broken facial bones, and a great many stitches were taken to replace his right ear, which was nearly torn off. One of the few things he had to be thankful for was, he did receive excellent medical care. But the most tragic thing of all was that his family was gone. His friends at the bakery told him their names had been placed on the selection list on the day Edward disappeared and then were deported.

Edward's name had not appeared on the list probably because it would have been too difficult to explain his absence when they filled the list for deportation. It might have been Heinrich meant to use Edward in some way. He would never know what Heinrich had in mind. Edward retained his place on the "protectorate" list. This, of course, meant his job in the bakery was still intact. However, his bitterness did not diminish, though he denied any knowledge concerning Heinrich Himmel's death.

His status remained unchanged until a day in late September 1944 when his name did appear on the selection list, which was always posted for everyone to see. Edward hadn't the slightest idea why he was chosen, but when the day came for the departure, he was among those who left for Auschwitz.

Disposition was made upon arrival at Auschwitz. Most of the people's fates were determined at the time they descended from the train. Those who were near the point of starvation, those who were sick beyond likely recovery, the elderly and the children too young to be of any help in the factories were sent directly to the gas chambers. Only the able bodied were allowed to live. Due to the better than average rations and the medical care Edward received, he appeared to be in good health, and so his life was spared.

The war was nearing its end at this point. The Russian liberation forces were coming through from the east, and soon, the heavy bombing of the installations was occurring in increased frequency. In November, the gas chambers were being dismantled, for the Germans still thought they could hide the truth from the world. The mass graves were being opened up and the bodies burned to destroy all evidence of the atrocities.

On January 18, 1945, the march of the prisoners began. Only about two thousand were allowed to remain—those who were housed in the infirmary and those only because of the extreme haste in which they were forced to leave. Mass murdering took place on those who were too ill to leave the barracks. Thousands of prisoners were shot to death before the movement began. Many thousands jammed the roads to places where it was hoped they could build fortifications against the allied forces. Those who were unable to keep pace were shot to death and their bodies dragged to the side of the road to be picked up later and heaped on trucks. They were then hauled to the local cemeteries and thrown into mass gravesites.

After many days of hard walking, blisters on one of Edward's heals became so painful he had trouble maintaining his walking. Edward said it might seem a miner thing, but it became infected to the point where the pain became unbearable. Like all the others who were incapacitated, he was shot and dragged to the side of the road and left for dead.

Darkness came on as he lay there on the cold ground. Gathering all the strength he could, he slowly dragged himself from the area and finally into the woods not too distant from the road but affording some protection from being seen by the troops.

All life experiences during the intervening time remained blocked from his memory. When he at last opened his eyes, a young woman sat in a chair beside his bed sleeping. "Where am I?" he asked, bewildered and confused.

The girl immediately roused and came to his side. In a language he understood perfectly, she said, "Ah, you have returned to the living. I didn't hold out much hope for you when you were brought here. You must be some tough individual."

In the night, her father, looking for wood for their fire, had stumbled onto him. Realizing he was alive but unable to move him by himself, he brought blankets from the house to try to keep him warm in the freezing temperature. The Russian troops came through early the next morning and helped her father move him into their house.

"I found three bullets in your body, but I think I found them all," the girl said. The girl's name was Maria Zelinski, the return name on the letter arriving at the Hayes residence, after which all these matters came to light for Mark and Claire.

"You reminded me of a squirrel," she said to Edward when he had become accustomed to the situation.

"Of a squirrel?" he asked in astonishment.

Maria laughed. "Of a squirrel I once found in the forest. Another animal had attacked it. Dying when I found it, I took it home and nursed it back to health just like I did you. That's why you reminded me of a squirrel."

Claire sat shaking her head. "It was another nine years before he came to America. What did he do during the time after 1945?"

It was still a sad plight for Jewish people. There was practically nothing for them to return to their homes for. Their neighbors had looted their homes of everything of value. The people didn't want the Jews back. Hundreds of Polish Jews were murdered when they did return. Often, they were forced onto trains and then pushed to their deaths. Edward tried to settle in a town near Maria, but the young ruffians of the community made life miserable for him, calling him Jew boy and threatening to take him for a "ride." "Too bad you didn't escape through the chimney," they taunted him.

Edward got a job enabling him to earn his room and board working for an elderly farmer who had a truck farm. This was work of which he had learned a great deal before they were forced to leave their home. He was quite isolated from the world all the while he worked there. He saw Maria fairly often, but feelings of guilt kept him from making any permanent commitments. Then one day, the old man for whom he worked passed away.

Edward remembered the name of the town his uncle Joseph had emigrated to in the United States, but he had no other address. Someone there told him of the way they had handled a similar situation once in contacting someone in America. They simply wrote the name on the envelope, leaving a space and then putting the name of the city and state below. In the space, they wrote, "Please deliver to my Jewish uncle." Because considerate postal workers handled the letter, it found its way into the Jewish community.

"I can't imagine how any people could have been persecuted for so many years," Claire said when the story was concluded.

"I certainly didn't realize nearly six million Jews died during the Holocaust," Mark exclaimed. "That was almost one third of the entire world's Jewish population."

Never in the history of man had there been an instance of such a widespread wholesale slaughter of a people. Probably that's what made it so difficult to believe as being fact. This launched Mark on a directed effort to find the reason God would allow something so devastating to occur. When Mark and Claire contemplated the things concerning evil, they had grasped a degree of understanding how God uses it to teach truth—how evil is meant to reveal good. But it had not prepared them for such a massive display of evil as this had exposed. They learned of the experiences of one Jew during the war years. There were nearly six million other similar stories never to be told.

Nearly two weeks had gone by since Mark related the story of Edward's experiences to Claire. Mark sat in his study room putting his books away after completing his time of study when Claire came and sat with him.

"Are we about to have a study class?" Mark teased.

"It just may turn into that. Something really does concern me, Mark," she said. "It's bothered me ever since you told me about Eddy's experience. It's about the relationship Eddy was forced to enter into with the German officer. I'm not blaming Eddy. I certainly know he had no choice in the matter. But well, I know Christians often feel contempt for ones who practice homosexuality, and I know the Bible teaches it as being wrong. But I guess what bothers me is the way it seems to be looked upon as being such a horrible sin, like it's worse even than kidnapping, or rape, or murder. I'm not sure. Is it blown out of proportion, o-or don't I understand something?"

"I've looked into the subject a little in my studies in both the Old Testament and the New Testament," Mark said. "I wrote a paper on it once, hoping to teach it in our Bible class, but I never got the chance. You are certainly right in thinking of it as being shameful and even by God. There's not a lot of scripture devoted to the subject, but most of what there is seems pretty clear." Mark wanted to approach this subject cautiously. "With God, sin is sin, whether it's a seemingly small lie or a man going on a mass murder spree. But Christ justified every sin, no matter how horrible it is, through His death, burial, and resurrection. I guess I don't think I have to tell you that."

"I think it's the shame it generates that I'm curious about." Claire was eager to deal more directly with her own concern of the matter.

"I remember how serious a matter the Bible showed it was during Noah's lifetime," Mark said. He found what he was looking for in the sixth chapter of Genesis. "It speaks here of the numbers of humanity becoming great, and many daughters were born to them. Sons of the adversary came down from heaven and took daughters of humanity to be their wives. Children were born to these daughters, offspring, which became masters great in name: great men of renown. They were evil men influencing the human to enter into their evil ways. They influenced humanity to actually make idols, which depicted the male anatomy, and then worship the idols they made. And dishonoring their bodies among themselves with ultra-prostitution was the evil most displeasing the Lord God. This angered God, and He regretted having made humanity. That's interesting, Claire, considering He did not say, He regretted bringing about creation—rather, He regretted having 'made' humanity. I think it was because humanity was so vulnerable to those superior beings. The Lord God determined to bring a flood upon the earth and wipe all He had made from the surface of the ground—the human to the moving animal and to the flyers of the heavens. But Noah was a righteous man and found grace in the eyes of the Lord God, and Noah walked with God. Noah built the ark, and with his wife, their three sons, and the wives of their three sons, those eight came safely through the flood.

"The entire earth was scattered over by the descendants of Noah's three sons—Ham, Shem, and Japheth." Of course, this followed the days of the flood. "Noah became drunk from the wine made from the vineyard he planted and exposed himself in his tent. Ham saw the nakedness of his father and told his brothers. The brothers, Shem and Japheth, placed a garment upon their shoulders and, going backward, placed it over their father so they could not see his nakedness. Scripture states, when Noah awoke, he knew what his small son (grandson, Canaan) had done to him. What the sons of God caused to occur on the earth, before the flood, apparently was recurring.

"It would be altogether unrealistic to suppose that for a man to see another man's nakedness would be something considered sinful in itself. More would be required to warrant the resulting wrath of the Lord." Mark knew some might consider his conclusion to be conjecture, but it seemed his explanation was the only logical conclusion. "When Noah awoke from his wine," Mark continued, "he was aware Canaan had entered into an unnatural relationship with him. Noah placed a curse upon Canaan, the son of Ham. All the descendants of Canaan would become the servants of Shem and Japheth. The amazing fact coming from this curse placed upon Canaan was the fact Noah was blessing the Lord by carrying out the Lord's desires through the curse."

"I think in answer to your question, the Lord was forced to place a curse upon such an abomination because it was introduced, by those evil celestial beings, upon flesh too weak to overcome the temptation. Surely, the wife of Ham was a descendant of one of those evil sons of God," Mark emphasized. "It's quite evident many giants were in this land of Canaan and probably descendants of those sons of God. When Moses sent spies to check out the land, they came back with word those giants were much too powerful for them to battle against. Goliath, the giant David slew with a slingshot and a pebble, was from the same land. It seems clear the sin of Canaan was the same sin previously bringing about the destruction of humanity. The Canaanites became a wicked and treacherous people. They multiplied and in time came to include peoples known as Hittites, Girgashites, Amorites, Perrizites, Hivites, and Jebusites. These seven nations were a menace to Israel for most of those many centuries. It stands to reason they have continued to multiply since those days." Mark went on to explain. "For all those centuries, from the time Israel received the Law of Moses well into the times of Judah being the only remaining nation of Israel, God's people continually served the images of the heathen nations. Many of the kings of Judah and of Israel caused the people to follow the abominations carried out by the heathen, whom the Lord had cast out of the land of Canaan to make room for His people. In the groves throughout the land, they carved abominable images of the male and worshipped those images. The Lord considered this a form of idolatry and to be prostitution against their true God. These were the people causing the destruction of Sodom and Gomorrah and tried to take the daughters of Lot and enter into ultra-prostitution with those of his house.

"Paul tells us in the book of Romans the truth of God has been made known to all men, for God has revealed it to them—first through the things He has made, then through the Law of Moses, and finally through the Son of God Himself. God makes Himself known to all men, but they do not glorify or thank Him. Their unintelligent hearts are darkened, and while claiming to be wise, they prove they are really stupid. They change the glory of an incorruptible God into an image of a corruptible god.

"Results of the influence of the curse upon Canaan have become evident throughout the world. Paul carefully lays down description of the way men have proceeded. God gives them over to doing the things they desire in their hearts, dishonoring their bodies among themselves in prostitutions. They alter the truth of God into the lie and exalt others above God. Then God gives them over to dishonorable passions. Female with female, male with male—they change the natural use of their bodies and crave one another instead. When a society reaches a certain point of depravity, they turn to homosexuality. Paul says they are effecting indecency then get proper return for their own deception. As they no longer test God or recognize Him as God, He gives them over to a disqualified mind to do all sorts of sinful acts. Paul lists more than twenty injustices they go on to commit. He said those who commit such things are ones knowing the just statutes of God. He says they know the ones committing such things are worthy of death, yet they not only continue to do them themselves—they endorse others doing them. Paul began all this by saying God's indignation is being revealed through this irreverence and injustice. It seems clear homosexuality is a measure of the depth of man's depravity. And it seems equally clear the more prevalent homosexuality becomes, the more intolerable it will be with God. God could not allow it to run its course in the days of Noah, nor will He allow it to run its course in the days ahead. Only the presence of the Holy Spirit holds it in check today. We can only imagine what the world will be like when the Holy Spirit is withdrawn from the earth. Except the days shall be shortened, all humanity would be destroyed.

"Jesus said, as it was in the days of Noah—thus, it shall be in the presence of the Son of mankind. It has become widespread throughout the world. It is indeed a shameful thing, but as evil as the world will become, we may thank God His grace will save all humanity from its own destruction, and God will become all in all."

The road back to reality for Edward was not a very smooth one, as might be expected. Mark was careful not to force his way into Edward's life, but at the same time, he was relentless in his effort to get Edward to associate with him and other neighbors. Opportunities to relate to him were hard to come by during the winter months, yet even the association from a distance, so to speak, had served to prevent Edward from retreating into the old pattern.

On what might have been the first warm day of the following spring, for it was only mid-March, Mark carried Deanna outside to enjoy the sunshine. Edward was standing in the alley. Mark put Deanna on the ground, after which she began walking toward

Edward. Pulling away from Mark's hand, he let her go to him. A broad smile covered his face, and a look of affection appeared. Deanna walked straight to Edward with outstretched arms, giggling as she went, now almost on a run. Edward reached out for her to keep her from falling.

Edward was almost as gleeful as Deanna was. "Pretty," he said. "Such a pretty little girl," he said to her again.

As though she knew what he was saying, she enjoyed it as much as Edward did. Clearly, he had found a friend as well. Over the summer, Edward played with Deanna often. They were truly fascinated with one another.

One evening, Edward sat on the steps leading to his back porch, with Deanna sitting on his lap. His eyes moist as he recalled events of his own childhood, he said to Mark, "I remember good times, my sisters and me, we be small. I do not remember they be this little," he said, looking at Deanna. "But I remember good times. On Shabbat, I look for three stars in heavens. That mean it be Shabbat already."

Shabbat was the Jewish term for what we call the Sabbath. It was the seventh day of every week, the day of rest, and for them, the seventh day was Saturday. Each Friday evening, Shabbat began at sundown and continued until sundown the following evening. In Edward's home, it had been the custom for the youngest child to stand watch and let the family members know when three stars had appeared in the sky. Visibility of the stars was the official indication Shabbat had begun. Each of the three children had taken their turn at carrying out the responsibility but only as long as it was fun and they remained eager to do it. When it became drudgery, it was discontinued. It was meant to create excitement for the little children and make them feel they were an important part of the festivities.

Mark was glad Edward talked about his childhood, for it seemed to him to be a very good sign. "What was Shabbat like in your home?" Mark asked, having genuine interest.

It had been the most enjoyable of times in their home. Mr. Rydz had stressed the observance of the day, insisting every Shabbat was just as important as any festival day. Following breakfast each Friday morning, Mrs. Rydz began the challah dough-making process. The kitchen table was soon covered with a mixture of yeast, flour, and cracked eggs. In later years, Ersa and Naomi were permitted to help with this responsibility. They kneaded the dough and then left it to rise on its own. Sometime later in the morning, they punched it down then kneaded it again to let it rise once more. After school was out, or just past midafternoon, it was again time to punch down the dough. This time they were allowed to mold it into whatever shapes they might choose. This was special fun for the youngsters. They brushed the loaves with egg white and sprinkled them with poppy seeds.

"Daddy say poppy seeds stand for manna falling from heavens while our people they wander through wilderness," Edward told him.

The loaves were covered and allowed to rise for about one hour before baking. There were at least two loaves of challah: one for the evening meal, and one for the late morning meal of Shabbat. A third meal was customary, just before sundown. No cooking was allowed on the Shabbat, so everything had to be prepared the day before; however, no challah was prepared for that meal. "At sundown, Saturday was Havdelah candle ceremony—candlelight and wine. This show separation of Shabbat from rest of week," he said.

"Daddy say, in old times, no fire allowed on Shabbat. Lighting candle show end of restriction and give light as darkness come. We not pass challah at evening meal—we pass spice box instead. Ersa and Naomi, they bless candles. I bless wine and spices.

"I remember good, like maybe yesterday. Mama put challah on challah plate, cover until it be blessed. Just before ghetto, Ersa and Naomi, they light candles and they bless. I remember, Mama cry when we leave candlesticks at ghetto. So little time, we leave many things, we leave quickly. If only we do it now," he said, as tears filled his eyes.

"I know it could never be exactly the same Edward," Mark said affectionately, having shared somewhat in Edward's grief. "You could have a family of your own and raise them to enjoy the things you enjoyed so much. No one can ever take away the love you have for your family, but you can begin a new life here in America and create your own traditions. Someday, your children can remember the same kind of experiences you talk about."

"Maybe I have daughter like Dee-Dee. Maybe I have two

daughters like Dee-Dee," he said, with a faraway look. "Maybe like Ersa and Naomi," he added thoughtfully.

Mark poured over the scriptures every available moment. No time spent in Bible study can be considered time wasted, but while he benefited a great deal from his studies, he seemed no nearer his objective. But one evening, while looking intently into a study of the book of Ephesians, he observed an interesting, though perplexing arrangement in the use of the pronouns displayed there. Why had Paul used with regularity, the pronouns *we, our,* and then for no obvious reason, abruptly changed them to *you* and *your*? The same was found to be true going in reverse order, regularly using the pronouns *you* and *your* then changing them to *we, us,* and *our*.

At casual examination, it seemed Paul was alternating their uses indiscriminately. Yet he knew Paul would have good reason for his choice of words. Mark was at a loss to explain why he hadn't seen this before. More than that, why hadn't others written about it? Then he recalled Harold Mason bringing it to his attention. *I wonder what Harold has found,* he thought.

On a more analytical examination, Mark found some interesting factors. He immediately recognized the fact of Paul's entire message becoming directed mainly to those of the nations. It was only natural to assume the *yon* and *your* would refer to those of the nations, whom he was addressing. At the same time, he was aware Paul had directed his message first to the Jews. Many Jews had become members of the body of Christ. Why then should they not comprise those whom Paul referred to as *we, us,* and *our.* After all, Paul was of the Circumcision and Benjamin, which made him a member of the house of Judah.

It opened doors of understanding amazing even to Mark. The Holy Spirit had certainly revealed many matters of understanding to Mark but none more clearly than this. While Paul was writing to one group, he was associating them with the other, and both groups were considered to be "saints." He had already determined only an Israelite was considered a saint, for only an Israelite becomes ceremonially consecrated to the Law of Moses. It was likely common understanding the two groups were the Circumcision and the Uncircumcision. But it was much more. Those of the nations could not be Gentiles and also be saints according to the very definition. These saints could be none other than the lost tribes of Israel—the people God once cast away, but whom He was now bringing back to Him. "Isn't it precisely what God promised to do?" he asked himself.

What Mark had uncovered startled him. Suddenly realizing if what he had found was true, Paul was addressing people of all the nations of the earth, as his direction of ministry stated, but it was people who once had been members of the ten tribes, making up the house of Israel, who were responding. It seemed the only accurate conclusion to the truth Paul had established: he was addressing those Israelites from among the nations who were believers in Christ Jesus.

Mark was well aware of Paul's reference to Old Testament scriptures along those lines, but it hadn't occurred to him to make the association in that way. Hosea states, "I shall be calling those who are not My people, 'My people,' And she who is not beloved, 'Beloved.'" It went on to say if He did not save a seed, they would become as the city of Sodom. And if the number of the sons of Israel should be as the sand of the sea, the residue shall be saved. It was clear! Paul was calling out that "seed," while the entire residue is being saved since that day.

All this told Mark the true believers today are really those Israelites who have lost their identity but are being taken back by God in fulfillment of His promise. This was precisely what Paul was called out to accomplish; to bring the two houses together.

"Young lady! Why don't we put the food in our mouth instead of on the floor?" Mark was trying to give Deanna what was left of her jar of baby food. "If you don't want it, I guess I'll have to eat it myself," he said, pretending to put it in his own mouth.

As though she understood Mark's antics, she giggled and swung her hands in the air all the more.

The doorbell rang. Handing the nearly empty jar of baby food to Claire, he went to answer the door. Standing outside the door was Edward. In all the time they had been neighbors, this was the first time he had found occasion to approach them in their home.

With a broad grin appearing on his face, he said to Mark, "I have news to tell you. Today, I write to my lady. I ask her to come to America. I ask her to be my wife. Already I send letter. I wait to hear from her."

This was wonderful news to Mark and Claire, as positive a step in the direction of making a new life for himself, as Mark could imagine. It was a matter he had prayed for faithfully and he was indeed happy for Edward.

"Maybe I have little girl like Dee-Dee. Maybe my lady like it here too. Maybe we have good life in America." The smile broadened, revealing the confidence Edward felt in having made the decision to ask Maria to be his wife and lifetime companion.

The smile disappeared from Edward's face. "I have something to ask, Mr. Mark. It is Jewish custom when man take wife, he ask his brother, or best friend, if he stand up with him. I have no brother, so will you be best friend?" he asked.

But only after he had finished stating his request, did there appear any evidence of worry on Edward's face. It seemed his concern for making the request properly had precluded any concern for whether it might be accepted or rejected.

Mark was elated with Edward's request. He had never been asked to be the best man at a wedding, though he always knew he would consider it a matter of greatest friendship.

"You are first friend to know I ask my lady to marry me, so if you not want to be best friend, it is all right."

Mark was quick to answer. The fact Edward had approached him in this way gave him a wonderful feeling of trust. "I would consider it an honor and a privilege to carry out such a request," he said to Edward. "And when Maria accepts your proposal, I hope you will tell me so I can be the first to congratulate you."

Claire was doing the dishes as they talked, taking in the entire conversation, and was equally happy for Edward. "When do you think Maria will be coming to America?" she asked.

"Maria and me, we talk much about marriage in letters. I see how happy you be and how much family you be. I decide I be happy in America. I decide Maria be happy too. When I tell my uncle what I decide, he give me money and say, 'Send it to Maria so she come to America.' I did it today already." The broad smile returned to Edward's face. "Maria already tell me she like to be my wife, so you not have to worry about congratulating, you talk about."

Now a smile appeared on Mark's face. He reached out to grasp Edward's hand. "Congratulations, Eddy. I wish you every kind of happiness. And thank you for telling Claire and me and confiding in us. I will be very happy to be your best man."

Mark had wondered about Maria's life in the ghetto and the Holocaust years. It had puzzled him as to how she had been allowed to stay at home all during the period while most Jews underwent such extreme persecutions. This seemed a good opportunity to get Edward to talk about the past, and so he did ask.

Edward was quite eager to tell the story of Maria's survival. Though much more simple as to detail, it was no less unique than most any of the stories of survival of his people.

Maria Zelinski and her family lived near a city later chosen as a site for one of the many ghettos. Maria became a close friend of a girl living next door. The two of them were almost inseparable. The ugly clouds of the coming dangers were well formed all about them. The local gendarmes had begun their movement to remove all the Jewish members of the community and place them in the ghettos. It wasn't a matter looked upon by all as being such a terrible thing. The Germans always tried to make the Jewish people think it was for their own good. Maria's parents were not taken in by this deception, however.

As circumstances would dictate, the two little girls were out playing together when the officers came to gather up the Jewish families of the area. Being frightened by all the excitement, the two girls hid under the porch of a house nearby. Maria's older brother became so incensed by the treatment they received; he struck out at one of the officers. In retaliation, a number of them opened fire upon him. Not only was her brother killed in the melee, but also a stray bullet struck Maria's little friend in her forehead. She was killed instantly. Maria remained hidden until the officers had gone, taking her family with them. Fortunately for Maria, the gendarmes knew nothing of the incident. It was decided by the family to quietly bury their daughter and keep Maria as their own. While several families in the neighborhood knew of Maria's identity, not one reported the incident to the authorities.

CHAPTER 23

"Good morning, Joseph. What brings you out so bright and early?" It was a beautiful morning, and Mark realized he was thinking how Joseph's presence was always a nice way to start the day.

"Ah!" Joseph said, showing a degree of concern. "I'm afraid I have something urgently needing to get done. You have busy schedule. I understand if you are not able to handle problem. You see, Edward and Maria, they set wedding date for only two weeks, too soon! Can you believe that? We not get announcements to friends and relatives, much too soon! How we get announcements out to everybody, I ask you?" Joseph was indeed hoping for a solution.

Mark immediately wanted to lessen Joseph's need for concern. "We better not waste time," he said. "Let's draw up a plan for what we need. You give me the information, and I'll work it out from there. If I have to, I'll finish them after hours tonight. You can pick them up first thing in the morning."

"You take big worry off me, Mark."

"Just a matter of priority. We have to determine what's most important then go from there. I have to admit, seeing things go well for Edward is pretty high on my priority list. I won't mind if I have to stay late."

"Having you for friend is one fine asset, Mark." His affection for Mark was evident. "You bring Edward out of past and make him see he have future now. For one year, I not make him see that. You are good friend. I can't thank you too much."

Almost apologizing, Mark was saying, "I do appreciate your kind words, but really I think it's Deanna who deserves credit for bringing Edward out of his past, as you say."

"What's this? A story behind what you say?" Joseph asked. "Your little Deanna did that?"

"A story, I suppose. Deanna did find her way into Edward's heart. She brought back some beautiful memories for him, memories of his own sisters and how much he loved them. I do think she was the key. He believes now as a family they can find happiness and create memories for children of their own. I think it was God Who worked it out by His Own counsel. He chose Deanna to bring it about."

"You be good friend! Now I think we better get this organized so I can leave and you can do your work. I have Edward tell you about your part in wedding. I think he should do that. Oh! I think also Edward has one more favor to ask of you and Claire. But I leave it to Edward."

Edward took care of his responsibilities well. The same evening, he called on Mark to tell him of the rehearsal. The wedding was scheduled for a Tuesday afternoon, having something to do with being preferred because considering the six days of creation, more things created on Tuesday were said to be good than on any other day. Maria would not arrive till Sunday before the wedding, but it would still allow adequate time for rehearsal.

Mark had told Claire there would be another request from Edward. "I hope she wants me to be her maid of honor. Every girl wants to have the honor at least once," she said. It was indeed the request Edward would make. Claire readily accepted.

"Maria, Maria not know people in America. I tell her you be nice people. She say you ask Mrs. Hayes be my attendant. Now I ask. You accept," he said with a shrug of his shoulders. "Maria be happy you both be best friends."

With Mark and Claire not being Jewish, there could be no formal ceremony performed in the synagogue. However, an informal ceremony did take place there. The bride wore a full-length white gown with a short veil. The maid of honor and the bridesmaids wore gowns of the same pattern, each a different color. The men wore dark business suits.

Even though it was an informal ceremony, it was nonetheless a gala affair. Joseph was well known by all the worshippers of the synagogue and well liked. Each had been issued an invitation. It seemed every worshipper made arrangements to attend.

The fathers of the bride and groom signed the legal agreement of the betrothal shortly before the wedding was to begin. The couple's names were placed on the marriage contract along with the date and location to complete their contractual obligations. After the groom formally stated acceptance of his obligations, two men, unrelated to the groom, signed it as having witnessed the formality.

The wedding canopy, still called chuppah from ancient times, though solid in structure, was portable and provided cover for the bride and groom as well as for the rabbi and the attendants. One of four of Edward's friends stood at each corner post according to traditional weddings. A beautiful lace-trimmed fabric hung from the top of the chuppah, with a corner draped low from the center of each side. With the rabbi and the two attendants already standing in the chuppah as honorary parents of Edward, Joseph and his wife escorted the groom there. Just as had the parents of the groom, both parents of the bride escorted her to the chuppah where she stood next to the groom. This came as a pleasant surprise to everyone, for it was not made known beforehand, Joseph provided means for Maria's mother and father (foster parents) to attend. They arrived only hours before the ceremony.

The bride and groom drank in turn from the cup of wine. The rabbi asked if the ring belonged to the groom. It was the principle function for the two witnesses who were in the chuppah to verify it did indeed belong to him. The groom then proposed to the bride reciting the marriage formula, "Behold, thou art betrothed unto me, with this ring, in accordance with the Law of Moses and Israel."

Then he placed the ring on her ring finger. This too was according to tradition, so it might readily be seen as proof of their consent to marry.

The Keturah, the marriage contract written in Aramaic, was then read aloud. The rabbi recited the seven benedictions over a glass of wine. The bride and groom drank from the glass, and then the groom smashed it with his foot.

The entire party faced east during the ceremony in honor of the old temple site in Jerusalem. The smashing of the wineglass is thought to be in memory of the destruction of the temple in AD 70. The wedding began and ended with the temple clearly in mind.

It was a beautiful ceremony. The people were warm and friendly and in no hurry to move away from the company of the bride and groom. An attractive couple, they showed no hint of the hardship they had endured during their young lives. Indeed, through the happiness displayed, it was evident they were on their way toward beginning renewed lives together in an all-new world.

Mark and Claire were finally able to move to the table where the gifts were neatly stacked. There the Keturah lay in full view for everybody to inspect. "What a lovely piece of artwork!" Claire exclaimed.

Mr. and Mrs. Zelinski were friends of people in Poland who were extremely talented in the kind of scribal art this Keturah revealed. Being such a delicate work, it was one any Jewish family would no doubt be grateful to own and very likely treasure for a lifetime.

"Mr. and Mrs. Hayes, what did you think of the Jewish wedding ceremony?" Rabbi Jonathan Steindler approached them as they admired the Keturah.

"It was lovely, Rabbi Steindler," Claire said to him. "All the ceremony was lovely. It seems apparent, Rabbi, we were observing a great deal of tradition here today. This was the first Jewish wedding we've attended. I'm glad we could be a part of it."

"It's nice to see you people again. Things were pretty hectic the other evening. I wasn't able to spend much time with you. I've heard much about the three of you. Oh, don't look so surprised! I heard about little Deanna too. Yahweh works in marvelous ways."

Mark was pleased the rabbi was told of the role Deanna played in Edward's life.

The rabbi was getting up in years and probably could have retired some years before had he chose to do so. Being tall and slender, the black robe and cap made him appear all the more so.

His hair was turning white, but the change in his hair was noticeably lagging behind his already snow-white beard. Indentations at the corners of his mouth created the allusion of a perpetual smile, which seemed to verify he was genuinely happy and a good-natured individual. He found a row of empty seats and invited them to sit with him.

"I must say, Edward has talked a great deal about you since the wedding plans began coming together." He took Mark's hand and grasped it between his own. "I am happy for Edward and Maria and for Joseph. Joseph and I have been friends for many years now. He confided in me about his family all through those terrible war times. We could only observe all those tragic events happening, knowing we could do nothing about them. For many years, it was not known Edward was alive. When Joseph received the letter from him, it was one of the happiest days of his life. Then came the disappointments of the last year, Edward shutting himself off from the world. It's apparent your family turned his life in the right direction."

"You're right," he commented, getting back to the subject of the Keturah. "That's as beautifully hand scribed as anything I've ever seen, and it's truly the most meaningful wedding gift a Jewish couple can receive. Few wedding gifts will ever exceed this one in appreciation." "I can also appreciate it, Rabbi. It's truly a beautiful piece of work," Claire said, "and no doubt every stitch was hand done and the thread colors so beautifully coordinated."

"You're also right about our tradition, Mrs. Hayes. There is much tradition in a Jewish ceremony. I suspect you didn't know, centuries ago, it took a minimum of one year for a Jewish bride and groom to reach matrimony."

"That's interesting. It's hard to imagine a young person of today having that kind of patience," she said with a laugh.

"So true," he said while waiting for them to be seated. "As you may well imagine, Jewish weddings have been going on for several thousand years. Many changes have taken place over the centuries, but what you saw today is basically what survived from our illustrious history—that is, the wedding ceremony with the nonessentials stripped away."

Claire was about to ask him if he would tell them about it, but it proved to be unnecessary. Many guests had congregated around them. The rabbi enjoyed his opportunity to talk about the history of their tradition, an eloquent speaker who dearly loved to talk about anything concerning their history and their people. His people truly loved him and never tired from hearing his discourses.

"It used to be the parents entered into negotiations for their children," he said enthusiastically. "The young man's father was required to go to the girl's father and purchase his daughter to become his son's bride. Can you imagine a man actually buying his son's bride?" he said with a chuckle. "It was customary for the married couple to live with the parents of the groom. Therefore, it was the household of the bride losing the worker, and so compensation was to be made for the loss. The money negotiated also helped assure a future for the couple starting out. They were then required to wait for at least one year. That was called the betrothal. Following the betrothal, the groom went directly to the chuppah where he waited for the bride. With much rejoicing, friends and members of the family led the bride to the groom's chambers. There the wedding ceremony was consummated.

"In those days costly dinners were presented for all their friends and families. Often, the poor of the community were invited to the dinner, sometimes creating hardship for them. By the time of the Middle Ages, much of the extravaganza was done away with, leaving only the rudiments of the ceremony. Now there's only one gala affair. Probably, the greatest reason for eliminating the betrothal was because Jewish families were increasingly forced to pull up stakes and leave quickly, often in the middle of the night. Many betrothed couples were separated and unable to complete their plans."

Mark had been observing a nine-cupped arrangement of candleholders. He walked over to the table where it was being displayed.

"What a beautiful arrangement," he said, awed by its sheer magnificence. "May I ask of its purpose?"

"That's a hanukiyah. Each of those nine cups holds a candle to commemorate the Hanukkah festival. This particular one is among the finest hanukiyahs you will likely ever cast your eyes upon. I can't give you an accurate evaluation of it, but I can assure you it is quite a valuable item. It has become somewhat of a Jewish custom to place something of value within the house. That's in recognition they might be forced to leave quickly. Something of such value can be stashed in their belongings and taken along. When their time of trouble is over, they may sell the item and then begin life anew in a new location with the proceeds. It has been a very common event for the Jewish people down through the centuries. Not something we like to think about, nevertheless, it has become not at all uncommon. Joseph has told you of the terrible times caused by the Holocaust, but the Jews have been subjected to similar treatment for many centuries, on a lesser scale, of course.

"Many of our festivals are of somewhat doubtful origin, perhaps coming down from pagan practices, but Hanukkah commemorates a well-documented Jewish event."

Those words almost put Mark in shock. "That seems an extraordinary statement—festivals could be based upon pagan practices? I never heard it before," he said, still reeling from the effects.

The caterers indicated it was time for everyone to be seated lor the dinner. The bride and groom, with their wedding attendants, were ushered to the most prominent table. Soon, all had found their places. The rabbi blessed the meal then asked God's blessing upon the couple so they might have a long and happy life together. Many toasts followed, and the wine flowed in abundance. A joyous time of dining and consuming of wine was underway.

When most of the people were finished with the main course, someone remarked about the Rabbi's and Edward's fondness for lemon flavor. A delicious lemon souffle was served, and some members from their table began passing their desserts to them.

"Looks like I'm not the only one who enjoys lemon souffle," Mark said casually.

Claire began laughing. "That reminds me of a time I took a lemon cake to a reunion of Mark's family," she said. "There were three lemon cakes setting on the table."

At a table a short distance away, several young men were gesturing and laughing. They appeared to be practicing a cheer for leading their team to victory.

"I believe the cheering section is planning something," the rabbi said, smiling broadly. "I can't wait to see what's next."

The young men were enjoying their bit of humor, and they had gained the attention of most of the people in the room. Each of them picked up their desserts, and carrying them, they approached the table where the wedding party was seated. After placing them on the table in front of Rabbi Steindler, Edward, and Mark, they began their cheer.

We had our salad and steak today,
you guys can have our lemon souffle,
eat, 'til you've had your fill.
Hoo-ray! Hoo-ray! Hoo-ray!

A round of applause soon became a standing ovation.

"One thing's sure," Rabbi Steindler said once it became quiet, "the lemon souffle is much better than your verse. But I have to say, your enthusiasm is greatly appreciated."

Much singing and merriment followed the dinner. Never had Mark or Claire been part of a more unrestrained show of joy and happiness from people among their friends. Mark wondered how any festival could be more joyous than this celebration for Edward and Maria and what a display of love and affection from all. The later the hour, the more they drank. The more they drank, the merrier they became, and the more visible their love was for one another.

After much celebration, the bride and groom were at last ushered from the synagogue while being showered with rice. It became quiet for a moment but only for a moment. Though the hour was late, there was little evidence of the festivities ending very soon. As though expected, many congregated around the rabbi to hear what he would say. Everyone wanted to hear about the Jewish customs it seemed, as though they were eagerly awaiting the words for the first time. There were no objections from Rabbi Steindler.

It was Joseph who determined the direction of the conversation. "Rabbi Steindler," he said, as it became quiet, "I detected some surprise with Mark when you say, some festivals are doubtful as to how they began. I know Mark is curious about things like that."

The statement the rabbi made had seemed to Mark a rather

peculiar one. "That's true, Joseph, I guess I assumed all festivals were carefully spelled out somewhere in your scriptures. It comes as a shock to find I was wrong. After all, Purim is clearly stated in the book of Esther, and the details of Passover were equally as explicit in the book of Exodus. Both observances were to be strictly upheld and taught to each succeeding generation."

"That's a very interesting matter, Mr. Hayes," the rabbi said. "A number of festivals seem to have been practiced in similar ways by the heathen nations. They carried out similar rituals when in the acts of worshiping their gods. It seems more important we know to Whom we worship and do so in the right spirit. It is of the utmost importance we give all glory to the God of Israel.

"Perhaps you have heard of the great teacher Hillel? The man lived during the era of Jesus Christ, the man on Whom the Christian church bases its belief. It is even thought Jesus may have sat under Hillel's teaching. Oh yes! We recognize Jesus as being one of the greatest of Hebrew rabbis. Hillel was a great scholar who traveled from Babylon to Jerusalem in about 40 BC to learn under the tutelage of Avtalyon and Shemaiah. Tradition teaches the fact those two great teachers descended from pagans, which converted to Judaism. It teaches that Hillel came to view God's message in the Torah as universal.

"Hillel shared his leadership with a teacher by the name of Shammai. Their personalities differed sharply. There's a story telling of a heathen coming to Shammai claiming he wanted to convert to Judaism if he could teach him the entire Torah while standing on one foot. In anger, Shammai drove him away. But Hillel answered the heathen kindly, saying, 'What is hateful to you, do not do unto your neighbor. This is the entire Torah; all the rest is commentary. Go and learn it!' According to the story, the heathen was converted. Those words are remarkably similar to what Paul said about the commandments in your scriptures and indeed what Jesus Himself taught," he added.

The idea the Torah might be universal, suddenly fit nicely into what Mark had learned from the writings of the apostle Paul. He told the rabbi, "Paul tells us in the book of Romans the truth has been descried to man since his beginning. Maybe that harmonizes with what you told us. He says in spite of that, man has ignored the truth and built idols for worship, instead. The pagans did have their idols, didn't they?"

Rabbi Steindler gave a nod in recognition of what Mark had said. "Anyway, this festival was derived from the rededication of the second temple in 165 BC. In those days, the Syrian people were trying to destroy the Jewish belief. For many years, they attempted to convert the Jews to the Hellenistic way of believing by attracting them to the Greek life and culture. Those who held tenaciously to the Mosaic principles were not willing to pay homage to Zeus, the Greek sun god. A few of those of the upper classes did willingly convert, but later, it became necessary for the Syrian ruler to charge those who did not give in willingly to be forced to do so. Mattathias Maccabee spurred on the Jewish people. His son Judah then organized them. Though their numbers were many fewer than the Syrians were, they battled successfully and regained the temple.

"The candle-lighting custom came to symbolize Jewish survival against all odds. According to the tradition, when Judah Maccabee regained the temple, there was but one sealed vial of oil in the sanctuary. It provided only enough oil to burn one day. What should have been only enough oil to burn one day burned on for eight days."

The rabbi smiled broadly. His eyes sparkled as he continued speaking. "You may well imagine the light of the oil came to symbolize the light of Judaism, neither one being extinguished, but rather continuing to burn supernaturally throughout even the darkest hours. On the other hand, the Maccabeans were so outnumbered they should logically have been slain in a single day. The belief and determination of those few overcame the brute strength of the Syrians, and Judaism was preserved.

"One new candle is to be lighted each day and left burning for the remainder of the eight-day period. The ninth holder is for the 'servant' candle, which is used to light the other eight. It is called the Shamash and is not to be extinguished."

"What a beautiful story!" Claire exclaimed. "Are all your festivals as colorful in meaning as Hannukah?"

"I believe they are," the rabbi answered. "Perhaps you and Mr. Hayes would like to attend a Purim spiel sometime? Purim is the most joyous festival of them all. In our synagogue, the children act out a little skit as a reader narrates the story. In fact, it is the story of the book of Esther, of which I'm sure you are familiar. That celebration will not occur until early March, but maybe you can attend sometime in the future. You will be welcome.

"It's doubtful even the festival of Purim is based upon an actual historical event. I'm sorry, Mark," he said. "I don't mean to startle you. We, as in all synagogues, observe it just as we are admonished to do. But the fact is, in all the history of that great kingdom, there is no record of there having been a Jewish queen or even a queen by the name of Esther. There is no record of there having been a ranking Jewish official, and no one by the name of Mordecai stationed second only to the king himself. So there is no record of there having been a Jew holding either of those positions. It is a matter of record any king was to choose his wife from among the seven prominent families of the lands, and those choices were scrupulously maintained, making it doubtful King Ahasuerus could have married a Jewess even had he desired to do so."

"I must admit, Rabbi, what you are saying rather shakes my confidence in believing every word of the Bible is inspired by God, literally, God-breathed. That's what I've always believed."

"I understand, Mr. Hayes. I too believe every word of scripture is God-breathed. It's not that we don't believe the authority of the book—we only doubt it should be seen as an actual historical event. If you will read the book of Esther carefully and with certain thoughts in mind as you read, you will see a greater purpose than you've recognized before. We, of this synagogue, have written the story into a little skit. That's the Purim spiel I mentioned before. In it, a narrator tells the story, while the children act out the scenes through dialogue. As each scene unfolds, the hand of God is seen, always creating the proper situation to move it closer to His desired conclusion. In other words, God intercedes in every stage of its unfolding to reveal His will all along the way.

"Truly, Mark, it depicts the people of Israel having been scattered about the world and being persecuted everywhere they locate. God allows every persecution. Greater still, He remembers every persecution in order to bring victory to His people in the end. We look to the book of Esther more as a book of promise, for it reveals us as being God's people, and one day, we shall no longer be in the servitude of our enemies. We enter into the joy of looking forward to the day we will be free from our oppression, something more prophetic than fact."

The explanation made a great deal of sense to Mark, even though it would require a rather radical departure from his previous thinking. "It has become quite a puzzle to me why God seems to require so much suffering from His people," Mark said thoughtfully. "Everybody suffers to some degree, but your people seem always to get the brunt of it from every direction," he added. Mark knew this would not come as a news bulletin to anyone in this group, but he wanted to hear all he could from the Jewish point of view. Perhaps he could find the answer to why they seem to be required to bear more hardship than any other people was.

Joseph again spoke up, saying, "Our people have been persecuted ever since they dwelled in Egypt. They know what it is to be badly persecuted."

"That's very true, Joseph," the rabbi said. "The Egyptians had already made the Israelites to be their servants and do hard labor in serving them. They were further embittered by being forced to make bricks for building walls around some of their cities."

The rabbi directed his comments to Mark and Claire, though everyone present listened carefully to every word. "This went on for many more years," he said. He continued, "The king of Egypt who placed the burden upon them died. New kings ruled over them, one who was even more wicked than the former. Moses had been born and called out by Yahweh. He had heard the cry of the people. When Moses informed the new pharaoh he must let the people of Israel go, he became angered and placed even more cruel exactions upon them. Pharaoh instructed the superintendents chosen from the Israelites. They would no longer be furnished with the straw to mold the bricks as had been done before. Now they would have to go into the fields themselves and rake up the crushed straw. The number of bricks they were required to make would not be decreased. When these quotas were not met, the superintendents were beaten and called slackers for not doing their jobs. It did no good when the people complained to Pharaoh and tried to convince him the burden was too great for them. Through Moses, they cried out to Yahweh again. From that day, Yahweh began to show His hand in the matter of taking His people from the land of Egypt. But it also set the stage for a long, long history of suffering and persecution for our people."

"Rabbi," Mark began cautiously, "all this suffering, I mean, how do you respond to all the suffering and hardship that's placed upon your people? Don't you feel as though God is placing too many burdens on you? Don't you feel He's being unfair and perhaps singling you out? I greatly admire the Jewish people for their patience and perseverance. But I think I would be inclined to lash out at Him for being unfair."

"We are God's chosen people. We are being molded so we may carry out our responsibility to the rest of mankind. Indeed, being perfected through our suffering is molding us. Our suffering only began at the time of the great Exodus. It continues with every generation. If it means suffering until every last man on earth has come to know God, so be it."

CHAPTER 24

Mark's family had finally arranged to attend a Purim spiel at the synagogue where Edward attended services. Deanna was only six years old at the time, but she had been totally fascinated with the program, especially the clackers. Edward told Deanna, many times over the summer, about the sukkah they would build in the fall, promising she could come over and eat in a real "tabernacle" out in the backyard. This excited Deanna.

Edward had a son, David, almost two years old, and a daughter, Evon, three. They named their children after their own parents, the boy after Maria's father and the girl after Edward's mother. They laughed about the arrangement, saying it was better than the alternative. Bratislav was a fine Polish name, but it somehow didn't seem appropriate for an eight-day-old Jewish American boy. Deanna loved Edward as much as ever and equally enjoyed being with the children, often pretending she was their mother.

Each year in the fall season and on the first day of the seventh month, Tishri, the Jewish community begins twenty-three days of almost continuous religious observance. The first day marks the beginning of the Jewish New Year and is called Rosh Hashanah. This observance continues for ten days, ending with Yom Kipper. The ten-day period is known as the Days of Awe, or Days of Repentance. Yom Kipper is considered the most important of all Jewish holidays. It is to be treated with solemnity with fasting and much prayer. At sundown on the tenth day, the New Year has "officially" arrived. Preparation for Sukkoth immediately begins and continues until day fifteen. Sukkoth begins on the fifteenth day and lasts for seven days. In the land of Israel, it ends with yet another holiday on the twenty-third day, Shemini Atzeret. Outside the land, the day is not observed, and it all concludes on the twenty-second day of Tishri called Simchat Torah.

The present occasion was Sukkoth. Sukkoth is an observance for those who were born in the land, but many of those of the Diaspora celebrate it wherever they are. A sukkah is a booth built by the family to commemorate the temporary shelters used by the Israelites during their wilderness wandering following the exodus from Egypt. A great deal of latitude is permitted for building this booth, or sukkah, but essentially, it is to be small and is meant to cause hardship such as their fathers experienced. Also termed a tabernacle, it must have at least three sides. The roof is to be open, covered with tree branches and leaves, and at least a few stars must be visible through the roof. Tradition requires some household furnishings of value should be placed there since in those ancient times, they carried with them all they owned. They could eat one meal in the sukkah or every meal according to preference. The same is true of sleeping in the sukkah, except they are not required to sleep there at all. However, more is expected of those living in the land. Edward and his family did faithfully eat their meals there. Sukkoth is a time of great joy and merriment, and many of their friends visit and share food with them. Gentiles are welcome, for it signifies a time when they are to make peace for having oppressed the Jews.

From the day the booth was erected, and the furnishings put in place, Deanna had pleaded with Mark and Edward to allow her and Evon to spend one night sleeping in the booth. After much discussion, it was decided to let them remain there until they fell asleep. Building some simple wooden frame structures to be used as beds, they placed them in the booth. Padding them with blankets, they placed sleeping bags on them. It would be an evening of enjoyment mainly for the girls. Each family prepared food dishes, and so the Hayes family came to join the Rydz family to dine under the stars out in the "wilderness."

Evon was as excited as Deanna. Before it was even dark, they lay snuggled in their sleeping bags. It was a cool evening. The families carried lawn chairs into the yard where they sat visiting.

Not wanting to spoil the evening for the girls, they even wrapped themselves in blankets to keep warm. David crawled onto Mark's lap where he got warm and soon was sound asleep. As it neared ten o'clock, they began getting things together to go in for the night.

Since Mark was already holding David, he carried him inside the house and put him on his bed where Maria took over the task of getting him into his pajamas and tucked in. From inside the house, Mark heard the panicked cry of Edward's voice, "Fire! The sukkah's on fire! Flurry, Mark! Fire! Fire!" By the time Mark was outside, he saw Edward, silhouetted against a mountain of flames, running from the sukkah carrying one of the girls. Racing to the sukkah, he found it filled with dense smoke and rapidly becoming an inferno. Reaching the cots where the girls slept in their sleeping bags, he found no one in them. Following the sounds of her cries for help, he stumbled onto Evon's body. She was out of her sleeping bag, crouched low against the back wall and trying desperately to get away from the scorching heat but with no place to go. In a single motion, Mark swept Evon into his arms and, in a spinning motion, threw their combined weight against the weakly constructed frame, crashing through to the outside.

Immediately, the booth was a mass of flames, but the rescue was over almost as quickly as it began. A neighbor had called the fire department, which arrived in only minutes. The building was small, quite uncomplicated in structure, and therefore, the fire was quickly extinguished. Edward was asked not to disturb anything inside the booth and to try to keep anyone else from entering.

Still coughing from having inhaled smoke into her lungs, they thought it advisable to take Evon to the emergency room as a precautionary measure. Evon was kept overnight in the hospital so her condition could be closely monitored. The worst effects of her ordeal were seen as symptoms similar to rather severe sunburn. To be sure, there were some very relieved parents.

The police were out early the next morning to seal off the area. It reeked of being an act of vengeance, and when it was learned of Edward's ethnic stock, it became the direction of investigation. Being plainly an act of arson was never questioned. Mark and

Edward were asked to reenact the episode in order to determine the amount of the elapsed time. From the time they left the yard to go inside the house to the time Edward was outside again was estimated to be no more than ninety seconds. And the time elapsing from the moment Mark heard Edward frantically shouting and the time he saw the flaming booth would have taken no more than another thirty seconds. They all agreed it might have taken even less time than the estimate indicated. When Edward went running to the booth, almost directly in his line of vision while leaving the kitchen door, he saw a figure standing beside his garage. It was dimly outlined but undeniably the form of a person illuminated by a yard light casting its light from a yard a short way up the alley. "It look more like boy than man," Edward had informed the officers. "Maybe little man," he added.

The primary concern for the police was of what knowledge did the arsonist have about the girls sleeping in the booth; specifically, was it a case of attempted homicide, or was the person or persons even aware someone was sleeping inside?

A team of investigators from the state fire marshal's office arrived late in the morning. Their main concern was to determine how the fire was started and what caused it to burn out of control so quickly. A number of photographs were taken of the burned out structure. Mark and Edward heard much of the conversation between the police and the fire officials, as they shared their findings. They pointed out what they called a flammable liquid spall pattern, which was caused by a liquid puddle burning at a much higher temperature than the surrounding area. Also, there was a distinctive V pattern at the foot of one of the wooden frame cots where the puddle stopped, and the extreme heat blazed upward igniting the bed coverings. By these, they were able to determine the fire originated with a highly flammable liquid of some type: probably gasoline. Near the spall was found a charred wooden match. One officer said, "A second match probably ignited the fumes." In the yard, near the chain-link fence separating the two properties, was found an empty mason fruit jar containing residue and still giving off the strong odor of gasoline. It was thought the gasoline was tossed through the window and so the window frame was dusted for fingerprints as well as the container. "It sure looks like the work of an amateur," one of the officers remarked. "That would also coincide with Mr. Rydz's conclusion it was a boy he saw standing by the garage. The next question is whether perhaps there is a boy in the neighborhood who has anti-Semitic feelings, assuming, of course, that was the motive. Can you offhand think of anyone?" the officer asked more pointedly.

Mark thought of the conversation between himself and some neighbors, taking place at a time shortly after Edward moved into his house. They had discussed Edward's reluctance to speak to anyone for a time. He explained the experience to the officers, apologizing to Edward as he spoke. "Harry Downing lived on the other side of Edward. We were talking when Lincoln Bailey, he lives across the alley from Harry, happened along. Something was said of the possibility of Edward being Jewish. Lincoln made it quite plain he disliked Jews." Mark apologized again to Edward.

"You say what you need to say, Mark. I know what Lincoln think. He tell me before."

"I think what I remember most plainly," Mark continued, "was him saying, 'So far, we did a good job keepin' the Niggers out of the neighborhood. Guess we blew it well when it came to keeping the Jews out.' I never thought it was more than just a lot of big talk, though."

"Are you suggesting he has a son who might be influenced by his father's 'big' talk?" an officer asked.

"Yes, sir, I am! His son, Ezra, is about twelve or thirteen. I've heard him yell some rather degrading remarks directed toward Edward. I'm not sure if Edward heard or not."

"What remarks?"

"Like a, 'Move out, Jew boy!' and 'Hey, Jew boy! Go back to Poland.' And one day, it was, 'Go back to the ghetto, pig.'"

"I hear what he says, good!" Edward said, holding his head low.

The officer thanked them both. "We'll have a talk with the Bailey boy and his father. If we can put a little scare into the boy, we just might find out who our arsonist is in a hurry."

"I hope the authorities don't go too hard on him. I doubt very much he knew anyone was even in the booth," Mark said as they were leaving.

"I suspect you're right, but the laws are quite specific as to the definition of first degree arson. Even though it's only a booth, it's designed to be lived in, even if only temporarily. The fact is, someone was dwelling inside, whether he knew it or not. Unfortunately, the state of Iowa needs to put some teeth into the law. Anyway, that's pretty much out of our hands.''

On the night following the investigation, Mark had trouble sleeping. He spent the evening, in fact much of a sleepless night, reconstructing in his mind what became evident to him. Though concerned about the ethnic situation and the crime itself, something else also occupied his thoughts. When Edward entered the burning booth, it was Deanna whom he gathered up and carried to safety. Edward had later stated he knew it was Deanna but he was unable to see his own daughter Evon through the smoke. It was evident Deanna had been in the most immediate danger, for when Mark entered, her bed was engulfed in flames. Edward had performed a very unselfish act. Under what must have been extreme emotional pressure, he chose to save Deanna rather than to look first for his own daughter. There was no question in Mark's mind Deanna would have been critically or even fatally burned or suffocated, from the extreme heat and smoke. Mark wondered if he himself could have made such a proper and unselfish decision. Thankfully, he would not have to answer the question for himself or for anyone else.

The longer he laid in bed, the more wide-awake he became. There was no way Mark would be going to sleep very soon. His eyes were as wide open as they were when he looked into the blazing fire. And of course, thoughts of the blazing fire were still a big part of the problem. He thanked God over and over for the deed Edward had done. There was little question in Mark's mind, if Edward had chosen to pass by Deanna and look for Evon in the smoke-filled booth, Deanna would surely have died in the blaze. Once again, he reached out in prayer to God, thanking Him for causing Edward to respond as he had. As it turned out, not only was Deanna alive, but also Evon was safe and sound. Clearly, the fire was an attack on Edward because of his ethnic ties, and even though it was the work of a mere child, it was almost an everyday occurrence for those people. Those aggressive attacks were waged often. "Thank You, my God and Father," he repeated.

"And, Father," he continued, "I want to ask a special favor of You. It is most difficult for me to comprehend why You have deemed it necessary for Your chosen people to suffer so much more than all other people. I ask You to reveal the answer to me. Please reveal to me the reason and what their rewards will be for going through it. May You give to me a taste of their suffering, if it is required for my comprehension? Amen!"

Mark opened his eyes, just as wide-awake as before. But what happened next could not have been a dream, for sleep was far, far from him. In but a moment's time, he became sensitive to the sound of train wheels as they pounded over gaps between the sections of rails. Standing inside a cattle car, at about eye level, he peered out through the narrow opening between the slats. The heat was stifling. The smell of body odor caused him to hold his breath 'til he could hold it no longer, for the car was filled with stinking bodies like his own. Deanna was sitting on the floor of the car, her slender, emaciated legs directed backward beneath her. She wrapped her arm around Mark's leg as her limp body shook from intense sobbing. Looking down upon the top of her head, he saw an oily, unkempt mass of lice infested hair. Claire sat beside her, presenting no more pleasant sight to his own reddened and tear-dimmed eyes. Having been brought from the ghetto, each still displayed bleeding welts caused by the whips used to drive them to the train station. There they had been herded into cattle cars, in which they had been confined and in which they were now riding.

Looking once again out through the narrow opening; oh, how he longed for him and his family to be free. Oh, to be on the other side of that wall. Gladly he would take his chances out there. A small herd of sheep stood grazing on a hillside. Even those sheep were better off than they were. No matter what their chances, they would be better than for those in the cattle car, packed in like sheep and not being treated nearly as well. At least there was a chance for freedom outside. The countryside in all its beauty made it so much harder to endure the confines of that crowded car.

"You're being taken to the east' where you'll be housed and given jobs in defense plants. You'll be helping the war effort." Those were the words they heard while being forced to leave the ghetto. But the rumor abounded, stating they were being taken to an extermination camp. Only those who refused to believe the rumor held out any hope at all. "I heard we're going to Sobibor," Mark heard someone say. "I heard we're going to a gas chamber in Auschwitz," someone else exclaimed.

"Daddy," Deanna said weakly, "I don't feel good."

Mark reached down and felt her forehead. Her face was reddened and hot with fever, and her body trembled.

The rhythmic clack of the wheels began to slow. They continued to reduce speed gradually until the train was barely moving at all. Inching its way along for a time, with one final thud, it came to a complete stop. Soon, the rattle of the padlock was heard as a key was being inserted. The snap made as the lock opened, then the removal of the key, and finally the long bar securing the door, moving out of position, was followed by the squealing sound made by the grease- starved rollers under the huge door as it came sliding open.

Several uniformed officers stepped into the car. "You've reached your destination. Get your belongings together! You'll be told where to go from here!" one of them shouted. Appraisals were made quickly as to where each family was being directed. At this point, it was merely from which side of the train they would exit. There were no whips being used now, but little patience was evidenced as the officers prodded the passengers along.

"Officer," Mark called out to the man approaching them. "Officer, my little girl needs medical attention. She is very ill! Please, may we see a doctor?"

"When you are properly registered and have taken showers and receive your issue of clothing, there will be ample medical facilities for everyone." He spoke loud enough for everyone to hear. "We have the finest doctors available at our disposal. Nothing to worry about," he shouted, showing little concern.

In a little while, they were ushered off the train and into a corridor, which led them into a large room. There they were further separated, sometimes even within families. It was moving more slowly than Mark could endure due to Deanna's deteriorating condition. Her forehead felt as though it were burning up with the fever. Much more than being listless, she could hardly raise her head from Mark's shoulder.

"Please, sir!" Mark called out as he saw the officer he had talked to before just a short distance away.

"What is it this time?" he asked impatiently. His complexion was reddish in color. His face was mostly covered with an auburn beard, as was the color as his hair. He was a large, towering man with huge hands. In spite of his physical features, he was no less a German than any other of the SS men. "You called to me, did you?" he asked.

"Please, sir," Mark repeated, "my little girl is very ill! Could we please see a doctor right away?"

Feigning affectionate concern, the officer said to Mark, "Let me see the child. Hold her out to me so I may look at her." When he did so, with a mighty swing, he slapped Deanna across the side of her head with his open gloved hand. Spun sideways by the force, her neck snapped. Making a short gasp, her head then fell limply against Mark's chest as he quickly drew her to him.

"She will be fine now." He pretended to restrain laughter by puffing his lips and cheeks outward while snickering.

Claire let out a scream in horror. Mark's temper immediately flared. Taking a step toward the officer, he then thought of Deanna and Claire and quickly backed away.

The officer had already placed his hand on his weapon. "That would be very foolish," he said.

Claire wanted to hold Deanna. As weak and as tired as she was, she wanted to hold her little girl.

"She's finally resting, Claire. Let's let her sleep."

Those who still remained were told to undress. "Remove all your clothing," an SS officer announced loudly. "Find a hook along the wall, and hang your clothes there. Be sure to remember the number you find at the hook. The next room is the shower room. After your shower," the officer continued, "you'll be issued a clean set of clothes. The clothes you were wearing when you came in will be carefully marked, so you'll get your own clothes back after they've been cleaned."

From there, they were directed into the next room, being prodded along quickly. A small bar of soap was issued to every person in the room.

"Deanna isn't breathing, Mark," Claire said, realizing the extent of what had happened to Deanna. "Oh, dear God! She's dead, isn't she? How could he do such a thing? The man is an animal." Claire was screaming in her anger.

"Shh, please, Claire, these people are capable of anything. I don't want anything to happen to you! Please!" Mark pleaded.

"But we're going to die anyway!" she whispered. "Don't you know that? Isn't it obvious to you too?"

"I know," he said softly. "Yes, we're going to die, probably right in this room. But let us die bravely, my darling. Yes, Deanna is gone now, but soon, we shall be together again. We are God's chosen people. This is our role. All men will come to know our God but only through our suffering. We must count it a privilege. Think of this as being the way the countless numbers from all nations will find life from out of these eons.

"Pray for those responsible for this. And pray for all God's people, Claire. Pray for His will to be accomplished very soon."

Standing there in the shower room, embracing one another and holding Deanna's lifeless body between them, the sound of escaping gas was heard from over their heads. Drifting downward from the inconspicuous heads mounted every few yards in the ceiling throughout the room, the gas settled upon them. At first, a cough was heard then another and another. Murmurs followed, and then as the people began to realize what was happening, great fear gripped them. Between the coughing and choking were laments in prayer arising all around. People fell to their knees as the grief from seeing their loved ones breathing their last settled upon them. From somewhere across the room came the lament: "Praise to the glory of our God. Glory to the God of Israel." The words trailed off as the voice became silent. As the coughing and final gasps for breath of life was leaving them, it became more and more quiet.

Mark lay there breathing his last nostril fulls of deadly gas, holding Deanna's body to him. Claire, lying beside him, whispered with her dying breath, "I love you, Mark. We will be together soon." Then came the sound of a voice filling the entire chamber. "They *devised it to you for evil, but I devised it for good—I, the Elohim of Israel.* " Then Mark exhaled his final breath.

As quickly as the trance began, it ended. Mark's eyes were wide open, for he had never been asleep. He was reminded immediately as the story of the sons of Jacob came to mind. What Mark heard spoken in the chamber was very similar to what Joseph said to his brothers those many, many centuries ago in Egypt.

Jacob loved Joseph more than any of his other sons, for Joseph was the son of his old age. When he was seventeen years of age, Jacob made him a distinctively colorful and beautiful tunic. When the brothers realized their father loved Joseph more than he loved them, they were jealous of their brother and hated him. One day, when they had been away longer than Jacob thought they should have been, he sent Joseph to find them to see if all was well. Joseph found his brothers where they grazed the sheep. When they saw their brother coming, they plotted to put him to death. But Reuben, the elder, convinced them to put him in a cistern and leave him there, for he intended to come back for Joseph and restore him to his father. But a caravan of Ishmaelites from Gilead, bearing perfume and balm, happened by, and Judah convinced his brothers to sell Joseph to them for twenty pieces of silver. Slaying a goat, they dipped the tunic in its blood and then gave it to his father to identify. Jacob mourned the loss of his son for many days.

In Egypt, a eunuch of King Pharaoh, an Egyptian and head of the executioners, bought Joseph. The Lord was with Joseph, and he became a wealthy man. He gained favor with Pharaoh when he interpreted dreams dreamed by Pharaoh. He foretold of the great abundance of crops continuing for seven years: bumper yields of all their grains. But a great famine would follow, also lasting for seven years. The famine would cover the entire land of Egypt and all the surrounding countries, including the land of Canaan where Joseph's family lived, just as would the seven years of good yields. During the good years, they should store up the abundance of the surplus to see them through the coming lean years. Of course, only those in the land of Egypt knew about the prophecy. In anticipation of what would occur, they built great bins to store the harvests of the good years. King Pharaoh was unable to find another man in all of Egypt with the wisdom of Joseph, so he placed Joseph over all the affairs of the kingdom, making him subject only to himself. And so Joseph became a man of great influence in Egypt and all the surrounding territories.

In due time, Jacob and his sons were forced to go to Egypt and purchase grain for food and for feeding their livestock. There they were reunited as a family and given a place to dwell. Five years yet remained of the great famine. Had they stayed in their homeland, they would have perished from starvation. The king allotted them a tract of land called the Land of Goshen, where they remained well beyond the great famine. Yet when Jacob died and the brothers were alone with Joseph, they were fearful Joseph would remember what they had done to him, and he would bring revenge upon them. But when they fell down before him and pleaded with him, Joseph said, "And you, you devised against me evil, yet the Elohim devises it for me for good, that it may work as at this day, to preserve alive many people" (Gen. 50:20).

Mark pondered the passage, considering what the connection might be to his own experience. Soon, he was reminded of the struggle God required Job to go through. God had placed Job in the hands of Satan so he might try and test him. The story of Job was there to illustrate that every member of humanity is destined for trial and to be tested by Satan. The entire world became aware of what the German authorities had forced upon the Jewish people, and surely, they would be an inspiration to all humanity. This verified the understanding of Mark that no matter what Satan is allowed to bring into men's experiences, all things are according to the will of God and according to His Own council. Indeed, God devises all things to work out according to His will in bringing men to the point of salvation. Not only is it true for Israel, but also it is true for all mankind.

He was very sure the message of grace was at the heart of the experience of the trance he had just experienced. Everyone in the room had undergone physical death, but there was far more to preservation than mere physical life. No matter the terrible things the physical body might be required to go through, it only concerns the physical body. Joseph had been made the savior of his people by protecting them from physical annihilation. God had permitted six million Jews to be physically annihilated, but not one soul would be lost, for nothing can separate the soul of man from God for the soul is eternal. By God's grace, every soul shall be preserved to enter into the kingdom of the Son of God's love and become part of the new creation. Mark understood the grace of

God. He longed for the day to arrive when all creation would understand it equally as well.

CHAPTER 25

To make sure Deanna knew she was an adopted child was not a problem Mark and Claire Hayes would yet have to deal with. The explanation was covered at the earliest possible time in her life. Feeling strongly about it, they had explained the matter to her before she was even five years old. As the years went on, she was told about her natural mother's death at the time of Deanna's birth and of being premature by a full month and weighing only four pounds the day she came into the world. They told her how much they both loved her natural mother and of it being her mother who named her. She had chosen to name her child after Claire because she thought of her as a dear friend. "That will help you realize what great friends we were and how much your mother and I loved one another," she told her.

The matter of her father's death had been treated differently. It bothered them in not having been entirely honest with Deanna.

"Your father was taken ill and died quite suddenly," they said. It was true in a way, but Mark especially felt guilty about their way of approach. She was told of the terrible accident and of his confinement to a wheelchair and would have been as long as he lived.

Five years elapsed since the night Lincoln Bailey's twelve-year-old son Ezra tossed gasoline through the window of the booth in Edward Rydz' yard. It was a frightening experience and one Mark did not deal with lightly. Ezra readily admitted to the police he had set the fire. He was extremely upset when he realized the children were asleep inside. By all accounts, being reprehended seemed to have served a good purpose, for he truly seemed to become a wiser young man for his experience.

In spite of the good coming to Ezra, Lincoln had taken offense toward Mark, blaming him for causing him "so much trouble." Mark remained calm, but he minced no words when explaining the seriousness of the situation the girls were faced with. It was then Lincoln lashed out at Mark. "I don't know where these brats get their screwed up ideas, but at least he didn't know someone was in the shed," he stated, raising his voice in anger. "There weren't nobody hurt. I don't know why you couldn't a just forgot the whole dang thing. I'll be surprised if this doesn't go on his police record. We can thank you if it does." For a while, Mark was afraid he might have to defend himself against Lincoln. Their relationship continued to be cool since then. Lincoln had eight children, all boys. Ezra was the oldest, and Mark was convinced he was the best-behaved one of them all, and just maybe it was because of that particular discipline.

Deanna came running down the sidewalk from the garage. Opening the screen door, she stopped to wipe the tears from her eyes, and then finding her mother, she went to her outstretched arms, crying as if her heart was breaking.

"What on earth is wrong, Deanna?" she asked, brushing away the tears, which continued to stream over her cheeks. "It's only two o'clock. Why aren't you in school?"

"It's Sammy! He's been telling lies!" she sobbed. "He's been telling them all over school. Everybody's making fun of me, Mama. Oh, Mama, I don't know what to do!"

"Oh now, surely, it isn't so bad. Kids can say cruel things sometimes, but they don't really mean to be hateful," Claire said, trying to sooth her hurt.

"He meant to be cruel a-a-and hateful too."

When Claire heard the words Sammy related to Deanna, she was at a complete loss for words.

"Sammy said my real daddy killed himself. He said Daddy shot himself through the head with a gun. He told all sorts of lies! He said there were brains on the ceiling. Mama, he told all those awful lies. And everybody heard him."

Claire's heart was aching as much as Deanna's was. They knew quite well Deanna would have to be told, but they had hoped they could delay it until a much later time. She prepared to do what must be done.

"Sammy said the police had to scrape Daddy's brains off the ceiling and wallpaper. He lied, didn't he, Mama?"

"Deanna, darling, I want to tell you the entire story. You're getting to be a big girl now, and I think you should know what really happened," she said. "First, we have to call the school principal. I suspect he's very concerned right now about where you are."

The time spent in placing the call and waiting for the opportunity to talk to Mr. Young gave Claire a chance to gather her faculties and determine how best to handle the situation. Mr. Young understood and was quite relieved. Yes, they were very concerned about Deanna's disappearance.

"Miss Drake reported to me Deanna was missing. We looked everywhere we could think to look. We didn't want to alarm you, but we were about to call you," he said.

Claire sat down on the couch with Deanna where they would be comfortable. "When your parents were young and hadn't been married very long, your daddy had to work late one evening. In fact, his work kept him until about ten o'clock. As he was driving home, a car sped through an intersection approaching from his left and slammed into him broadside. Your daddy was badly injured and taken to the hospital. The man who ran into him was charged with drunk driving."

"I knew about the accident, but I didn't know the man was drinking," Deanna said.

"Your daddy was paralyzed from the waist down and confined to a wheelchair from that day on. Your daddy was very bitter about the whole thing. He had a lot of trouble understanding why God would allow something so terrible to happen. He blamed God for it, but, darling, I want you to understand, that's something we all tend to do when things go against us. It seems to be part of the process of accepting what happens. We become angry, and when there's no other place to vent our anger, we put the blame on God.

"Your daddy always had to depend on someone to pull his

wheelchair up the steps until a ramp was built from the garage to the back door. He was unable to get in and out of the bathtub by himself. It was even very difficult getting in and out of bed.

"Honey, I'm only saying these things in hopes you can have an idea what your daddy had to go through. It must have been very frustrating to realize how limiting his disability was and to have the feeling with him constantly. He came to know Jesus as his Savior, and he learned to live with the situation. He became a much happier person. He found a job as a bookkeeper in the courthouse. He enjoyed his job and did his work well. From the time Mark and I moved into this house, we were the best of friends. We were together doing something practically every week. We had a Bible study class, and we studied many things from the Bible. Your daddy was a good student. Mark said we learned many things we wouldn't have learned had it not been for your daddy wanting answers."

"I wish I could have known my daddy."

"Oh, darling, I wish too you could have known him. He was a fine man, and you would have loved him very much."

"Tell me more about Daddy."

"I'm afraid the story gets even more sad now!"

"Will you tell me anyway?"

With a loving smile, she pulled Deanna closer to her. "One day, Mark and I decided we would take a vacation. We talked about where to go. Then we decided to ask your mama and daddy if they would go with us. It was then we learned your mother was expecting you. She wasn't sure her doctor would let her travel, being pregnant." Claire looked into her little girl's eyes. "I had never seen your mother so happy," she said, running her fingers gently through Deanna's hair. "I know it was probably the happiest day of her entire life. Your daddy was grinning from ear to ear because he was as happy as your mama was. And I'll tell you something else—it was a very happy day for me too because that was when she told me if she had a little girl, she wanted to name her after me. That's how you came to have my name."

Deanna smiled at Claire. "I like my name," she said. "It sounds like I'm already grown up."

"By the time we actually took the trip, your mother was having some sick days, but she insisted on taking the trip anyway. By the time we returned, it was obvious she needed to see the doctor. She was treated, and it was thought she was all right. By November, she was more ill than ever. The doctor ran tests, and that's when it was learned she had cancer. Your mother would not allow anyone to operate on her until her baby was born. She wanted you more than anything in the world even if she didn't live. The doctor didn't think she could live long enough to give birth to you. On December fifteenth, she was stricken with a problem with her lungs and couldn't breathe. Your daddy thought your mother had passed away. We all thought she had. When the ambulance left, we thought your mother had died.

"Getting her to the hospital was so urgent the attendants couldn't wait to take your daddy in the ambulance. Mark was going to take him. It was early in the morning, and no one was dressed. We ran home to change clothes so we could take Victor to the hospital. That's when we heard the gunfire.

"Darling, I'm so sorry! But it never even crossed your daddy's mind you could be born alive. His only thoughts were of being alone to deal with his problem. Abbie would never be there to help him, to take him to work, to bring him home, to cook meals, to keep him company, to laugh with him, to cry with him. He didn't give things time enough to know how they might turn out, that's true, but your daddy saw so little hope, a-a-and, darling, he never even thought about having a little girl to help take her place. If he had known, he never would have taken his life."

Deanna was sobbing bitterly.

"Darling, you don't know how I've dreaded the day I would have to tell you that story, and I didn't know it would be so soon. I hoped you would be older, when you could deal with it much easier.

Please don't blame your daddy. If your mother hadn't had such a strong will to give birth to you, you wouldn't have been born alive.

"If Sammy had the understanding we have, he never would have said the things he did. I know children can be cruel. But don't blame Sammy. That too is part of growing up. He may never realize what he did was wrong, but if you forgive him and ignore anything he may say in the future, he'll stop talking about it. Honey, please try to put it all behind you. But don't ever forget, your mother and father would have loved you as much as Mark and I love you, and that's an awful, awful lot." Tears were felling from Claire's eyes too.

"I love you too, Mama."

The back door opened. Mark entered the door, looking exhausted. "I should clear out some jobs at the shop, but I'm just too tired!" he exclaimed. He approached Claire, gave her a kiss on the forehead, and then received a kiss on the cheek in return. "You haven't started supper, have you? How about me taking my two lovely ladies out to dine at some fancy restaurant? I hear McDonalds give excellent service!"

"Are you sure you didn't read my mind? That's exactly what I was going to suggest," she said, as she took him by the arm, leading him to the living room.

"You're acting strange, Claire, is something wrong?"

"Mark, Deanna had a devastating experience at school today. I think I did a pretty good job of dealing with it this afternoon, but she was hurt terribly bad."

"Did she somehow hear about Victor? Is that what it is, Claire? Oh, boy! I was afraid this would happen. I should have told her long ago."

"She heard it from Sammy Bailey, so you know she got it pretty straight. Mark, she's sleeping now. It really did her in. But I think she took it very well. Frankly, I'm quite surprised at how well."

"I'm not! No one could do it better than you could."

"Well, I hope you're right, but I think you need to cover the spiritual aspect of it. I assured her Victor and Abbie loved her, and you and I love her very much. She needs to know God loves her, and I rather left it for you."

Approaching the door to Deanna's room, Mark knocked lightly. He could hear her stirring and then heard her call, "Mama?"

"It's Daddy! Is it all right if I come in?"

She was sitting on the side of the bed when Mark entered. "I heard what happened at school. I know how upsetting it must be. I'm sorry, honey! I should have talked to you long ago. Do you want to talk about it? If there's anything you want to discuss, we'll do it right now."

Deanna seemed to be quite calm. Apparently, the nap helped calm her. "I know my real daddy didn't mean to go and leave me. An' I know you and Mama love me. It's the kids at school. They all laughed at me, like I should be ashamed. I'll just have to drop out of school, Daddy. I can't face all them making fun of me."

"I had something alarming happen to me when I was a boy. It seemed like the end of the world. Just when I thought the worst had happened, a stranger came to me and comforted me. It was like he came from out of nowhere."

"You mean, like you blinked, a-a-and there he was? Like that?"

"Oh, it wasn't something supernatural, just a stranger walking the railroad tracks. He was hungry and stopped for something to eat. But I think it happened because God thought I needed help. He stopped at our house for food. After Mama prepared him a meal, he stayed the entire afternoon and visited with me.

"About three weeks before that, my puppy was hit by a car and killed. I was awfully disappointed when he died. I had learned to love him very much, and then he was taken from me. I had a pretty hard time dealing with it. On that particular day, I went to the post office to get the mail. A man started making fun of me. Well, I thought he was making fun of me. He was just teasing me, but I felt sorry for myself and decided nobody liked me. I even thought my daddy didn't like me."

It occurred to Mark he had been about the same age as Deanna when he had his experience. "I was eleven years old too when he came to visit me in the garden. He seemed to be a very wise man. He returned thanks at the table when we ate. I'll never forget him praying, so genuine, so sincere."

Deanna interrupted, "After Mama talked to me, I came upstairs and prayed about Sammy. I don't know if God heard me. Nothing really changed. I still felt like crying."

"Honey, I'm glad you asked God to help you 'cause that's the best thing you could have done. I'll tell you something, something it took me a long time to learn. God always hears our prayers, and He always answers them. The problem is, sometimes, we aren't listening when He answers." Mark gave Deanna a loving hug. "I mean, God is always faithful. He will never fail us when we call on Him with a problem. When our problems seem to go away, we tend to forget we even prayed. But sometimes and that's what's kind of hard, God wants us to deal with them. The fact is He had a reason for letting us go through the problem in the first place because there is something He wants to teach us. That's why each one of us was placed here on this earth, so God can cause us to learn to be strong so we will be prepared for whatever God has in store for us."

"That is hard, Daddy, 'cause I know Sammy knows what my daddy did, and he'll probably go right on telling everybody."

"Okay, honey, let's talk about it. There's something God wants you to learn from this experience. What do you suppose He wants you to learn?"

"I don't know! Maybe I should love Daddy anyway? Even if he did kill himself?"

"If you've learned that, you've come a long way."

Mark felt Deanna was doing remarkably well in understanding the situation. He wanted to do everything possible to make it clear to her.

"Remember, I told you about the stranger who visited, and I told you about the death of my puppy. I know having a puppy die isn't very much like having your daddy die, but I learned something from the experience. I asked the man, 'Why did my puppy die?'

The man told me pretty much what I told you. God wanted me to learn something, something He felt I could learn best in that way. But he told me something else. He said God even had a role for my puppy to live out on this earth. I realized whatever my puppy was supposed to learn, he must have learned, or God wouldn't have let him die.

"Most of all, 1 learned God has a purpose for everything in this universe. He didn't create anything to be tossed away when He's through with it, for He will never be through with it. He has a place for everything in His great plan and purpose."

"You mean even puppies and animals like that?"

"Yeah, even animals like that."

"The stranger died the same evening after our visit. It was a devastating thing for me too. He had become the most wonderful friend I had ever known, but I was much better able to handle his death then. You see, I knew whatever God wanted the man to learn, he must have learned it, or God wouldn't have let him die. I always kind of thought God wanted him to teach me something before he died too because I sure think I learned something wonderful. I also know your daddy learned what God wanted him to learn too. For some reason, God didn't require your daddy to go on suffering in his paralyzed body. He did suffer very much, Deanna, and it would have been very hard for him to go on alone. That's probably why we couldn't have any children because God wanted us to have you as our little girl. The whole thing is, I'm sure it all worked out exactly the way God meant for it to be."

"Mama says if I ignore Sammy, he'll probably stop talking about it. I think I'm gonna tell Sammy I know what my daddy did but God still loves him and I do too. Then we'll stop talking about it."

Mark kissed Deanna again. "I think you're going to handle this situation very well, baby."

"Daddy! I'm not a baby!"

"No, you certainly aren't. You are my lovely little lady, and your mother and I decided tonight would be a great time to eat out in your favorite restaurant. Let's go find your mother, and we'll be on our way to McDonalds."

"Not so fast, you two," Claire said, as they came rushing through the kitchen.

"Come on," Mark said. "We're on our way to McDonalds."

"Not until Deanna gets washed up and into a clean dress, were not.

Mark and Deanna looked at each other and grinned. "Well, maybe not," Mark said.

Apparently, Deanna's problem with "life" had been handled adequately, for it was never a problem afterward. Sammy soon forgot about the matter. Deanna kept a picture of both her parents on her dresser. She often asked about them. As she grew older, she often told them what wonderful parents they were to her and how she loved them for it. Mark never ceased being a devoted Bible student. He went on confining his studies to the Bible itself. He would rather be wrong in his own misunderstanding of the meaning of scriptures than from accepting someone else's error, he often said. Teaching the class, which gathered at the Family Center, continued strong for another ten years. It was then Leland Bartholomew was given the opportunity to interview for a job in television on a station in Omaha. Mark had always known Leland provided the fuel, which kept the fires of enthusiasm going strong. The membership dwindled drastically after Leland left the area and took his new position. They kept the class, but it dropped to a disappointingly few who attended.

In 1976, Deanna dated a man for a few months, whom she admired very much. When asked whether she would have married the man, she said, "Perhaps but I'm not sure. There was a lot I needed to learn about him. If I had loved him as much after a year or so, I might have wanted to marry him."

They met one day after Deanna had decided to make divinity as a treat for some girlfriends she had invited over to spend the evening.

Not having the required corn syrup, she went to the supermarket to purchase it. She stood looking over the various brands and types of syrup the shelf contained until she found the one she was looking for. Reaching for the bottle, her hand made contact with another hand reaching for the same bottle.

"That was sure a coincidence," said the man next to her.

She was about to make a curt remark like, "Sure, nothing short of a coincidence." But turning in his direction, she saw the most beautiful head of deep auburn hair she had ever seen. I wonder how many girls I know would give both arms for hair like that. Maybe not with all those curls, but wow! The color of his hair! Standing as close as they were, he appeared to be about six inches taller than she was. Catching a glimpse of his profile, it revealed a near perfectly straight line, interrupted only by an ideally proportioned nose. Casually but neatly dressed, he wore a pair of gray wrangler jeans, a canary yellow T-shirt, white socks, and a pair of brown loafers. She wasn't sure whether the young man had a reddish complexion or if she had embarrassed him by her stare. As they turned to walk up the aisle, Deanna said, "You really don't have to buy the syrup, you know."

Again, his face registered a flush of red. "I-I-I assure you, I did come in to buy white corn syrup, 'though I honestly can't remember anything else I came for. Anyway, I wouldn't be using a line on a married woman." He watched carefully for any reaction.

"Now you're fishing," she said, becoming a little embarrassed herself.

"Shall I call you Miss or Mrs.?"

Hesitating whether to continue the conversation, she realized she was impressed with him. She made her decision. If this doesn't work out, I'll just not see him again. "My name is Miss Deanna Hayes."

"And your address."

"Maybe we should limit this to a phone number for now."

Deanna was the first to walk by the cashier.

"Pardon me, Miss," he said to the cashier, "but could I have a little piece of your tape to write on? I have an important telephone number to write down.

"Now for the number, Miss Hayes."

When he had the number, she said to him, "If you do call, I'm not sure I'll be talking to you."

"I don't understand! Why wouldn't you talk to me?"

"How would I know it's you I was talking to?" she said.

"Oh!" he said, thrusting the thumb side of his fist into his forehead. "I'm sorry! My name is Theodore Landon. Everyone calls me Theo."

Deanna could hardly remember driving home from the market. After she set the syrup on the kitchen counter, every thought of making divinity was gone from her head.

A wonderful relationship developed from the meeting. He was a fine young man, courteous and well-mannered. Both Mark and Claire thought the world of him. He didn't claim to be a Christian, but he seemed to enjoy talking about things of the Bible and even seemed to be somewhat knowledgeable concerning it.

After they had dated only a few months, Theo was killed in a senseless act of violence. Only a couple of weeks previously, he had told Deanna he was a hemophiliac. After taking Deanna home, he drove straight toward his own house. Having traveled only about a block off the more heavily traveled road, he suddenly had a tire go flat. While changing the tire, four teen-aged boys stopped, feigning an offer of help. It was decided, as later pieced together, the boys perhaps thought he was resisting being robbed. He received a deep gash on his arm and then was left to bleed to death. As a bleeder, death probably took only a few minutes, the blood being unable to clot properly.

A large handful of nails were found about midway between the place where he had stopped and the thoroughfare from which he turned off. The four boys were seen cruising the area soon after the tragedy was reported. When the car was stopped, a box of nails matching the description of those found at the scene and in the tire was found in the car. They soon confessed to slashing Theo's arm, not realizing he could have been so seriously injured.

Mark had long thought about trying to write an anthem in commemoration of the two hundredth anniversary of the founding of our country. The memory of the young man gave him the incentive to give it his best effort. This song was written in 1976, in memory of Theodore Landon.

This Our Mighty Land

From byway to the mountains, from stream to ocean sand:
a hush of tranquil beauty prevails across our land,
for there in His achievements the truth of God reveals
a love and harmony.
Give courage to the weary: bring hope unto the worn
for love is where our strength lies,
a joyous life of faith and peace is born.
Whatever be the color, reach out a helping hand, f
or under God we all are one,
in this our mighty land.

Old Glory shines a beacon from highest mount unfurled,

a warning toward aggression to powers 'round the world:
we'll fight to save our freedom, pursuit of happiness,
and keep our honor pure.
When danger stands before us and justice is in view,
we'll keep our banner waving—
the stars, the stripes, the red, the white, the blue.
United we'll assemble directed by God's hand;
with faith a must, in God we trust,
in this our mighty land.

We lift our hearts in singing from shore to distant shore,
with Vic 'try bells still ringing on wings of joy we soar,
we cherish "Independence" in these United States,
the home of brave and free.
While many die in valor that all be not in vain:
like others gone before them
they give their lives so freedom might have reign.
We'll choose the ones to serve us, who love their fellow man,
in God be blessed, with happiness,
in this our mighty land.

CHAPTER 26

Two years passed after the day of Theodore Landon's tragic death. Deanna had gone into what the doctor termed a mild depression. Both Mark and Claire remained greatly concerned for her, but time had done much to heal the hurt. The concern might have been precipitated by what her natural father had done—in taking his own life. Since then, she went to dances at the Coliseum a few times. She went to movies with acquaintances from high school days and men she worked with. At the Prom Skating Rink, she met a young man who was an avid roller-skating enthusiast. They talked and skated together over a few weeks when she realized skating was about the only interest he had. He wasn't interested in visiting the movie theaters or going to dances, and most of all, he was not interested in things of the Lord. She came to realize on the evenings she wasn't with him at the prom, he was there skating by himself. Deciding it had been his good looks and his skating ability that attracted her, she was glad she discovered it so early in their relationship. He certainly did one thing well: roller-skating.

But now Deanna had met a man who had swept her off her feet in no uncertain way. Six feet two, slender, dark wavy hair, a year or so older than Deanna, dark green eyes, beautiful teeth showing through every smile, jaws firmly set, confirming an already present look of extreme confidence—all in all, he was quite a handsome young man. Every time Mark saw him, he was wearing a suit, or a sport jacket, or sweater, and never had he seen him not wearing a tie. He always looked like he had just stepped out of a bandbox, Mark had commented. "I always think of him as Barbie's boyfriend. What's his name? Ken? And frankly, the likeness to DM disturbs me," he said. "Of all the people she could have fallen in love with, her choosing DM Holliday's son seems almost too remote even for chance.

"They must not screen their applicants for those jobs," Mark had said jokingly. "If DM Holliday had known she was my daughter, I doubt very much she would have been accepted."

"That doesn't sound like you, Mark," Claire had responded quickly. "You were always the one who said, 'We mustn't interfere in Deanna's life. We can help her make decisions, but ultimately, she must decide for herself.' What happened to your principles? It sounded like good advice to me."

"I know! I was just hoping for something better for my daughter." "Hey! Hold on a minute! How can you say Donald isn't what Deanna needs? How can you say they aren't exactly right for each other? Maybe Deanna is so special to you, you're not in a position to make an honest evaluation."

"It bothers me, Claire. He's disrespectful to others. Have you heard how he addresses me? How he always calls me Hayes? It's never Mr. Hayes, not even Mark! Just how's things Hayes? Or beautiful night, Hayes!"

Claire was trying hard not to burst into laughter. She knew exactly what Mark meant. It had bothered her a little at first, but she soon gave way to the assurance it was just his particular manner. She had no problem in accepting him just the way he was. But Mark was actually sulking. His pride had gotten squarely in the way. "The problem is, Mark, there is likely not a man on this planet who's good enough for your daughter. Isn't that what it's all about? Have you ever let Donald know how you feel about being called 'Hayes?'" she asked.

"No, I guess I haven't. I'm just remembering what Donald's father did to Victor the night we visited his church? He almost ruined Vic's life. I remember how relieved I was when Vic started coming out of his depression. DM was concerned with building esteem in the eyes of his congregation. And do you remember the time he called me a heretic on the radio?"

"You realize, don't you?" Claire said to him. "You're remembering what Reverend Holliday did. We're talking about Donald. You surely can't hold Donald responsible for things his father did."

"Of course, you're right. I guess I'm assuming Donald is a chip off the old block. I'll have to try to expect more of Donald."

Mark mellowed after giving considerable thought to the matter, but none of the facts had really changed. When it all began, Deanna had been working in an office supply store with a fine Christian gentleman, near retirement age, and a man whom she admired greatly for his Christian-like conduct. "He not only claims to be a Christian, but I think he lives a Christian life," she told her parents. He had mentioned to Deanna how the staff placed in charge of the Summer Bible School classes at the church was looking for volunteers to help in teaching the children. She had already scheduled her vacation but then found the plans for a trip to Florida with some girl friends had fallen through. The idea of teaching children had appealed to her so much she readily volunteered and was accepted.

Donald was the assistant minister at the Pentecostal Tabernacle Church where the Reverend DM Holliday presided as pastor. He had attended the Southern States Seminary, in the south, where he graduated in the top ten percent of his class. His father would probably remain as pastor of the present church until he retired or until eventually giving over all the pastoral duties to his son then stay on as his assistant.

Donald headed up the Summer Bible School, and Deanna's association with him progressed from there. They had dated a little more than a year, and now there was mention of a marriage ceremony.

Claire was uneasy about Mark's feelings toward Donald. Of course, the choice was Deanna's to make, but it was important Mark have a good relationship with his future son-in-law if indeed there was to be a marriage. Those matters were no secret to Deanna. She had sensed coolness on her father's part. But she was also aware of Donald's often-careless manners. It puzzled her how he could be so meticulous about his appearance and yet at times be so crude when conversing with those with whom he associated.

"Why don't you have a little talk with your father," Claire had said to Deanna. "There's no point in trying to change Donald, but maybe you can convince your daddy he's not so bad just as he is."

"Daddy, it's very important to me for you to like Donald," Deanna said, as she approached Mark on the subject. "I love him very much, and I know he loves me."

"Honey, I don't dislike Donald." Mark was surprised at the straightforward way Deanna had spoken to him. Had his feelings really been so obvious? "I-I-I just want you to marry someone who will be thoughtful and considerate of you at all times. I'm not sure it would happen with Donald. I-I-It doesn't seem to me he shows proper respect for others. I should think being considerate of others to be one of the first requirement for a minister."

"He's always considerate of me, Daddy. I know he takes after his father. Mr. Holliday is quite blunt in some of the things he says. And he's not one to hesitate in voicing his opinion on any matter. Donald is very much like him."

Mark had to interrupt. "Please, honey, I know his father all too well! I have come to accept the fact God made every one of us as He chose and for His Own special reasons, but it still gives me consolation to know I don't have to be involved with him. Let's just be concerned about Donald. Do you think I'm the only man Donald addresses by calling them by their last name? Doesn't it strike you as being disrespectful?" He looked at his daughter through loving eyes. "Honey, I could live with being called 'Hayes' for the rest of my life. But I don't think I could live with the thought of him not showing you the respect you deserve."

"Daddy, I'm sorry he does that. It seems to me you're the only one he addresses that way. Believe me, I've noticed it, and it bothers me. Daddy, if it means so much to you, I'll stop seeing him for a while. Maybe when he realizes why, things can be different."

Mark took her in his arms and hugged her. "I love you, honey. I'll always think of you as my little girl, and I want only the best for you. Don't say one word to Donald. I'll get used to whatever he calls me."

"Daddy!"

From the tone of Deanna's voice, Mark knew what she was about to say.

"Donald asked me to marry him. I haven't said I will yet. I've been waiting. Well, I just wasn't sure if—"

"If I would approve? Is that why you hesitated to give an answer?"

"Oh, Daddy, I love him so much, but I've got to know you approve of him. I couldn't stand knowing you were disappointed with our marriage."

"You are what's important to me. You're still my baby, and if you'll be happy with Donald, that's what it will take to make me happy."

Deanna had gone to a great deal of trouble trying to keep her little secret from Mark and Claire. She prepared Sunday dinner for her family and had invited Donald as their special guest. The surprise Deanna and Donald had planned was, immediately following dinner, Donald would stand up at the table and, addressing Mark, ask for his consent to marry his daughter.

"Mr. Hayes, I am very much in love with your daughter, and I would count it a great honor if you would give your consent for me to marry her. I will love her until the day we are parted in death."

Mark could hardly believe what his ears conveyed to him. There was equal surprise registered on Deanna's face. It wasn't surprise in hearing Donald asking for Mark's blessing, for that was the whole purpose for the event. The surprise was because of the respect he showed her father when asking. Mark had no intentions of rejecting his request, but accepting it was much more pleasant now.

"Daddy, I want you to know I love Donald as much as he loves me, and I would like both you and Mama to honor his request." She sat down after she spoke.

Slowly, Mark stood up. "I've thought about this moment many times," he said. "I might just as well have saved my concern because right now, I don't remember a word I planned to say." He reached for Claire's hand and held it between his own hands. "Deanna's mother and I have always been greatly concerned for her happiness. We did not seek to give her many things, only the things which are good and the things which will make her the most happy. Now we can only hope and pray we've taught her to know how to recognize those things. I know Deanna loves you very much, Donald, and I hope the two of you will be just one half as happy as her mother and I have been. We always wanted Deanna to marry a Christian man, and we feel you are a Christian. That's very important to her mother and me. And if you ever do anything to cause her unhappiness, you'll be dealing with me."

Mark gave Deanna a wink as she stood up to give her father a hug.

An October wedding was planned, and all the wheels of preparation were set in motion. They would be married in Donald's church. DM Holliday would be officiating the ceremony. This was no problem for Mark, for they had no particular church in which they attended. Deanna was glad there would be a church wedding. Just the tradition alone seemed to require a church where the ceremony could take place, and being as well-known as Donald was would help assure there being many in attendance, making it even more memorable for her. There would be enough pictures to fill many photo albums. The church would be filled with autumn leaves, enough to look like the outdoors. The janitor would likely be vacuuming up leaves until spring.

Just as soon as the wedding date was selected, Deanna called her grandmother Lane to tell her of the event. The same evening, Mr. and Mrs. Lane came calling on them.

"Have you selected a wedding gown, dear?" she asked Deanna. She looked around the room to watch the expressions on everyone's face. When no particular look of surprise or uneasiness appeared, she said, "I've thought about this day many, many times. I still have the gown your mother was married in."

Deanna gave out a gasp of excitement. "Oh, Grandma! Could I please? Could I wear my mother's wedding gown?"

Mrs. Lane held out her arms as Deanna came running to her. "I would have been disappointed if you refused me," she said, trying to hold back the tears of happiness. "I want you to know it was also my wedding dress. You will be the third generation to wear it. I looked it over right after I received your call. It may need some reinforcement here and there, but I think it will hold up as long as you don't wear it to clean house in or something."

"Oh, Grandma! You're wonderful. You've made me so happy." Mrs. Lane had something else for Deanna. Because of Deanna's extreme happiness from receiving her mother's wedding dress, Mrs. Lane seriously thought about waiting for another day.

"Grandma, I'm so happy. I'll be wearing my grandmother's and my mother's wedding dress. I can't wait to see it."

"I have something else for you," she said, deciding at that moment to give it to her. "I'm afraid everything I'm offering falls into the 'something old' category." She reached into her purse and pulled out a container serving as a jewelry box. "The original container was lost many years ago," she said mysteriously. "Would you look inside, then I'll tell you about it."

Deanna looked inside the box and then gently lifted its contents. "Don't be afraid! You won't break it!"

What she saw was a rich velvety green stone set inside a beautiful eighteen-karat gold border. It was distinctively emerald and a large one. "A perfect emerald of this size is quite rare and very expensive," Mrs. Lane said. "Unfortunately, this one is flawed like most of them this large."

Most emeralds of this particular era were cut "en cabachon"; however, this one was faceted in the finer step cut, or emerald cut, with the corners being mitered and producing an octagonal shaped stone. This particular cut brought out the greatest display of color depth. Its greater length was placed on the vertical plane. A wide gold band, appearing as braided gold, outlined the general shape of the stone and closely surrounded it. Made somewhat in the "art nouveau" style—which inspired the free-flowing patterns of flowers and fernery around the turn of the eighteenth century—also used in decorating furniture, pottery, silver, glass, architecture, and paintings, this was of an elaborate broad leaf design. It gave the entire necklace an overall diamond shape. In each of the four points of the design was placed one-half of a greenish-black pearl. Each was expertly chosen in just the proper size for the overall concept and coordinating well with the color of the gem.

"Oh, Grandma, you said this is for me, but I can't accept something so precious to you. Thank you anyway."

"Nonsense! You not only can accept it, you must! It's the only way I'll ever be free from the guilt of not giving it to your mother. Oh, I had every intention of giving it to her. I just wanted to wait until she was older. It was so beautiful; I couldn't bear to part with it yet. I thought she would have enough years to enjoy it after I grew old. Anyway, I insist you take it so you can treasure it as much as I have. Besides, the high neckline of the wedding gown worn by such a beautiful young woman will bring out all its beauty."

Miss Deanna Claire Hayes became Mrs. Donald Marshall Holliday III. They would go by the arrangement of Reverend and Mrs. Donald M. Holliday. The ceremony was beautiful. The bride was stunning in her white floor-length gown. Made of chiffon and trimmed with lace, it defined a high neckline with the sides joined by tiny round, white pearl buttons, and closed by loops from the opposite side. Seed pearls were sprinkled throughout the bodice. The emerald green gem, set in the gold frame, hung from a choker chain providing its prominent display. The bride's attendants wore emerald green chiffon gowns with slippers dyed to match. The bride's attendants carried bouquets of white roses, while the bride's bouquet contained roses dyed emerald green to further enhance the eloquence of the stone.

Flash cameras were allowed, except during exchanging of the vows and while the professional photographers were taking their pictures. Everyone said it was like holding the wedding out in the woods, seeing the entire podium engulfed in such an array of multicolored leaves. Being carefully selected in great numbers, with spotlights strategically located to bring out the most of the beauty, they created refreshing effects through light and shadows. The entire church was decorated in fall colors. She and Donald were extremely happy. They spent their honeymoon in Florida. Deanna joked about taking the vacation she missed when she stayed home to meet Donald.

On March 5, 1979, a son was born to Deanna and Donald. Breaking the established tradition, they retained the middle name but christened him Dennis Marshall, instead. A little more than two years later, on April 30, Deanna gave birth to a daughter, Cora Elizabeth.

During the early years of Deanna and Donald's marriage, Mark and Donald had numerous arguments over scriptural differences mainly because Donald didn't care for Mark's understanding. But what was probably their most heated argument came after an episode having its beginning when Deanna and her family were visiting. Cora was to enter the hospital to have her tonsils removed, and they wanted to ask Mark and Claire to take care of Dennis for a few days. This would give them freedom to go to and from the hospital, and when she was released, they could devote all their time to Cora.

Dennis came bursting through the room, and on reaching the bathroom, he found the door closed. "Daddy! Someone's in the bathroom, and I have to wee-wee."

"Deeennis!" Donald shouted. "Just say you have to use the bathroom!"

"But you don't know what I have to do."

"It doesn't matter, Dennis! You shouldn't say those naughty things. All you have to say is you want to use the bathroom."

"I'm sorry, Daddy," he said, becoming more desperate, "but I still have to go."

Mark was disturbed over the way the situation was handled, but he refrained from further comment.

Dennis did come to stay those few days. He had received a new sled for Christmas that winter. Mark had promised to take him to the park where he could slide down some hills. It was a bitterly cold February day, and Mark carried the sled home from the park. Dennis followed at a short distance, trudging along in a pair of overshoes that were a full size too large for him. With each step, his overshoe touched the snow before his shoe could settle down inside, making a shuffling sound as he walked.

As Dennis sauntered along, Mark said to him, "Boy! This cold sure makes the weenie shrivel."

The shuffling noise abruptly stopped. Mark turned to determine the problem. Dennis had stopped in his tracks and was just standing there. A bewildered look covered his face.

"What did you say, Grandpa?"

"I was just commenting on how cold it is. Aren't you cold?"

Dennis was indignant. "That's not what you said!"

"I just said—" Mark was about to repeat his words when Dennis interrupted him.

"Don't say it again, Grandpa!" Dennis gave out a big sigh. "That's not nice! It's just not a nice thing to say!"

"Hmmm." Mark contemplated. "How would you say it so it would sound nice?"

"I guess we just don't talk about it, that's all. God punishes us for saying things like that."

He was quiet for a moment. "Grandpa?"

"What!"

"What does shrivel mean?"

Mark sighed. "Oh, let me see. You like raisins, don't you? I saw you eating one of those little boxes of raisins one day."

"Yes!"

"Well, a raisin is simply a shriveled up grape."

"Oh!" Dennis interrupted again. "I guess we're not supposed to talk about that either."

Mark thought about the conversation all the way home. The circumstances certainly were not in any way proportionate to the situation occurring in the life of Victor. Yet he could see potential problems coming down the line just from Donald's way of approaching the matter.

"I think I'm going to have a talk with your son-in-law," Mark said, as he met Claire after entering the kitchen.

"My son-in-law?"

"I don't like what I see!" Mark was very serious now. "I know Donald loves Dennis as much as any father could love his son, but I don't like what I see him doing to Dennis."

Claire had purchased a doll for Cora. It cried, it laughed, it wet, and it did about everything real babies do. Claire and Mark were bringing Dennis home after his stay with them. Not wanting Dennis to feel neglected, Claire brought along a tractor and trailer set. The occasion was that Cora was over the worst of her time of recovery. They would have a little party to celebrate, with cake and ice cream everyone would enjoy.

Dennis had been home barely ten minutes when Mark saw him whispering something in his daddy's ear. He could see the puzzled expression on Donald's face. After enjoying the refreshments, it was down to visiting for the adults and playing with the new toys for the little ones. Donald said, "Well, Hayes, why don't we go to the living room where we can be more comfortable?"

Once they were seated, Donald got right to the point. "Dennis told me what you said to him. Why in the world would you say such a thing to a four-year-old? You don't use vulgar language. Why would you talk to my son like that? Deanna and I are trying our best to keep him away from gutter talk. Now you use it and apparently think nothing of it."

Mark was disturbed, but he remained calm. "Actually, Donald, I just wanted to confirm what I already suspected. I think you're acting like a prude and you're teaching Dennis to be the same way. And I also think you're being overprotective."

Now Donald was angry, and he immediately raised his voice to Mark. "Do you realize the number of programs there are on TV, which children should not be watching? Do you realize what kids are exposed to—the violence, sex, vulgar language, use of alcohol and drugs and tobacco? In most sitcoms, they fill the half hour with shows teaching our children to be disrespectful to others. When the entertainers aren't teaching sex, violence, and how to commit murder, they're teaching them disrespect for their parents and elders. It only prepares them for the worse crimes. I wouldn't think of allowing my child to watch an afternoon of soap operas. But the worst thing is the disrespect. Four-year-olds are probably the most vulnerable of any age. By the time they learn to recognize who the police are, and the school principals, and the ministers, they'll already know they're not required to show them respect. You don't suppose these kids use vulgar language out on the playground, do you, Hayes?"

Donald was being facetious, and Mark knew it, but he wanted Donald to continue for he was playing into his own argument beautifully.

"I saw something just the other day, Hayes? I could hardly believe it, and it just about says it all. There was this huge billboard depicting a picture, which a small child had drawn in stick figures. One figure was pointing a gun at another. The caption beneath the drawing asked, 'How can we take the crime out of this picture?'" Donald had calmed down and was more patiently explaining his feelings. "I think it should occur to those people where to begin. They need to keep the crime out of the picture in the first place. Dealing with crime is like mopping up after the bucket of water has been overturned. We have no choice but to try to mop up the mess, but we'd better learn to keep the bucket upright."

"You know what should be done, Hayes?" Donald asked.

"I'd be very interested in your opinion."

Without giving Mark a chance to finish stating his thoughts, Donald continued, "Nobody's going to listen to my solution. There's too much money and greed involved in the entertainment field for those people to allow anything to change."

"Maybe I can't do anything about it either, but I'd like to hear your solution,'' Mark said.

"Of course, nobody has all the answers, but I think I know where it all has to begin." He gave Mark a puzzled look. "Are you trying to change the subject?"

"Not at all! I do have something I want to say, but I want to know how you plan to solve the problem of crime first."

"There needs to be some rigid guidelines set up, ones to keep undesirable television and movie films out of the reach of children. They talk about how hard it is to keep children from coming into contact with it. Maybe if the directors of the networks and cable companies and even the station and theater managers were put on trial, it would create a different way of approaching these matters. Since children can't be tried as adults, why not make the adults responsible for what goes on? Make them punishable for the garbage they expose our children to. It really is garbage, Mark! Of course, ultimately the parents are to blame, but it would be much more effective if we prevent the problem from occurring in the first place."

"I like your proposed solution, and once the plan is put in place, the law should be extended to include the parents when it's proven they were negligent. And they should enforce the laws already passed to prevent merchants from selling tobacco and liquor to minors."

"Now what's this other business all about?" Donald asked. "Okay, let's get down to business. You've done a fine job of showing one side of the problem. I insist there are two sides. Like the old saying, 'There are two sides to every story.' It seems to me any truth is found somewhere in the middle. The point is you're so intent on keeping Dennis away from sin, you're forgetting about the perfectly normal curiosities children have to deal with. Eating a meal is quite normal, but in the strict sense, overeating is sinful. Sex is normal, but misapplying it is to commit sin. Conversing with someone and hearing what they say is normal, but listening to a raunchy story is sinful. It's all in how we deal with important everyday situations. Children have to learn how to handle any given situation. We have to be there to help them learn properly. I don't believe what I said to Dennis was so bad, but I've seen several situations come about, which do seem unhealthy to me. I'd like you to at least hear me out." Mark told Donald the entire story of the experience Dennis's grandfather had when he was a child. He told of him being invited to a friend's place on the farm and engaging in intimacy with his Shetland pony. "'God will surely strike you down,' he heard said by the pious father who thought he was being righteous." He told Donald of how frightened Victor was and how tortured his life was until he was able to deal with it rationally.

"I saw the torture and torment in Victor's life. I know too well what he suffered. I don't want Dennis to go through anything like what Victor went through. I owe it to Victor if to no one else. I loved Victor like a brother. If I can prevent a similar thing happening to his grandson, I surely want to do so.

"Donald, I know you love Dennis with all your heart. I could never doubt that. But please, please don't ever let any of your children think normal, everyday body functions mustn't be discussed." The conversation opened doors. Mark was much better able to talk with Donald after that. He came to appreciate Mark's grasp of the real meaning of grace and even more so as the years of discussions continued.

CHAPTER 27

The people of Mark's hometown had been preparing for a centennial celebration for a period of four years. Considering the fact of Peru, Iowa, having a population of less than two hundred, quite an accomplishment was taking place. In the beginning, the major concerns were for raising money to defray cost of the various activities themselves. Several thousand dollars would be needed to carry it off. Sales of a cookbook were hoped to be one of the major sources of income. This was made up entirely of recipes contributed by local residents, some having been handed down through several generations. Four years seemed to Mark a long time to plan a weekend. He reckoned it was a good thing others were doing the work, for he hadn't been able to generate much enthusiasm in those early days of preparation. The impossible, it appeared had been accomplished. Everyone became actively involved in some way. Altogether, Mark and Claire bought about a dozen cookbooks.

Mark's favorite cake was a recipe of his mother's and contributed by his family. Actually, two sisters and Mark contributed the same recipe. And no wonder, it was the best raisin cake ever baked, bar none, at least in Mark's opinion. Because of the fine dishes Claire was able to prepare, she fell in love with the book, buying the additional copies for friends and relatives.

When visiting with his sister, Edith, she and Mark made a list of all the last names of the people they could remember having lived in the town and the surrounding area. The letters of 228 names were placed on a sheet, creating a maze of letters. A second sheet supplied the names to be located. The remaining letters spelled out words meant to be a clue concerning what the centennial was all about.

Recalling those names brought nostalgic moments tumbling back through time For Mark, some names long forgotten. On Wednesday and Saturday evenings of those years so long ago, everyone came to town for shopping, especially the farmers and their families. When Mark and his young friends chose sides to play cops and robbers, the entire center of town was their playground. The area around the lumberyard, the stockyards not yet having been torn down, the winding Rockey Creek bed, usually dry except for a trickle, the station, which pumped water from Clanton Creek to the huge tower where locomotives regularly stopped to take on large volumes of water, the out buildings behind the store fronts—there was no end of places to hide. They could have remained hidden all night.

Whatever happened to all those kids? Mark wondered. Carl Dawson moved out west somewhere, right out of high school. Allen lived in the northern part of the state. Liked what he did very well, he had heard. Randy died in a farming accident. What a tragedy it was. Harold and Ralph Kale still lived there. After inheriting their father's farm, they divided it equally between them. Harold bought a farmhouse and moved it onto his property. And Craig, Mark had no idea what happened to him. It sure would be great checking up on some of those old friends. And Diane Halsey, she married Randy. Of course, Tom lived in Oregon now.

Mark lay resting on the couch. Claire was shopping with Maria. The weekend scheduled for the celebration was less than six months away. As he was reminded of those childhood experiences, he began thinking of what it would be like to return to those days.

If only he could go back in time, even if only for a short time. He would wander through those hills and over the fields. He would walk those railroad tracks and along the creek bottom. The memories kept streaming back, one event after another, just like something written down in the recesses of his mind, needing only to be opened up and read once in a while. Wouldn't it be grand to just relive it all, and just like—like—?

Near the Town of Of Peru

Like a melody that keeps haunting me,
as an old familiar song:
just a memory that keeps taunting me
to go back where I belong.
It's so grand to be where I once was free,
just to stroll about the land—
in a quiet place at a change of pace,
in the heart of nature land.

In a lovely valley,
nestled in the hills,
where nature's on review:
there we'll build a cottage,
near the town of Peru.
We can watch the sunsets
burning in the west,
aflame with scarlet hue:
just outside our window,
near the town of Peru.
A place of rare enchantment,
a land of paradise,
from the rays of morning light;
like a great concerto,
nature plays the score,
'til the dark of night.
Birds sing in the treetops,
gentle breezes play,
where skies are country blue:
all around our cottage,
near the town of Peru.
All around our cottage,
near the town of Peru.

During the remaining six months, Mark determined what he would do about the song he had written. He talked to Donald and

Deanna almost immediately about allowing Dennis and Cora to appear on a parade float. He would arrange on the float a living room scene with Cora sitting or standing somewhere in the room. Dennis would be near her, perhaps playing a piano, but singing his song as a boy would sing a love song to his sweetheart. Of course, Dennis would only be mouthing the words, for he would have a professional sounding recording made, and someone concealed from view would make sure the record continued to play as necessary. Dennis would need some rehearsing in order to synchronize his lips and actions with the recording. And of course, Cora would need some rehearsal in knowing how to appear star struck over her lover.

They arrived in Peru early Friday to prepare the float. It had rained all week but cleared nicely on Friday. People were already streaming into town, and the celebration would not officially begin until Saturday. It suggested something he remembered hearing as a boy, referring to the Saturday afternoons of an era even long before Mark was born. "Biggest little town between Des Moines and St. Joe," they said. However, in those days, farmers came to town in horse-drawn buggies.

On Friday evening, Mark took the entire family out to the farm where the original delicious apple tree had stood for so many years. Of course, the original tree was gone. Even the old iron fence had been removed. It was now a problem in trying to determine exactly where it was originally located. The Stark Brothers Nursery, who purchased the rights to the tree, furnished most of the known information.

They gave speculation the original tree had provided roots for a tree growing in the same spot. If it was true, then it still grows more than 125 years since its discovery. Donald was excited and wanted to discuss any facts known about the tree. Unfortunately, little was known except for what was furnished by the nursery.

Stark Brothers Nursery had donated one hundred, four-to-five-foot delicious apple trees, one for each of the years since the birth of the town. These were to be auctioned off to the public. Many of these had been planted throughout the community. "One day, those will be a pleasant reminder of this community's heritage," Donald said. "I even like the old farm where the orchard was located."

The parade, originating in the "Old Town" and proceeding down the "back hill," was under way. What a rewarding sight it was to Mark, watching the color guard of the veterans of foreign wars leading the way, while the Interstate Thirty-Five public school marching band marched closely behind. Then came the car seating the grand marshal, followed by the king and queen of the festivities. The local fire truck preceded a stream of antique cars, giving way to the floats, interspersed with clowns, funny cars, and specific organizations representing their objectives, nearly all from Winterset.

He could hear the music coming from the float they had created and then caught a glimpse of it a short distance back. "Don't they look sweet!" Claire exclaimed, as they came into full view. The recording played loud and clear, and Dennis carried his part to the letter. Cora stood near Dennis, acting the part of a young lady being charmed by the words and voice of her lover. It was hard to determine whether Mark was more proud of hearing his song or of watching his grandchildren performing so well. "They sure did it right, didn't they?" Mark said after they passed. Proceeding on through town, the parade ended at the former school grounds.

All of them stayed around for the remainder of the festivities, unwilling to miss anything if it could be avoided. Dennis and Cora entered every contest they were eligible to enter. For the novelty of it, Deanna entered the husband-calling contest but soon withdrew after hearing some of the other contestants. "I would be no competition for those girls," she joked. The afternoon was spent visiting with Mark's family. They didn't often get a chance to visit, and so they welcomed the few remaining hours and indeed made the most of it. Soon, it was time to return home.

Mark was aware Donald wanted to discuss something with him, though he had no idea what it concerned. He evidently felt the trip home from Peru offered ample opportunity. Sitting in the seat beside Mark, he casually remarked, "Remember the little talk we had a couple of years ago, about the problem over Dennis," he said with a grin.

"I remember." Mark was a little embarrassed when the subject was approached. "Maybe it wasn't in the best taste," he apologized.

"Forget it, Hayes! The fact is the little episode led into some very helpful conversations. Think we got pretty good mileage out of that. I'm serious, Hayes, I'm really coming to appreciate you. You made me very angry, but even then I was seeing a lot of good common sense in what you said. I read the Old Testament where everything is according to the Law of Moses. Then I read Paul's epistles, and everything there is about the new covenant and nothing but grace.

"Grace seems so obvious when I read where Paul talks about the new covenant being written on the heart and how God will judge all humanity for the things hidden in the mind, according to his evangel. It seems so clearly shown to be our own conscience condoning us or condemning us in the day of judgment."

"It's comforting to hear you say it. I mean, you're taking such a liking to the evangel of grace. Still," Mark added, "everyone is subject to judgment."

"What really disturbs me is I recognize, even my discipline for the kids, especially my discipline for the kids, was based on the Law of Moses. It shouldn't be. There's even more to it than that. I'm disturbed about what my church teaches. I don't know how I can continue. It's difficult having to teach things I no longer believe."

"Tell me about it. I haven't felt comfortable in a church building in more than twenty years." Mark looked at Donald apologetically. "I didn't mean to sound flippant. I certainly know what you're up against. Have you talked to DM about it?"

"You don't talk to DM about such things."

It might well have been the first thing the two had ever agreed on where Donald's father was concerned.

"I don't expect you to solve my problem, Hayes, I just wanted to talk to someone, I guess. That's another thing."

"What?"

"Calling you Hayes! Would it offend you if I stopped?"

"Stopped what? Stopped calling me, Hayes? Of course not!" Donald looked at Mark, shaking his head. "I never thought I'd be talking to my father-in-law this way. You may never have been aware of it, but your daughter was the most boring individual in the entire Quad Cities when she began discussing the subject of

Mark Hayes. I used to think you must have brainwashed her. 'Dad says this, Dad says that, Dad did this.' I can tell you, it got very annoying. Calling you Hayes seemed to be the only way I could vent my exasperation, the only way I could compensate for all her disgusting respect. After a while, calling you by your last name became so natural it seemed the only right thing to say. I really want to call you something different, Mark," he said with emphasis.

"Very well," Mark said with a grin. "How about the name you just used? Mark!"

"Sounds good to me, Mark. Mark it is!"

Just as he assumed he would, Mark had long grown used to what he once considered disrespect, but their conversation had helped tremendously. "I'll give your problem a lot of thought. If I get any ideas, I'll let you know. I'll sure give it earnest attention in my prayers." "What was it like, Mark, growing up in a town as small as Peru? Wasn't it terribly boring?" Donald had shown considerable fascination with the community, but he also had some pretty strong reservations. "I might be able to handle it now, but I don't know about it as a kid."

"I guess if you don't know any different, you don't know what you're missing," Mark replied with a chuckle.

Claire had overheard the latest subject of conversation. "I'm sure glad Mark's never been serious about wanting to move back there. I don't think I could handle it. There isn't even a supermarket within ten miles," she said. "Or a theater, or a drugstore, or a skating rink. I could go on and on."

"Seriously, what was it like? What in the world did you do for entertainment?"

"I'll have to admit things were pretty mild compared with the city boy's lifestyle," Mark said. "It's what you grow accustomed to. Did you ever watch a child who seems to have every kind of toy imaginable to play with? Then give him a clothespin and a rubber band, and watch what he plays with. I think the simple things are often the best. I think it would be a little like comparing radio with television. Think about having only radio to listen to, as we did, and no television to add pictures to what you hear. Come to think of it, I guess radio did furnish the bulk of our entertainment. It seems to me our imagination often provides a more vivid picture to a story than an actual picture can. I remember the program called *I Love a Mystery*. I don't think it would be possible to film many of the things I imagined, and I don't think it was harmful. I'm positive of this much. The concepts we visualized were far healthier than the things actually portrayed on television today. Maybe radio provided us with a pretty good babysitter."

Donald was interested and wanted to pursue the subject. "Surely, you had more to entertain you than the radio."

"Saturday nights in the summertime provided a great deal of fun. Silent movies were shown in the park. I suppose the late thirties was when they were replaced with 'talkies.' They were still paid for by the merchants but were free to the public. I can still see in my mind the huge screen standing on the far side of Rockey Creek. The people sat on blankets, or in chairs, watching from the other side. It never took but a few well-placed drops of rain to play havoc with plans for the evening at the movies," Mark said with a chuckle.

"A hitching chain reached from one end of the park's length to the other and threaded through holes in the large posts. Cars, and oh yes, a few buggies—buggies were nearly a thing of the past, but there were still a few. They lined up along the hitching posts. You know the chain is still there? I hope it never gets taken down."

"By the 1940s, it cost a dime to see the movies, and the 'theater' was moved to an area between a couple of buildings, with the ends sealed off to contain the area, but still playing under the stars. Following the previews each week, a serial continued throughout the entire summer. Probably running no more than seven or eight minutes, it was a fast-moving film, designed to place the hero in an incredibly dangerous situation at the close of each segment. Of course, this enticed the youngsters to bring their parents to town again next week. Gene Autry, Roy Rogers, Hop-along Cassidy, Tom Mix—those were only the western Films. I think they were the movies responsible for bringing the crowds back week after week, though.

"They used to have pig roasts on Armistice Day. I'm not sure they had them every year, but I remember some of them. Those celebrations brought people to Peru who never came for any other reason. I sure remember the one of 1940. We were all in short sleeves. Don't seem possible a storm could come up so fast, but by the middle of the afternoon, it was like the bottom fell out of the thermometer. It really plummeted! Most people went scurrying home for warmer clothing. And most didn't bother coming back. They had scheduled a big dance, but they couldn't begin to heat the building, so it was called off early.

"The saddest thing of all was the delicious apple tree being killed by the freeze. I remember the tree was struck by lightning one time, bolted together and the crack filled with cement. Looked like it ought to stand there forever. It had already been there since the civil war when it was discovered growing out of an old tree stump. I guess Mother Nature had different ideas.

"During the war, in 1943—no, probably 1942—we had a huge nationwide scrap drive. It was promoted through the school system, at least in our area. We kids were to collect all the scrap we could find and take it to the railroad siding where it was sorted and weighed, and the weight recorded so each student would receive credit for what they collected. I'll never forget it as long as I live. I had collected all of one small broken chisel and an empty toothpaste tube, and was I ever discouraged. I was a pretty negative kid anyway, and it seemed to be about the way my life progressed in those days. But then what seemed the best thing ever happening to me happened. I remember the strong feeling I had. It must be a sign or something, I thought. My life seemed to have been nothing, but maybe now God's going to let me do something really important.

"George Simpson, a neighbor, he was a friend of the family all my life. Well, he was depressed because of his son. His son enlisted in the navy right after Pearl Harbor, and while they cruised somewhere in the Pacific, his carrier was reported lost at sea. There was no word of possible survivors. Anyway, I asked Mr. Simpson if he had some scrap out on his farm I could turn in for the drive. He told me whenever parts became available, he would probably repair it and put it to use.

"I accompanied Mr. Simpson to his farm to help him with some chores one day. While I was there, I saw his barnyard literally strewn with old pieces of equipment. Some of it was big machinery. I must have looked pretty sad, or wide-eyed, or something. Anyway, he walked up behind me and said, 'I suppose

I can give you a few pieces of this old steel for your project.' I remembered what our teachers said, and without considering I might offend him, I repeated it to him, 'Our teacher says if we lose the war, ain't nobody gonna need their scrap anyway.'

"Well, Monday morning, I walked to school just like always. I always looked at the big mounds of scrap material piled along the railroad tracks. That's where they sorted it and got it ready for loading onto gondola cars to be shipped to foundries and melted down to make war equipment. There looming above all the other stacks stood a huge threshing machine, the very threshing machine I saw on Mr. Simpson's farm. Much of the other equipment, if not all of it, was piled up beside it. It put my class over the top, and I can tell you it went a long way toward boosting my ego. And Mr. Simpson was just as proud as I was.

"Come to think of it, I have an idea the old iron fence surrounding the original delicious apple tree went to the scrap drive."

What had once seemed hard feelings, or at least strained feelings, were much different after that day. They often discussed scripture at length, reminding Mark of the days when he and Victor enjoyed their deep studies together. Donald never stopped talking about leaving his father's church, yet he hadn't the financial means to pull up stakes. "It's mostly a longing for something entirely unreachable," he would often say.

With the events actually soon unfolding, one might have wondered if Donald was a prophet, though it certainly wasn't a prophecy he would have desired to make. What occurred was indeed a tragedy of tragedies, yet it changed the direction of Donald and Deanna's lives forever.

"Minister, Wife, Brother Killed in Accident"

The headlines covered almost half the front page of the local newspaper. The article began: "Well-known area minister, DM Holliday, and his wife, and brother, Walter Holliday, whom they were visiting in Thibodaux, Louisiana, were killed in a fiery automobile accident. Reverend Holliday was pastor of the Pentecostal Tabernacle Church, in Davenport for nearly thirty years. His brother was an executive for Gulf West Textiles, located in Thibodaux. Also killed in the crash were the driver of Holliday's limousine and the driver of the other car."

"Mark, come here quickly!" Claire said to him, as he was arriving home from work.

"I know, dear! I heard the news on the car radio," he said, not really needing to confirm the headlines. "Let's go see Donald. They'll want to fly down to Louisiana immediately, I'm sure. Maybe we can do something to help, keep the kids maybe."

"I just this minute saw the headlines," she said, hardly having had time to discern whether to read the paper or run for the car.

"Grab the paper! I'll tell you about it on the way," he said, as they hurried to the car. "DM and Carla were visiting his brother down near New Orleans," Mark said, as he pulled away from the curb. He had purposely parked the car on the street. "They were traveling up state, on highway 65, along the Mississippi River, just north of Ferriday, I believe it was. They had been visiting some of those old mansions on the cotton plantations, car pulled right across the road in front of their limousine. They hit broadside."

"How awful!"

"The announcer on the radio said it was a fiery crash. Said no one escaped alive. The driver of the limousine, even the driver of the other car was killed too."

"Do you think Donald knows yet?"

"I'm sure they know! I don't think the media would give out the names so quickly if they didn't."

When they arrived at their daughter's home, Donald was on the phone contacting the textile mill. "I don't know what arrangements Uncle Walter may have established for himself. I'm trying to reach the vice president now. I suppose he can tell me who Uncle Walter's attorney is." Donald blotted his forehead with his handkerchief.

"Your uncle probably did use a corporate attorney. I have an idea he'll take a lot of pressure off you. It seems more and more, contingency plans are laid out in situations like this," Mark said. "Then it's a matter of carrying them out as prearranged."

In a short while, Donald was put through to a Mr. Rathburn.

When the conversation concluded, Donald was noticeably calmer. "Mr. Rathburn is going to try to contact their attorney and have him call me," Donald said. "He said the attorney, let's see, I wrote his name down—C. Evan Chandler. He said Evan was contacted almost immediately and has been busy making arrangements. Says Evan will work with us in any way he can. Mr. Rathburn was aware Dad's family is the only relatives Walter has. He said if there is anything he can do for us to please let him know. Oh, dear! I hope our attorney's head is screwed on better than mine is. I feel so helpless being a thousand miles from it all. Well, I guess the best thing to do is stay here by the phone 'til we hear something."

"The newspaper article said they had been visiting some old mansions on the cotton plantations in northern Louisiana when the accident occurred?"

"Dad said Uncle Walter had been asking them to come down and go through the mansions in the Tallulah-Lake Providence area for years," he responded. "Walter visited them many years ago then talked about them ever since. I remember how neat it seemed when he told Deanna and me about it. At one time, I guess there were many of those old mansions along the Mississippi River. I suppose it was a long rime ago now. Some of those plantations were miles from the river. Yet the long distances didn't keep them from using the river for transportation. Those owners maintained a narrow piece of property giving them access to loading the big barges docked along the riverbank. Many of them built their mansions on those access strips."

Donald stopped and then thrust the palms of his hands into his forehead, as though suddenly realizing something. "Dear God! I'm rambling on like talking can make the whole problem disappear. Like all I have to do is think about them having a good time and it becomes so. Why do we have to have such tragedies?" He sat shaking his head, knowing the full impact had not yet set in.

The telephone rang, bringing him the call he anxiously awaited.

The bodies had been immediately taken to the Noble Funeral Home in Ferriday, where they were made ready for burial. Walter's body would be shipped by plane to Thibodaux. They arranged shipment of Donald's parent's bodies to the Moline airport by way of the best route. Donald would take care of matters at his end, as soon as he was made aware of the plane schedules.

Between the two of them, they decided to conduct the Davenport services previous to those in Thibodaux. It would allow sufficient time for Donald and his family to attend the services for his parents before going to Louisiana to attend services for his uncle. This too was tentative to schedules.

There was the matter of a will to be read; however, there would be a limited audience for that. DM Holliday and his family were the only close relatives Walter had, possibly the only relatives. He would have to refresh his memory of the will on that matter.

CHAPTER 28

Soon, Donald was giving serious consideration to leaving his church. The people had shown much love and offered their sympathy for Donald and his family's sorrow, but he made up his mind he would be changing vocations as soon as circumstances warranted. Any exact figures as to the amount of the inheritance were never mentioned, except it would probably be a substantial amount. There was no other living relatives, which meant the entire estate would go to Donald after it was probated. A charity with headquarters in New Orleans was to receive one million dollars, after all outstanding debts were settled. Walter Holliday and his wife had lost their only child, an infant daughter, to a rare blood disorder—a disorder passing down through several generations. Walter already contributed heavily to the foundation, but now he was leaving them the additional sum.

Nearly a year passed before the estate was settled and the check issued. Donald received a letter from the attorney, C. Evan Chandler, informing him of the amount and asking for the name of the bank where it might be deposited. Within ten days, a check for the sum of $4,595,072.00, was issued to his bank in Donald's savings account.

"Not even in my dreams did I consider such a large amount," he said to Mark and Claire, as he and Deanna discussed the matter with them. "Deanna and I have devoted a lot of time over the past year to thoughts of developing an area of retreat back there in your hometown. I really fell in love with the place. With Uncle Walter's inheritance, we may be able to build the things we've dreamed of having."

"It should be a wonderful place to raise the kids," Deanna said.

The thought of moving had taken Mark by surprise. "I wasn't aware you were even considering such a proposal. Tell us about it! Sounds exciting!"

"As a matter of fact, it was little more than a dream until we received word of the money from Uncle Walter. We often talked about it. But it didn't seem very realistic thinking. The first thing I'm going to do is announce my resignation as pastor so they can begin looking for someone else then hope they come to an early agreement on a replacement.

"In the meantime, we'll check into purchasing the property, which includes the farm where the 'original delicious apple tree' was located. The main attraction would be the site of the tree. We would try to promote the idea of what the tree really means to the world, how approximately seventy percent of the entire world's delicious apple production can trace its origin to this tree. That thought alone makes the whole thing worth pursuing," he added. "We've had a lot of other ideas, nothing very concrete as yet."

"I guess I could easily envy you two for going to Peru to live," Mark said. "It'll be hard enough not having you near us here. Be doubly hard with you being where I've secretly thought I'd like to finish out my days." Mark had said much more than he would have, had it not come as so much a surprise to him. He had made the comment entirely without proper thought.

"As a matter of fact," Donald said, "Deanna and I have talked about another matter a great deal too. You're retired now, nothing to keep you and Mom from doing pretty much whatever you please. Why not come along with us. We'll build a retreat together."

Mark was trying hard to become disinterested in the matter. He hadn't forgotten the statement Claire made the day they returned from the centennial celebration. She made it quite clear it would be hard for her to cope with the lifestyle it would entail. "I'm afraid we've rather carved our niche for the rest of our lives. To tell you the truth, we dearly love the home we have. The place is easy to take care of. We love the yard. All our friends are here. Not much left of the Bible class, but we enjoy the fellowship we have with those who are left. No, I'm afraid you better not count on us. But

I'm certainly all for you being able to do something you truly enjoy doing with your lives. And I sure like the idea of your promoting the original apple tree." Claire had remained silent on the day of the discussion, but she brought up the subject of life in Peru during a discussion taking place a few days later between the two of them.

"Do you think you would really like to retire to living in Peru? I mean, with all things considered, do you think you would be happy there?" she asked.

Mark had already determined in his own mind to discourage every suggestion involving moving from their present home. "I know I wouldn't be nearly as happy as I'd be right here in this house. This is where I want to live the rest of my life, right here in the 'White House,' with my 'lovely lady.' Does that answer your question? Besides, we have some years to go on our fifty-year term." Mark grinned, stood up, then walked to where she was sitting and placed a kiss on her lips.

"I had no idea you felt so strongly about it," she said, laughing as she spoke. "But you know, I've been giving it a lot of thought. I think it would be fun living back there, being close to Deanna and Donald and the children. It would be a good environment for Dennis and Cora."

The more Mark thought about the conversation, the more it puzzled him. Until the present time, there seemed to be no desire in Claire's mind to live in Mark's hometown. Suddenly, it seemed she was all for the idea. Of course, wanting to be near their daughter and grandchildren would be a most logical reason for changing one's mind. Perhaps there was no real reason to even suspect an ulterior motive.

His first concern was of the surgery she had undergone just four months before. A lesion appeared on her back actually causing her some discomfort as early as the late spring. Having been located in an area hard to be observed and not really anticipating it could present a danger, she largely ignored it until it began to itch and become quite annoying. It became painful and blood appeared on her clothing. Only then had Claire thought about going to a doctor or even thought to be concerned. When Mark saw the lesion, he insisted she see her doctor immediately. The lesion was removed surgically, and the biopsy showed it to be a malignant melanoma.

Dr. Melvin Winslow was reasonably sure all the cancerous tissue had been removed, leaving little concern of metastasis to other tissues having occurred.

"This tumor developed from an already existing mole, which is probably the most common way for them to occur," he had said.

Claire recalled how as a child she always sunburned in the summertime before she would get a tan. That too was a very common occurrence among those developing melanoma. "You have a number of other moles in close proximity to this one," he cautioned. "You would be wise to watch them closely. If there's a change in color, or enlarging of the surface, or rising of the lesion, you had better see me right away. You may never have another problem, but the chances are you will. We should be able to control it, but it's important for any lesions to be found early."

There was no hesitancy on Mark's part in bringing up the subject. "Tell me, Claire, are you worried about a recurrence of the melanoma?"

At first, her face flushed somewhat, then she turned pale. "I-I suppose I am a little worried." She hesitated as she spoke. "It's probably all these books I've been reading. They're enough to scare the daylights out of a person. Now every time I get a headache, I think of the recurrence of cancer. I've been feeling kind of drug out lately. I think what concerns me is something I read about the 'radial growth phase.' The author was saying if the tumor is stopped during that phase, there is almost one hundred percent correction by surgery. But if it continues to the elevation stage, it also means the lesion may be going deeper and may develop into more dangerous situations. In other words, it can enter into the lymph system and, from there, into the blood stream. Then it can spread rapidly throughout the entire body. I remember the lesion I had was well into the radial growth stage. It was really rather nasty looking. This writer talks about the possibility of little malignant cell colonies having existed outside the original lesion and going undetected and continuing to grow deeper and then spread."

After a very brief discussion, an appointment was made with Dr. Winslow.

After weighing in at the doctor's office, a loss of twelve pounds was registered from her final weigh-in after surgery. Almost from the moment the doctor saw Claire, he registered signs of concern. After examination, Dr. Winslow strongly suggested the necessity for some tests to determine if and to what extent metastasis had taken place. He then indicated preference to ultrasound. Sonograms were made for body imaging. This would reveal if and where metastasis had taken place by showing foreign growth structure. When the pictures were viewed, it was quickly realized the melanoma had indeed metastasized and permeated throughout her entire body. The diagnosis was disheartening, though Dr. Winslow tried to be encouraging.

"Even in severe cases," he said, "the prognosis is often better than for some other forms of cancer. However, these cells have traveled freely to virtually every part of your body by way of the blood stream." From then on, it was more than clear, Dr. Winslow was not optimistic about her chances of recovery. "I don't recall ever having seen melanoma develop and spread so quickly. I know it's little comfort at a time like this, but I want you to know there was nothing you could have done differently. All indications were the lesion was entirely gone after surgery, but apparently, there remained some undetected malignant cells at the time allowing them to penetrate into the blood stream. I truly am sorry," he apologized.

"As I said, though, there is hope. I have a suggestion for something, which may be helpful. A treatment has been developed for advanced melanoma. It's in the form of a vaccine. It's not designed to prevent the disease, as most vaccines are. The object in this case is to cause the body to develop immunity to its own cancerous cells. A substance shed by the melanoma itself is cultured and then injected back into the body. In some cases, it has proven to slow the growth. You must realize your body has been seriously weakened. It's incredible you feel as well as you do. I must warn you, however, of a more serious problem—I should say, the ultimate problem. It could come by way of almost any organ of your body because of the extent of the metastasis. This treatment will at best only prolong the inevitable. Why don't you talk about this option between yourselves and then let me know what you decide. If it is to help at all, it will surely need to be done quickly."

The process was initiated on the following day. Several of the moles on her back showed early signs of discoloring. Cells were removed and placed in the cultures to begin the vaccine formation.

Winter was underway. Considering the initial rapid growth from the discovery of the lesion to the time they could view the sonograms and the extent of metastasis, there was no question the treatment had slowed the growth dramatically. But even so, Claire weighed barely one hundred pounds. Her body had weakened to the point of needing a great deal of additional rest, and stronger medication was needed for the pain. She insisted on spending the time at home rather than being confined to a hospital. This offered no problem for Dr. Winslow, as long as he could see her from time to time. Mark was with her almost every moment.

Claire had tried to initiate discussions a number of times, but Mark discouraged all attempts toward talking about what he should do with his life after she was gone. Had the matter concerned any other subject, it would have seemed Mark's approach was of a childish nature. It was as though, as long as he could put off dealing with the inevitable, he would not be required to deal with it at all. Claire, of course, recognized the difficulty, and it was she who forced him to face the facts.

"I want you to make the most of every moment we have left." Mark started to place his hand over her mouth, but she stopped him from doing so.

"Mark," she said, "you must face the inevitable. It's a matter of time now, and you must come to grips with it."

He watched her expressions as she spoke the words, wanting her to be still. Don't say another word he wanted to say. Suddenly, he burst into tears. Sitting at her bedside, he began weeping uncontrollably. Claire reached out for him, pulling him close. Placing his head upon her breasts, his body shook with each sob.

"I'm sorry, Claire," he finally managed to say.

"I know," she said. She remained quiet until he regained his composure, then she began speaking again. "Now we are aware that God is working all together for the good of those who are loving God, who are called according to the purpose" (Rom. 8:28).

Mark rose up and looked into her eyes. Claire had quoted a verse he had repeated often. It was one he chose to use in similar situations, always trying to encourage those to whom he was witnessing. "But I love you so much, Claire."

"Is that a verse only applying to others, Mark? Are you telling me it's fine for you to use it to comfort others, but it somehow doesn't apply to you?"

"Please, Claire, I can't bear the thought of you leaving me. It just doesn't seem fair."

"Does anyone ever feel death is fair?" Claire purposely raised her voice to show anger, hoping to jar him from his inability to deal with reality. "Who are you to think God shouldn't send adversity your way or only send it to others? You! You're the one who talks about the plan and purpose of God, how every event dovetails into every other event to carry out His carefully designed program."

With his handkerchief, Mark wiped the tears from his eyes. "I'm sorry, Claire. You've been my very life for so many years."

"Maaark! I'm not trying to hurt you! You needed a swift kick in the pants. You've got to get matters into perspective. Consider yourself having been kicked, and make up your mind to get on with your life."

Claire's brief display of anger was ended. She spoke softly now. "You've lived a lifetime feeling strongly God has a definite objective for you to carry out. I feel just as strongly there's good reason for you to think so. I'm sure I'll be going to be with the Lord soon, but I must know you are strong.

"I must know you are ready to carry out God's purpose for you. I don't know God's reasoning any better than you do, but maybe your goal can be better reached with you being alone. That could very well explain the reason he chooses to take me from you. You must be aware His objective will be realized and exactly in the way He intends it should be. Mark, whatever's in store for us, we'll be together soon, and I'm sure it will be for all eternity. I love you so much. You've given me many wonderful years. No one could have made me happier than you've made me."

Of course, the words made perfect sense, but Mark was not prepared to accept them.

Donald went about the matter of checking out the property he was interested in purchasing. Actually, several properties occupied the area he desired to develop. If he could purchase a strip reaching from the original delicious apple tree site to the highway running into town, he would be well pleased.

It would have seemed much better had Mark been able to accompany him on those trips, having been so much more familiar with the area, but Mark would not leave Claire for the length of time required. As for dealing with the owners, Mark wouldn't have known any of them any better than Donald did. Far too many years separated them from the days Mark remembered. Besides, he had never really explored that part of town when he was a boy. He often joked about having grown up living by the tracks. "Nobody was very far from the tracks in my hometown," he had said many times. The man, who owned the farm where the apple tree once stood, didn't particularly want to sell. He told Donald he had no reason to. "Everything has its price," he then added. "But the price for the land would be pretty doggoned steep if you really want to know."

From then it was a matter of negotiating terms to buy the sixty-acre farm. When the asking price had become firm, Donald was in a position to negotiate with the owners of the smaller properties. Whether or not they would finalize this deal depended upon the purchase of the adjacent properties.

After the fourth trip back there, Donald was able to make the purchases. An apartment was secured in Winterset where he and his family could reside until things were better organized.

"Mr. Hayes, there's something I must say to you." Dr. Winslow had stopped by the house to see Claire. After he finished his examination, he and Mark left the room where Claire was resting. As they walked, he handed Mark a prescription, saying, "This one is to be filled for you. It will help you get some much-needed rest." He stopped and squarely faced Mark to be sure he had his full attention.

"I don't quite know how to say this, but by all the odds, Mrs. Hayes should have succumbed weeks ago. I don't know what it can be. There's no way your wife can recover, yet she refuses to give up. Mr. Hayes, I don't pretend to know how to explain it, but it's like something is preventing her from letting go. I think only you hold the key to what's happening. I've seen an unusual degree of love between the two of you. In fact, the degree of devotion seems incredible to me. Like I said, Mr. Hayes, I can't explain it, but I think you are somehow keeping her from giving up this life. Whatever strong tie you have to her, you must break it. You must let her go! Please, Mr. Hayes, let her go! She'll be much better off."

"Call me anytime at all. If there's anything I can do, I'll be there. Good day! Oh, and be sure you take the medication as I've directed," he said, as he turned to leave. "If you don't get some rest, you're heading for serious illness yourself."

Mark returned to the room where Claire lay sleeping on her bed. He sat down in the chair beside her, the place where he had spent so many hours over recent weeks. He watched her varying expressions as they changed from a noticeable grimace to one of comparative relaxation. There were tears in her eyes. Even as she slept, she endured pain. Mark hadn't noticed that particular pain before. Nor had he seen the tears before as she slept. Tears filled his own eyes as he began accepting the reality of the situation. Claire was little more than a mere skeleton lying there between the sheets. Her eyes were deeply set in darkened cavities. Extremely gray in color, her skin clung closely to her facial bones. What he observed frightened him.

Her eyes slowly opened. Then they focused upon him. A faint smile appeared, not a pretty smile but certainly a genuine one. "I'm so tired, so very tired," she managed to say. "Mark, how can I help you? How can I help you to be strong?" She struggled to express the words she wanted to say. "I must go soon! But I must be sure you are ready to face life alone." Once again, she closed her eyes and fell asleep—the same tortured kind of sleep Mark had seen just a few moments before. Again, her face grimaced, and the tears once again filled her eyes.

"What have I done?" he cried out, fully realizing the extent of her deterioration. "Oh, God! Help me! Help me to face what's happening. Give me strength, Father. Let Thy will be done, not mine! Please Father take her. Take her and love her as I have loved her. And please, please give me the strength to go on. Please, let the bond existing between us remain. May we remain as one, even when she is gone! Amen!"

Mark sat quietly, grasping her hand between his hands. He felt a gentle but unmistakable pressure from her fingers. Then her hand fell limp. He looked upon her face, and there was the smile of a wonderfully peaceful lady. No longer did he see the grimace of pain, or the tears, which had filled her eyes. Even the vision of her sunken eyes disappeared, and gone was the gray skin stretching from bony feature to bony feature of her once beautiful face. Mark was once again observing the beautiful smile he had seen so many times—the smile made possible by being freed from the torture she had endured and of being in the presence of the Ford she loved even more than she loved Mark. And every bit as important was having the knowledge Mark had faced the reality of his situation and truly accepted it.

Claire was free, free from the frailty of these "soilish" bodies—bodies subject to pain and suffering. Whatever God meant for Claire to learn from this life surely had been learned, for God would leave nothing unfinished. He would do the same for Mark. And He would do the same for every other creature in the universe. What a happy time Claire must be realizing now in the presence of her Lord and Savior! Mark could only be happy for her, knowing her pain and suffering was over and God's objective for her was established and established for all eternity.

Mark bent down, his lips meeting with her lips. He kissed her tenderly. After raising his head, he looked into her eyes, and then he closed her eyelids. "Farewell, my lovely lady. Farewell for just a little while."

CHAPTER 29

While Donald diligently dealt with the purchase of the land in Peru, he had still found time to inquire about a burial plot for Claire's remains. "The man said there were still some spaces in the western section overlooking the valley," Donald said. "It was cold and wintry the day I was there, but it certainly was a beautiful place, Mark."

"I guess I was in no condition to think clearly at the time I should have been taking care of those matters," Mark said. "But I'm glad I hesitated. I do want Claire to be buried in the Peru cemetery. We may have difficulty arranging anything on such short notice, but I think things can be held up in cases such as this."

"I really don't think things will need to be held up, Mark. I spoke with the caretaker of the cemetery. He gave me his telephone number and said to give him a call. All you need to do is purchase a plot of ground and he'll handle the rest." Donald had been thorough in his investigation. "I told him no decisions were made concerning the plot. I said I was just feeling it out in case you wanted to buy a plot there. As soon as all the plans for burial are settled, I'll give him a call if you'd like me to."

Mark was greatly relieved to think the problem would be taken care of. "It rather creates another problem, though," Mark said as an afterthought. "We'll need someone to handle the graveside services. As a matter of fact, we haven't decided who'll do the services at the funeral home."

"I was thinking about that last night." Donald had waited for the subject to come up, not wanting it to sound like he was trying to orchestrate the details. Being well aware Mark was not thinking clearly, he only wanted matters to go smoothly. "I was thinking about the man who used to MC your Bible study classes. Wasn't his name Leland?"

"Leland Bartholomew! Of course! From Omaha, it's only about a ninety-minute drive. He might do it. Anyway, I know he'll want to know of Claire's passing. I'll give him a call."

Mark checked through the stack of business cards, which he kept handy in a corner of his desk. "I'll try the television station first," he said.

Soon, Leland was on the line. "Hello! What can I do for you?" "Mark, Mark Hayes speaking."

"Mark! How nice to hear your voice! What a pleasant surprise! I think of you so often, I just never seem to get around to calling. What's new in Davenport? How are the classes going? Still packing them in?"

"Not really. A, Leland, I'm afraid my call is not with good news. I'm sorry I couldn't be calling about something more pleasant." "What is it, Mark? Something happen to Claire or Deanna?" "It's Claire. Claire passed away yesterday afternoon."

"Oh, dear God, no! Not Claire! Oh, Mark, I'm so sorry! A greater lady never lived. You have my deepest sympathy, Mark."

"I know, Leland. I know you care deeply, and I wanted you to know. I also want to ask a favor of you," he said.

"Anything I can do, just consider it done."

"The burial will be in a little town called Peru. The town's located in Madison County, Iowa."

"Sure," Leland interrupted. "Winterset's the county seat. I've been through there many times. Highway 92 and 169,1 think. Never heard of Peru, but I'm sure I can find it from there."

"I don't know how busy your schedule is, Leland, but I was wondering if I could impose upon you to conduct the graveside services?" There was no hesitation on Leland's part. "Sure, and it is certainly no imposition. And let me know when the services will be in Davenport. I'm coming for the funeral too. Suppose they will be in the funeral home. Who's doing those services, Mark?"

"The fact is we haven't made those plans yet."

"Be glad to do that too. Just say the word!"

"Well, the word is, if you're sure you don't mind."

"I would consider it a great privilege. Say, Mark, I have a talk show airing in less than four minutes. The funeral won't be tomorrow, will it?"

"Probably the day after. Yes, we're thinking Thursday morning," Mark answered.

"I'll catch a plane to Moline, rent a car, and drive back to Omaha. Maybe we can spend some time together in Peru."

"Leland! Don't hang up yet! We're going to make plane reservations from this end. And we'll have a rental car waiting for you. It'll all be paid for. You just catch the plane. Many thanks, Leland."

It hadn't occurred to Mark to inquire if Leland had married. When Leland arrived, Mark was pleasantly surprised to see the woman who accompanied him. They had driven directly to Mark's home from the airport. "This is Deborah, my wife," he said as they entered the house, introducing her to Donald and Deanna as well as to Mark.

"I hope I haven't put too much pressure on you, Leland. I know this is not something you're accustomed to doing, and it doesn't give much time for preparation."

"There were so many nice things to say about Claire, the only pressure was in making the best choices," he remarked. "No, Mark, hosting talk shows has given me a lot of good experience in finding things to say. At least I hope it shows as being good experience."

Several members of Mark's family attended the graveside services. Had there been more time for preparation, the women of the Methodist Church would have furnished refreshments in the church basement. Even so, Donald's arrangements were thorough. He had arranged with a catering service, which the minister had recommended, to furnish the food and serve it in the Methodist Church basement. Donald was pleased it went so well and especially on such short notice. The minister had done very well in estimating the number of those who might attend.

They arrived at the church. Some of Mark's family had not met

Donald and their children, nor had they met Leland. After their plates were filled and the drinks served, the fellowship began in earnest. It was an enjoyable visit with Leland and his lovely wife, with Mark renewing an old friendship and Donald getting to know the man Mark already knew and loved so very much.

Mark had the opportunity to confide in Leland. "I must confess, Leland, when I first saw Deborah, I was quite shocked."

"I know exactly what you mean," he replied. "I wondered if you would notice the resemblance. I think knowing how much she reminded me of Claire helped even more in my falling in love with Deborah."

There was indeed a strong resemblance, and Leland was pleased it hadn't gone unnoticed.

''Oh my," Leland sighed, "I so often think about the evenings we spent in those Bible studies. Those were some of the most enjoyable times of my life. I certainly learned a lot. Those people attending just lived for the next class to meet. And seeing the faces light up on some of those people, especially the elderly ones. Most of them never heard the truth like you were presenting it. Come to think of it, I hadn't either. Your class was the hardest thing for me to give up when I chose to leave and go to Omaha.

"I'll never forget the day I first met you and Claire in Chad Worthington's waiting room. I was hearing some strange comments coming from the seat nearby. I couldn't help but recognize the perceptive value of what you were presenting. I guess I liked your comments the moment I heard them. I'll never forget the message you presented on my radio program Viewpoint. I'll bet you remember it too, Mark."

Mark smiled. "Yes, I sure do! It certainly launched our Bible study class. It started some very enjoyable times for me too. I still have a stack of printed copies of the message."

"I remember the week before," Leland continued, "when DM called you a heretic? I never in my life had anything upset me like whoops\" Leland became flustered when he realized what he had done. "I sure put my foot in my mouth that time. I'm sorry, Donald.

There was no call for those unkind words. I apologize! I don't know what to say. Leland Bartholomew at a loss for words."

"No problem, Leland." Donald laughed heartily. "I've heard the story from Mark. What's more, I knew my dad quite well. And I know he probably deserved anything ever said about him. He could be one big pain in the neck sometimes."

"I'll have to admit, he never failed to get the best of me. I thought I had one over on him that day by matching Mark against him in his rebuttal, and then he pulled that fast one. I was so angry I saw red. How in the world did Mark ever allow DM's son to marry his daughter? Something had to have gone awry there," Leland said with much amusement.

"I really think it had something to do with his determination to get even with Dad somehow," Donald explained. "I think Mark figured if I were a member of the family, he would be in control of the situation. As a matter of fact, you will be pleased to know Mark did have the last word in the scenario. He used his grandson to carry it off. I'll tell you the story sometime when we're not in the presence of the ladies."

Deanna laughed. "I don't think ladies of today would be very shocked with what Mark said to his grandson, though it did come as quite a shock to Donald."

Donald told Leland the story, while even those nearby seemed to be greatly entertained. "I responded very much the way my father would have," he concluded. "He would have looked upon it as a very vulgar way to speak to a four-year-old child. Of course, Mark saw the innocence of the remark and purposely set me up so he could show me how foolish I was. I took the bait, and I was really sore. I couldn't understand why he would talk that way to a child. After he let me explain my solution for the crime problem, he lowered the hammer on me, telling me I was a prude. I was angry at the time, but I began to realize I wasn't looking at grace properly. I was looking to the Law of Moses to deal with life's problems. We're not expected to live up to the law. We're expected to do our best with life, of course, but we're to understand what grace is all about. Grace covers our shortcomings."

With tongue in cheek, Donald continued, "Anyway, I think Mark had that in mind all along. He thought, 'I'll just let him marry Deanna, then I'll convert him over to my way of thinking and be even with DM once and for all.'"

There was hearty laughter, and then there was a perceptible

return to a more somber atmosphere. At this point, Leland changed the subject of conversation. "I heard the news about your father and mother being killed in a terrible accident. It made news all the way to Omaha, on the front page of the Omaha World Herald. His brother was also killed, an executive in the textile industry, wasn't he?"

"Those things are pretty hard to take. Seems ironic, facing death as an expected part of life," Donald remarked.

"May I ask why all of you are moving to Peru?" Leland asked after a brief period of silence. "It doesn't exactly seem like the hub of the world down here."

"No, actually, that's down the road a piece." Mark managed to pick up on the humor of Leland's remark. "It struck me funny you should say that. When I was a boy, we would often hear about the mythical place called Podunk Center. Haven't heard the name in many years now, but it was meant to describe a small town as being just a wide place in the road in an out-of-the-way place. Well, about nine miles southwest of Peru was just such a place, and someone actually named it Podunk Center. The place even had city limit signs. Over the door of the gas station was a wagon wheel, and directly under it was a sign reading—"

Leland and Donald shouted the words in unison, "The Hub of the World!" Everyone at the table burst into laughter.

"A number of years ago, there was a humorous article written in the papers about the town being for sale. I think they were asking twelve thousand dollars, if I remember right, for an entire town, mind you!"

Again, there was laughter.

"I wasn't trying to avoid an answer to your question, Leland," Mark apologized. "Actually, this was my hometown, but it was Donald who decided to move here. It was right here the original delicious apple tree took roots, just a chance growth out of an old tree stump during the Civil War. Talk about the handiwork of God. Makes you realize things often aren't according to the chance we suggest."

Donald entered the conversation. "When my uncle Walter Holliday was killed, his estate would have gone to Dad, but with Dad being killed too, I was the only living heir. It was a sizeable inheritance, so we plan to see what we can do about promoting the delicious apple site. I suppose il it doesn't work out, we'll farm the ground. We have a lot of big ideas, but nothing in the planning stage yet.

"Some of those ideas include a restaurant and a small motel, twenty or thirty rooms, maybe more. We want it all oriented toward families with wholesome entertainment. We had the idea of hiring musically talented people as waiters and waitresses who could also furnish the entertainment. We're thinking about tram rides on scenic trails down through the valley. The hired people would be trained in all areas of dealing with the public, thinking about other things too, about a wedding chapel. Since the water problem has been alleviated, we even thought about a water recreation of some type. The biggest problem will probably be in finding others willing to buy stock in the project. We want to invest rather heavily into the thing, but it will require much more capital than we can provide."

Leland was impressed. "Really, you have quite an area to draw from. There must be five or six county seats within forty miles, not to mention Des Moines. I suppose it's also about forty miles? You're only about ninety miles from Omaha and Council Bluffs. I'll sure do all I can to help. I can put you on a talk show. You can reach all of our viewing audience."

His expression changed from one of excitement to a more serious one. "What about your plans, Mark?" Leland asked. "I remember you talking about a premonition you had. Something kept prodding you, something God wanted you to accomplish. Whatever became of your premonition, Mark?"

"It's still a bewildering thing to me. I've spent practically a lifetime of thinking God has something for me to accomplish. But I'm still no closer to realizing what it is. As Claire lay dying, it seemed my dream was dying at the same time. It seemed everything I hoped for was escaping me. Then suddenly, the desire came back as strong as it ever was. I sensed Claire had refused to give up until she knew I was thinking along those lines again. I don't know, but as I sat there looking at her emaciated body, I had the overwhelming feeling I must return to Peru and live out my days. But it was just as clear I should take Claire with me. It was then I made the last-minute decision as I did. I feel I made the right decision. But I still can't be any more sure. I do feel Claire is somehow a part of God's objective for me. I really don't know how she could be, being gone this way."

"I apologize, Leland. I'm carrying on as though you should know exactly how I feel. I don't know how I feel."

Leland had great respect for Mark. If Mark felt strongly about any matter, he was confident it was no mere whim. Besides, he had known him for more than thirty-five years, and he had been aware of Mark's premonition all that time. "I won't doubt your wisdom for one moment. Say, Mark," he spoke as though something had occurred to him for the first time, "did the thought of writing a book ever seem like the right thing for you? I know you're not interested in developing a new denomination. Still it is a wonderful way of understanding. You said yourself the things you taught were the explanation of the plan and purpose of God for having made the eons. What about the idea of you writing a book, basically a story of your life and how God directed you from one truth into the next through your own life's experiences? It seems to me it would be a most worthy undertaking. Anyway, let me know more as things develop. I know they will because I know you. And hey, Donald! What you and Deanna have planned sounds really exciting. Let me know the minute you think of a way I can help you. We cater heavily to things like your enterprise. Might be able to help a whole lot."

"It's been a genuine pleasure to visit with all of you. I only wish it could have been under more pleasant circumstances. Being closer now, maybe we can get together more often. And, Mark, Godspeed with your desires. I have every confidence you will do it well, whatever it is. Now I think Deborah and I had better be on our way back to Omaha so you can spend some time with your family."

"Thanks, Leland, and thanks for coming to my rescue. You gave a superb service, as I knew you would." Mark could hardly release his grasp on Leland's hand.

"Wouldn't have wanted it any other way."

Mark enjoyed a nice visit with his family and a few old friends but soon became exhausted from the strain. It had been an exhausting day in general, and the proverbial let down was setting in.

"You need rest, Mark," Donald said. "I think we should get you to the apartment so you can get a good night's sleep. We can decide tomorrow where to go from here."

As Mark waited his turn to be seated in the barber chair, he thumbed through pages of a magazine he took from the rack next to him. In the lower corner of a page, a small ad read: "Put Your Stories into Print." Little else appeared besides the form to fill out and mail for more information. Mark had seen the advertisement several times, but he had no reason for interest. But having seriously thought about following Leland's suggestion on writing a book, this notice immediately caught his attention. Taking a course in writing seemed the logical thing to do, especially in consideration of his lack of writing experience. Maybe he should enroll, he thought. Why not! It sure wouldn't hurt to enquire. Anyway, what did he have to lose? Why not cut it out and mail it? With the barber's approval, he had clipped the advertisement. The decision had launched him into his writing career.

As he returned to the apartment, he thought about Leland's suggestion. Had God placed those words of encouragement upon Leland's lips? He began thinking about some of the things he had learned—things, which brought him much joy and peace of mind. He thought about the very reason God subjects us to evil and the real meaning of grace and how its meaning has been concealed by the eternal torment doctrine. And even the eternal torment doctrine itself, the Christian world should welcome the truth of his understanding.

Mark began to reminisce. Just what had he learned over the years, which might be of use in helping others? His thoughts went back to the day he met his friend in the garden so many years ago. It was in those early years he first became aware of the feeling he had. Beginning with that event, he began recalling to memory all the things standing out in his memories—anything seeming significant at all. Learning there would be a future life for his puppy seemed to be the matter awakening him to knowledge of another way of believing in God.

Step by step, event by event, memory of them came to mind. The reason for many of those events seemed to be self-explanatory. Each event seemed to blend as though developing a special continuity. Meeting the man as he had in the garden certainly was the beginning. That was far too wonderful to have happened in any way other than by God's design. The day he spent the afternoon at the south rim—becoming closer to God than ever before in his life— without a doubt, that clearly was by the hand of God. What would have happened had he been thrust into a world of such confusion for him? God Himself had made arrangements for him, allowing him to remain at home until he matured enough to meet the need.

And when he did make the decision to leave his hometown and set down roots, why did he particularly make the choice he had? Had he gone anywhere else, it seemed obvious he would never have met Claire, especially in light of the unique way they did meet. What about the night he met Claire? Had he gone to Omaha, or Kansas City, it wasn't likely their lives would have crossed. He and Claire were meant for each other. It was impossible to even imagine having lived his life apart from her. Some kind of bond had formed the evening they met, for very soon, they both knew they were in love. From then their love only grew stronger. How could it have been anything but the result of God's direction? The way they purchased their home, their rent having been applied as down payment.

Even meeting the couple next door and becoming such good friends surely was more than coincidence. Then being able to help in the spiritual needs of Victor and Abigail. It hardly seemed necessary to mention the circumstances by which they came to adopt Deanna.

Without Deanna, they would have had no children. Except for the love for the Lord and the love and devotion they felt for one another, love for Deanna was their greatest joy. What an incredible story it was to recall.

Then there was the experience gained from knowing Edward. They were given firsthand knowledge into the plight of the Jewish people. And getting acquainted with Rabbi Steindler had helped him to properly comprehend God's continued role for the nation of Israel.

As Mark pondered the memory of those many events, it occurred to him it would be a wise thing if he were to write them down in outline form while they were so clear in his mind. He had the feeling he should preserve the clarity of each of those moments. If he should decide to write a book, it certainly should give him an edge.

Renting the apartment had proved to be the practical thing to do. Over the winter, Donald stayed there on several occasions conducting business as he checked out land purchases, finally being able to buy the land he was interested in. He and Deanna hadn't wanted to disrupt the school program for Dennis and Cora, so there were no plans to move there before spring.

Mark spent most of the winter in the apartment. It had given him time to work on the writing course. He spent some time with the family, being able to visit more with them than he had in many years. He managed to get to the cemetery a number of times, but on each occasion, it was much to too cold to linger for any length of time.

Spring arrived, getting ready to clothe the area in its most beautiful attire. Having waited all winter for a day such as this, he drove to the cemetery and parked his car next to the big iron gate at the entrance. It wasn't noon yet, but the temperature had reached the mid-seventies. Removing his coat, he placed it over the rear cushion of the seat. Entering the cemetery, he followed the graveled lane as it wandered back through the grounds. Arriving at the site of Claire's grave, he discovered the flowers accumulating over the winter had been removed. Upon the grave, he placed the flowers he brought. "White roses—Claire would love the white roses," he said, speaking softly.

From where Mark stood at the grave site, he looked out over the valley. Observing the signs of springtime everywhere before him, his immediate thoughts were of a certain fulfillment in having brought Claire's remains here. One could hardly wish for a nicer final resting place. She would be pleased. He sat down in front of the stone. This would be an ideal place to commune with God. Not only would he be close to God, but also he would be in the presence of Claire as well. Mark turned himself over to God as he knelt down and bowed his head in prayer.

"Where, my gracious God and Father, do I go from here? Do

only memories remain for me? Are mere memories capable of replacing a lifelong premonition? My hopes, my dreams—all are yet unfulfilled. Is there something more for me to learn? Am I to be a teacher of others? I am Your servant. How may I serve You? Take this frail vessel, and use it in some way. Use me, oh, God, to move your plan and purpose ever closer to Your objective. Still the longing I feel in my heart. Thank You, my God and Father, in the name of the Lord, Jesus Christ."

When his prayer was ended, his eyes focused upon the stone laying before him and the names and dates placed there. The date of Claire's death had not been engraved. Secretly, it pleased Mark, for somehow, her death didn't seem quite so final.

"Claire! Claire! I love you so much! I miss you, but thank you for all those wonderful years. I'm so incredibly thankful for those beautiful memories. Thank you, my love."

Lowering his head, he rested his face on his hands. With eyes closed, he sat quietly, savoring the memories, which filled his mind and heart. Tears of joy and tears of extreme sorrow intermingled and gently fell from his eyes. Mark felt sure somehow that book would be written.

CHAPTER 30

"I just stopped to give a hand with painting your basement. You said you were going to do it today." Deanna entered the house, stopping to give Mark a kiss on the cheek as he held the door open.

"You're right! I was going to do some painting, but I've decided to wait until fall. I'm pretty involved in my book right now. I just don't want to leave it even for a short time. Besides, the painting can wait."

"Donald told me you've selected a title for your book, said you sounded excited about it."

"Since you put it that way, yes, I guess I am excited. I already had a title, even thought it was a pretty good one. Then I discovered someone had used it. As a matter of fact, I ran across a second book with the same title. That idea was taken care of. Actually, it was truth concerning the eons, which ultimately helped with my decision.

"The most enlightening thing I ever learned about scripture was the study of these eonian times. That's what put me into my deep studies in the first place. I've believed for many years, the eons were made in Christ Jesus so those celestial beings could know God. God established a plan through which He could reveal Himself to all His creation. He would make a fleshly body of visible, tangible flesh. Then He would transfer the souls of the celestial beings into these fleshly bodies. But between the original creation of those beings and the new creation created through the blood of Christ is a huge chasm. It was no problem for God to envision a perfect creation coming out of it, but it would require a tremendous work to bring it about.

"I visualize this great period of time as being required for God to deal with every one of His universal creatures. So the marvel of the eons is the survival of the soul throughout their duration. A spiritual soul cannot undergo death, but it does go through a dying state, and it does so while embodied in human flesh.

"It's very hard for men to believe, I mean, to believe all these physical beings we see around us make up such a temporary state of an eternal creation. Anyway, the eons are only a brief intermission in a vast, vast realm of eternity. I see the eons or ages as being a bridge. Darkness fills eternity as it was, and brightness of the glory of God fills eternity as it becomes and a bridge connecting the two. I see humanity emerging from this bridge and Christ Jesus leading the way into the light. As a matter of fact, I would like to see a picture of that on the dust cover: Many billions of members of humanity walking over the bridge into the perfect light of the glory of God. The faith of God is being transferred to creation by way of this bridge through Christ Jesus. When that picture first came into view for me, even the title came naturally. *Bridge of Eternity* seemed the natural result."

"Daddy, I think your title is very appropriate." Deanna was excited with what she heard. "You make it seem like the best thing that can happen is for the eons to end."

"Frankly, I guess it is!" Mark laughed as he spoke. "But we mustn't be impatient. Paul spoke of sufferings not being worthy of the impending glory. He, of course, was talking about the sufferings of those of the body of Christ, but the same is true for all of us. God's program is moving exactly as He planned, and this earthly suffering is only for a moment compared with eternity. Entering into the eternal kingdom of the Son of God's love will far outweigh any comparatively brief time of suffering spent here in the flesh."

Mark confided in Deanna how he marveled of the way his scriptural understanding had grown over the years. "It seems amazing how we learn by bits and pieces, little by little, something here and something there, and then they begin joining together and becoming more complete truths. It seems God never allows us to discover a truth all at once. I suspect it would take away from the real joy of discovery. The real joy can only come after we have diligently searched for answers and then realize the Holy Spirit has revealed the truth to us. The fact is I just had such an experience."

"I didn't have a chance to tell you before, Deanna," he said, wanting to keep her informed of his work. "But I've come to an understanding, which is helping me complete my book. And I am excited about it."

Mark hesitated before going on. "Maybe I'm being eccentric, I don't know, but I just can't make myself finalize this work until I've shared it with Claire. It used to be we never settled upon any point of view until we had shared it completely. Of course, it's been different since she's gone. It's become so important. I-I-I-I just have to share it with her. I want her to be a part of it. I am eccentric, I guess."

"No, you're not eccentric!" she said. "I know how much you and Mama enjoyed your studies. And if you are eccentric, all I can say is it must be a wonderful thing to be. If you told me Mama would take part in the discussion, I might think differently." Deanna smiled as she spoke those words.

Mark was a bit embarrassed by what Deanna said. "Maybe we're getting closer to the truth now," he said. "Oh, I know the difference, but it really seems like she's here with me sometimes, again sharing the wonderful things of scripture. And it's as though she's learning right along with me. Anyway, I want to present these things to her before I put it into its final form. If only Claire could be here with me now."

"Deanna," he said lovingly, "I enjoyed so very much all those times your mother and I discussed the scriptures. So many of the matters we discussed over the years have become clear to me now. What I would give if Claire could be sharing these things with me now."

"Mama would have loved to be a part of what you're learning. Daddy, I miss her so much. My grandchildren miss her too. Roger showed me his report card the other day, and he asked me if I thought Grandma would have liked it. I told him she would have been very proud of him and she would have been the first to tell him so. She was so much a part of all our lives." Deanna's eyes moistened.

"And, Daddy, I think she will be a part of what you've learned," she added with a loving smile.

Mark knew Claire would clearly recall the passage of scripture found in the first chapter of Colossians telling them that even the celestial beings would find salvation through the blood of Christ. They discussed that many, many times. Yet they could never understand how celestial beings in spirit form and having no blood could be saved through His blood. "Here's what we do know, Claire. Christ is the Firstborn of every creature, for in Him is all created. That in the heavens and that on the earth, the visible, the invisible, thrones, lordships, sovereignties, and authorities—all is created through Him and for Him. And He is before all, and all has its cohesion in Him.

"Both Habakkuk and Zephaniah, in about 518 BC, tell us that God is giving the house of Judah over to the penalties of the Law of Moses. He had already cast away the ten tribes. Thus, God had given up all hope of any of His people turning back to Him by their own choice. But if it was to continue in that manner, the entire human race would have gone the way of Sodom and Gomorrah, and all humanity would spend eternity in the lake of fire.

"Now the old creation must die but not in that way, for they must become a new creation. All along, God had a plan to restore humanity to Him. Claire, you remember how most of Christendom expects to be called up to heaven as members of that body, but we determined that was not true. The body of Christ," Mark explained, "was led by Christ as the complement of the eras. The first era was in days of Zechariah, when the Spirit of Christ was among the people teaching ten thousand of them to walk holy and flawlessly. They would become a monument to future generations that God would once again be their God and restore them as His people. These ten thousand, which Zechariah called 'mortals of a miracle,' were all from the house of Judah. And, Claire, this became a premonition of salvation for all mankind. The second era came in the days of Paul's ministry. The total number was 144,000, 12,000 from each of the twelve tribes of Israel, all walking holy and flawlessly with Christ. Claire, where today do we see anyone walking holy and flawlessly? There is not one!

"At the midpoint of the tribulation period the 144,000, because of their flawlessness, will be resurrected and taken on clouds to heaven, and also because of their flawlessness, their witness while on earth brings on the fall of Satan. The power of Satan will have been destroyed, and he is cast to the earth.

"Claire, what happened to Adam soon after God made him out of the soil of the ground and then breathed into him the breath of life is a very important event. You will remember how God told him not to eat of the tree of the knowledge of good and evil. Some will tell us," he said to her, "if Adam had not disobeyed God, we wouldn't have been subjected to all the hardships we are confronted with. Of course, that may be true, but what they don't realize is that led to the very object of God's plan and purpose for the eons.

"God created the sovereignties and authorities and powers of the universe, but they did not know Him. This did not come as a shock or surprise to God," Mark said to Claire, "for this was part of His plan all along. Faith can only be observed by visible means, and nothing about the spirit realm was visible. God had already created Christ in the form of the Elohim, thus, becoming the Firstborn of all creation. The Elohim made the eons in Christ Jesus. Elohim means 'I am coming to be.' I like to explain the meaning of Elohim in this way. The Elohim is the Spirit of Jesus Christ coming-to-be Jesus Christ in the flesh. Now Jesus became the visible image of God that would reveal God to every creature.

"Adam's blood is contaminated with sin, a-a-a-and all humanity inherits that same contaminated blood. Now God is bringing all the celestial beings into this visible world to know God by way of humanity. Therefore, the contaminated blood of humanity is also inherited by the celestial beings by way of humanity.

"According to the Law of Moses, Claire, and found in the seventeenth chapter of Leviticus, God would set His face against anyone eating blood, for the soul of the flesh is in its blood. God Himself assigned to them to make a propitiatory shelter over their souls on the altar, for the blood in the soul makes a propitiatory shelter. It further states the soul of all flesh *is its blood.*

"As we return to the passage in Colossians, we learn why the body of Christ is so important in all this. The entire complement, 144.000, delights to dwell in Christ. For now through Christ, they shall reconcile all creation to Him. The reason for such a statement is because of their spiritual walk here on earth. The mere fact that the members of the body of Christ will be resurrected proves the very righteousness of Jesus also dwelled in the 'body.' Because of His righteousness, the body would also reconcile all humanity to Him. Thus, peace was made to all creation, whether those in heaven or those on the earth. This made peace for all through the blood of Christ. The purified blood of Christ has replaced the contaminated blood inherited through Adam.

"The truth I just told you about, Claire, not only verified that we are the sovereignties and authorities of the universe, it goes a long way toward verifying that all humanity will find salvation, but there is much more. I want to show you further proof of that from the fifth chapter of Romans. I know you understand these verses from our other studies, but it plays such an-an-an important part of the study we're in now. It first reminds us that sin entered into the world though Adam and then death passed into all humanity. But because the law had not yet been given, sin was not taken into account. The death, burial and resurrection of Christ nullified the dying state for those from Adam to Moses. Therefore, what occurred for them also occurred *for all humanity*. Claire, these verses clearly show that the dying state inherited by all humanity is no longer charged against anyone.

"But then the Law of Moses came in that the offenses should be increasing. Even so, where sin increases, grace increases all the more.

"Paul says he knew nothing of sin as a child and he knew nothing about coveting until the law said he should not covet. Sin latched on to the precept and produced all manner of coveting. The cross of Christ had taken away the dying state inherited through Adam, but when he reached the age of accountability, sin caused him to sin through the knowledge of the law. Once he lived apart from the law, yet at the coming of the precept, sin was revived. But sin only affects the body while it is alive. When it dies, either through salvation or by physical death, sin has no power over the flesh. Paul said, 'A wretched man am I! What will rescue me out of this body of death?' Then he answers his own question, 'Grace! I thank God, through Jesus Christ, our Lord.'"

Mark had discovered something in the scriptures he was sure few students were aware of. This was because he believed relatively few accept the view that all humanity will be saved, therefore, they are not looking for such truth. He was very anxious to share these findings with Claire. He learned that the fifteenth chapter of First Corinthians was a virtual outline of how God would bring about the salvation of all. Some in the congregation believed there would be no resurrection. Paul began by stressing the fact that there is a resurrection.

"In the early verses, Paul had brought up the matter of the evangel He had taken to them. The Corinthians accepted it, and they believed it, and they were saved by it, providing it was a genuine salvation. The Corinthians," he said, "were among the first to accept his evangel that Christ died for their sins according to the scriptures. He was entombed and roused on the third day according to the scriptures. He was seen by Peter and the twelve. Then He was seen by more than five hundred at one time. Many of those were still alive, though some had died. Then He was seen by James and the apostles.

"Last of all," Mark stressed, "Christ was seen by Paul himself as if by a premature birth. Paul says he was the most sinful of all the apostles and not even competent to be called an apostle because he persecuted the ecclesia of God. But by the grace of God, he is what he is, and God's grace, which is in him, did not come to be for nothing. But more exceeding than all this, he toiled, but he said it was not him that toiled. It was the grace of God which was in him. Thus, whether he or the other apostles, they all herald and all the Corinthians believed.

Now Paul wants to prove beyond doubt Christ was resurrected. If Christ is being heralded for His death and resurrection, how is it some of these Corinthians are saying there is no resurrection of the dead. Then Paul declares this. If there is no resurrection, neither was Christ dead. And if this is so, their faith is for nothing, and they are found to be false witnesses. And if the dead are not being roused, neither was Christ roused.

"Paul states emphatically! Christ was roused from among the dead. He is the First fruit of all who are in the grave. For through a man (Adam) came death, through a Man (Jesus) also comes the resurrection of the dead. As in Adam all are dying, so also in Christ shall all be vivified yet each in his own class. But how these verses became so confusing to Christendom is a great wonder," Mark exclaimed. "It must be without much argument Satan's greatest achievement, for these words clearly indicated that just as all humanity became sinners through Adam, then all humanity shall be made alive through Christ.

"Claire, the word fruit is one of those words that may be either singular of plural. It has already been stated that Christ was the First fruit (singular) to be roused from death. The second use of the term is listed as the first of three classes to be raised in Christ. Thus, this First fruit is plural. It must refer to the 'body of Christ' for they shall be one in Christ. The second class is made up of those who shall be present when He sets up His kingdom. The third class occurs at the consummation of the eons, whenever Christ gives His kingdom over to His God and Father. That is when the sovereignties and authorities and powers shall be nullified and become a new creation by way of humanity. That also is the time when the last enemy, death, shall be destroyed—that is, at the consummation of the eons. Then Christ shall hand the entire kingdom over to His God and Father that God shall be all in all.

"Now Paul asks what those are doing who are baptizing. Claire," Mark began to explain, they baptized as a witness that they were cleansed of their sins. If the dead are not being roused, then baptism is for the dead only. And why are they baptized for their own sake? The Corinthians boast of how Paul fights wild beasts in Ephesus.

What does it profit him if the dead are not roused? He might as well be eating and drinking for he will die tomorrow anyway.

"This part about the planting of seeds is hard to comprehend, but I think Paul was stressing the point that everything planted must die before it can become a new creation. But whatever is being sown is sown a naked kernel, like wheat, and God gives it a body according to His will. But he includes fleshly bodies in his explanation—bodies of beasts, of men, of flyers, and of fishes. These are the terrestrial bodies, but there are also celestial bodies, but all these receive a different glory.

"I remember, Claire, how Sidney comforted me by telling me

my puppy would go to heaven. I often wondered about that, even doubted it sometimes," Mark said with a chuckle. "Well, I think the truth is right there—he will be different when he is resurrected. Paul goes on to say the sun will have a different glory. In the new heavens and earth, there will be no need of the sun. Perhaps its glory will become the light of Christ shining as the glory of God.

"Paul centers upon the human seeds. He states that if there is a soulish body, there is also a spiritual body. The first man, Adam, became a living soul—the last Adam became a living spirit. Therefore, the first was soulish, the last was spiritual. The first man was out of the earth, soilish. The second man was the Lord out of heaven. Now such as the soilish one is, so shall his descendants be soilish, and such as the Celestial One, such are those also who are celestials. As we now wear the image of the soilish, we should be wearing the image of the Celestial.

"Claire, again, we come across that one word should. It causes a great deal of confusion among those who believe in the salvation of all, which shouldn't really be a problem if we recognize Paul is speaking to members of the body of Christ. The next paragraph settles the entire problem. 'The salvation of all' has been kept secret since the days of Paul's ministry. Paul is about to reveal that secret to us in this next paragraph.

"He tells us that flesh and blood cannot enjoy an allotment in the kingdom of God, nor will corruption enjoy a place with incorruption. Most Christians believe the following event takes place at a resurrection of what they believe is the body of Christ. It is here that Paul reveals the secret. As the verses that follow verily, this resurrection takes place at the consummation of the eons. This secret pertains to all humanity at the 'last trump.' He says *we all* shall not be put to repose but we all shall be changed, in an instant, in the twinkle of an eye, at the last trump. At this time, all those living on the earth shall already be incorruptible. At the sound of the trumpet, those in the lake of fire shall be roused up incorruptible to meet those on the earth. It is then we shall all (humanity) be changed in the twinkle of an eye.

"That corruptible, in the lake of fire, must put on incorruption, and then as mortals, this mortal must put on immorality. So when those corruptible ones put on incorruption and the mortal ones put on immortality, then these words of prophecy shall have come to pass:

'Swallowed up was Death by Victory.
Where, O Death, is your victory?
Where, O Death, is your sting?'

"Paul continues by saying, 'The sting of Death is sin, yet the power of sin is the law. Thanks be to God, Who is giving us the victory, through our Lord Jesus Christ.'

It was nearing sundown. The day was warm but cooling nicely after the evening breeze began stirring the air. Mark often made it a point to come to the cemetery at this time of the day, for he dearly loved the view of the sunset from Claire's resting place. He sat where the horizon was directly behind the stone. Because of the unique cloud cover in the western sky, it promised to be a beautiful sunset, and just as Mark had supposed, it presented a spectacular display. Having watched in awe, he reverently bowed his head. Silently, he gave praise to God for the beauty he observed.

But this visit with Claire was different. Great joy was stirring in his heart. Since the day Claire died, he believed he would somehow share his discoveries with her whenever God should permit him to realize the fulfillment of his premonition. Mark wanted her to recognize the rewards for finding the truths they had worked on together for so many years. They had studied together for most of their married lives. He indeed wanted her to learn how all those concepts had blossomed into such marvelous and wonderful truths. He loved her so much, and he often prayed for these things to become as vivid to her as they had to him. His book was complete, and he had vowed not to contact a publisher until he had shared it all with her.

Once again, Mark bowed his head in prayer. "Gracious God, and Father of the Lord Jesus Christ, it is my prayer Claire has shared these wonderful truths with me this day. Amen!"

CHAPTER 31

This would be the first season the holiday retreat enterprise would be in full swing. The lodge provided thirty nice but not expensive rooms and dining facilities for up to three hundred guests. A garage provided housing for the maintenance equipment and three battery operated trams. Also kept in the garage was a limousine for special services.

Donald appeared on a television station in Omaha, the station where Leland Bartholomew was host for a talk show. Mark was already aware of Leland's ability to promote any cause, and Donald was also an excellent speaker, presenting himself well. The program had reached a large audience and proved to be very effective.

Something over sixty acres of ground, with nearly one hundred red delicious apple trees and the same number of golden delicious apple trees, graced the upper portion of the sloping hillside. These were only a short distance from where the original tree thrived for so many years following the Civil War. In the previous fall, the contractor engaged to do the landscaping took Donald and Mark for an aerial view of the park. Mark had marveled at the symmetry of the rows as they stretched in both directions. They could hardly have been spaced more perfectly. All but a half dozen or so lived from the time of planting, and those not surviving were replaced. Donald took precautions to make sure they received everything needed to become healthy trees.

Mark was taking his daily stroll around the park where he spent the entire morning of every nice day. He left the orchard and then paused for a time while he sat on a park bench within hearing distance of the voice coming from the address system of the tram. Visitors were learning how the tree was discovered in the early 1860s, how the fruit samples were taken to various county fairs across the Midwest, and finally recognized by a representative of the Stark Brother Nursery out of Louisiana, Missouri. The great potential was soon recognized. He loved to hear the story, and it pleased him that something was being done in recognition of its importance.

Walking across the beautifully manicured lawn toward Rockey Creek, he thought of the memories of the beauty of those spring seasons. But none of those spring times had produced anything to rival what surrounded him now. The excavators had done a remarkable job of adjusting the terrain with their bulldozers and end loaders, leaving a gradual descent toward the road that led into town. It was also made sure all rainwater would eventually drain into Rockey Creek. A sprinkler system carried water to the entire area. The creek banks were widened and terraced to adequately carry off any excess rainwater. Most of the summer, any water found in the steam was carry off from the sprinkler system. All the large stones found during excavation were moved to the creek banks, while the banks of the stream became a virtual rock garden throughout the entire length. A nursery had been contracted to plan a perennial plant growth to coordinate color with the change of seasons. Plenty of rich green shrubbery abounded to enhance the color in any season. Layers of beautiful hues cascaded down the terraces to the waterbed cut a little deeper in order to keep the flooding of groundwater to a minimum.

Leaving the orchard, he stayed near the blacktop trail prepared for the tourist runs of the tram rides. The trails followed along either side of the stream, allowing constant view of the rock garden. At the southern end of the creek, the trail turned westward to wind back through the park, permitting close view of the flower garden arrangements. For the return trip, a stone bridge at the lower end of the park permitted crossing to the other side of the stream. He was proud of Donald's accomplishment. Indeed, it was a beautiful and relaxing place to be, away from the staggering pace from the rest of the world. Sometimes, he walked the trail at night observing the landscape lighted by the many streetlamps. He always enjoyed being seated on one of the park benches and listening to the happy voices of those riding the tram as they rode along the stream. The world would probably scoff at such simplicity, enjoying nature in all its beauty and intrigue, but Mark considered it the world's loss.

Purposely staying close to the trail this morning, he hoped Cora would just happen along to keep him company. Cora often did come looking for him, knowing where he would be about this time of the day. Mark loved his granddaughter, and she loved him as much.

A new song filled the mind and heart of Mark. Both the words and melody came to him quite naturally as he strolled along the bank of the stream day after day. Loving the Word of God as he did, he was always seeking new ways to express it. It was just a matter of arranging the words to rhyme while maintaining the proper thoughts.

Most of the thoughts had been on his mind for many years, but his understanding of grace was so much clearer now.

These Days of Grace

God gave His Son
upon the Cal'vry cross,
where Jesus died
while suff'ring shameful loss.
I praise His name
for all He's done for me,
to show God's grace
through all eternity.
My Lord arose
with great triumphant ring,
He conquered death—
oh, grave where is thy sting?
Christ came down from above
and filled my heart with love;

He lives in me
all through these days of grace.
He walks with me
along life's weary way,
He talks with me
and cares for me each day.
Though days on earth seem long,
He fills them all with song.
He lives in me
all through these days of grace.

Beep, beep came the high-pitched sound of the tram horn. "I came to give you a ride to the lodge, Grandpa," Cora said, as she pulled up beside him.

"I thought maybe you came to spend some time with me. Such a beautiful day, not a cloud in the sky."

"I'd love to, Grandpa, but I came to tell you something," she said. "Do you know an attorney by the name of Thomas Harmon? He stopped a few minutes ago. He just happened to be driving through Peru and thought he'd take a chance on seeing you. Said he'd stop back about ten-thirty. He'd be glad to make an appointment with you if you're busy."

"Gosh, I hope you informed him of the heavy schedule I'm carrying these days," Mark said with a chuckle. "There's hardly enough time in the mornings to get all the way round this park. I didn't get back until nearly twelve-thirty yesterday. Did he give any idea what he wanted?" "Not really! He said you would either be extremely pleased, or you'll think it a complete waste of time. Unfortunately," he said, "I'll have to discover which it is."

Mark and Cora sat at a table near the entrance of the lodge. A few tables were occupied, mostly small groups sipping coffee and eating rolls or doughnuts. A man entered, and recognizing Cora, he came to their table.

"Thomas Harmon," he said, holding out his hand to Mark. "You're Mark Hayes, I presume. I met your lovely granddaughter. I must thank you for getting my message to Mr. Hayes," he said, directing his words to Cora.

As Cora left them, Mark motioned for a waitress. "May I order a pot of coffee and some rolls? I highly recommend their hot Danish rolls with butter," he said.

Seeing the pleasure registered on Mr. Harmon's face, Mark placed the order.

"I've heard a lot about the holiday retreat. Just never stopped by before this morning."

"We hear that a lot," Mark said with a chuckle. "I'm kidding. This place is doing very well. Really, it's exceeded everyone's expectations. We have a number of bookings already for the wedding chapel. I believe about two dozen for this summer and fall. Motel reservations are mostly for overnighters, but we realize we haven't very much to offer for vacationers yet, unless, of course, it's someone just looking for a place to enjoy the quiet and beauty of nature. Frankly, that's what I enjoy the most—the quiet and beauty of the place. It always seems God is much nearer in this beautiful place. Of course, God is everywhere," he added. "I usually tell people I'm vacationing here permanently."

"From what I've seen today, I find nothing to convince me your wrong," Mr. Harmon replied.

"You really should stop in when you have some free time. We have a nine-hole miniature golf course with some rather attractive and unique arrangements. And if you like to ice-skate, our rink is open the year around. This idea of ice-skating in the middle of August almost blows my mind. The people around here sure like it, though."

"You know, Mr. Hayes—"

"None of that Mr. Hayes stuff! Just call me Mark," he said. "Okay, Mark, I have twin great-grandsons about seven years old. I think I just discovered how I can make a hit with them. I promise to bring them here before this summer ends."

The man's expression changed. "Before I cause your death by curiosity, I guess I'd better tell you why I'm here. Do you remember a medical doctor by the name of Charles Waters, Mark?"

"Yes, sir! I certainly do! Don't tell me he's still alive!"

Mr. Harmon chuckled. "That's not as strange as you might suppose. He died only about six months ago. He was 104 years old, died in a nursing home in Greenfield."

"That is amazing! Dr. Waters was county coroner when I knew him. He was a kindly man. Being just a kid, I thought it hard to believe he could be so considerate of me."

"Then I guess you know why I'm here," he said.

"No, can't say that I do. Oh, wait a minute!" Mark began to laugh. "I know why. Our visit concerns a Bible! He promised to return it to me if it became possible." Mark chuckled. "It's got to be the Bible."

Suddenly, Mark's expression changed to utter amazement. "It is the Bible, isn't it? It can't be! But it is, isn't it?"

"Yes, sir, it is, Mark! That's just what it's about!"

Mr. Harmon watched Mark. The look of amazement changed to one of seriousness, and then his eyes moistened, but it was from tears of joy. A smile covered his face, a smile showing joy in what he was thinking.

"I had no idea what was involved with the book," Mr. Harmon said. "But from the expression on your face, you just made my day. It's been at least thirty-five years since I drew up his will. Of course, I forgot about the request being in it, that is until he died and I read the will again. He had been very specific I should try to locate you in the event of his death. When I read the will, my thought was it couldn't be very important to anyone after all those years. Really, I didn't give it any more consideration.

"As a matter of fact, the rest was quite by accident. Not the most orthodox method, I'm afraid. About two weeks ago, I attended graveside services of a friend in the cemetery up the road from here. As I returned to my car, I happened to see the name on the marker of your grave site. Later, I stopped in the post office and made some inquiry. That's when I realized you and the writer was the same person. The rest was easy." "What do I need to do to claim the book?" Mark asked.

Mr. Harmon reached for his briefcase. "Nothing, except take it." Unlatching the case, he reached inside, and pulling the book from it, he handed it to Mark. It was indeed the same book, though the pages were yellowed from the years of being exposed to the day-light rather than being packed away somewhere.

"I think Dr. Waters probably kept it in his library at home. Judging from my own experience with things like that, I suspect Dr. Waters went searching through the courthouse for it sometime after the lost person was identified. Those things have a way of getting buried under the dust. Anyway, I'm glad I was able to help fulfill his promise to you."

Mr. Harmon was gone. Mark was alone, sitting quietly and drying his moistened eyes with his handkerchief. There in the lower right-hand corner were the small but distinct gold letters—SIR. Remembering well the moment he first saw those letters, he carefully opened the book. As he turned to the first page, the upper corner broke away and fell to the table. But something else claimed his attention, for at the first page of scripture was a narrow strip of paper. Curiously, he opened the note and read the type written words, "The house of Israel—then and now." And in Sidney's own handwriting were the added words, "See that Harold gets a copy."

Immediately, the memory of having seen the note before came racing back, but even during all those years, not once had it entered his mind—that is, not until this very moment. It wasn't the book title that put Mark in awe; it was the note written by Sidney that caused him such wonder. He had long believed God had arranged for his coming in contact with both these men: Sidney, who wrote the note and had introduced him to the most enlightening truth he could have hoped for; and Harold, whom he considered the one most responsible for his studies developing as they had.

Mark closed the book but determined to catch one more view of the Bible verses he and Sidney Rawlings both loved so very much. He made an educated guess as at about where to find the passages. Carefully, he opened the book again and even more carefully turned the pages until he came to the place. There, just as he remembered, was the passage carefully and separately underlined with pen following a straight edge.

Those were the verses that instilled so much assurance in Mark. Whenever his confidence in what he believed would wane, they always gave him renewed determination to go forward with his understanding. It all began on that warm summer day in 1939. As he had done so many times before, he thanked God for the experience of that day. Then once more, he read those beautiful words: "Faithful is the saying and worthy of all welcome (for this are we toiling and being reproached), that we rely on the living God Who is Savior of all mankind, especially of believers. These things be charging and teaching (1 Tim. 4:9-11).

ABOUT THE AUTHOR

A dear friend and I had studied the scriptures together for years, but it wasn't until he gave me a brochure setting forth a study of the eons that a revelation of truth completely changed our direction of thinking. It established the premise of the salvation of all humanity. It teaches that even the lake of fire is contained in the eons and comes to an end.

I read many articles showing scripture to prove the point, but none showed me how God was bringing about that goal. I determined that with God's help along the way, I would write a book proving the salvation of all. That was more than fifty years ago. I began a verse by verse study, particularly of Paul's epistles. I learned that much of Paul's knowledge on the matter came from the book of Isaiah. Isaiah was told to write to God's people about the new covenant, but in a way, they would not understand. They would see with their eyes and hear with their ears, bur they must not comprehend.

Paul was given understanding of those scriptures and given the call to take the message to the entire world, especially to the ten lost tribes of Israel. He revealed many things to those making up the body of Christ or compliment of the eras, but when the body was complete, the truths he taught again faded out. This was due to the eternal torment doctrine hiding the truth. The truths are still there, but the translators have managed to deny them by the apostasy of Satan and his evil doctrine to intercede. I believe God is allowing those truths to become known once again. The end times are coming into view. What could possibly anger the antichrist more than the truth that all humanity shall be saved?

www.ingramcontent.com/pod-product-compliance
Lightning Source LLC
LaVergne TN
LVHW050921080826
845145LV00001B/158

* 9 7 8 1 9 6 0 4 9 9 9 4 3 *